12/97

| | DATE DUE | | |
|---|---|---|---|
| | | | |
| | | | |
| | | | |
| | | | |
| | | | |
| | | | |
| | | | |
| | | | |
| | | | |
| | | | |
| | | | |

Also by Pete Hautman

♠

DRAWING DEAD

SHORT MONEY

THE MORTAL NUTS

MR. WAS

# Pete Hautman

# RING GAME

SIMON & SCHUSTER

SIMON & SCHUSTER
Rockefeller Center
1230 Avenue of the Americas
New York, NY 10020

SIMON & SCHUSTER and colophon are registered trademarks
of Simon & Schuster Inc.

Designed by Irving Perkins Associates

Manufactured in the United States of America

1  3  5  7  9  10  8  6  4  2

Library of Congress Cataloging-in-Publication Data
Hautman, Pete, date.
Ring game / Pete Hautman.
p.    cm.
I. Title.
PS3558.A766R56    1997
813'.54—dc21        97-18286  CIP

ISBN 0-684-83242-9

ISBN 0-684-84718-3 Signed Edition

For
Elaine

♠

*I don't expect you to understand this, but it's a great comfort to
a girl to know she could not possibly sink any lower.*

—*Barrie Chase to Robert Mitchum,* Cape Fear

CARMEN ROMAN WAS PISSED OFF. She sat with the bottoms of her Birks
pressed against the steel dashboard, arms wrapped around her knees, watching
Hyatt Hilton pilot the delivery van, his feet working the gas and the brakes simultaneously, the tips of his long fingers wrapped around the bottom of the
steering wheel the way a possum would grip a branch: thumbs on top. Hyatt
was excited, showing pink tongue between large, bright, charmingly crooked
teeth, telling her about something he'd seen on TV. She watched Hyatt's lips
moving. Now and then a little glob of spittle would make it all the way to the
windshield, like when he said "perfect," which he did a lot.

She shifted her gaze to the street, seeing the storefronts, the traffic, the
pedestrians, letting the images in, but retaining none of it. She did not know
*what* Hyatt was talking about. She didn't *care*. When he'd called her that morning Hyatt had told her he had a surprise for her, like he was going to give her a
present, or take her someplace special. He hadn't said anything about doing
water deliveries. He hadn't said anything about driving all over South Minneapolis in his creaky old Econoline van selling cases of Evian.

Then she heard him say, "A hundred thousand dollars. Minimum."

Carmen turned her head back toward Hyatt. "What?"

"That's what they pay."

From a distance, or at first, people often mistook Hyatt for a kid from out-
state, a broad-shouldered farm kid, six-feet-several-inches tall, skin the color of
a flesh-tone crayola, untended white-blond hair, eyes sky blue and empty. A kid
who had perhaps sprouted too quickly, vacant of mind but overflowing with

good intention. Closer inspection, however, would reveal a patina of twenty-year-old acne scars on his cheeks and neck, fine lines radiating from the corners of his eyes, and a sort of rodent intelligence glinting from his unequal pupils. He claimed to be twenty-nine years old, but Carmen believed him to be closer to forty.

"Who? Pay who?" She pulled her feet off the dashboard, scooted her butt back in the seat and gave him her full attention.

"Whoever's got the goods, Carmenito. And that's not even counting the book deals. Like that guy got his wee-wee cut off? You don't think he's rich now? It'd be *perfect!*"

She had no idea what he was talking about. It would be "perfect" to get his wee-wee cut off? Hyatt was strange, but not that strange.

Hyatt stopped the van in front of a small convenience store. Hand-painted signs in the window read: WE ACCEPT FOOD STAMPS. WIC WELCOME. CHECKS CASHED. Hyatt consulted a small notebook. "Four cases," he said. "You want to give me a hand?"

Carmen crossed her arms and turned her face away. She was not a goddamn teamster. Hyatt shrugged, got out, opened the back of the van, lifted out two cases of Evian, the half-liter bottles, carried them into the store.


Carmen Roman had met Hyatt Hilton last summer when she'd been working for Axel Speeter, selling tacos at the Minnesota State Fair. Back then, Hyatt had been involved with the Amaranthine Church of the One—a sort of New Age, vitamin-gulping, sprout munching bunch of health nuts who thought they could live forever. He had tried to convert Carmen, but any lifestyle that demanded abstinence from tobacco and alcohol was not for her. She'd told him to buzz off.

A few months later Hyatt had called again and said that he'd left the church and would she like to join him for a drink, a real drink, and she'd said yes. They'd been seeing each other ever since and, for the most part, it had been fun. Hyatt liked to get dressed up, take her places, catch a buzz, dance a little. He had a BMW with leather seats. He gave her presents. He'd given her a watch, which she didn't like, but which got her a two hundred twenty-seven-dollar credit when she returned it to Dayton's. He'd given her a tortoiseshell Dunhill cigarette lighter, worth three hundred bucks, he'd told her, which she'd kept because the dark reddish-black surface of the shell matched her hair color and because Dayton's wouldn't take it back, the customer service woman claiming that they had never stocked such an item.

Carmen lit a cigarette with her Dunhill and watched the smoke flatten against the windshield.

A hundred thousand dollars? What had *that* been about? Maybe she should have been listening closer. Of course, knowing Hyatt, whatever he'd been saying, he would repeat it until he beat it to death. She watched him come out of the store walking his jerky, loose-jointed gait. He grabbed two more cases from the back of the van and carried them into the store.

When Hyatt had first told Carmen about his Evian business, she thought she'd struck it rich. He claimed to have the exclusive Evian franchise for the Twin Cities area. Later, he amended that to Minneapolis. Then, the first time she visited his rented house on Lyndale Avenue, she discovered that what Hyatt actually had was a garage full of empty Evian bottles and a landlord with a larger-than-average water bill. She'd spent that whole stupid afternoon in his garage, watching him fill and cap bottles.

What Hyatt Hilton had was a franchise on counterfeit Evian. He bought the empty ersatz bottles from a plastics company owned by a bunch of Norwegians off the Iron Range—most of them ex-hockey players from Virginia and Eveleth who called themselves the Range Boys, guys who'd never made it out of the semipros. He paid the Range Boys five bucks a case for the empties, filled and capped them using a miniproduction line he'd set up in his garage, then sold them a case at a time to corner groceries, gas stations, and restaurants. Forty cents a bottle wholesale for an item that would go for a buck and a half or more over the counter. It looked like a nice little business, except that when it all added up he was driving all over town delivering Evian making no more than he would have as a regular truck driver.

That was pretty much the story on Hyatt Hilton. He looked good on the surface, but lately Carmen had been noticing signs of wear. His BMW was eight years old and showing rust, his clothing was a couple years out of date, and her Dunhill lighter had probably come out of a pawn shop.

Maybe she should move on. The excitement just wasn't there anymore. Hy was fun to be with, sure, but his stories were going into reruns. He was obsessed with the Amaranthine Church, which he claimed had been his idea. He'd started the church with a couple of partners a few years back and then, he said, just when the money started to roll in, his partners had kicked him out. She was sick of hearing about it. So he'd gotten fired. So what. She needed more variety in her life, and fewer Evian deliveries. Carmen ashed her cigarette on the floor of the van. Where the hell was her big surprise?

Maybe she could cruise the country-western bars, find some guy with lizard boots and one of those big hats. A guy with a little danger and excitement in him. All she'd have to do is wear something to show off her shape, throw on some lipstick, play with her hair a little—they'd be all over her in a second.

But what was this about a hundred thousand dollars? Probably more of Hy's bullshit. She returned her sandaled feet to the dashboard and examined her toenails' bright red polish, needing some touch-up around the tips. She could fix herself up real nice. Get any guy she wanted. What the hell, she was only twenty-three.

Hyatt hopped back into the van, grinning, tucking a handful of small bills into his shirt pocket. "Just three more stops," he said. He twisted the key, dropped the gearshift into drive, and pulled out onto Lake Street.

Carmen flicked her cigarette out the window. "Stop the truck," she said.

"Why?"

"I said stop."

Hyatt pulled over to the curb. "What's the matter?"

"I'm not having fun."

Hyatt elevated his pale eyebrows, pushed out his lips—one of his many peculiar facial expressions—and made a sucking sound through his front teeth. "You're not?"

"No."

"Oh. Well, don't forget, I've got a surprise."

Carmen crossed her arms. "I want my surprise now."

She watched his face go from startled to puzzled to amused. "You can't wait till later? I was thinking we could go to someplace nice, relax, tip a few."

"That's my surprise?"

Hyatt shook his head, smiling now.

"Then what is it?"

Hyatt put his hands on her shoulders and turned her toward him. "You want me to just give it to you? I was sort of hoping for more, you know, ambiance."

Carmen set her jaw and stared back at him.

Hyatt sighed. He released her and turned up his empty palms as if demonstrating a new coin trick. He rotated his hands, showing her the carpet of fine white hairs on their backs. He folded his hands as if in prayer, interlaced his long fingers, then turned them palm up. In the basket formed by his meshed fingers lay a tiny, gray velvet box.

Hyatt said, "For you."

Carmen took the box and opened it. A diamond ring, a single large stone—maybe three carats—surrounded by a spatter of ruby chips. Carmen felt her heart filling her chest, the rock hitting her like a nose full of Peruvian blow.

Carmen slipped the ring onto her finger.

"Is it real?" she asked.

Hyatt said, "Sure, what do you think? You think I'm proposing on a piece of glass?"

Carmen wasn't sure she'd heard him right. She said, "What?"

"I'm asking you to marry me, Carm. Tie the knot. Wear the big white dress."

"Me? The big white dress? Are you nuts?"

"I'm serious." He didn't look serious. He looked like he'd just eaten somebody's canary.

Carmen was intensely suspicious. "You want to marry me? Why?"

"Because I love you."

"Bull *shit*." She held the ring in the sunlight, letting it dazzle her eyes.

"Because you look like Sophia Loren. I always wanted to marry Sophia Loren."

"More bullshit." The ring fit her perfectly. She said, "No offense, Hy, but you're gonna have to do better'n that."

Hyatt put the van in drive and pulled out onto Lake Street. "Okay," he said. "I'll tell you everything, how it's gonna work and what we're gonna do. You're gonna love it. It's *perfect*."

*In close contests . . . psychological factors can be decisive.*

—*Arnold Schwarzenegger*

JOE CROW GRIPPED THE BAR, felt the worn knurling press into his palms. He closed his eyes and envisioned the barbell floating up from its rack, hovering effortlessly under his control. He imagined his arm bones as titanium shafts, his tendons as steel cables, his pectoral muscles as powerful turbines. He slowly counted, visualizing the weight descending, lightly touching his chest, floating up again. He counted three reps in his mind.

Two hundred fifty-five pounds. He'd be lucky to press it once.

To the bodybuilders and powerlifters at Bigg Bodies, benching two fifty-five would be part of their warm-up routine, but to Crow it was a lot of iron, seventy pounds more than he'd been able to handle a couple months back when he'd started working out at Bigg's. Twenty pounds more than he'd pressed last Friday. A big jump, but he was feeling good. Feeling strong.

He had a rule. *Always play your strong hands.*

What he should really do, he should ask someone to spot him, lend a hand if he got stuck with the bar pressing down on his ribcage. That would be the smart thing. Unfortunately, his choice of spotters was limited to two: Beaut Miller, who was taking time out from his duties as assistant manager of Bigg

Bodies to build up his already overdeveloped chest, and the aromatic Flowrean Peeche.

Of all the human oddities that frequented Bigg Bodies, Crow found Flowrean Peeche to be the most bizarre by several orders of magnitude. She was working the pec deck at the other side of the chest room, twenty feet away but well within smelling distance. A frightening symphony of grunts, growls, and snarls erupted from her throat as she squeezed out a last few reps. For a five-foot-three-inch female, she was astonishingly powerful.

Flowrean had been wearing the same unwashed heather gray sweats ever since Crow had started working out at Bigg Bodies two months ago. She did her workouts barefooted and barehanded. Twisted shanks of thick hair explored the space surrounding her head, framing her imperturbable features in an explosion of black tendrils. Around her neck, six dead goldfish in various stages of decomposition were strung onto a braided steel wire.

Despite her over-the-top body odor and her dead-fish necklace, Flowrean radiated a kind of regal beauty. When not contorted with momentary physical effort, her olive-gold skin, deep brown eyes, and full, dark lips gave her the look of a placid, self-satisfied icon. Her bearing was that of a queen in exile, her aroma that of a hydrophobic bag lady.

Crow caught her eyes in the mirrored wall. For a fraction of a second he found himself held by them, then her lids closed. She rotated her head and opened her eyes onto another scene.

Flowrean seemed to live inside an invisible but palpable bubble. She spoke to others in the gym only when she could not avoid it, and when she did speak, she was both abrupt and succinct. Crow suspected that Flowrean Peeche saw other human beings as phantasms—less real and important than the dead goldfish around her neck.

The only other potential spotter in the chest room, Beaut Miller, was pumping up his chest on the cables. In a pinch, Crow decided, he'd take the nose-wrenching Flowrean over the dangerous wit of Beaut, whose favorite gag was to come up behind a guy doing pull-ups and yank his shorts down to his ankles. None of the regulars did pull-ups when Beaut was in the vicinity.

Ah well, thought Crow, having no spotter might inspire him to perform better. Once the bar touched his chest, he'd have no choice but to shove it back up. He planted his feet firmly, centered his back on the bench, and lifted. The barbell came up off the rack, and his muscles went into overload, desperately trying to prevent the weight from dropping onto his face. The bar wavered, loose plates clanking. Crow kept his elbows locked, trying to reassure his panicked muscles.

"That looks heavy, guy." Beaut Miller's hoarse voice came from behind.

Crow felt his concentration split. He thought, I should just rerack it.

"You want a spot there, guy? You don't want to drop it on your face."

Through gritted teeth, Crow muttered, "No thanks." He lowered the bar toward his chest, blocking Beaut's presence from his mind, stopping the bar just before it touched his T-shirt.

Now up, he commanded, squeezing his chest, forcing his arms to straighten. Miraculously, the bar began to ascend. He allowed himself to think of Beaut watching him control the weight, pushing it slowly skyward.

Something icy cold slapped him on his bare thigh. Crow flinched, the barbell tilted to the left. He felt himself losing control, seeing it happen in slow motion. The five and ten-pound weights slid off the left end of the bar and hit the rubber floormat with a clang. That end of the barbell, suddenly fifteen pounds lighter, whipped up. All four weights on the right end slid off and slammed onto the rubber. The right end of the bar kicked up then, and the last pair of forty-fives crashed down to his left. Crow was left holding the empty bar, his arms shaking violently. He racked the bar and sat up. His leg was wet.

Beaut stood shaking his golden mane, holding a half-empty squeeze bottle. "Jeez, guy, I'm sorry as hell. Didn't mean to splash ya." He upended the bottle and jetted a few ounces of water into his mouth. "A guy oughta ask for a spot if he's not sure he can handle it." His pale blue eyes widened, as if a new thought had entered his mind. "A guy could get hurt."

Neither bodybuilder nor powerlifter, Beaut was your basic gym rat—whatever part of his body he could see in the bathroom mirror bulged meatily, including his prognathous jaw. He made no effort to achieve a symmetrical physique, choosing to conceal his less-than-impressive legs beneath billowing leopard-skin-patterned Zubaz and relying on his jutting chest to divert attention from his spongy abdomen. Beaut wanted mass and, at six-three and upward of two hundred sixty pounds, he had it. With his double-wide shoulders, his twenty-inch biceps, his deep tan, and his curly bleached locks, Beaut cut an impressive figure at the local T.G.I. Friday.

Crow wondered how Beaut would respond to a ten-pound plate thrown at his head. Probably just let it bounce off his skull, then try to dismember the thrower. Maybe it would be worth it.

Flowrean, sitting at the pec deck, had paused in her workout to watch the two men facing one another. She caught Crow's eye, then looked quickly away, her mop of black hair whipping across her face. Crow wished she wasn't there, watching. Having an audience, especially a female audience, made him want to do something stupid. He called up another of his rules, forced himself to look at it: *Never act in anger.*

Beaut held out the water bottle toward Crow. "You want some?"

Crow stood up and walked away. *Walk away from bad hands early.* He proceeded into the main room, a large open area that contained most of the back, shoulder, and arm equipment, and the cardio gear—four stationary bikes, a pair of Stairmasters, and a rowing machine. He remembered the first time he'd walked into Bigg Bodies and seen the long rows of weight-training equipment, the padded benches covered in cherry-red vinyl, rack after rack of neatly stacked iron plates, a two-tiered rack of dumbbells stretching out across a sea of pebble-gray carpeting. He had quickly realized that the size of the gym was exaggerated by the mirrored walls, but somehow that knowledge had not taken away from the majesty of it. He still liked to imagine himself in an endless room, an illusion shattered only when he encountered a reflection of himself.

Behind the counter near the entrance sat Arling Biggle, better known as Bigg, reading a magazine, wearing his usual red, white, and blue silk warm-ups. He looked up from his reading, caught Crow's eye, smiled, and winked. From his perch behind the counter, Bigg had a view into every corner of his mirrored establishment. Crow was sure he had seen Beaut's little trick with the water bottle.

Crow stepped onto one of the Stairmasters and began climbing, determined to think about something peaceful, like fishing, which was what he planned to do as soon as he finished his workout. Drive up to Whiting Lake to his old man's cabin. Throw a line in the water. It was a three-hour drive, but he'd be there by four o'clock, plenty of time to land a monster. Throw out a buzz bait, reel it in. Throw it out, reel it in. If the buzz bait didn't work he could maybe try a spoon, or even one of those weird lures his father made out of spark plugs or strips of auto body. Load up his line with a twisted scrap of Dodge minivan, throw it out, reel it in.

According to the computer readout on the Stairmaster, Crow had climbed seventeen floors when Arling Biggle leaned a meaty forearm on the handrail and looked up at Crow. "Beaut give you a hard time there, Crow?"

Crow let the fishing thing go and pulled himself back to the here and now. "You saw that?"

"I thought you guys were going to go at it."

Crow nodded. "So did I."

"Probably a good thing you didn't."

"Maybe. How come you keep him around? He must cost you business."

Bigg looked like a short, aging version of the Incredible Hulk with a shaven scalp and thick sideburns that began in front of his ears and followed the line of his jaw to the tips of his Fu Manchu mustache. The look, Crow believed, was designed to make people want to laugh—then think better of it. Bigg's round, unblinking blue eyes, a little white showing all the way around the iris, had a reptilian quality that belied his clownish whiskers.

Bigg considered Crow's comment. He raised his short, thick eyebrows, pushed out his lower lip, and contracted his trapezius muscles. His thick neck disappeared, and his cantaloupe shoulders rose a full three inches. He held the pose for an instant, then relaxed. Crow took it for a shrug.

"Beaut's not so bad, once you get used to him. It's like with Flowrean: Once you get used to the smell, you kinda get to like it."

"I can hold my breath around Flowrean. Beaut's tougher to ignore."

Bigg smiled and nodded. "I know what you mean. But when Beaut's doing his workout, he's on his own time. Just another member. Technically speaking, he hasn't broken any of our rules." He ticked off the three Bigg Bodies rules on his stumpy fingers. "One: Beaut racks his weights. Two: Beaut gives a spot if you ask him nice. Three: Beaut pays his dues on time." He laughed. "Course, they come right out of his paycheck." He gave Crow a flat smile. "Unlike some of our members, who pay no dues whatsofuckingever."

"You should've thought about that when you bet those queens."

"You're the luckiest son-of-a-bitch I ever played cards with," Bigg said.

Crow stopped climbing. The treads sank to the floor, bringing him down to Bigg's level. "Is that what this is about?" he asked.

Bigg looked over his shoulder into the chest room. Crow followed his gaze, saw Beaut watching them, a white grin shimmering on his tanned face.

If that Joe Crow had started working out ten, fifteen years ago, Bigg thought, he might've been one hell of a powerlifter. He had the classic powerlifter's build: small and compact, with muscular thighs, short arms, and naturally sloped shoulders. He'd never make it now, of course. Not at his age. A guy couldn't expect to walk into a gym for the first time at thirtysomething and expect to compete, no matter how good his genes. Crow had pissed away his life when he could've been a champion. A real shame.

Bigg had been a competitive powerlifter until 1979, when, a few days after squatting nine hundred twenty pounds in the Tri-State, he'd blown out his left knee. Playing golf, of all things. He'd gone on to a brief career on the pro wrestling circuit under the name "Studly Doo-Rite," then spent a few years working as a personal trainer, occasionally collecting bills for a furniture rental company just for laughs. Eight years ago, at the age of forty, he'd bought Smithy's Auto Body and turned it into Bigg Bodies, the Choice of Twin Cities Bodybuilders.

Bigg gave Crow a cuff on the shoulder and returned to his stool behind the counter. Crow continued his climb to nowhere on the Stairmaster again, that dreamy, blank look returning to his face. It was the same look he'd had when Bigg had bet those three queens, the same look he'd had when he'd shown Bigg his straight and won himself a lifetime membership to Bigg Bodies. In fact, it was pretty much the same look Crow *always* had. Bigg found such complacency to be enormously irritating.

Maybe he should tell Beaut to turn up the heat, drop a plate on Crow's head or something. That might be interesting. He'd have to think about that. One thing for sure, he didn't want to watch Crow working out for free every day for the rest of his life.

He picked up the magazine he had been reading, but nothing had changed. Bigg Bodies had failed, once again, to make the Mpls./St. Paul magazine list of "Best Twin Cities Workouts." Not even a mention. In fact, no one who worked at the magazine had ever visited Bigg's, much less worked out there. Never mind that Bigg had trained three of the last five Mr. Minnesotas. Never mind that he'd been training champions years before those pencilnecks at Bally's had moved in on the market with their chromium "fitness centers" and spandex discotheques. He'd been to one once. A bunch of geeks standing in line waiting their turn to use the ten-pound dumbbells. No serious bodybuilder had ever worked out twice at a Bally's.

Running a gym was a pain in the ass anyways. Up at five-thirty every morning, dealing with all these 'roided-out kids with their big talk and nothing egos, listening to a bunch of pinheads grunting and farting their way through their sets. It was undignified. Work his ass to the bone and then get screwed over by some pencilneck reporter who probably got a free membership to Bally's for writing the article. Maybe he should close the joint, get into selling amino acids and protein supplements instead. Or buy a couple more stretches, build up his limo business. That was easy money, renting out those white Lincolns to wedding parties and such. Easier than running this damn gym.

Arling Biggle crumpled the magazine in his meaty fist, dropped it into the overflowing trash can behind the counter. None of his customers read anything but muscle mags anyways.

Beaut Miller watched his chest in the mirror as he performed his fourteenth set of cable crosses. He wore a fluorescent orange T-shirt with the neck and sleeves cut away, a narrow strip of ragged cloth surmounting each mountainous shoulder, the neck and armholes cut low, almost to his waist, showing his pectorals to maximum effect. An impressive chest, especially in its current pumped condition. He loved the way his serratus muscles popped when he did cable crosses. He wished he had a better audience. He wished some kid he'd known in high school would walk in and get an eyeful. One of those kids who used to give him a hard time, back when he'd been Little Leslie Miller.

Almost anybody would do for an audience. Anyone other than Miss Stinkypants, who didn't give a shit about anybody. Beaut sneaked a glance at her in the mirror. Flowrean was on her back, ankles crossed, bare feet in the air, pressing a pair of fifty-pound dumbbells—a lot of weight for a gal her size—giving forth a hoarse grunt of effort with each rep. The bitch was probably on the 'roids. Probably had to shave every morning.

Beaut tried not to get too close to Flowrean, ever since the time he'd accidentally—well, sort of accidentally—poked his elbow into one of her tits, and she'd jumped him like a psycho bobcat from hell, all claws and screams and kicks—he'd lost about a yard of skin in three seconds. Stone bitch. It was right around that time that she'd started wearing her goldfish necklace. She was still a looker, but nobody'd want her now. A little B.O. was one thing, but those dead fish hangin' over her tits, that was too much. Beaut couldn't figure out why anybody'd want to smell that bad. Any other gym, she'd've been eighty-sixed, but Bigg, he had a thing for Flowrean Peeche. Bigg was funny that way.

Looking past her reflection, he saw Crow coming back into the chest room. Beaut hadn't minded a bit when Bigg asked him to give the pilgrim a hard time. It was a pleasure. He'd about sprained his abs trying not to laugh when those plates had slid off—Ka-clang! Kangkangka-kang! Kuh-chlang! Beaut grinned at Crow's reflection, performed a final rep with the cables, and let the weight stacks slam back into place. He turned and crossed his arms and waited, wondering what the frozen-faced little wimp had in mind. Waiting for the close-range eye contact. Give him that fuck you look, see what he did with it.

Crow stopped in front of Beaut, looking up. The moment of eye contact didn't feel as satisfying as Beaut had expected. Crow's gaze was too calm. Beaut felt Little Leslie tugging urgently at his frontal lobes. He flexed his jaw muscles until his teeth pulsed painfully, causing his chickenshit alter ego to bury itself deeper in his brain. Fucking Little Leslie, any little thing, and he'd shit his pants. Beaut tipped his head back, pointing his chin, holding Crow's eyes, ignoring Little Leslie's frantic scrabbling, thinking that if Crow didn't look away soon, he'd have to either step back or give him a short one to the solar plexus.

Crow said, "You have an opportunity here, Beaut."

Beaut was so startled he felt his jaw go slack. Have I been dissed? he wondered. He wasn't sure, but that was how it felt, like the guy was fucking with him, like the guy was the fucker instead of the fuckee. Beaut concentrated on holding Crow's gaze—he wasn't going to be the first one to look away.

"You have the opportunity to do nothing." Crow's eyes were calm, almost sleepy. Almost inviting. Something in his voice frightened Little Leslie badly.

Beaut said, "What the fuck are you talking about?"

Crow's brown eyes remained flat and opaque.

Little Leslie was going into crisis. Beaut heard himself say, as if from a distance, "Someday somebody's gonna fuck you up good, Crow."

Crow smiled. "It will be worth it."

Little Leslie moaned. Beaut watched Crow turn and walk away.

A few weeks before, Beaut had been leaving T.G.I. Friday's when a drunk, a guy Beaut had had a few words with earlier that evening, had come roaring across the parking lot in a Chevy Blazer. Beaut had jumped out of the way with no room to spare—he'd felt the Blazer's bumper tick the heel of his shoe. The way he'd felt then—once he realized he wasn't hurt—that was the way he felt now. Numb, and relieved that he hadn't wet his pants.

Beaut heard a noise, turned his head to see Flowrean looking right at him, laughing, snorting through her nose, white teeth flashing in the fluorescent lights, goldfish dancing.

Crow took a leisurely shower, keeping his eyes open, half expecting Beaut to follow him into the locker room and try something. He didn't want it to go anywhere, but he wasn't going to cut back on his shower time.

Beaut didn't show. That was good. Crow wasn't sure it had worked, getting in Beaut's face that way. A bully like Beaut, the way to put the fear into him was to let him know that you didn't care if you got hurt. It usually worked. You could never be sure what a guy like that would do, but he had another rule: *Always bet into weakness.*

A few weeks earlier, during an otherwise astonishingly unproductive afternoon, Joe Crow had taken up a pencil and, on the cover of the Minneapolis Yellow Pages, scribbled a list of things to remember when playing poker. That original list had contained seven items. Since then, he had added more rules as they occurred to him. He was up to about twenty-five. He thought some of them were pretty good.

On his way out, Crow glanced back into the chest room. Beaut was alone, pumping himself up again with the cables. Bigg gave a glum nod as Crow passed the front counter. Crow crossed the hot parking lot to his GTO, which was parked over near Bigg's two white rental stretch limousines. He tossed his gym bag onto the passenger seat, cranked the engine into life, and rumbled out onto the street. Minutes later he was on the freeway entrance ramp winding out the big V–8, slamming the transmission into third gear when he noticed, just above the wiper blade, a red smudge, as if someone had planted a kiss on his windshield.

*When you go fishing, beware the fish.*

*—Crow's rules*

**M**ID-AFTERNOON ON WHITING LAKE: The thermometers tacked to the walls of the lakeshore cabins had peaked half an hour ago, some at eighty-one, some as high as ninety-two. Later, holding sweating cans of Pig's Eye beer, the owners of the cabins would stand around their smoking Webers and argue about how hot it had gotten, each defending their own thermometer's accuracy, citing location, poor vision, and manufacturing problems as the reason other thermometers disagreed with their own. The air was beginning to move from west to east, making the flat surface of the lake shimmer. Out on the big water, the surface began to jiggle in spots, forming near waves. Water that had been soaking up the July sun now threw off shards of light. From the shore it looked like sparks dancing just above the surface.

To the two men drifting in the battered aluminum johnboat three hundred yards off the point of Pine Island, the sparkling effect was not noticeable. Axel Speeter first became aware of the afternoon breeze as a tugging sensation on his arm hairs. He looked at his forearm, at the forest of white hair, making sure that what he was feeling wasn't something about to bite him. A variety of bloodsucking insects had been feeding on him all week, and he was tired of it. They never seemed to bother Sam O'Gara, the other occupant of the boat. Sam, about half Axel's girth and a foot shorter, had been staying at his cabin on Pine Island for most of the summer, and he claimed he hadn't given up but a thimbleful of blood. "The bugs know not to fuck with Sam O'Gara," he said. "Besides, you're bigger. You got more blood."

Sam was fishing with a lure he'd carved from the taillight lens of a '65 Mustang. He twitched his rod tip, let the makeshift lure settle back toward the bottom, jigged it up again, let it settle, over and over, every five seconds, just like a damn robot. He'd been applying the same technique for over two hours without a strike.

A deerfly buzzed Axel's nose, veered away, did a loop around Sam's greasy red baseball cap, landed on the bill for half a second, then buzzed off, apparently deciding not to fuck with him. Axel reeled in his line and examined the dying leech hanging from the hook. He lowered it back into the water. The three small walleyes he'd caught were hanging alongside the boat, waiting to be gutted, filleted, breaded, and fried. Axel was ready to call it a day, but he knew better than to suggest returning to the island. Sam would automatically object, and they'd be guaranteed another hour on the water. He pulled his cap low over his eyes and let his gaze wander down the shoreline. Maybe he should buy one of those cabins, have his own boat, his own place on the lake, fish when and where and for however long he wanted. How would Sophie feel about that? He shook his head, trying to derail that train of thought. The whole reason he'd come up here was to forget about Sophie and that crazy damn daughter of hers. The whole situation made him physically ill. He hadn't had a good night's sleep since Carmen had announced her engagement.

He said, "Hey, Sam."

"What?"

"How's it going? You holding your end of the boat down?"

Sam smiled and squinted, causing the number of wrinkles on his face to quadruple. "They ain't biting, but I'm stayin' dry."

It was a very Sam O'Gara thing to say. Axel did not know what the one fact had to do with the other, but when Sam put them together they sort of stuck. He remembered meeting Sam back in fifty-nine at a poker game in Sioux Falls. Sam hadn't had the wrinkles then, but he'd had the mouth. Axel let a wave of nostalgia wash over him.

"Hey, Sam."

"What's that?"

"How about you let me try out one of those Sam O'Gara originals."

Sam looked surprised, but pleased. "What you got in mind?"

Axel thought for a moment. "You got anything in a fifty-nine Chevy?"

For the first quarter of the three-hour drive up from the cities, Joe Crow had kept himself entertained by listing, one by one, all the women he had ever known to wear red lipstick. He tried to imagine each of them kissing his windshield, but could not come up with a plausible image. He was repeatedly forced to the conclusion that someone had mistaken his car for someone else's, which seemed unlikely, since there were very few lemon-yellow '69 GTOs remaining in this universe. But it was better than any of his other ideas.

After a time, the question began to grate on him. He tried to push it aside in favor of other mental exercises, but the lipstick print kept reminding him that his car had been kissed. He finally turned on the windshield washer and watched the lipstick smear, then disappear. His mind set free, he began to brood about other things. Beaut Miller muscled his way back into Crow's thoughts, leering and flexing his ridiculous arms. As soon as Crow recognized Beaut, he propelled his mind in other directions. Fishing, poker, highway signs, the way the engine made the hood vibrate, how his body felt after a good workout, music . . .

He'd listened to both of his Led Zeppelin eight-tracks too many times. He had to find some new music, but eight-tracks were as outdated and hard to come by as leaded premium gasoline—another requirement of riding the Goat. Maybe he should sell it and get another car. Something that would get better than nine miles a gallon. A Mercedes, a Land Rover, a BMW convertible—even a Volkswagen would be nice. Something with a cassette deck in it, or a CD player. Anything but an eight-track. He supposed he could take it out, replace it with a cassette deck. But the eight-track was original, it had come with the car. It was part of the whole classical sixties shtick that the Goat represented. If only he could find some decent tapes. Something besides Robert Plant's screeching vocalizations.

He thought about Laura Debrowski.

She had called from Paris a week ago, all chipper and bright.

Crow had asked her straight out, "So when are you coming home?"

The line crackled. "I don't know. I want to get this CD nailed down. These guys are good, Crow. I'm gonna make them the first French post-grunge superstars." She was talking about *Les Hommes Magnifiques,* the band she had discovered when she and Crow had flown to Paris last April for an open-ended vacation.

Crow had lasted less than two weeks in the land of baguettes and Camembert before heading back to the states. Debrowski stayed in Paris to work with *Les Hommes.* Their parting had been awkward. Crow didn't like to think about it. The phone conversation had been awkward, too.

"Hey, did I tell you I moved to a new place?" she said.

"No, you didn't. You're coming back sometime, aren't you?"

"Why? You miss me?"

"I'm keeping busy."

"Playing cards?"

"Some. So, things are going okay with that band?"

"Pretty good. How's Milo doing?"

"Pretty good."

After they exchanged a few more conversational packets and said good-bye, he realized that he had failed to get her new phone number and address. Or she had failed to give it to him.

Crow downshifted and depressed the accelerator, felt himself sink back in the seat. He watched the speedometer needle swing across the display. Ninety, ninety-five. He upshifted. One hundred, one-o-five, one-ten . . . there, he felt the fear hit him—visions of a blown tire, a tie rod giving way, wildlife jumping into his path. Crow held the speedometer at 110 for half a minute, feeling alive, then lifted his foot from the gas. The big engine slowed the car quickly to a sedate sixty-five. Hadn't blown a tire, cracked a rod, hit a deer. Hadn't got nailed by a trooper. Had he broken his thought pattern? For a brief moment, he could not remember what he had been thinking about. Then it came back.

Debrowski. He was still thinking about her. She would've liked that burst of speed, he thought. She was a fast car type of woman. Crow smiled at himself. Ah well, better to brood on her than on Beaut Miller. He imagined the two of them meeting. He did not think that they would like each other.

These days, thinking about Debrowski on the other side of the world brought sadness and loneliness. Thinking about Beaut and Bigg made him agitated and tense. The stew of emotions blended imperfectly; he arrived at the Whiting Lake landing feeling nauseous and jittery. Summoning all of his cerebral powers, Crow kicked Laura Debrowski and Beaut Miller and Arling Biggle under a large piece of mental furniture where he wouldn't have to look at them. For the next two days, he promised himself, he would think only about the fish.

"Hey, Sam."

Sam grunted, staring intently at the point where his line entered the water.

Axel pointed his rod tip toward shore. "Somebody's at the landing, waving at us."

Sam didn't move his head. "How come you think they're wavin' at us?"

"On account of we're the only goddamn thing on the lake, that's how come."

Sam raised his chin and squinted toward the landing.

"That would be my kid," he said.

Axel frowned. "Your kid Joe Crow?"

"No. Joe Stalin. Who the hell you think? Course it's my kid. What the hell you think we been doin' out here? Can't see the landing from the cabin now, can we?"

"I thought we were fishing."

Sam pulled in his line and waved the homemade lure in front of Axel's nose. "You think I'm gonna catch a fish with this piece a shit?" He set his rod in the bottom of the boat and started yanking the cord on the outboard. It usually took him seven or eight vigorous pulls to get it going.

As he reeled in his line, Axel said, "You know, I got a problem with that Joe Crow."

Sam paused in his efforts. "What's that?"

"I said I'm pissed at that kid a yours."

Sam gave the cord another yank. The motor sputtered and coughed, then settled into an unsteady putter. He adjusted the choke and dropped the motor into gear. The prow of the boat slowly swung around. They moved toward the landing.

Sam leaned toward Axel. "What did he do this time?"

*I chose my wife, as she did her wedding gown, for qualities that would wear well.*

—*Oliver Goldsmith*

HYATT HILTON SET THE CASE of Evian on the carpet and perched his lanky body on the waiting room chair. He said to the receptionist, "Nice day, huh?" and gave her his most disarming grin.

The receptionist smiled back at him—a quick flexing of her prim lips and a crinkling of the eyes—then returned to a sober perusal of her computer screen. Her hair was cut so short that Hyatt could see glare from the overhead fluorescents on her scalp.

"So, I guess you get to meet a lot of interesting people," Hyatt said.

"Mr. Chance will be right out," she said, granting him another smile, this one even more brief than the last.

Hyatt settled back in his chair and propped his feet on the case of water. He could always sense the way people reacted to him, and he used their reaction to divide humanity into three camps. There were the Suckers. There were the Assholes. And there were the Players.

The Suckers loved him. They saw the innocent kid in him, the farm boy. They bought their own first impression and stayed with it, too unimaginative to imagine he could be anything different than what he appeared to be. In Hyatt's experience, 20 percent of the human race were Suckers. Hyatt liked Suckers. He more than liked them. He loved them the way a dairy farmer loves his cows.

Most of the rest of humanity—79 percent, to be precise—fell into the Asshole category.

Assholes usually started out looking like Suckers, but at some point—sometimes it took seconds, sometimes days—their perception of him evolved. He had seen it, again and again. He would meet an individual, shake hands, see them taking him in, and then something would happen. Eyes would narrow slightly, chin would come down a quarter inch, arms would cross. Sometimes they would actually step back, expanding their personal space. It was not a good feeling, to watch a Sucker turn into an Asshole.

Generally speaking, Hyatt did not like Assholes. This receptionist was an Asshole.

The remaining 1 percent of the population were Players, those who, like Hyatt, understood the Sucker/Asshole equation and who had the smarts, the guts, or the position to take advantage of it. Hyatt didn't like Players, even though he was one. They were the competition.

He had been puzzling for some time as to how he should classify Carmen Roman, soon to become Carmen Hilton. She seemed to straddle all three camps. The more time he spent with her, the less he understood her.

His old friend Drew Chance was more easily classified. His reputation was a part of the public record. The simple fact that he made his living packaging celebrity gossip and personal tragedies into ninety-second news bytes was sufficient to define him as a Player.

Drew Chance was the host and executive producer of *Hard Camera,* the half-hour weekly TV news magazine that had recently gone into syndication. A few months back, Hyatt had read a newspaper article about the amazing success of the locally produced program and had realized for the first time that Drew Chance was actually Andy Greenblatt, a guy he'd used to play pool with at Moby Dick's back in the seventies. The realization that he had important contacts in the media had inspired Hyatt to devise his wonderful, perfect plan. His one shot at fame and fortune. His ticket out of the bogus Evian business and into the big time. Andy Greenblatt. Who'd have thought it?

It was Drew Chance who had broken the story of Sister Hulda Flood, the trailer park Madonna who had discovered an image of the Blessed Virgin Mary in the scum-crusted water of her backyard pool. That story had gone on to appear on both *Dateline* and *American Journal,* making both Sister Hulda and Drew Chance Productions a pile of money. According to the article in the *Star Tribune,* DCP had made better than six figures on just that one deal. Drew Chance had also reenergized the story of the Sandusky twins, the fourteen-year-olds who had gained notoriety last year when they were tried as adults for murdering their eight-year-old sister. They'd pled not guilty, claiming that she had jumped off the roof of their apartment building of her own volition. The jury had believed them. A few months after the trial, Drew Chance had convinced the twins to confess their guilt during a live edition of *Hard Camera*. The story was titled "Flying Lessons," and it had sold big overseas. DCP had made a few bucks on that one, too.

Yeah, Drew Chance—or Andy Greenblatt or whatever his name was—was definitely a player. Hyatt did not necessarily *like* Players, but he understood them. He could work with them.

"Mr. Hilton?"

Hyatt looked up. "Andy!" He stood up. Hyatt Hilton was a good fourteen inches taller than Andy Greenblatt.

Drew Chance's eyebrows drew together. He had those perfect news anchor eyebrows: dark, mobile, and expressive. His hair, curlier and more abundant than Hyatt remembered, glistened under the fluorescent lights. Drew's mouth fell open, then widened into a smile, showing a complete set of large, well-formed teeth, also more abundant than Hy remembered.

"Well I'll be butt-fucked. It's Hy the Guy."

Hyatt said, "How's it going, Andy?"

"I'm killin' 'em, Hy. God *damn*. You're looking *good*. Man, I thought you'd be dead or in jail by now. God *damn*. Is your last name really Hilton? I don't think I ever knew that. God *damn*. Somebody asked me, I would've said it was the Guy. Hy the Guy. Still got all your hair and everything."

"I see you got yours back, and then some."

Drew laughed and shook Hyatt's hand. "It's a rug, you moron."

"I brought you a present, Andy." He pointed to the case of water. "You like Evian, don't you?"

"Evian? Sure, what's not to like? Everybody likes Evian."

"Thirteen hundred dollars?" Sophie Roman let her mouth fall open.

The saleswoman, who dealt with such exclamations on a daily basis, nodded seriously. "It's a very good price," she said. She had introduced herself as Glinda, but she looked and talked more like the mayor of Munchkinland. Her three-inch heels and elaborate hairdo brought her up to an even five feet.

"Good for who?" Sophie asked, fingering the lacy fabric.

"An excellent price, considering all the beadwork. It all has to be done by hand, you know."

Sophie turned to her daughter. "It's too much," she said flatly.

Carmen pushed out her lower lip, but said nothing. Glinda made herself invisible.

Sophie said, "When I got married, I bought a dress for one hundred twenty-nine dollars, and it was beautiful."

"When you got married," Carmen said, "I wasn't even born yet."

Sophie digested that, shook her head to clear it. She retreated to her original position. "It's too expensive," she said.

"I only get married once, Mom."

"I sure hope so."

"Besides, Axel's going to pay for it, isn't he?"

"Not if it costs thirteen hundred dollars he's not." Sophie moved to another mannequin, this one wearing a dress with no beadwork whatsoever. "How much is this one?" she asked Glinda.

Carmen said, "I don't do big bows, Mom."

Sophie frowned and began to stalk the showroom floor, looking for something without beadwork or bows.

"Did you have a certain price range in mind?" Glinda asked, following her.

Sophie said, "Yes. Under three hundred dollars."

"No way," Carmen said. The expression on Glinda's face confirmed Carmen's analysis.

Sophie sucked in her upper lip. "We could check out some other shops."

Sensing a critical moment, Glinda asked, "Might I ask when the wedding date is?"

Sophie and Carmen spoke as one. "August ninth."

Glinda smiled sadly and shook her head with obvious relief. "All of our dresses are made to order. The fastest we could possibly deliver would be in about eighteen weeks. I think you'll find this to be the case at any quality bridal shop."

"I told you this was happening too fast," Sophie said, giving Carmen a triumphant look.

"The date's set, Mom. It's Hy's lucky day."

"I don't see what's so lucky about it."

"It's lucky 'cause he gets to marry *me!*" Carmen giggled and turned back to Glinda. "What about all these dresses you've got hanging here? You don't sell them?"

"These are our display models. They aren't for sale."

"I think we should go to J.C. Penny," Sophie suggested.

"I'd rather cut my throat."

"You've got some pretty fancy tastes for a girl with a baby in her belly."

Carmen rolled her eyes.

Glinda said, "We do sometimes sell our display models, but only when they're discontinued. Unfortunately, they're all size ten."

Carmen perked up. "I'm a ten up top."

Sophie said, "You'll be a ten down below by August."

"I'm sorry to say, we really don't have any available right now," Glinda said. She did not look sorry.

The other saleswoman, who was styling a dress nearby, said, "We do have one, dear. You know." She lowered her voice. "The Madonna."

Glinda turned to look at Carmen, tapping a long pink fingernail against her chin.

"The Madonna?" Sophie said, envisioning a saintly, mother-of-God edition of the classic wedding dress. "May we see it?"

Glinda smiled. "Why not?" she said. "We might be able to get near your price range with that one. Plus alterations, of course." She gave Carmen another appraising look and said, "You know, this might just work on you."


After Hyatt left, Drew Chance cracked open an Evian, pressed the intercom button on his phone and told Melissa to hold his calls. He leaned back in his ergonomically correct, black leather BackSaver Executive swivel chair. With a grunt of effort, he lifted his feet up onto the desk. As always, the desktop was empty except for a leather blotter, the telephone, and the remote control that controlled the bank of four monitors on the opposite wall. Drew believed that an empty desk was conducive to concentration. He lifted the Evian to his lips and sipped. It tasted like tap water, right down to the slightly swampy flavor that Minneapolis water developed during the summer months. Drew looked at the bottle. Imported from Évian, France. It seemed sort of silly to ship water all the way across the ocean, especially if it tasted like it had just come out of the kitchen faucet. It was all marketing. The right sales pitch, a guy could sell ice to an Eskimo.

That was pretty good. Drew sat up and pulled a notebook from the right-hand drawer. He uncapped his Waterman fountain pen and wrote: *Like selling ice to an Eskimo.*

Drew liked to write down a good line when he thought of one. He would use it during one of his hard-hitting news stories, and it would come across as if ad-libbed. He returned the notebook to its drawer and his feet to the desktop. Once again, he considered Hyatt Hilton. Hy the Guy, man, he'd been crazy back in the old days, and he hadn't changed a bit. Hy had spent an hour pitching his story, and Drew still didn't know what the guy was talking about. Something about a big wedding with lots of local celebs, a beautiful virgin bride, an evil cult of blood-drinking vampires, and a handsome courageous hero. Comic book stuff.

Drew had told Hy that he didn't do fantasy. "Real-life drama, Hy. All I do is the real stuff."

"This is what I'm saying, Andy!"

"Please. It's Drew."

"Drew! It's what I'm saying, it's real! I mean, what if it was real? What could you do with a story like that?"

"You mean it actually happened? In what universe?"

"Right here! Only it hasn't happened yet. I'm asking you, what if it *did* happen?"

Hy had even promised the story for the second week of August, which was—statistically speaking—the slowest news week of the season. That was according to the magazine *TV Journalist!* Hy was dreaming up some crazy stuff, but Drew was intrigued. A surrealistic real-life comic book thriller on a slow news week? What was not to like?

Of course, Hy had been sort of vague on the details. Drew still didn't know who, where, or why. Hy said he had all that, but he wanted money in exchange for exclusive rights to the story. A story that had not yet happened.

Drew had told him where to get off with that. "Hy, you ever hear of a thing called journalistic ethics?"

"We're talking story of the decade here, Andy."

"Yeah. You want to talk story of the decade? Suppose those guys that blew up that building in Oklahoma had come to me first, before they did the deed, and I'd paid them a few thousand bucks for the exclusive. You know. To be there with a film crew when it happened?"

"You'd have had one hell of a story."

"I'd be in jail, you moron."

"I'm not talking about blowing up anything."

"I don't know *what* the hell you're talking about. But until it happens, the checkbook stays closed."

"But if I tell you where to be, and when, and if you use the story, then there would be some money, right?"

"*If* there's a story."

"There will be. How much?"

"That would depend. If it got picked up by any of the national shows—they start bidding, the sky's the limit."

Hyatt had liked that. "Okay, but I need some kind of guarantee."

That had been a tough one. How could he contract for an exclusive on a story that hadn't happened yet and which, from the sounds of it, was going to involve some criminal activities? After mulling it over for a few seconds, Drew had an idea.

"How would you like to become one of our freelance reporters?" he asked.

Hy placed his hand reverently upon his breast. "Me?"

"Sure. That way it would be your story for sure. We write up a contract, and you're locked in. Anything you bring us, you get a piece of the pie."

Hyatt had bought it. He'd signed the standard contract and left the *Hard Camera* offices with a smile on his face.

Drew was smiling, too. The risk was all on Hyatt. If the story ever happened—which it probably wouldn't—Drew could see it going much bigger than the local market. He could see it going all the way to the top. *Jenny Jones. Geraldo Rivera. Dateline.*

He could even see it as a Movie of the Week.

*One God, One Way, One Life.*

—*First Maxim of the Amaranthine Church*

POLYHYMNIA DESIMONE, FIRST ELDRESS of the Amaranthine Church of the One, watched the long white thread depending from Rupert Chandra's slim ass. When Rupe moved from one side of the small stage to the other, the thread wafted behind him. When he stopped, it hung straight down, ending in a small bit of fluff. The thread originated from within the left hip pocket of his powder-blue linen trousers—from the lining, perhaps. She wondered whether anyone in the audience could see it.

Not likely. Rupe was in fine form. The Pilgrims were seeing what he wanted them to see.

Polly sat with her long legs crossed on one of two director's chairs set eight feet back from the edge of the stage, a pink-lipsticked smile fixed on her face. The spotlight in the floor behind her illuminated her platinum wig, producing a halolike effect. She wore a sleeveless, white silk brocade sheathe dress with a stand-up collar fastened at her throat by a ruby-studded brooch in the shape of a double helix. When she stood, the skirt would end six inches above her knees. Rupe called it her "dragon angel" outfit.

Rupe prowled the lip of the stage, his arms writhing, hands grasping, pulling ideas from the air, rubbing them into his chest, words welling up and pouring from his mouth. A Pakistani lilt elevated the end of each thought, making room for the next. The microphone clipped to the pocket of his electric blue silk shirt transmitted his words throughout the building. Even the restrooms had piped-in sound. That was the secret to a successful Extraction Event: Fill their minds with ideas. Never give them time to have their own.

Rupe was saying, "Energy is everywhere. I take it from here, and here"—he clawed the air and slapped his hand to his chest—"and where others see thin air I see life energy, there for the taking, the manifestation of the idea of life which you already have in you, my friends, for by the simple act of accepting your destiny you have begun a process that will regenerate your telomeres, strengthen your mind, and empower every cell in your body like the athlete who causes his own muscle cells to divide and increase in number, a process which only a few years ago scientists insisted was an impossibility but which has now been proven beyond the penumbra of a shadow of a doubt, my friends, for as the bodybuilder's muscles grow so will your telomeres grow and there is no stopping you now for you have taken the first and most difficult step and you are on your way and together, together we will live to see humanity spread to the stars and beyond and already you can feel your cells responding as I feel with each and every one of you, my friends, for today is the end of your long journey toward death as you take your first steps outside the festering murk of the Death Program and into the clear, clean thought of life, for you have seen the Death Program from the outside and you know it for the ugly little thing it is, and now is the beginning of your true life, not your pseudolife, because for millions of years life on this planet evolved through the mechanism of pseudo-life also known as death which was created by the mindless forces of evolution, my friends and, like the dinosaurs who ruled the earth for forty million years, it has had its day, for we are the RE-evolution, the evolution of the self-aware—" Rupe closed his mouth, snapping off the chain of words.

Polly let her breath out. She had a habit of inhaling when Rupe launched one of his megasentences, then trying to hold it until the sentence ended. Usually, she couldn't do it.

After three seconds of silence, Rupe began to speak again, more slowly. "Think about it. Think for yourself. Today, for the first time, we have the awareness, the knowledge, the intelligence to move evolution forward, to cause the very cells of our bodies to experience constant rebirth through telomere technology, channeling the powers of the mind, teaching ourselves to step out of the Death Program and to think for ourselves, to cast off the chains of the Death Program and take your time for I say to you again and again and again and again that we . . . have . . . all . . . the . . . time . . . in . . . the . . . world. We do not have to die anymore, my friends. Death is the *old* program. We are on the *new* program of cellular regeneration. We are the next step in the evolution of humanity, the first step beyond the boundaries of our former lifespans. We don't have to wait ten thousand generations to evolve. We see the opportunity to *live*. And we take it."

God, he was good. Polly could talk for an hour at a time if necessary, but Rupe could keep it up for two or three times that long. He just kept getting better. Never repeated himself, never faltered. The only imperfect part of him at that moment was that goddamn thread. It was all she could do to keep from jumping up and pulling it off him. Polly forced her eyes to the side. She looked past Rupe's thread-ridden ass and out at the room full of Pilgrims. They had twenty-seven today, two hundred fifty dollars a head for the one-day Extraction. She knew nearly all of them from previous Extraction Events. Greta Hoffmann, her pink rinse lighting up the front row, had been attending Extraction Events for two years. Greta, one of the forty-four Faithful who made up the ACO's core membership, could always be relied upon to slip a little something extra, a contribution to her "Life Account," into Rupe's pocket. Five hundred dollars was her usual offering. Sitting beside her, a young couple named Williston held hands and followed Rupe's movements across the stage, necks stretched forward, mouths open, looking like a pair of baby robins waiting for a dose of predigested worm. This was Bruce and Janice Williston's second Event. They had yet to embrace the Life Account concept, but Polly judged them to be ripe to enter the ranks of the Faithful.

There were only two new faces in the room—a bearded grad student type and a fearful-looking woman in her late fifties. The woman looked like a potential immortal. Polly wasn't so sure about the grad student, but the fact that he'd paid his two-fifty to be there was a good sign. The fact that this Extraction Event had attracted only two new faces concerned her greatly. Without a continual influx of new members, the church's energy would sag in time. Work on Stonecrop would come to a halt.

Polly was counting on next week's Anti-Aging Clinic to bring in a new wave of Pilgrims. They had beefed up their print advertising for the clinic, running ads in *New Age Health,* the *StarTribune,* the *Pioneer Press,* and *Senior Times.* Calls had been coming in all week. Polly was hoping for a full house.

Rupe would be winding down soon, and it would be her turn to speak the language of life. She decided to come down hard on the membership challenge: *To grow is to live. To live is to grow.* As she was formulating her opening, she saw the door at the back of the hall open. Hyatt Hilton poked his head into the room. He grinned at her, making sure she saw him, then disappeared. Polly's smile wavered. She stood abruptly and left the stage through the curtained wing, followed by a concerned glance from Rupe.


Polly found her Head of Security, Charles "Chuckles" Thickening, slouched in a chair in the dressing room playing with his GameBoy. The handheld video game looked tiny in his meaty brown hands. He glanced up briefly, flashed his gold canine tooth, then returned his attention to his game. Chuckles's face was the color of sooty brick, with mobile, purplish lips and large, expressive eyes. He had a closely cropped head with a double helix shaved into each temple, one gold earring, and a thick gold chain draped across his fifty-three-inch chest. A crude tattoo depicting a grinning skull adorned his left forearm.

"Why aren't you on the door?" Polly demanded.

Chuckles's thick fingers massaged the GameBoy, producing a series of beeps. "Me, I'm on break. It quiet in here." The dressing room was the only room in the building that did not have Rupe's discourse piped in. "Chip, he's up front," Chuckles added.

Polly snatched the GameBoy, her pink nails raising parallel weals on Chuckles's wrist. "You don't take breaks when we're on."

Chuckles rubbed his wrist and kept his eyes on the GameBoy. "Chip, he can handle it."

"If Chip could handle it, I wouldn't have hired you. Hyatt Hilton is in the building."

Chuckles sat up. "Again?"

"I just saw him in the auditorium. Find him. And before you put him back in the dumpster, find out how he got in, and what he's doing here."

Chuckles pushed up off the chair and trotted down the hall toward the front of the building, his thick torso gaining speed.

"And cover up that tattoo!" she shouted after him. Polly tossed the Game-Boy on the long dressing table. She took a cigarette from the pack she'd stashed above the mirror and lit it. Puffing angrily, she paced the room. What was Hy doing? The last time he'd tried to disrupt a meeting, Chuckles and Chip had tossed him in a dumpster. Apparently, he hadn't got the hint.

What did he hope to gain by making trouble for the church?

Maybe Rupe was right. Maybe they should've paid Hy off when they'd expelled him. Given him enough to live on for a year or two. Severance pay. She could understand how Hy might feel bitter, but it wasn't as if he'd given them any choice. Well, hell, it was too late now. If Hy wanted a fight, then that's what he'd get.

Polly sucked her cigarette with renewed fury, producing a glowing ash two inches long. The sudden influx of superheated nicotine produced the sensation that her wig had come alive. She ground the butt into the floor and kicked it under the table. Rupe would be freaking. He could talk for a long time, but he was nearing his limit, and he didn't like being on stage alone. Chuckles could handle Hy. She had to focus and keep the show going. *To grow is to live, to live is to grow.* That would be her theme for the next half hour. She checked her reflection in the mirror. Not bad, she thought, for thirty-eight.

Polly DeSimone had worked as a model—mostly runway work—back in the eighties. She had been valued for her regular, instantly forgettable features and her ability to change outfits in seconds. She still looked good, and she planned to keep it that way. Aging and death were disgusting, small-minded concepts. It was remarkable, really, that she and Rupe were among the first to have discovered the key to cellular regeneration. It was right and fitting that they should be rewarded for bringing this knowledge to others, even though— she had no illusions here—many of the Pilgrims would never develop the mental powers to regenerate their telomeres and bring about the cellular rebirth necessary for them to achieve true physical immortality.

Polly stepped back from the mirror and turned her body this way and that, checking for loose threads.

Thirty-eight years old, and she didn't look a day over twenty-five.

As soon as Rupe saw Polly return to the stage he segued into his finish. "I love you," he said to the audience, spreading his arms wide. "How can I not? I'll know you for a thousand years. I'll know you forever." He paused for ten full seconds, the longest period of silence since he had taken the stage two hours earlier. Midway through the moment of silence, spontaneous tears welled from his soulful Pakistani eyes, streamed down his cheeks. His arms began to shake. The thread on his ass quivered. He screamed, "I can feel your cells!"

That was Polly's cue. Rupe's knees were shaking so hard they could see it from the back of the hall. Polly jumped up and wrapped her arms around him. She helped him to his chair. As he sat down, she pulled the thread loose from his back pocket and let it fall to the stage. Polly turned to the enraptured audience.

"Why is this man crying?" she asked quietly, layering a measure of anger over her voice. The faces in the audience underwent a communal cringe, as though they had been found guilty. Polly darted her eyes from one anchor point to another, as though accusing each individual Pilgrim, though in fact she was looking at no one in particular. "I'll tell you why he's crying," she said. "He is crying because he knows that there is one person in this room who does not believe." Long pause. "One person who does not wish to see the future." She put a hand on Rupe's shaking shoulder. "This man, this good and generous man is crying because he knows that despite everything he has done, one of you will die!" She shot out a finger, pointing at Bruce Williston. He gasped and squeezed his wife's hand so hard she let out a yelp. Polly stepped to the lip of the stage, holding him with her accusatory finger, then releasing him, scanning the audience with her long pink nail, searching for betrayal like a dowser with a witching wand, finally letting her arm fall to her side and turning her back to the audience. She smiled at Rupe, who continued to produce a river of tears. It was amazing how that man could cry.

Polly raised her hands above her head, then spun around, breasts thrust out, chin up, lips pouted, legs apart.

She said, "Look at me." She did a pirouette, all the way around, inviting them to see her as a woman. "How old am I?" she asked. "Come on, don't be shy. Talk to me. How old am I?"

Greta Hoffman, who knew the routine, raised her hand.

"Twenty-five," she said.

"Why, thank you," said Polly, bestowing the full luminosity of her smile on the elderly woman. "Any other guesses?"

One of the newcomers, the grad student–type, called out, "Thirty-six."

With tremendous effort, Polly forced her smile to widen. "Oh dear," she said. "Okay, one more." She pointed at Bruce Williston. "What do you think?"

Williston licked his lips. "Twenty-six?" he asked. Like most of the Pilgrims in the room, the Willistons had seen this act before. They knew what to say.

Polly laughed. "Much better. Thank you."

Greta, who loved to play this game, asked, "How old *are* you?"

Polly said, "I am sixty-one years old."

The Pilgrims began to clap. Polly beamed, drinking in the applause. She forgot about Hyatt Hilton. She forgot about the thread on Rupe's ass. She even forgot, for the moment, her true age.

*Let other people have their problems.*

—*Crow's rules*

"**W**HAT'S WRONG WITH AXEL?" Crow asked.

"Ax? Nothing wrong with him a two by four upside the head wouldn't cure."

"He's hardly said a word to me all afternoon. Keeps giving me that evil eye."

Joe Crow and Sam O'Gara were sitting on Sam's small porch, looking down the hill through the trees toward the dock, where Axel Speeter was cleaning the three walleyes he'd landed that afternoon. Sam's hounds, Chester and Festus, were sleeping at the foot of the steps, emitting occasional snorts and grumbles, occasionally joined by a hollow, bonking sound from a nearby birch tree from which Sam had suspended about twenty steel hubcaps by wires. Every time the breeze picked up, the hubcaps clanked against one another. Sam called them his wind chimes.

"Yeah, well he's got a bone up his butt, and he thinks you put 'er there, son." Sam fished a Pall Mall from the pocket of his plaid flannel shirt. The sun was sinking into the treetops, but it was still warm, in the eighties. The heat never seemed to bother Sam. He wore flannel all summer long.

"Me? What did I do? I haven't even seen Axel since last summer, at the fair."

Sam ignited a wooden match by flicking it with his thumbnail, sucked the flame onto the tip of his cigarette. "According to Ax, that's when you put in the bone."

Crow stood and faced his father. He had known him for nearly two decades, ever since Sam had reentered his life at his high school graduation, claiming to be his old man. Even now Crow had a hard time imagining his mother taking on this wizened old coot's seed, though she had confirmed, somewhat reluctantly, the truth of Sam's claim to parentage. Still, at times, he doubted it. Other times, he felt as if he was looking into a time-warped mirror, seeing himself in another thirty or forty years—three inches shorter, features obscured by massive wrinkling, and not giving a shit about much of anything. Whatever the facts surrounding Crow's ancestry, the two had become friends.

Crow looked back down through the trees. Axel had finished filleting the walleyes and was sitting motionless at the end of the dock, staring across the water at the last shards of sunlight. For a few seconds, Crow felt himself wrapped in silence. No sound, no movement, no sensation. Then a breeze crossed his neck and the hubcaps began to bong mournfully, and a twisting cloud of blue tobacco smoke floated into view.

Crow said, "You want to tell me what the hell's going on here, Sam?"

Sam grinned through the veil of smoke, his weathered face crinkling in a hundred places. "Son, one thing you got to learn about Ax, you can't take him too serious. He's spent half his life mad at me, and we're still fishing outta the same boat."

"So what am I supposed to have done?" Crow stepped off the porch and started pacing, scuffing pine needles with the toes of his canvas shoes, kicking at pine cones. One of them hit Festus, causing the hound to leap to his feet and bay.

"Easy there," Sam said. The hound shook its head, recognized Crow, and sank back down. Sam continued. "You didn't do nothin,' son. Ax ain't been the same since this wedding thing."

"Wedding thing? What wedding thing?"

"It weren't your fault, son, no matter what that old cocker thinks. It's that little gal Carmen that's got his pecker in a twist."

Crow stopped. "I should have known this had to do with Carmen. What kind of mess has she made this time?"

"She got herself knocked up and engaged is what."

"And Axel blames me? I didn't knock her up, that's for damn sure. She's not my type."

"Well, you're the one introduced her to the one that done it, son."

"I did?" Crow furrowed his brow, thinking back. He shook his head. "I don't remember fixing up Carmen with anybody. I wouldn't do that to anyone."

"That a fact? What about a fella named Holiday Hilton?"

"Holiday . . . wait a second. Not *Hyatt* Hilton."

"That's what I said."

"Carmen Roman and Hyatt Hilton?"

Sam nodded. "You got 'er."

Crow climbed back onto the porch and sank into a chair, wearing a stunned expression. After a minute had passed he said, "I suppose it's like atoms."

Sam said, "Say what?"

"Atoms. The odds of any two of them colliding are trillions to one. But they're running into each other all the time."

Sam's lips parted slightly. He gave his head a quick snap, tossing off his son's words. "Yeah, well, whatever. Anyways, that's why Ax is acting like a jerkball. He says you're the one put those two together."

"I was there when they met, but I didn't introduce them."

"That don't matter to Ax," Sam said. "You was within a country mile of the deed, Ax is gonna put it on ya."

Crow nodded slowly as a memory returned.

The way it happened, he recalled, he'd been minding his own business, just happened to be in the wrong place at the wrong time, the same way he always got himself in trouble. He and Debrowski had decided to visit the Minnesota State Fair. Debrowski liked to look at the horses; Crow went for the memories.

Debrowski had traded in her usual black-leather-and-chains biker ensemble for a pair of dagger-toed red, white, and blue cowboy boots; a pair of powder-blue Wranglers so tight Crow could hear the seams creaking; and an embroidered western shirt with mother-of-pearl snaps and silver collar points. Crow, by contrast, had once again applied his sole fashion strategy, which was to put on something clean and hope for the best. On that day he had thrown on olive chinos and a white T-shirt.

Crow said, "Howdy, podna. What have you done with Laura Debrowski?"

Debrowski grinned. "You like it, don't you, Crow?"

Crow wasn't yet sure. "Don't you need a cowboy hat?" he asked.

"I don't wear them."

Crow nodded as if that made sense. They rode to the fairgrounds in Crow's Jaguar XJS. On the way there, Crow found it impossible to stay off the subject of Debrowski's outfit. He kept looking over at her.

"Aren't those boots going to make for uncomfortable walking?"

Debrowski laughed. "You're so sweet to worry."

"It's just . . . I never thought of you as a cowgirl."

"It's for the horses," she explained. "I used to ride in exhibitions, you know."

"Sometimes I think you used to do everything."

"Pretty much," she agreed.

"Only I never knew anybody who dressed up to impress the animals."

"Horses are smart."

Crow didn't argue. For all he knew, horses might be the true rulers of the planet. Or maybe it was the cats that were in charge. He sure as hell hoped it wasn't people. On the way from the parking lot to the fairgrounds his thoughts returned to the matter of Debrowski's ensemble.

He said, "Tell me something. How did you get into those jeans?"

Debrowski winked. "Crisco," she said.

They hadn't stayed at the fair long. Debrowski headed straight for the barns. Crow begged off the horses, pleading a fashion deficiency, and went for a walk down the Midway, absorbing the music, the rattling of the rides, the shouts of pitchmen. Trashy, cheap, and strident, but if he let his mind float back to the age of, say, ten—he could still taste the excitement.

Crow and Debrowski rendezvoused an hour later at the seed art exhibit in the Horticulture Building.

"Get me out of here, Crow," Debrowski said, staring at a portrait of Michael Jackson made from pinto beans, wheat berries, sunflower seeds, and quinoa. "My goddamn feet are killing me. Besides—" Crow felt her hand on the back of his thigh. "—Those stallions, Crow, they sort of make me think of you."

Crow swallowed and hoped he wasn't blushing. "Absolutely, then, let's get going," he said. "Only we've got to say hi to Axel on the way out."

"Who's Axel?"

"One of Sam's old buddies. He's got a concession here at the fair. Used to give me free tacos."

Debrowski shrugged her assent. They threaded back through the crowd. Crow fell in behind her so that he could watch her jeans, make sure they didn't split open or anything. They exited the Horticulture Building onto the grassy mall. He pointed out a brightly painted concession stand: AXEL'S TACO SHOP. "Over there."

They were almost to the taco stand when Crow heard his name called. Looking around, he spotted a pale head jutting above the mass of fairgoers.

Crow said, "Oh my god. Is that Hy the Guy?"

Debrowski said, "Who?"

Hyatt Hilton caught up with them, holding out his hand. "It's Joe Crow, isn't it?"

Crow shook Hyatt's hand. "How's it going, Hy. Still in the dope business?"

Hyatt waggled his head. "I found peace," he said, offering his hand to Debrowski. "Hyatt Hilton," he said. "One God."

Debrowski gave him a formal smile and a brief handshake.

Crow explained. "Hy used to be my coke connection."

"Ah," said Debrowski.

"A former existence," Hyatt said.

"So what happened, Hy?" Crow asked. "You make enough money to retire?"

Hyatt ignored the question. "I'm with the Amaranthines now."

"The what?"

"The Amaranthine Church of the One." Hyatt's eyes spun with zeal. "One God. One Way. One Life."

Crow took a step back.

Debrowski said, "He's talking about that immortality cult, Crow. They had that article about them in City Pages."

"It's not a cult." Hyatt frowned. "That was lies. They twisted what we said."

"So you don't really claim to be immortal?"

"Oh. That part was true. You should stop by our booth," Hyatt said. "We're in the grandstand. First floor, between Miracle Chef and the pro-life people."

"Thanks, Hy, but we were just on our way home." Crow gave Debrowski a nudge and started walking.

Hyatt followed them. "I'll walk you out."

"We have to stop and say hello to some friends first," Crow said over his shoulder.

Hyatt said, "That's okay. I've got plenty of time."

Carmen and Sophie Roman were working Axel's taco concession. Crow approached the front of the stand and waited for Carmen to notice him. She finished making change for a customer, then turned her sleepy eyes on Crow.

"Hi, Carmen," he said. "How's it going?"

"Can I help you?" she replied.

"It's Joe," he said. "Joe Crow. You remember me?"

"I don't think so," she said.

"I'm Sam O'Gara's son."

Carmen smiled. "Oh, sure."

"Is Axel around?"

"I don't think so."

Crow could see he wasn't going to get much from Carmen. He looked past her and called out, "Hey, Sophie."

Sophie, who was lowering a rack of tortillas into the deep fryer, recognized him at once. She wiped her hands on a towel and leaned over the counter. "Axel's gone off someplace," she said. "I don't know when he'll be back." She looked tired.

Crow gestured toward Debrowski, who was standing behind him talking to Hyatt. "This is Laura Debrowski."

Debrowski looked up and smiled. "How you doing?"

Crow said, "This is Sophie Roman and her daughter, Carmen." Sophie nodded politely. Carmen's bored, sleepy expression did not change.

Hyatt stepped in. "I'm Hyatt Hilton," he said, holding out his hand until Sophie shook it. He released her, then repeated his self-introduction to Carmen. "You look like Sophia Loren," he told her. "Back in the sixties."

Carmen woke up. "Really?"

Sophie rolled her eyes. She said to Crow, "If you see Axel, tell him to get his butt back here, would you?"

Hyatt and Carmen had moved down the counter. Crow heard Hyatt ask her if she would like to live forever.

"What for?" Carmen asked.

Crow saw his opportunity to give Hyatt the slip. He grasped Debrowski's elbow and led her up the mall toward the fairgrounds exit.

Debrowski said, "Where did you find him, Crow?"

"He used to work at this health food store," Crow said. "He and this woman—I think her name was Polly—and her husband. Ambrosia Foods, down on Lyndale Avenue. Melinda used to shop there."

Debrowski grunted. Crow's ex-wife was not one of her favorite topics.

"She spent a fortune on vitamins and weird herbs. After a while, she even had me going there."

"That I can't see. Aren't you the guy who just ate two corndogs?"

"I didn't go there for the health food. Hy had a little cocaine business going on the side. He was the guy. Hy the Guy. He had a theory about how cocaine should only be used with these multivitamin supplements. They were called Coca Boost, and they came in a plastic bag and cost ten bucks a half dozen. I always left there with a bunch of stuff I didn't want." Crow laughed. "Hy was the only coke dealer I ever met who made his profits on accessories. Anyway, the coke was always good."

"That's all that matters," Debrowski said dryly. Joe Crow and Laura Debrowski had met in a CA group.

Crow remembered two other things about that day at the fair. One was that Debrowski's feet had hurt so bad she'd had to take off her boots and socks and walk barefooted all the way to the car. The other thing was that she had lied about the Crisco.

Crow and his father were still sitting on the front porch. A few minutes earlier, Axel had marched past them carrying the filleted walleyes. He hadn't said a word. They could hear him banging around in the kitchen, cursing Sam's meager collection of kitchen utensils.

Sam had finished his cigarette and now had his lower lip packed with Copenhagen. "So this fella Hilton, he as bad news as Ax thinks?"

Crow shrugged. "Maybe. Maybe not. He used to be into health food and dope, but by the time he met Carmen, he said he was involved with some flaky church. I don't know if that's better or worse."

"Prob'ly both."

"You think I ought to try to talk to Axel, or just let it slide?"

"Hold that thought, son." Sam got out of his chair and went into the cabin. Ten seconds later he was back in his chair cracking open a Budweiser. "Ax says we're eatin' in a minute." He poured a few ounces of beer into his mouth, swallowed, belched, leaned over the low railing, and spat tobacco. "I was you, I'd go ahead, try and talk to the son-of-a-bitch. God knows he can't get any crankier. There's just one thing I gotta ask you."

"What's that?"

"This fellow Hilton, is he the sort likely to hit ol' Ax over the head and try to steal all his money like Carmen's last boyfriend?"

Crow thought for a moment. "I don't think so."

Sam nodded sharply. "Good. Then you tell him whatever you got to. Only don't tell him nothing he don't need to know."

Axel appeared in the doorway, nearly filling it.

"Let's eat," he said.

*I don't remember finding a sailor, however modest, who was not frank to admit that at cribbage he was champion of his ship.*

—*John Scarne*

"**A**RE YOU HAPPY NOW?" Sophie asked.

"Happy about what?"

"The dress, what else?"

Carmen shrugged. "It's okay." She bit into her scone. They were sitting at one of the upstairs tables at Café Latté, looking down on Grand Avenue.

"It better be okay."

Carmen grinned. "Axel's gonna freak when he sees it."

"He's going to freak when he sees the bill, that's for sure. It's going to wind up costing nearly five hundred dollars." Sophie Roman stirred her cappuccino. Carmen was right. Axel *would* freak when he saw the Madonna dress. It certainly was not like any wedding dress Sophie had ever seen before. Not at all like the chaste, God-fearing frock she had expected. But Carmen had loved it. Carmen had gone nuts for it.

Sophie tried to reconstruct the way it had happened: Glinda brought out the dress. Carmen put it on. Sophie said, "No way, young lady. Absolutely not."

That had been a mistake. The next thing she knew they were shouting at each other, right there in Bridal Shoppe. Then something had happened inside her, like a pipe broke, and all the fight had drained out of her and she'd agreed to buy the dress. It often went like that when she argued with Carmen. Sophie just didn't have the legs to keep on slugging. Carmen was a young woman; she had the endurance to go all the way. Sophie chose to reserve her energies for more important matters—although she could not at the moment imagine what could be more important than the selection of a wedding dress.

So they'd bought it.

Carmen said, "I can't believe you let me buy it."

"What's done is done," Sophie said, wondering how the purchase had suddenly become *her* doing. "Now show me what you've got from the caterer."

Carmen pulled a sheaf of paper from her purse and handed it across the table. Sophie propped her reading glasses on her nose, looked at the first page, turned to the last line of the last page, then reviewed the entire four-page document from front to back, her mouth becoming increasingly smaller. She could feel another fight coming on, another fight she knew she'd lose. But she couldn't stop herself.

"When I married your father we fed seventy-five people for two hundred and sixty-five dollars."

"What did you serve them? Oatmeal?"

"We had an Italian wedding." She pronounced it *eye-TALY-un*. "We had lasagna and spumoni and red wine in those basket bottles, and it was very elegant."

"That was twenty-two years ago," Carmen argued.

Sophie stabbed her finger at the paper. "What's this 'Wild Mushroom Tarts'? What are Wild Mushroom Tarts, and why do they cost a hundred twenty dollars?"

"Hy likes mushrooms, Mom."

"Well I like Rolls Royces, but that doesn't mean I have to drive one. I don't see the meatballs on here. We have to have Swedish meatballs."

"Hy's a vegetarian, Mom. He wants the reception to be meat-free."

"What about Axel? If you want him to pay for this, you'd better have Swedish meatballs. He loves those things. Besides, they're cheap."

"Maybe we should go Mexican," Carmen said, putting a sneer in her voice. "Have Axel cater the damn thing himself. Feed everybody Super Tacos and Bueno Burritos. We could set up a taco stand in the reception hall."

Sophie actually seemed to be considering the suggestion. Carmen quickly said, "I'm just kidding."

"It *would* save a lot of money," Sophie said.

"Look, I don't want you and Axel rolling burritos when you should be in the wedding party. I want this to be nice. It's my *wedding*."

Sophie bit down on her wooden coffee stirrer. "Maybe we could invite fewer people," she suggested.

"We already cut it down to one hundred and sixty. Hy wants a big wedding."

"Speaking of the wedding, have you found a church yet?"

"Not exactly. But we've got a preacher."

"A preacher? What kind of preacher are we talking about?"

"I don't know. Does it matter?"

"Well, we *are* Catholic."

"Yeah, right."

Sophie blinked. She parted her lips to speak, then gave her head a quick back-and-forth jerk, as if trying to flick a bead of sweat from the tip of her nose. "Well, anyway, you want to make sure it's a nice church. Big enough to hold everybody."

"Uh-huh. I'm sure it'll be fine, Mom."

Sophie looked back down at the caterer's estimate, frowning. "I still don't see why we can't have meatballs. Hyatt doesn't have to eat any if he doesn't want to."

Carmen tasted her coffee, added two more pouches of sugar. She agreed with Sophie about the meatballs. She liked Swedish meatballs, too. But Hy wanted a vegetarian spread, and that was that. She had to keep it together here. Sophie would bitch right up until the *I dos,* and then some. But it really wasn't up to her—Axel would be paying the bills. Still, she had to start with Sophie if she was to get the wedding she and Hy wanted. She hadn't broken it to Sophie yet, but Hy didn't want to get married in a church. He said he'd had enough of churches. He wanted to do the deed at the reception hall, wherever that turned out to be. Some place nice. It had to be big. They were going to have a big wedding with lots of people. Hy said a lot of celebrities would be there, like the guy on that TV show. What was his name? Hy had a list of people he wanted to invite. Hy said the more people they invited, the more *perfect* it would be.

♠

Axel placed the last piece of walleye in his mouth and chewed slowly, fixing his green eyes on Joe Crow. He said, "So what you're saying is, he's not a friend of yours."

"That's right," said Crow. He watched the way Axel's chewing made his jaw muscles pulse up his temples, all the way to the top of his bald crown. The old man had a big head, which suited the rest of his body. He must've been a monster when he was younger, Crow thought. He still looked like he could eat nails.

Axel put down his fork. "But you don't much like him."

"I wouldn't want to go fishing with him. But if he was in the boat, I wouldn't jump out."

"Then how come you introduced him to Carmen? You know how impressionable she is."

Sam pulled off his baseball cap and whacked Axel across the shoulder with it. "Dammit, Ax, he's been tryin' to tell you he didn't do nothing."

Axel looked at his shoulder, then back at Crow.

"But she'd never had met him if it wasn't for you."

"That's right," Crow admitted. "He followed me and Debrowski over to your taco stand, and then he introduced himself. I think he was trying to convert her."

"Convert her to what?"

"He was involved in some sort of church."

"He doesn't strike me as the church-going type."

"I don't think it was the church-going type of church. Anyway, Debrowski and I took off. We were trying to get rid of him, actually."

"You left him with Carmen."

Crow sighed. "I didn't know he was going to want to marry her. Besides, what was I supposed to do?"

Axel set his jaw, leaned forward, then rose up to his full height of six feet four inches, his bad knee popping. He said, "I always liked you, Joe. You're a straight shooter." He walked to the door and looked out through the screen toward the sunset. "Unlike my future son-in-law, who I wouldn't trust to piss out the right hole." Axel opened the door and stepped out onto the porch.

Crow turned to Sam and said in a low voice, "Carmen isn't his *daughter*, is she?"

Sam shook his head. "Ax is kinda funny on that point. See, him and Sophie, they're shackin' up. So in his head, it's like her kid is his kid."

"Axel and Sophie are living together?"

"Pretty much."

Crow smiled. "They must be driving each other nuts."

Sam lit a cigarette, tipped his chair back, propped his feet on the table next to his plate. "Sometimes I think they already done it, son. She's what they call a *fate accomplished.*"

Later that night, Axel and Crow sat down to a game of cribbage, a dime a point. Sam had made the cribbage board from the valve cover off an old Ford 289-cubic-inch V–8. The pegs were fashioned from cotter pins. Axel was up five bucks, which was fine with Crow. He'd be better off losing, considering Axel's touchiness. Sam watched for a while, drank a few more beers, made some unwelcomed suggestions, then tottered off to bed.

"He likes his juice," Axel said.

Crow nodded in agreement. He had mixed feelings about Sam's drinking. Sometimes he thought that his father would be better off if he gave it up. Other times, he couldn't imagine it. Maybe an alcohol-free Sam wouldn't be Sam anymore. He might become somebody else. As for himself, Crow suspected that he'd been a more interesting person when he'd been using. Funnier and more relaxed. According to the CA and AA people, such thinking was both fallacious and counterproductive. Nevertheless, Crow still had those thoughts, though they didn't come as often these days. Crow now thought of Sam as the family drinker. As long as Sam drank, Crow didn't have to. If Sam clambered aboard the water wagon, Crow might have to jump off to make room.

"Never could understand it." Axel had been nursing the same Budweiser since dinner. "I drank that much beer I'd be pissing all night long."

"This didn't used to be an island, you know."

Axel picked up his newly dealt hand, frowned at his cards. "You ought to be more respectful. He is your old man."

"Yeah, maybe. He's old, anyway."

"All the more reason to be respectful."

"He ever tell you how he came to buy this place?"

"He said you and him came into some money."

"Yeah. I was going to buy a cabin up here. Next thing I know, Sam goes and buys one."

"And you're complaining 'cause he stole your idea? Seems to me it's a good deal for you, kid. You hang out for free and when he dies you get your cabin after all."

"I suppose. But sometimes I wish I had something of my own right now. You know. You've got your business at the fair, and Sam's got his place in St. Paul. Me, I'm living in a rented duplex and playing cards for a living."

Axel sorted through his cards. "You keep dealing your opponents shitty cards like these, kid, you'll do fine."

"The point is, I wish I had my own island or something." Crow felt awkward now, with Sam gone. He wasn't sure why he was saying this to Axel.

Axel selected two cards from his hand and threw them into the crib. "Of course, I don't need good cards to whip your rookie ass. Back in the merchant marine I was cribbage champ three years running."

Crow added his two cards to the crib. Axel cut the deck and Crow rolled the starter card. A jack. "Two for his heels," Crow said, moving a cotter pin forward two holes. He hadn't played cribbage in years, but its strange rules and customs and language had quickly come back to him.

Axel grunted, squinting at the jack with his straight eye. The other eye stayed on Crow, who could not imagine how a guy could make sense of the world with eyes pointing two different directions. Axel emitted another grunt, then laid down a card, calling it out. "Four. Sam and me, back in our heyday we used to make our living playing cards. Best times I ever had."

"It must've got old or you'd still be doing it. Ten."

"I was the one got old. Fifteen two and a run of three." Axel pegged five points. "Why don't you buy yourself a little business? Get yourself a stand out at the fair?"

Crow laughed.

Axel gave him a sharp look. "What's so funny?"

"Nothing," said Crow.

Axel stared at him, his eyes catching light from the flyspecked lamp hanging over the table. "Don't talk out the side of your mouth to me," he said, his voice sharp.

Crow sat back, startled.

Axel said, "Don't give me this crap about you want your own island then laugh at my piece of dirt."

"Sorry!"

Axel was shaking his head. "Jesus Christ, Joe. First you fix up my little girl with that son-of-a-bitch Hilton, then you laugh at what I do."

Crow laid down a three. "Eighteen and a run of four. And I told you, I didn't 'fix them up.'"

Axel frowned as Crow pegged four. "Whatever. Look, I believe you when you say you didn't do it on purpose. Everybody makes mistakes. When I was your age I did some pretty dumb-ass things myself. Just don't treat me like I'm an old cocker doesn't know what's what. I don't need you walking on my eggs."

"Okay." The hell with respectful, Crow decided. Axel might be his elder, but he could be an elderly ass. "I won't walk on your eggs anymore if you'll lay off me about Hyatt Hilton. It's not my fault if Carmen's stupid enough to marry the guy."

"Carmen is not stupid. And she didn't go looking for the guy. Somebody brought him to her."

"Fine. Okay. I give up. I was the matchmaker. I went out of my way to introduce Hyatt to Carmen for the sole purpose of making your life miserable. I confess."

Axel lifted his eyebrows. "Good." He laid down a ten. "Twenty-eight."

"Thirty."

"Thirty one." Axel pegged two. "Can I ask you something?"

"Sure."

"What exactly do you do? I mean, besides playing poker."

Crow laid down his last card, a ten, and pegged a point for the go. He hated that question. He didn't really know what he did anymore. The last time he'd been able to answer it had been a few years ago, when he'd been working as a small-town cop out in western Minnesota. He'd gotten fired from that job and hadn't seen anything resembling a paycheck since.

Everyone who asked him what he did got a different answer.

"Well," he said slowly, "this weekend I'm hanging out with a drunk, who thinks the world is made out of car parts, and a cockeyed, cribbage-playing taco-seller with a bone up his butt on account of he needs to blame somebody for a situation he can't do a damn thing about."

Axel glared, then his mouth fell into an open grin, and he began to chuckle. The chuckle enlarged into a laugh. His face, always ruddy, bloomed deep red, and his green eyes filled with tears. Crow watched, astonished. Axel was not a man who laughed easily, and certainly not like this. It was all the more bizarre because Crow didn't think that what he'd said was funny. He'd been genuinely angry. Within a few seconds, Axel's laughter took on a wheezy quality, and he started coughing—big, gasping coughs that sounded as if his chest was filled with Jell-O.

"Are you okay?" Crow asked.

Axel nodded, still coughing. He waved his hand in a don't-mind-me gesture.

Crow found himself thinking how hard it would be, if Axel died, to get that big body down the hill and into Sam's boat. As soon as he had that thought, he felt ashamed—it was the sort of self-centered, unfeeling thought that he would expect of a guy like Hyatt Hilton.

Axel's coughing fit subsided. He thumped his chest, clearing his throat, wiping tears from his fading cheeks.

"That's funny," he said in a ragged voice. "Bone up his butt. Sounds like something your old man would say. I needed a good laugh."

"I thought you were going to blow an artery. You scared the hell out of me."

Axel gave him a flat smile, his eyes bright. "Yeah, right. Probably scared you were going to have to haul my dead ass off this island."

Crow laughed. If Axel detected a hollow quality to the laugh, he didn't show it. Crow picked up the crib, looked over the cards, threw it down. "No points. It's your deal."

Axel scooped up the cards and squared the deck. "I wanted to ask you something, Joe. That fellow Hilton. I really am worried that Carmen is making a mistake here."

"Can't say I blame you."

"I was thinking about having him checked out. You know. See if there's anything Carmen ought to know."

"Like what?" Crow asked. He was afraid he knew what was coming.

Axel picked up his can of beer, looked at it, set it back on the table. "Like if he's got a record. You do that sort of thing, don't you? Find out about people?"

Crow shook his head. "Not really."

"I mean, when you're not hanging with the old cockers. You used to be a cop. You know how to investigate people, right?"

Crow shifted uncomfortably in his chair. He did not want to get involved in this. No matter how it came down in the end, somebody was going to hate him for it. He felt a burning in his gut. He'd just come up here to go fishing with his dad, that was all, and now this. Maybe he should simply say "No," and live with the consequences. At least he'd be done with it.

Axel, reading the direction of his thoughts, said, "I need your help, Joe. It's bad enough she wants to marry the son-of-a-bitch, but if she married him and it turned out he was a wife-killer or a bigamist or something, hell, I just couldn't stand it that I didn't check him out. You know the guy. You used to be a cop. You know how to find stuff out. Help me out here."

"I don't know," Crow said, unable to look at Axel's face. "I'm kind of busy these days."

"Look, I'll pay you for your time. You could at least find out if he's got a record. What's that take, a phone call?"

Guilt smothered anger; there was no way out. He couldn't say no. The fact was, he hadn't told Axel the whole story. He could almost smell the incense and old wood of St. Mary's church on a Saturday morning, see the red light above the confessional door. He felt like a kid who'd gone to confession and left out his most grievous sin. What was the penance for that?

*Death is a very dull, dreary affair, and my advice to you is to have nothing whatever to do with it.*

—W. Somerset Maugham

"POLYHYMNIA DESIMONE?"

"Yes?"

"I'm calling from Drew Chance Productions."

"Drew Chance?" She'd heard the name someplace. The voice was familiar, too. "Yes?"

"Have you ever been on TV, Polyhymnia DeSimone?"

Polly frowned and tightened her grip on the steering wheel of her eco-green Range Rover. Her instinct was to look around for the hidden camera—a van with tinted windows, or a helicopter. There was a charter bus crowding her on the right. The car in front of her was some guy in a Saturn and, behind her, two elderly women in a minivan. No aircraft in sight.

Why would anyone want to film her?

"Ms. DeSimone? Are you there?"

"Yes. Who did you say this is?"

"I'm a reporter with *Hard Camera*. Is it true that you claim to be immortal?"

"Where did you get this number?"

"How old are you claiming to be this week? Are you collecting Social Security yet?"

"I—" Polly's brow ridged. She brought the heel of her hand down hard on the steering wheel. "Hy, is that you?"

"I'm sorry, but I can't reveal my true identity."

"You son-of-a-bitch. How'd you get my number?"

"I got your number, darling. I got all your numbers."

"Good-bye, Hy." She dropped a hand to the console, disconnected the call, then said, loudly and clearly, "Call Rupe." The phone dialed itself, rang twice, three times. "Answer the goddamn phone, Rupe," she muttered.

"One God." Rupert Chandra's creamy voice filled the Range Rover.

"One Way, One Life. It's me, Rupe," Polly said. Her voice, by contrast, was sharp as broken glass.

Rupe's voice rose. "Where *are* you?"

"Stuck in traffic. I'm sitting in the left lane on the goddamn freeway. Haven't moved in ten minutes."

"Polly, my sweet, the young lady is here, waiting for you."

"Listen, Rupe. I just got a call from Hy, pretending to be a reporter."

"Oh dear. What did he say?"

"I hung up on him. We've got to do something, Rupe. He's up to something. I've got a feeling."

"Please don't be so negative, my love. He's just trying to upset you, that's all. We confiscated all the flyers and destroyed them. In any case, no one would have believed." The document that had appeared on the windshields of every car in the ACO parking lot during the last Extraction Event had made several outrageous charges against the Amaranthine elders, accusing them of Satanism, child abuse, consumer fraud, and vampirism. The flyers had also included the obituaries of two former Amaranthines whose immortality had failed them in the worst way.

Rupe said, "The Faithful are safely in the fold, my dear."

Polly could almost see the beatific smile on Rupe's suntanned features. "I'm not worried about the Faithful. I'm worried about the Pilgrims. We don't need Hyatt trying to stir things up. I don't know what he thinks he's doing, but whatever it is, it's not for our benefit. We're in debt up to our ears with Stonecrop. We can't afford a hit on our cash flow."

"Eternity will provide, Angel. In any case, we've nothing to hide."

"Hide? Eternity? Listen to me, Rupe, I don't want to spend eternity in court, or talking to reporters, or dealing with the IRS, or in any other variety of hell on earth. If Hyatt is leafleting our parking lot you can bet he's sending the same materials out to the media. If the spotlight shines our way, it won't matter if we've done anything wrong. They'll be on us like jackals on a wounded lion. You saw what happened at Waco."

"That was another matter entirely."

"Was it? I don't think so, Rupe. If one reporter gets the idea that we're a bunch of satanic child-abusing vampires, we'll be preaching to a lot of empty seats."

The speaker produced a rushing sound: Rupe sighing into the phone. "I wish you wouldn't talk like that, my love. Let's discuss it later. In the meantime, would you please just get here and talk to this young lady? I don't know what to do with her. I showed her the contract, but she won't sign."

"What's her problem?"

"She wants to talk to you. Something about her hair."

"Jesus, Rupe, do I have to do everything?" The van in front of her had advanced a car length. Polly put the Range Rover in gear and inched forward.

Rupe said, "You know I don't like to talk to the actresses, Polly. I don't even like to meet them beforehand."

"All right, all right, I'll be there. Give her a cup of tea or something. And try to think of something that will scare off our friend Hyatt. Something that will leave a lasting impression. Something to make him feel mortal."

Polly hit the disconnect. She could almost see the expression on Rupe's face—like he'd just swallowed a cockroach. Ordinarily, she would have tried to be more diplomatic, but the traffic and Hyatt Hilton had her on edge. Later, she would give Rupe one of those foot rubs he liked. Make it up to him.

The phone chirruped. She reached down and turned it off, then cranked the steering wheel hard to the right. She leaned on her horn and nosed in between the charter bus and a new Mercedes—two vehicles whose drivers would not want to risk a fender bender, then forced her way, banging her wrist repeatedly on the horn button, across all three eastbound lanes, across the shoulder, into the ditch, and up the steep grassy embankment. When she reached the top she turned west, following the guard rail toward the entrance ramp she had passed a mile back, her jaw set in a grim smile. Maybe she had all the time in the world, but she damn sure didn't want to spend it sitting in traffic.

Carmen, holding the latest issue of *Modern Bride,* watched Hyatt hit the switchhook, then release it and punch the redial button. Hyatt listened for several seconds, then returned the handset to its cradle. He noticed Carmen looking at him and shrugged.

"She shut off her phone."

"What do you expect? That's what I'd do."

"All the money she's making off my ideas, you'd think she'd do me the courtesy of listening. If it wasn't for me, those assholes would still be peddling ginseng tea."

"I don't know why you're harassing her."

Hyatt shrugged. "I just want to keep them off balance."

"What was that about being a reporter?"

"I didn't tell you? I went and saw my friend Drew Chance today. I'm a reporter for *Hard Camera* now."

"Really?"

"I bring in a story, I get paid." He sighed. "I wish we'd get some nibbles from the other TV stations, though. I keep calling them, but they don't know me from Herman Munster. Maybe I need an agent."

"So call one."

"I did. I called a guy. He told me to write up a proposal. I'm not going to write up a goddamn proposal."

"Call that investigative guy on channel four."

"I did. They all think I'm some kind of crank. I leave messages, then they don't call me back. They think I'm just making things up."

"Well? Aren't you?"

"That's not the point."

"Maybe if you tone it down. Make it more, like, believable."

"If it was believable it wouldn't be news, Carm. You gotta look at the big picture. What I'm doing is laying down a base, creating a buzz. Think of it like butter on bread. Nobody gives a shit about plain old bread and butter. But then you slap on a piece of meat, and you got a hamburger. It's bread on the water, Carm. Media strategy. Setting the stage for the big finale. Looking at the big picture. Swinging for the fences."

Carmen said, "Ba-da, ba-da, ba-da. I still don't see why you're calling *her*."

"I guess I just like to give her grief."

Carmen rolled her eyes, then lifted the magazine on her belly. "Hey Hy, what's a 'trousseau'?"

"I don't know. Was he the guy in *The Pink Panther?*"

"It's in this magazine. Says I'm supposed to 'select my trousseau' four months before the wedding."

"Whatever it is, if you haven't selected it you're late. Why don't you ask Sophie?"

"She's having kind of a rough time right now. She thinks we're spending too much on the reception. Plus, I don't think she liked my wedding dress."

"Really? I thought they were all the same. Big and white."

"Mine's a little different. Anyways, she's kind of touchy right now. I'd just as soon not talk to her. Give her a couple days to cool off. I think maybe it was a mistake to tell her I was pregnant."

"If we hadn't told her that, she'd still be trying to talk you out of marrying me."

"That's true," Carmen laughed.

"Maybe I'll take her out to lunch," Hyatt said. "Show her my serious, trustworthy side." He composed his face, flattening his cheeks and drawing his eyebrows together while keeping his eyes wide open. He made his mouth short and straight. He had learned the expression from watching *Perry Mason,* but Hyatt, instead of looking dark and intent like Raymond Burr, came across as vacant and confused. "What do you think?" he asked, keeping his lips tight.

Carmen tipped her head to the side and looked at him carefully. "I think you'd better work on that one, Hy."

Hyatt let his face snap back to its usual smiling, nobody-home look.

Carmen said, "She's gonna figure it out, you know."

"Figure what out?"

"That I'm not really preggers. All she could talk about the whole time they were fitting the dress was how I needed to leave a little extra room. The thing's gonna be huge on me."

"That's okay. Nobody's gonna notice." He looked at his watch. "You about ready?"

"Ready for what?"

"It's time to go meet the preacher, Carm."


The refrigerator in the sacristy was secured by a padlock.

The Reverend C. Bruce "Buck" Manelli scowled and gave the door handle a futile tug. These damned Lutherans didn't trust anybody. Oh well, probably nothing in there worth drinking anyways. Protestants always went for the sweet, cheap, Kosher stuff—Manischewitz, or Mogen David, or worse. Although a few weeks ago, at First Family of Christ in Edina, the Reverend Buck had found the sacristy to be stocked with a decent California Cabernet, a bottle of tawny port, and, to his delight, a nearly full fifth of Bushmill's whisky. But not here. Not at Christ Free Lutheran Church.

"Should be called *Trust*-Free Lutheran," Buck muttered, then laughed at his own joke. He loved to laugh, loud and hard. *"Ha ha ha ha ha!"* Five shouted "has." He believed that laughter was good for the heart, and besides, life was funny. He opened the fake oak veneer cabinet above the sink. A pair of chalices, one old and worn, the other new and cheap looking. An open bag of whole-wheat communion wafers, presumably unconsecrated. A plastic-wrapped package of paper napkins. He grabbed a handful of wafers and munched on them as he searched the rest of the tiny room. The cabinet beneath the sink was jammed with Amway cleaning products. No surprise there—Gruenwald was a distributor. Buck sorted through the pile of magazines on the small table near the door—*Light and Life, Christian Single,* and the *National Enquirer.* In the table drawer, beneath a few old church bulletins, he found a copy of *Swing Set, The Bi-Weekly Journal.* Buck flipped through the magazine, smiling, then laughing as he carried it out of the sacristy onto the chancel area at the front of the church. He sat on a chair beside the communion table, eating the chewy wafers and reading as he waited for Hy the Guy and his bride to be.

*I had often remarked to my husband, Todd, how attractive I found Michelle, the cashier at our neighborhood A&P. Her wild red hair, bright blue eyes, and incredible shape actually made her A&P apron look sexy. What a waste for a girl with her looks to be stuck behind the counter, scanning frankfurters and weighing zucchinis! Of course, I*

*knew that Todd thought she was attractive too. Every time I went gro-
cery shopping I would come home and tell him I was thinking about
giving him Michelle for his birthday. I would tell him some tiny detail
I'd noticed about her—new earrings, or a little mole on the corner of
her mouth, or the fact that some of her coworkers called her Mish—
and Todd would laugh and pretend he didn't really care. But we would
always have extra-hot sex that night.*

*Imagine my surprise when I came home from my aerobics class
on my birthday and found Michelle in our bed wearing nothing but her
A&P apron and a large red bow . . .*

That Gruenwald, what a character. The Reverend Buck smiled and placed
another communion wafer on his tongue. Interesting how tasteless they were,
as if the manufacturer had attempted to create a food utterly devoid of character. There might be some sort of theological sense to that, but whatever it was,
he couldn't agree with it. It seemed like they could at least put a little salt in
them, or a touch of garlic. Maybe sell them in assorted flavors. Buck laughed
again, *"Ha ha ha ha ha!"* He'd have to suggest that to Hyatt Hilton. He could
see it now: Garlic 'n' Onion Communion Wafers. Extra Crunchy Cheese Hosts.

The priest would ask the parishioner, "Body of Christ?"

"Yes, the Spicy Jalapeño, please."

*"Ha ha ha ha ha!"* Maybe he shouldn't mention that idea to Hyatt. The guy
might actually run with it. Flipping through the magazine, the Reverend noticed one page that had been handled many times, a story titled "A Common
Confession." He skimmed the text: Young Courtney goes to church to confess
having had sex with her boyfriend, one of the altar boys. Turns out that Courtney and the priest have something unexpected in common. The Reverend Buck
imagined Andy Gruenwald poring over that story repeatedly, sweating right
through his collar. What a guy.

It was nice of Andy, though, to let him borrow his church for a couple of
hours.

The call from Hy Hilton had been unexpected. The last he'd heard, Hy had
been promoting his own brand of religion with that pair from the health food
store. Apparently it hadn't worked out. Hy had a talent for getting in his own
way. Always had. Now he was getting married. Poor girl, he'd probably screw
up the marriage, too. Buck placed another wafer on his tongue and sucked on it
contemplatively. It was all the same to him.

Since receiving his ordination certificate from the Northern California Insti-
tute of Theoretical Christianity three years ago, the Reverend Buck had performed more than eighty marriage ceremonies. He had a talent for it. He could
do anything from Catholic to Greek Orthodox to Baptist renditions of the marriage ceremony. It felt good to bring people together, to unite two individuals in
the sacrament of marriage, no matter what their faith, no matter how unwise

the union. Marrying people was, in many ways, the perfect part-time job. He usually received from one hundred to five hundred dollars per ceremony, depending on the generosity of the bride's father, and there was always plenty to eat and drink at the receptions. But most important, it provided both spiritual and material counterpoint to his primary profession, which was that of a divorce lawyer.

The Reverend Buck, also known as Buck Manelli, Attorney at Law, believed in balance. He believed in Karma, he believed in vertical integration, and he believed that in this day and age, it paid to specialize. He was a marriage specialist. He married them, and he un-married them.

He had agreed to perform the wedding ceremony for Hy the Guy because Hy was an old friend, and because he had agreed to Buck's standard fee of $250. This prenuptial meeting with the bride's parents wasn't usually part of the package, but Hy had insisted.

"The mom's kinda hinky," Hy had told him over the phone. "I don't think she trusts me."

Buck had gotten a good laugh off of that.

"Seriously," Hy had said. "I need you to meet with us. Put on your collar and convince 'em you're for real."

"I *am* for real, Hy."

"I know, I know. Maybe we could meet in a church. I mean, we want you to marry us where we're having the reception, wherever that is, but maybe if we have this meeting in a church it'd be, you know, more better."

So Buck had arranged to borrow Christ Free Lutheran for the meeting so that it would be "more better." Hy hadn't changed a bit. Big ideas, lots of weird details, but nothing in between. Buck gave this marriage six months, maximum.

The church doors opened and Hyatt Hilton entered with his bride-to-be and an older couple, the bride's parents, the people he was supposed to impress with his devoutness. The Reverend Buck swallowed the host and rose to greet them.

*Cabanne: Do the letters "L.H.O.O.Q." have a significance
other than pure humor?
Duchamp: No, the only meaning was to read them phonetically.*

CROW SAT IN HIS CAR, listening to the engine pop and sigh as it cooled. The aging First Avenue duplex looked the same as always. It had not burned down or changed color or moved so much as an inch. The building squatted quietly on its lot, waiting for its occupants in the fading evening light. Milo, his hind legs on the passenger seat, front paws against the door, stared out through the window.

Crow said, "We're home, buddy."

Milo twitched his ears. Crow interpreted that to mean that Milo was still mad at him.

He could have left the big black cat home alone for the weekend, but had instead decided to leave him at Zink's. Zink Fitterman had recently acquired a Chihuahua, an ill-behaved creature he called Mr. Bean, who barked more-or-less constantly. Zink had a theory that a couple of days in the company of a cat three times its size might socialize Mr. Bean, and perhaps quiet the barking. To test his hypothesis, he had offered to board Crow's cat for a few days. It hadn't worked. According to Zink, Milo had divided his time between sleeping, eating, sulking, and hissing at Mr. Bean, who had followed Milo everywhere he went, barking at every ear twitch, paw lick, and angry tail swish.

A lot like my weekend, Crow thought as he opened the car door.

Laura Debrowski, who lived in the downstairs unit, had received her usual prodigious stack of junk mail. Crow's mailbox contained an electric bill and a French postcard displaying a reproduction of the Mona Lisa. The sender had added a mustache and goatee to the smiling face and scrawled L.H.O.O.Q. across the bottom. Crow turned the card over and tried to read the back, but the evening light failed to bring Debrowski's minute script into focus. He followed Milo up the stairs and stood outside the door to his apartment. As always, he felt a nugget of fear. He didn't know why—it was not as if he expected some creature to lie waiting inside. Perhaps he was afraid of the opposite, that it would be devoid of all signs of life. Milo scratched impatiently at the door. Crow turned the key and pushed inside. The instant the door opened, the fear evaporated. Milo ran for his food bowl and began crunching stale kibble. Crow added Debrowski's mail to her growing pile, turned on a lamp, and sat down on the sofa with the postcard.

> Allo allo, Crow. You like my faux readymade, mek? Hey, on St. Germain this morning and saw a mek who looked like you. Later, I saw him again, but he didn't look like you anymore. My new place has a huge bathtub with brass fixtures and a bidet. The music scene here is for shit. You'd think people who make such great bread would have great music too, but except for Les Hommes, the bands bite. Last night I saw a new group—3 Frenchmen with accordions. You think America is ready for polka punk, froggie-style? How's Milo? How's Sam? Don't know when I'll be back. Paris misses you.
>
> —L.D.

No return address. No date. No clue as to the meaning of the letters on the front. He couldn't tell whether the card had been sent before or after their last conversation. And what was this "Paris misses you?" What about Laura Debrowski? Did *she* miss him? He looked again at the front, at the defaced Mona Lisa, at the L.H.O.O.Q. scrawled below, but could make nothing of it. He sailed the card across the room, where it lodged in the dead branches of his Christmas tree, sending a few dozen needles filtering through the branches. The Christmas tree had been Debrowski's idea.

Last December, two days before Christmas, he had heard a thumping coming up the stairs toward his apartment. He had opened the door, and a large, green, prickly mass of vegetation had fallen in on him, followed by a laughing Laura Debrowski. He remembered her saying, "You need a tree, Crow. It's Christmas, for Chrissakes."

And maybe he *had* needed a tree. It had made the room smell better, and it had been nice to have something green in the house. Now, half a year later, it was dead and bone dry. A fire hazard. He would have to do something about that.

Thirty minutes later, he was still sitting on the sofa. Milo had joined him. Crow's body had not moved, but his mind was spinning free, jumping from Debrowski to Arling Biggle to Axel Speeter to wondering whether he still had a frozen pizza in his freezer. Crow watched himself with grim amusement. How long would this ennui last? He listed in his mind the various forces that could shatter it. A telephone call. The cat demanding attention. An unexplained noise from outside, or from another room. Hunger. The need to urinate. Sooner or later, one of these forces would come into play. He wasn't worried about himself yet. He let his thoughts roam, steering them away from bad memories, of which he had many, and uncomfortable subjects, most of which had to do with the status of his relationship with Debrowski. He searched for a pleasant fantasy. A big fish. A heroic deed. He avoided thinking about sex, as such thoughts returned inevitably to Debrowski, which always wound up producing that hollow feeling he was trying to avoid.

One topic crept repeatedly back to the main screen. At first he refused to think about it. But it would not go away. Realizing that he couldn't box this one up, Crow relaxed his mind and let it roll. He shifted position, crossing his left leg over his right, folding his arms over his chest, his face drawn into a frown. The windows were black now, evening having become night. Crow thought, I didn't really *lie* to Axel. I just didn't tell him everything.

A few months ago Crow had been sitting on this very sofa in the midst of an ennui session similar to the one he was currently undergoing. His telephone had rung, and he had answered it. The caller had been Hyatt Hilton.

"How did you get my number?" Crow remembered asking.

Hyatt replied, "The phone book."

That made Crow feel somewhat sheepish, so he had indulged Hyatt with an exchange of telephone pleasantries. Hyatt quickly got around to the real reason he had called.

"I hear you're a poker player."

"Who did you hear that from?"

"Zink Fitterman. A good friend of mine is having a game tonight, and he asked me to round up a couple players. Zink said he'd play, and he said you might be interested. You interested?"

"Zink gave you my name? How do you know Zink?"

"I've known Zink for years."

"And he just told you to call me?"

"Actually, your name came up in conversation. He said he was baby-sitting your cat. If you don't want to play, that's cool."

"What sort of game are we talking about?"

"Friendly. Five-ten, maybe ten-twenty. Could go higher."

"Where?"

Hyatt gave him an address. Crow wrote it down on the back of a phone bill. Hyatt said, "They'll be dealing by eight. What do you say?"

"Just a second." Crow closed his eyes. Did he want to play cards? Absolutely. Did he want to play cards with Hyatt Hilton and a bunch of people he didn't know? One possible scenario occurred to him. He said, "This doesn't have anything to do with that church of yours, does it Hy? I'm not going to be betting against a bunch of tongue-talkers and Jesus freaks, am I?"

"I've cut ties with the ACO, Joe. It'll just be us mortals."

"Who's the host?"

"Bigg Biggle."

"Don't know him," Crow said.

"He's all right. He owns a gym. So what do you say?"

That was the night that Crow had won his lifetime membership to Bigg Bodies. It was also the night he'd told Hyatt Hilton how to find Carmen Roman. He hadn't done it on purpose. It was just one of those things. They started the game with seven players, but by midnight it was down to four: Crow, Zink, Hyatt, and Bigg.

In the middle of a hand of seven stud, Hyatt said, "Say, Joe, you remember when I saw you last summer at the state fair?"

Crow frowned at his cards and folded. "I remember."

"You remember that girl in that taco stand? Her name was Carmen."

"Yeah?"

"What was her last name?"

Crow replied without thinking. "Roman, I think. Carmen Roman."

"You know how I can get in touch with her?"

"In touch?" Crow blinked. "What for?"

Hyatt produced an abashed grin. "I thought she was sort of interesting. I'm trying to meet some new people, you know?"

"She's just a kid. Besides, you don't want anything to do with her. You know what happened to her last boyfriend? Carmen's mother ran over him with a pickup truck."

"No kidding? Was it an accident?"

Zink, who had been listening, said, "Way I heard it, she did it on purpose."

"It was pretty ugly," Crow said.

"It was in the papers and everything," Zink said. "The guy was robbing them or something, wasn't he?"

"Something like that," Crow said.

Zink said, "The way I heard it, the girl was behind the whole thing. It was her idea."

"Really?" Hyatt seemed more interested than ever. "Was she on TV?"

"The mother was, just for a second."

"They get paid for that, you know."

Biggle said, "Hey! You girls come here to talk or play cards?"

"What? Is it to me?" Hyatt looked at his cards. "I check." He turned back to Crow. "So, she's had a rough life."

"I'd stay away from her if I were you, Hy. Besides, what makes you all of a sudden get the hots for a girl you met way last summer?"

"I had a feeling with that girl. You say her name's Roman? She in the book?"

"That's how you found me, right?"

It was right about then that Crow had been dealt the baby straight that had beat Bigg's three queens and won him the membership to Bigg Bodies.

Apparently, Carmen's full name had been sufficient information for Hyatt to locate her. Without Joe Crow, it never would've happened. Now they were getting married. He should have told Axel the whole story, but he'd held back, not wishing to implicate himself further, and now—the price he was paying—he'd agreed to take a tour of Hyatt Hilton's life.

*It is our own vanity that makes the vanity of others intolerable to us.*

*—François de La Rochefoucauld*

F LOWREAN PEECHE ARRIVED AT THE gym at her usual time, 10:30 A.M., in a pink XXL T-shirt and oversize jeans, turned up at the cuffs. She looked like a little girl in daddy's clothes. The shirt was so big that only a few inches of her muscular forearms showed past the edge of the sleeves. Cuffs dragging, she shuffled past the front counter, ignoring Beaut, who was on duty, and headed directly into the women's locker room.

It was unoccupied, as usual. That was a good thing. Flo did not like people bumping up against her, touching her. Like Garbo, she wanted to be left alone. Unzipping her nylon barrel bag, she removed a discolored leather weight belt and her dead fish necklace. She rezipped the nylon bag and beat it several times with her fist to soften its sweat-hardened contents. When she opened it a second time, an invisible cloud of funk billowed from within, surrounding her with the sweet and sour effluvium of her last fourteen workouts. Flo inhaled deeply, her head swimming with a marriage of revulsion and hunger, an energizing, sensual kick that would get her out onto the floor and under the bars. It would also serve to insulate her from the other gym rats, most of whom had learned to give her plenty of personal space, especially since she'd started bringing her fish. A few of the less-hardy pilgrims made a habit of simply going home when they saw her emerge from the locker room. That was another good thing.

Bunch of muscle-brained geeks. Except for that Joe Crow. Ever since she'd seen him face off with Beaut she'd been thinking about him, the way he'd stood there like a polished stone, casting Beaut's brutish reflection straight back at him. That Crow, he didn't need a cloud of funk and fish to get his space. He had something that a lot of guys, guys like Beaut, couldn't get no matter how big they grew their pecs. Crow had attitude, a force-field that the more you pushed at it, the harder it got. Anyway, that's the way Flo thought of it.

In some ways he was just like her, except where she gave them stink, he gave them their own self right back at 'em. It was two real different things, but they worked the same, and that was what was important.

Flo hoped he'd be working out today. She kicked off her Nikes, stripped off her baggy jeans and panties in one motion, and regarded her bottom half critically in the greasy, finger-smudged mirror that covered one wall of the tiny locker room. She advanced one leg and snapped it tense. Muscle jumped and quivered, quads ridged and bulging beneath paper-thin skin. Leg day today, definitely. Work on that vastus medialis. She turned to view herself in profile, flexing her left ham, admiring the slash that separated the ham from her vastus lateralis. If she could get her arms like that, that would be something. What would that Joe Crow think? Did her muscularity scare him? She didn't think anything scared him. But did he like it? She scratched herself thoughtfully, lifting the bottom of her sweatshirt, nails catching in the black forest of curly pubic hairs, imagining her reflection in Joe Crow's eyes.

With her dusky-gold skin, molasses eyes, and full lips, Flowrean Peeche had grown up thinking of herself as African American. Not that her mother, Hanna—tawny-haired, green-eyed, and mozzarella-pale—had ever actually *told* her she was black, Flowrean had just assumed it. All the pieces were there. She'd grown up in a black St. Paul neighborhood. Her mother's series of live-in boyfriends had all been black. Flowrean's friends were black. She went to a mostly black school. She walked black and talked black, and she'd never thought much about it until one day she got home from school and her mother's latest boyfriend, Bubby Roode, cornered her in her bedroom and had his way with her slim sixteen-year-old body. Her mother had come home, not in time to salvage her daughter's virginity, but soon enough to catch Bobby with his silk boxers around his ankles. Flo remembered watching him make his final exit amidst a shower of imprecation and household items, holding his pants up with one hand, unlocking his Lincoln TC with the other. After he drove off, Flowrean had somehow expected a flood of motherly concern. What she got was a barrage of screaming accusations.

"But I didn't *do* anything!" Flowrean had protested.

Her mother took a frowning look at sixteen-year-old Flowrean in her cornrows and baggy black jams and torn orange tank top and said, "Girl, I don't know what you expect. You dress like a nigger girl, you're gonna get jumped like a nigger girl."

Flowrean, taken aback, had replied along the lines of, "Well that's what I *am,* Mama!"

That was when her mother had given her a smack across the mouth, then informed her that her father was actually a Portuguese-Canadian sailor she'd met in Duluth—dark-skinned, brown-eyed, and black-haired, yes—but not black.

Flowrean's metamorphosis from black to white occurred instantaneously and effortlessly. She got herself a white girl haircut, gave her hip-hop clothing to her black friends, then told them she couldn't hang with them anymore. Her speech patterns changed instantaneously as did her taste in music, movies, and television shows. She gave up rap for modern rock, Denzel Washington for Mel Gibson, and the *Fresh Prince of Bel Air* for *Beverly Hills 90210.*

She was no longer the skinny little black girl who let herself get jumped by Bubby Roode. That little girl was gone forever. The new Flowrean, the white girl, was still a virgin, and determined to remain so.

Shortly thereafter, Flo found a job at Denny's, moved out of her mother's house and into her own efficiency apartment, and started a weight-training program at the YWCA. That had been eight years ago. All that remained of the old Flowrean was a gap between her bottom incisors and an abiding appreciation for the music of Michael Jackson who, after all, had lighter skin than most Caucasians.

Flo's hand clenched, grabbing a fistful of her short hairs, giving them a sharp twist. The pain brought tears to her eyes, but it worked. Pain always did that, rescued her from the past.

She lifted her dead-goldfish necklace. The fish were getting sort of old. Two of the corpses—Arnold and Jussup, had dried out completely. She slipped the necklace over her head. Its aromatic intensity had lessened over the past week, but another of her pet goldfish would die soon, giving the necklace renewed life. Every week or so another floater turned up.

In the meantime, she'd have to make do. If she couldn't lay a taint, she'd blow 'em all away with attitude, just like Joe Crow. It came down to feeling right about yourself, and being there. Flo closed her eyes, took a deep breath, stepped up to the mirror, and placed her palms flat against its cool, oily smoothness. Opening her eyes a slit she said, breath condensing on the glass, "You're in the present, you beautiful thing. Be there."

She kissed the mist.

Arling Biggle breathed, "God's Blood!" His nose was less than six inches away from Flowrean's lips, on the other side of the glass.

Until Flowrean had entered the locker room, Biggle had been sitting in his six-by-eight-foot office reading a pornographic adventure novel, a story about a seventeenth-century English sea captain who was stranded on an island ruled by women. With each orgasm—he averaged about one every seven pages—the sea captain cried out, "God's Blood!" Biggle had been in the middle of a scene wherein the Queen of Isla Mujeres was having her attendants bind the Right Honorable Captain Richard MacGregor Smith, known to the islanders as Captain Dick, to the four posts of her royal bed, when he had heard the faint sound of the women's locker room door opening—his signal to close his office door, turn off the lights, then let himself into the narrow closet space that separated his office from the women's locker room. Sometimes it turned out to be a waste of time. It depended on who it was and which locker they used, and how quickly they dressed and undressed, and how good looking they were. He couldn't see into the shower, unfortunately. In fact, the only way he could get a really good look was when one of them would stand right in front of the one-way mirror.

He could always count on Flowrean to give him a show. Were it not for these displays, he'd have eighty-sixed her the first time she'd showed up with those goddamn fish around her neck, but with the glass between them, the smell just wasn't an issue.

Ten thousand cars could have cruised down Excelsior Boulevard at thirty-eight miles per hour without a problem. Even a dredlocked black man in a purple Cadillac with curb feelers and a white woman by his side *might* have made it past this Officer Johnson, badge number 2952. But not a lemon yellow 1969 Pontiac GTO. The car was a cop magnet. This was the third ticket Crow had earned since he had acquired the car six weeks earlier. His insurance rates, which were already over three hundred bucks a month, would be rising again. All in all, Crow thought, a lousy beginning to an unpromising week.

Officer Johnson, who looked as if he had been born about the same time the Goat had rolled off the line in Detroit, frowned at Crow's driver's license. Then he frowned at the car. He was working on a permanent frown. By the time he turned forty, it would wrap all the way around his chin.

"How long have you been driving this vehicle in the state of Minnesota?" Officer Johnson asked.

"Six weeks," Crow said, countering Officer Johnson's scowl with a sunny smile.

"You've got to get those plates changed, you know."

"I've got six months."

That has been a mistake.

Officer Johnson, badge number 2952, had put a little extra muscle into his scowl and returned to his patrol car to play with his computer. He wouldn't find anything. Crow had assumed ownership of the vehicle in a legitimate transaction, which had been duly notarized and entered into the public record at the courthouse in Alma, Nebraska. Crow thought about asking him to check into Hyatt Hilton's record while he was waiting for the plate to run, but he suspected that that wouldn't go over very well. The mere ownership of this saffron paean to gas consumption and virility pretty much killed any chance he'd ever had to come to friendly terms with Officer Johnson. To be fair, it wasn't really the cop's fault. It was the car.

He should have known better. Actually, he *had* known better, but his choices had been few. Crow had not gone looking for a muscle car. The Goat had come to him like a lost cat in search of a new owner.

Six weeks ago Crow had been driving a Jaguar XJS, one of the great road cars, from Las Vegas to Minnesota after a disastrous series of poker games at the Golden Nugget. He'd gone to Vegas with thirty-two thousand dollars—nearly everything he had—planning to play a little Texas Hold 'em, maybe enter some of the spring tournaments. Maybe even enter the big one, the World Series of Poker, where a ten thousand-dollar buy-in could win a million. Everything had gone according to plan. Unfortunately, it was someone else's plan. His thirty-two thousand had dwindled with alarming speed. The games were tough, his luck ran sour, and he began to doubt his own judgment. By the time the World Series of Poker got underway, Crow didn't have the cash to make the entry fee.

He blew his last three grand at the craps table. And he *never* played craps.

Then, crossing Nebraska, wondering if he had enough gas money to make it back to Minnesota, he noticed the oil light beaming at him from the dashboard.

"Not now," he muttered, looking out at the endless fields of newly planted corn. The oil pressure gauge read zero. That couldn't be right. He had checked the oil a thousand miles ago. The engine sounded fine. The gauge must be broken. Would that make the oil light come on? He had no idea. He kept his foot on the gas. There was a town coming up, another ten, twelve miles. He'd stop there and check the oil.

Two minutes later Crow heard a faint clattering sound. Was that the engine? It became louder, a troupe of manic tap dancers under his hood. Crow lifted his foot from the accelerator and was rewarded with a metallic squeal and the unmistakable reek of superheated metal.

Two hours later the Jag, its black exterior spattered with dead bugs and road dust, sat parked in front of Hansen's Garage, hood up, its back end still hooked up to the tow truck. Crow stood with the garage owner and his mechanic, staring down at the engine.

"He smoked 'er," said the mechanic in a nasal twang, avoiding Crow's eyes. Both men wore shirts with the name *Harl* embroidered on the chest. Harl the mechanic's baseball cap read "Go Big Red." "Smoked 'er good."

Crow felt a wave of despair and shame wash over him. He had abused his fine European automobile, and he was stuck in Alma, Nebraska, with fifty bucks in cash and a maxed-out VISA card.

"What will it take to get me back on the road?" he asked.

Harl the mechanic snorted.

Harl the garage owner said, "What you think? Three, four weeks?"

"Take longer'n that just to get the motor shipped out here," the mechanic said.

Crow said, "You telling me it needs the whole engine replaced?"

The mechanic stared at the ground. "You fried both cams, mister. You run your oil out, that's what happens."

"I checked the oil in Vegas," Crow said.

The mechanic shrugged, refusing to look at him. "This ain't a lawnmower," he said.

It took the two Harls another ten minutes to convince Crow that his car was, in fact, going nowhere.

Crow said, "Well if you can't fix it, how about you buy it from me?"

It took a few minutes, but Crow was finally able to coax Harl the garage owner into the driver's seat of the crippled Jag. A car salesman had once told him that was the key to making a sale. Get the guy in the car and let him imagine it's his.

"I dunno," said Harl, gripping the Jaguar's pink steering wheel, looking about as comfortable as an aborigine in a tuxedo. Reaching down with one thick-fingered, grease-rimed hand, he poked the pink leather passenger seat. The Jag had once belonged to one of the Crow's former clients, a flaky plastic surgeon who had custom ordered the pink leather upholstery.

"I dunno," Harl repeated.

Crow said, "It's a nice car. Worth twenty, twenty-five thousand."

Harl the owner shook his lumpy head. "Not like this it ain't."

"So figure it with a new engine. Cost maybe, what? Four thousand?"

"More like eight," said Harl the mechanic.

Crow said, "Okay then, eight. So it's worth, worst case, it's worth twelve."

Harl the owner stared at the pink leather knob on the shifter, moved his hand, pulled back before touching it. "Not in Alma it ain't."

"So you tow it into Lincoln. Sell it to a dealer."

"Prob'ly have to take 'er all the way to Omaha."

"So you take it to Omaha."

"Long friggin' drive, that."

"Look, I'm not trying to come out on this. I just want to get into something that runs. I've got to get back to Minneapolis." In reality, there was nothing waiting for him in Minneapolis. He just wanted to get the hell out of Alma.

"Can't say I blame ya."

"You're in the car business. I'm offering you a chance to make a few bucks."

"I dunno. You want twelve? I don't got that kind of money."

"So make me an offer."

Harl the owner shook his head, opened the car door. He stood and hiked up his jeans, recovering his confidence now that he was free of the Jaguar's hot pink grasp.

"No sir," he said. "I don't believe that I want to own this vehicle today."

Crow sighed. He felt the weight of the Jaguar on his soul, dragging him down and holding him on the bottom like a three thousand-pound pink leather anchor. He said, "Look, suppose I was to sell it to you for a hundred dollars? Would you buy it for a hundred?"

"Shee-it, I'd buy 'er for a hunnert," said the mechanic, suddenly interested.

Harl the owner gave his mechanic a disgusted look. "Since when'd you have a hundred bucks, Gunner?"

"I could get it."

Harl, of whom there was apparently only one, shook his head and said to Crow, "You sayin' you're gonna sell me this for a hundred bucks?"

Crow shook his head. "I'm just making a point."

Harl waited for more.

"I'm saying," Crow said, "I want you to buy this car off me. You've got me over a barrel here. I'm not going anywhere. We just have to find a price we can both agree on."

Harl pushed out his lips, then gave his head a quick shake. "Mister, I'm going to tell you something straight out. I don't need another broken-down car, especially a foreign one, especially one with pink insides. I don't have the kind of money you want."

"I can get a hunnert, Dave," the mechanic said.

The owner, whose name was now Dave, said, "He ain't gonna sell it for a hundred bucks, Gunner, so just shut your yap."

Crow said, "Maybe you've got something to trade."

For the first time, Dave showed a spark of interest. He said to Gunner, "Smitty still trying to sell off his Judge?"

"Last I heard."

Dave said to Crow, "You wait right here, Mister." He went into his cluttered office.

Gunner said, looking at the Jag's ruined engine, "I do believe she'd take a Chevy short block."

Crow tightened his lips and looked away. He had mixed feelings about the Jag, but replacing its twelve-cylinder powerplant with an outdated Chevrolet V–8 bordered on sacrilege, like pouring ketchup on foie gras. He walked away from Gunner and the Jag, stood at the side of the road and looked west, thinking again about Las Vegas, about the last hand he'd played, going on a hunch, going all-in, eight thousand four hundred dollars on a lousy pair of jacks. Why had he done that? Crow thought he knew why, but he didn't like to think it out loud.

It was the same impulse that caused young boys to leap from high places. The same urge felt by skydivers and war heroes: the thrill of stepping into the unknown; flouting the odds; wallowing in the brief, heady moment of "I don't give a damn." Even as he now regretted betting those jacks, he felt himself careening toward another such decision. He was going to let these Cornhuskers have his Jag. He was going to take whatever they offered, because he wanted to get into something that rolled, and he wanted it now, and he didn't give a damn.

He heard a rumble and screech. A bright yellow, three-decade-old Pontiac GTO pulled up to the gas pumps. The decal on the rear quarter panel read, "The Judge."

*For as long as Planet Earth shall spin through Space and Time, until the Eternity of Love shall shrivel on the Vine of Life, so Everafter shall our Endless Love shine upon this Universe.*

—*Wedding vows of Gerald Roman and Sophie Stevens, 1975*

WITH THE RIGHT STICK or the right carrot, it was possible to turn an Asshole into a Player. Hyatt had seen it happen many times. Businessmen and politicians and cops were particularly easy. What was more difficult, though not impossible, was to turn an Asshole into a Sucker. This was the challenge he faced now, sitting in Perkins over a poorly made vegie omelet, looking into Sophie Roman's harsh blue eyes.

The luncheon with Sophie had been Hyatt's idea. "I just want to get to know my future mother-in-law," he'd told her. Sophie had accepted his invitation with an ungraceful, "I suppose." Hyatt had suggested Cafe Brenda, an upscale downtown restaurant with a good selection of vegetarian entrees. Sophie had countered with, "How about if I just meet you at the Perkins?"

They'd spent the first half hour at Perkins eating and discussing the wedding. Sophie had not been impressed by Reverend Buck.

"I don't know," Sophie said. "He seemed kind of strange; laughing all the time. Why did he laugh when he shook my hand? I spent the whole meeting wondering if I had something stuck in my teeth. Besides, we're Catholic. I don't know if I like the idea of Carmen being married to a Quaker by a Lutheran."

Hyatt had told Sophie he was a Quaker. He'd met a Quaker once.

"The Reverend's a marriage specialist," Hyatt said. "Besides, Lutherans and Catholics and Quakers are pretty much the same these days. A lot of Catholics are marrying Quakers, you know. In fact, the Reverend was telling us that in Europe they go to each other's churches." Hyatt didn't know whether there were any Quakers in Europe, but he knew that Sophie was impressed by anything European. "Whichever one is closer, that's where they go. Methodists and Lutherans, too. It's all about creating harmony, and getting people together, you know." Hyatt had no idea what he was talking about, but he kept talking, watching Sophie, waiting for her eyes to glaze over. "The basic ceremony is the same, no matter what the religion is, and since a lot of people get married outside in parks and like that, it doesn't matter any more where you get married, either."

"I don't see why they don't have Jesus Christ at that church," Sophie interrupted. "How come it's 'Christ-Free'?"

Hyatt had wondered that, too. He had asked Buck Manelli about it. Buck had laughed. "*Ha ha ha ha ha!* Jesus, Hy, it's not like 'sugar-free.'"

That had confused Hy.

Buck had explained. "It's not like, 'Christ-Free,' as in free of Christ. It's like the *Christ* . . . Free-Lutheran-Church. Get it?"

Hyatt got it, but when he opened his mouth to explain to Sophie, he once again became confused. "It's just a name," he said. "They have as much Jesus Christ as any other religion. They have pictures of him on the walls. Did you see the pictures?" He was giving it everything he had, but Sophie, picking at her chicken salad, remained distant and cool.

Hyatt decided to change direction. "How are you doing on finding a place?"

"Fine. We found an American Legion hall that's pretty nice. Axel wants to take a look at it, but I think it'll be fine. I still don't see why you two don't want to get married in a church."

"It's because of the Catholic-Quaker thing," Hyatt said, once again plunging into the murk. "According to the Vatican, a union between a Catholic and a non-Catholic can be recognized by the church if it's sanctioned by the state, but not performed on consecrated ground. Remember when they started letting you eat meat on Fridays? That whole deal, with all the new rules, this was part of it. It's okay for Catholics to marry Quakers, but only if it's not in a church, and that's not me talking, it's the pope."

Sophie's eyes finally glazed.

Hyatt said, "You don't like me much, do you?"

Sophie blinked. "I just don't know if you're right for my daughter."

"I can understand that. I'm a few years older than Carmen, and you don't know me. I'm not a doctor or a lawyer. I understand that you want better for your daughter."

Sophie lit one of her long brown cigarettes. That was good, Hyatt thought. She wasn't talking back at him, putting all her energy into forming her own thoughts. She was listening.

Hyatt said, "I won't lie to you. I'm no altar boy. But I've never asked a girl to marry me before. Carmen is special."

"She's no altar girl herself," Sophie said dryly.

Hyatt allowed himself a smile, holding his breath to force a blush onto his face. He said, "I know she's had her problems. She told me all about that guy she was with before. Marriage will change all that. It'll be a new life for both of us."

Sophie flicked an ash onto the remains of her chicken salad. "You think so? I got married, that's when my problems really started to kick in."

Hyatt spread his hands, palms forward, and bowed his head, accepting the validity of her experience. Sophie continued. "Gerry had a good job at LeJeune Steel when I married him. He had a seventy-three Buick Electra, and he looked like Robert Redford's baby brother." Sophie squinted at Hyatt and frowned. "He was a big guy, about your size. Treated me like a princess. Two weeks after the wedding, I found out I was pregnant. You know what he did when I told him we were going to have a baby?"

Hyatt shook his head.

"He hit me." She touched her left cheek. "Here."

Hyatt held his breath again, clamping his jaw, closing his throat, and contracting his abdomen to produce a look of suppressed rage.

"When I was three months pregnant, he got fired from LeJeune and never worked another day as long as I knew him. We stayed married three years," Sophie said. "The worst three years of my life." She stabbed out her cigarette on a lettuce leaf.

Hyatt said nothing. He was still holding his breath.

Sophie said, looking at Hyatt's red face, "It was a long time ago." She let a hand flutter into the air, releasing him from his silent fury.

Hyatt let his breath out slowly, let his shoulders drop down. "I don't hate anybody," he said, "except a wifebeater."

"He came back a few years later, and we gave it another try, but it was the same story all over again. He hit me, and I stuck him with a paring knife. Stuck it right in his cheekbone."

"Jesus!"

"The funny thing was, I missed him when he left. Both times. But only for a few months. A man—even a terrible man—can make a woman need him. Even when he's the last thing she needs."

Hyatt nodded, not entirely sure where this was going.

"What do you think Carmen needs?" she asked.

Hyatt hesitated, letting the question hang tantalizingly before him. He believed he knew the correct answer, the answer that would make her happy. Carmen needed what Sophie craved for herself. It wasn't romance, or excitement, or intellectual stimulation, or children, or fame. Sophie was fifty years old, unmarried, and living in a mobile home. She wanted one thing above all others.

"Security," Hyatt said. "I want her to have a good home and a secure future."

Sophie smiled.

"I want what's best for everybody," Hyatt added.

"Good. Because you know what would be best for Axel? You know what he'd really, really like?"

Hyatt shook his head. Axel Speeter was a complete mystery to him. Like Carmen, Axel embodied qualities of the Sucker, the Asshole, and the Player—all rolled up into one.

What would Axel really, really like? Hyatt didn't have a clue, but he was sure that Sophie was about to enlighten him.

"Swedish meatballs," Sophie said.

"Excuse me?"

"He would like Swedish meatballs at the reception."

"That's it?"

Sophie nodded.

"I've got no problem there."

"Good!"

They looked at one another, enjoying the warm feeling of having successfully communicated. Hyatt wasn't sure where to go next, so he said, "Did Carmen tell you that I got a job with *Hard Camera?*"

Sophie's eyes widened. "The TV show?"

"Yes. I'm a reporter now, working directly for Drew Chance, the host."

"I know who Drew Chance is."

"It's just part-time. I'm what they call a stringer."

"You're going to be on TV?"

Hyatt nodded seriously. "Oh yeah. I'm gonna be on TV."


Joe Crow found Wes Larson sitting in the rearmost booth at Garrity's, nursing a mug of pale coffee.

"You're late," said Larson.

Crow had known Wes since college. Hadn't seen him in more than ten years, and this was the greeting he got.

"Sorry. I got a speeding ticket." He resisted the urge to prove it by showing him the citation.

Wes frowned as he digested Crow's excuse. Physically, he had not changed much. He still looked like a giant thumb with beady, unblinking eyes. Only nowadays, the thumb had less hair, wore a cheap gray suit, and was employed by the Minnesota Bureau of Criminal Apprehension. The thumb said, "You must have been driving too fast."

An unimaginative, suspicious, and humorless man, Wes Larson's view of the world had much in common with that of a laboratory rat memorizing a maze. By way of compensating for his negative qualities—all of which he easily admitted to—Wes had become methodical, punctual, scrupulously honest, and profoundly frugal. Crow liked Wes, but he had never particularly enjoyed his company. There had been a year in college when they had almost been friends, but it hadn't lasted. Being so different, they found each other fascinating to behold, but ultimately intolerable. Wes knew that he was boring, and that he made people uncomfortable. That was okay with Wes. He was who he was.

Having been born without an ounce of charisma, Wes had wisely married an ebullient, extroverted woman who did everything she could to preserve his existing relationships. For the past ten years the only contact between Crow and his old college acquaintance had been the birthday and Christmas cards he received every year from Wes and his wife. The cards always arrived in a timely fashion, and always included a short personal note in the wife's handwriting—despite the fact that Crow had never met her.

"It wasn't the speed, it was the car." Crow went on to tell Wes about his GTO, thinking he might get a kick out of it.

Wes said, as if explaining something to a child, "The newer cars get much better gas mileage, Joe. You should consider getting a Toyota."

"Next time I save up twenty grand I'll do that, Wes."

"Actually, the Corollas aren't that expensive, Joe." Two faint lines appeared on Wes's brow, effecting an extraordinarily earnest expression. "They are rated very high by the Consumer Union."

"I'll check into it."

"I've got two hundred thirty thousand miles on my Camry. The secret is to change the oil every three thousand miles." Wes was squeezing his coffee mug. His nails and fingertips were white from the pressure.

"Amazing." Crow decided to forget about bonding. It was too painful to watch Wes Larson talk about nothing. "Wes, let me tell you what I'm doing here."

Wes's chin bobbed once. He relaxed his thick fingers and rested his hands on either side of his mug. Blood returned to his fingertips. He remained upright and rigid, but Crow instantly sensed a lessening of tension in the booth. Wes

Larson was happiest when he had a mission, a plan, a goal to achieve. Small talk had always been his personal nightmare.

Crow explained that he had been asked as a favor by a family friend to investigate the background of one Hyatt Hilton. "All I really need to know is if he has any sort of criminal record. No big deal."

"That's all?" Wes asked.

"Yeah. I'm just trying to do this guy a favor." Recalling Axel's concerns about bigamy, Crow added, "Also, I need to know whether he's currently married. That's easy to do, isn't it? A simple computer check?" Crow cringed at his own words. He must sound to Wes the way Axel had sounded to him—begging a favor while minimizing the difficulty of the free services he was requesting.

"What do you have?" Wes asked.

"Name and address, that's all. He used to work at a place called Ambrosia, but I think they went out of business."

"And you want to know if he's a bad guy, and to know whether or not he's married, correct?"

"That's right."

"Tell me this. If I do this for you, does it take care of the time you dragged me out of the Viking and drove me home?"

"The Viking?" Crow hadn't thought about the Viking Bar in years. He wasn't sure what Wes was talking about. It could have described any number of drunken nights.

Wes said, "I always felt I owed you one there, Joe."

"You never owed me, Wes. But sure, this would definitely take care of it." It made a kind of weird sense, he supposed, that Wes would think this way. That thumb-shaped brain case must contain a complex array of scales—good and bad, assets and debits, income and expenses, right and wrong.

"When do you need it?" Wes asked.

"Sooner is better."

Wes nodded. "I'll call you," he said.


Val Frankel squared up the three-page contract and placed it face up on Polly DeSimone's black glass desk.

"I've never seen a contract like this before," she said.

"It's perfectly straightforward," said Polly. "You make two appearances, one week apart. We pay a flat fee of four thousand, eight hundred dollars. And you agree to complete confidentiality. We discussed all this on the phone. Is there a problem?"

Val lifted her cup of tea, touched it to her bright red lips, set it back on the desk. She could have been anywhere between thirty and forty-five years old. She had a narrow waist, surgically enhanced breasts, and the muscular legs of a dancer or waitress. Her makeup had been generously applied, giving her skin the look of calfskin. Most important, her hair was a rich, dark brown—its natural color.

"I understand that," said Val. "But what's this: 'Provider agrees not to reveal the trade secrets of ACO Ministries, nor to describe any ACO Ministries practices, rites, or beliefs to any person or entity, living or dead, until such time as provider shall die, or until the end of time, whichever shall come first.' I mean, isn't that kinda over the top?"

Polly tapped her pen on the glass surface of her desk. It was always something with these actors, but this was the first time she'd actually seen one read the contract.

"Is that a problem?" she asked.

Val smiled and shook her dark brown mane. "Not really. I mean, I already signed a confidentiality agreement before you even told me what the job was. I just think it's kinda weird is all."

Polly returned Val's smile, leaned forward, and placed the pen on the contract. "You're an actor. You should be used to weird."

Val rested her eyes on the pen, but made no move to pick it up. She said, "I do got a problem, though."

Polly tilted her head, still holding the smile.

Val said, "The hair thing. I got a problem with the hair thing. I like my hair the way it is."

Polly's smile flattened.

"It's the bleaching that concerns me," Val said. "It'll never be the same. Mr. Chandra said that I might be able to use a wig. Instead of bleaching it out, you know? That's really hard on the hair."

"A wig?" Polly sighed. "Look, Miss Frankel, you must have misunderstood Mr. Chandra. The hair is not negotiable. I really don't have time to discuss this any further. I explained to you last week that would be required. If you have a problem with us changing your hair color, you should have said something then."

"I didn't think I was gonna have a problem with it. But now I'm worried it's gonna go all brittle. Mr. Chandra said the hair wasn't that important."

Polly imagined herself giving Rupe his foot rub, dislocating one of his toes. What had he been thinking? The hair is not important? The hair was the closer, the thing that would dispel all doubts.

"Listen, Miss Frankel, I want you to forget whatever Mr. Chandra told you. You're dealing with me, and I'm telling you that the hair is not negotiable. Do you want the job, or don't you?"

"I could use the work," Val said slowly. "I use to do a lot of ad work, but it's mostly being done out of state these days, and I got a kid, too, you know. I need the money."

"Okay. I'll tell you what. I'll throw in another eighty dollars, cash. You go down to Horst after the shows, and they'll put your hair back where it was. Would that do it for you? Either say yes, or go look for another gig. Okay?"

Val squirmed for a few seconds, then leaned forward and signed the contract.

Polly stood up. "Be here at eight A.M. sharp on Friday. Be sure to wear something appropriate for a woman of sixty-five."

Val smiled, relieved and happy now that she'd made her decision. "I'll borrow something from my mom," she said brightly.


Charles "Chip" Bouchet, ACO Head of Security, removed the headphones and placed them on his desk. He reached up and rubbed the top of his head vigorously, reactivating his buzz cut where a band of short blond hairs had been flattened by the headset.

So, they were hiring another actress. Another false miracle. Compounding their crimes.

Chip was manning the Security Annex—what he thought of as the heart and soul of the ACO. From his swivel chair, he could monitor the four security cameras mounted on the outside of the building and the nine concealed microphones within the building. Seven of the microphones had been installed at Polly's request, for the purpose of monitoring church employees, and to eavesdrop on conversations between members of the flock. The other two microphones, one in Rupe's office, the other in Polly's, had been personally and secretly installed by Chip Bouchet, for the purpose of monitoring his employers.

Some of the things he had heard concerned him greatly.

For instance, he had learned that the Anti-Aging Clinics, where Dr. Chandra performed the miracle of age reversal, were staged, using professional actresses such as this Val Frankel woman. He had learned that the First Elders smoked tobacco and drank alcohol, both of which represented Death Program behavior. And he had heard Polly refer to him, her very own Head of Security, as a "pig-faced Nazi son-of-a-bitch."

Actually, he didn't mind the "pig-faced Nazi son-of-a-bitch" comment. He was inclined to forgive that, especially since he had a special relationship with the First Eldress. When she called him her "little Nazi," she meant it in an affectionate way. But the other things, especially the smoking, were clear violations of the Amaranthine Principles.

It's a terrible thing, when one's own religious leaders go astray.

*Vary your play.*

*—Crow's rules*

Bigg bodies was busy—typical for a Monday. Crow had to park between two of Bigg's white limos at the back of the small parking lot. Beaut, perched behind the front counter, glared at Crow as he entered the gym.

After the weekend's excesses, members were purging themselves by putting their bodies through another version of hell. All of the Stairmasters were in motion, as were the stationary bikes. Assorted groans, coarse shouts of encouragement, clanking iron plates, and the thud of dumbbells dropping to the rubber mats. The air was palpable, smelling of sweat and Ben-Gay and sweaty iron.

Crow stopped at the front counter. Beaut's eyes flickered, but he did not move. Like many bodybuilders, Beaut avoided physical effort when he was not working out, subscribing to the theory that muscular hypertrophy was encouraged by a combination of heavy-duty training followed by periods of lethargy.

Crow said, "Is Bigg in? I need to talk to him."

"In conference," Beaut said. His eyes flicked momentarily toward the office door behind the counter.

"With who?"

Beaut blinked, but made no further reply.

Crow shouldered his gym bag and walked around the end of the counter to Bigg's office door. Beaut watched him but made no move to intervene. Crow rapped twice on the door, then pushed it open. The tiny office was dark and empty. "Where is he?"

Beaut shrugged, a faint smile toying with his lips.

"Nice talking to you," Crow muttered. He headed for the locker room, leaving the office door ajar. Sooner or later Bigg would show up. In the meantime, he'd get started on his workout. Today was leg day. Squats, leg presses, leg extensions, hamstring curls, and calf raises. The leg workout would leave him barely able to walk, but ultimately he would become stronger, a goal which Crow no longer permitted himself to analyze. He quickly changed into his sweats and threaded his way through the gym, giving wide berth to an obese man doing a set of flyes with five-pound dumbbells, flapping his arms like a Thanksgiving turkey attempting a vertical takeoff. Crow headed for one of the two squat racks. The other one was being used by a pair of acne-riddled kids—high school football heroes cutting classes to get in an extra workout. He tossed his leather lifting belt on the floor, shouldered the empty bar, and cranked out a quick fifty reps to warm up his legs. The two kids watched him, amused by the spectacle of him squatting the empty bar.

As he racked the bar, Crow saw the light go on in Bigg's office. Bigg appeared in the doorway. What the hell? Had he been hiding under his desk? Crow added a pair of forty-fives to the bar. Bigg and Beaut exchanged a few words, then both looked at Crow. Seconds later, Flowrean Peeche came out of the locker room dressed in her baggy street clothes and headed out the front door. Crow fitted the bar onto his shoulders and lifted. It felt light. He must be getting stronger. He began a slow set of deep squats, pausing at the bottom of his lift, returning smoothly to a standing position. After fourteen reps he racked the bar and permitted himself another look at Beaut and Bigg.

Beaut was gone. Bigg sat in his place reading *Muscle and Fitness.*

Crow loaded two more plates onto the bar and did another set, twelve slow ones, his knees cracking. The noises coming from his joints had alarmed him when he'd first started working out, but now he thought of it as the audio portion of his workout. He racked the bar and leaned on it for a moment to catch his breath. Looking back at Bigg, who still had his nose in the muscle magazine, he tried to imagine that bulky body hiding beneath a desk in a dark office. It didn't seem plausible. There was a large closet with sliding doors at the back of the office. Could he have been hiding in the closet? That seemed weird, even for Bigg. Maybe the doors led to something other than a closet—another room, or a larger storage space. Crow tried to visualize the layout of the club. What was behind Bigg's office? The women's locker room? He'd have to ask Bigg about it, see what he said. But first, he had to finish his squats. If he walked away from the rack now, it would be too difficult to psyche himself up for another set.

He added a third pair of plates and wrapped his leather belt around his waist. He put Bigg out of his mind and focused on the set. Three hundred fifteen pounds for ten reps. Last week he'd done eight. Crow pulled his belt tight, centered the bar behind his neck, and lifted the loaded barbell off the rack. He stepped back and planted his feet solidly on the rubber mat. The bar bowed, and the plates clanked dully against one another. Crow made the rest of the world go away and slowly lowered himself into a full squat. He straightened his legs and returned to standing position. Like magic. The mind sends forth its command, the body responds. He repeated the movement. The second, third, and fourth reps were no problem, but he felt number five from his hamstrings up through his lower back. Six was worse. On the seventh rep, his right leg went soft on the way down. He almost didn't make the lift, coming to a full stop halfway up, but a moment of panic sent a final surge of energy into his thighs, and he was able to slam the bar back onto the rack. Gasping, he stood with his arms draped over the bar. Seven reps, and last Monday he'd done eight. This was not good. He bent his right leg and straightened it. Something had happened down there, inside his body. He walked a few steps to the nearest bench and sat down heavily, massaged his thigh, searching for a sore point, but there was no pain, only weakness.

One of the high schoolers asked him, "You okay, dude?"

"I think so." He stretched the leg, flexed it, stood and bent over, touching his toes. Everything worked. He decided he had torn some tiny, insignificant muscle fiber deep in his thigh. He would give it a few minutes, then resume his workout, hit the leg extension machine. This would be a good time to talk to Bigg. He crossed the weight room and rested his elbows on the counter. Bigg was chewing on something, making his sideburns quiver.

"You got a minute?" Crow asked.

Bigg closed the magazine and lifted his eyebrows.

Crow said, "Remember that card game at your house?"

Bigg nodded and swallowed. He dug into a paper bag on his lap and pulled out a handful of dried banana chips. Tossing them into his mouth, Bigg resumed chewing.

"You know that Hyatt Hilton?"

Bigg shrugged. "Wha' 'bout him?"

"Where do you know him from?"

Bigg leveled his eyes at Crow, who waited patiently, knowing that Bigg wouldn't tell him if it was raining outside without trying first to divine his reason for asking. Bigg swallowed and asked, "Why you want to know about him?"

"I was wondering how you know him, that's all."

Bigg licked his lips. "I thought he was a friend of yours. Why don't you ask him?"

Crow sensed that pushing the question now would cause Bigg to dummy up. "It's not important. I was just wondering how you two knew each other, that's all."

"That what you came over here to ask me?"

"Partly. Mostly I was wondering how you did that trick with your office."

"What do you mean?"

"A few minutes ago I looked for you in your office, and you weren't there. Then I see you come out. What gives?"

"What were you doing in my office?"

"Looking for you."

Bigg inflated his cheeks, staring at Crow as if making a decision. He let his lips part, expelling a cloud of banana-scented air, and pointed toward the glass-fronted cooler next to the counter, which contained an assortment of energy drinks, fruit juices, and bottled water. "Hilton's the Evian guy." The sudden return to the topic of Hyatt Hilton surprised Crow. Apparently, Bigg did not wish to discuss his magical appearance from within his office. Or maybe he'd just decided to be helpful. "He sells it cheap, too," Bigg added.

"That's how you know him? You buy water from him?"

"That's right." Bigg grabbed another handful of banana chips. He offered the bag to Crow. "Want some?"

"No thanks."

"Lots of potassium," Bigg said, chewing. His throat pulsed, sending the masticated chips toward his digestive system. He reached across the counter to grab a half-liter Evian from the cooler, cracked it open, and poured a few ounces into his mouth. The image of all those banana chips rehydrating inside Bigg's body made Crow slightly queasy.

"That's all you know about him? He sells you water?"

"Every couple of weeks he drops off a few cases." Bigg examined the Evian bottle.

"How did you happen to invite him to that card game?"

Bigg shrugged. "I didn't invite him. Zink did. You sure you don't want to try some of these chips?"

"Zink? Zink invited Hy? How do you know Zink?"

Bigg took another swallow of Evian. "I know Zink through Hilton. Hilton sells him Evian, just like me. Zink sells it out of his bar, though why anybody would go in that dump for any reason other than to get shit-faced I don't know."

Crow, who dropped by Zink's Club 34 a couple times a week for lunch, tried not to take Bigg's comment personally.

Bigg continued, "You buy from the regular Evian distributor, you pay an arm and a leg. Hilton's got the good price. He's got a nice little business. Hell of a lot easier than running a goddamn gym. You want to buy a gym, Crow?"

"No thanks."

Bigg gave the bottle another look, tasted it again. "To tell the truth, I don't know what people see in it. But what the hell do I know?"

Crow wondered—not for the first time—how a guy like Hyatt Hilton got an Evian distributorship. The stuff was everywhere. Every gas station, mom and pop, and newsstand sold the plastic bottles of Evian, all doing their part to drain every last drop of groundwater in France a half liter at a time. But why would an international company like Evian have anything to do with a guy like Hy?

"How come he introduced you to Zink?"

"Who?"

"Hy."

"I forget. It was a long time ago. You done grilling me, Crow?"

"I'm confused," Crow said. "Everybody knows everybody else, and people who shouldn't know each other are playing in the same poker game."

"It's a small fucking world." Bigg picked up his *Muscle and Fitness* magazine and pointedly began reading. "Don't forget to rack your weights," he said as Crow turned away.

The luncheon with Sophie had gone rather well, Hyatt thought. He pulled his van off the freeway at the Lyndale exit and headed south toward his house. He was a few minutes late, but Carmen was used to that by now, and besides, those extra few minutes with Sophie had made all the difference. She'd been delighted by his willingness to compromise on the meatball issue.

As he drove past the vacant storefront that had once been Ambrosia Foods, he thought about how the little things mattered so much. When he and Polly and Rupe had founded the ACO—back then they'd called it the Ambrosia Long-Lifer Club—and they'd started signing people up for their seminars and supplement program, he'd been amazed by the little things that would close a sale. He'd be pitching the program, telling people that the human body was capable of stepping out of the D.P., or Death Program, that eternal life was not an unrealistic goal, and they'd be listening but not 100 percent convinced of it. He'd try this and that—telling them that they could see their great-great grandkids or how a healthy body could support a dozen or more orgasms a day, or telling them their saggy triceps would firm up—you just never knew what would get them. One woman he remembered had cared about nothing more than clearing up the yellow deposits that had formed at the corners of her eyes. The fact that she could live forever was incidental. She did not want to live to be one hundred fifty years old if she had to do it with yellow eyes.

Hyatt pulled up in front of his house. Carmen was sitting on the front steps, waiting.

"You're late," she said as she opened the car door.

"Sorry. Sophie and I were working on the meatball issue."

"It's a good thing I'm not really sick. Which hospital are we going to?"

"Our Lady of Mercy." Hyatt pulled away from the curb. "In case you were wondering, Axel's going to get his Swedish meatballs."

"I'm sure he'll be thrilled."

"It worked for Sophie."

In the end, it wouldn't matter what they served at the reception. He didn't plan to be there anyway.

♠

Crow finished his workout without putting much into it. For his last few sets of seated calf raises, he used half the weight he was capable of handling, just going through the motions. Tomorrow, he told himself, he'd make up for it with a few extra sets. He kept thinking about Hyatt Hilton, wondering what he would find. The best outcome would be for him to discover some spectacular crime in Hyatt's past. For instance, if Hyatt had three wives and had murdered each of them, that would be good. Axel would really appreciate knowing a man like that. Carmen might like to know it, too. He hoped Wes had left him a message.

On his way out of the gym Crow made sure to thank Bigg for sharing what he knew about Hyatt Hilton, even though he hadn't told him much of anything. *Always be polite.*

He felt less like being polite thirty seconds later. Instead of a lipstick print on his windshield, he discovered a vertical crease four inches long and half an inch deep on his driver's side door. Since he had parked between two of Bigg's rental limos, and since Beaut Miller worked for Bigg, it was clear to him what had happened. The only question was whether Beaut had acted on his own, or done Bigg's bidding. Crow breathed deeply, trying to force it into perspective. It's just a bit of sheet metal, he told himself. It's not like he swung on me.

*Blood alone moves the wheels of history.*

*—Benito Mussolini*

**O**UR LADY OF MERCY TRIAGE nurse Deedee Feider had a theory about emergency room patients. If they weren't unconscious or bleeding, she believed, they were almost certainly faking. Every day she saw hours of valuable ER time being wasted on people who claimed to be having heart attacks or internal bleeding and who turned out to have nothing that a spoonful of Maalox wouldn't cure. People who wanted attention, that's all, bunch of crybabies. If it was up to her—and sometimes it was—somebody came in and couldn't show her blood or severe swelling, she'd give 'em a couple of Tylenols and triage 'em the hell out of her ER.

The girl with the long dark hair and the pouty lips was a case in point. Deedee saw her coming from way off. Coming in bent over like that, holding her belly like it was going to fall right off of her, giving that fakey agonized look—about as real as a six-year-old trying to get out of school. Her boyfriend was a piece of work, too. Tall, thin, and dumb as a sleeping cow. Before they even reached the registration desk, Deedee had them pegged. Nothing else to do on a Saturday afternoon? Desperate for attention? The girl had decided to fake an attack of some sort. Get her boyfriend to haul her down to the hospital. Inject a little life into their relationship.

Yeah, Deedee could read this one through a lead apron. If her boss, Jerome the Gnome, hadn't been standing there, she'd have shooed them off, sent them over to the free clinic, let them sit in somebody else's waiting room for four or five hours. But with the Gnome looking over her shoulder, Deedee had to follow procedure. Make sure they had their admission form filled out, check her vital signs, make sure she wasn't in shock or cardiac arrest, then sit her down until her name came up. Or longer. Other patients might show up in the meantime. Real, bleeding, dying patients.

"The old witch is gonna let us sit here the rest of the afternoon, Hy," Carmen said. "I could be dying. I could be having an appendix attack. There's been three people came in after us already got in."

"The one guy looked like he was dead. I think they had to get him in fast."

"I think he *was* dead. So what's his hurry?"

"I'll talk to her again." Hyatt stood up and approached the nurse. Carmen hugged herself and tried to look miserable. It wasn't difficult. She'd been sitting in that same plastic chair for more than an hour. She was hungry and thirsty, and she had a nasty headache.

Hyatt was back within a minute, looking discouraged. "She says we have to wait."

Carmen wasn't surprised.

"Maybe you could do something," Hyatt suggested.

"Like what?"

"I don't know. Start bleeding or something."

"Yeah, right."

"Maybe I should've beat you up or something."

"That would've worked great. You'd be in jail."

"Not if you refused to press charges."

"I wouldn't refuse."

"I'd rather wait in jail than here." He picked up a *People* magazine from the seat beside him and flipped through it. "A few more weeks, we're going to be here, Carm."

"Be where?"

"In *People*. Photos and everything."

"Yeah, right. If we're not still sitting here in emergency."

"We might be."

"Not if I can help it." Carmen took a deep breath and forced out a loud, high-pitched moan. All the heads in the waiting room turned toward her.

Hyatt shuddered. "Jesus, Carm. What the hell was that? You okay?"

"No. I'm dying. Can't you tell?" She made the sound again, something between a groan and a scream, drawing it out until she was sure everyone in the room was staring at her. She waited, remaining silent until their attention drifted to other things, then repeated the sound, this time punctuating it with a spell of dry coughing. Carmen looked over at the nurse, who was fixedly staring at the top of her desk. Carmen produced another wail of pain and despair, aiming this one directly at the nurse and holding it until she looked up and their eyes met. The nurse turned away, but both she and Carmen knew who was in charge now.

It too a full five minutes of howls, groans, wails, and coughs for them to come for her. A nurse appeared with a wheelchair and motioned for Carmen to have a seat. Carmen's histrionics instantly ceased.

As they entered the examination room the nurse said, "You know, you'll have to wait just as long as you would have outside. We only have so many doctors."

"That's okay," Carmen said. "I don't mind waiting."

In fact, she was counting on it.

"As far as his criminal record goes, he's clean, Joe."

"Like me." Crow pressed the phone to his ear and gazed into the Formica top of his small kitchen table. Overlapping green and blue boomerang outlines on a pale yellow background.

Wes Larson said, "No, not like you. Do you want to know what we've got on you?"

"Not really."

"Okay. But I've got it right here if you need it."

"Thanks a lot, Wes. I'm more interested in Hilton."

"Okay. I got a few hits on his name, but he's never done time. And he's never been married in Minnesota or Wisconsin, at least not under his own name which, it appears, is genuine. I have a Hyatt Hilton born in Biwabik, Minnesota, forty-five years ago this coming September. Does that sound right?"

"Could be." Crow wrote the date down on the phone book cover. "He doesn't look quite that old. You said you got a few hits. What's that mean?"

"You sure you don't want to know what they've got on you?"

"Not unless it's an outstanding warrant."

Wes did not reply immediately. Crow heard the clatter of thick fingers on plastic keys.

Wes said, "No warrants."

"I'm so relieved. What about Hyatt Hilton?"

"He was named in a few drug investigations. Identified as a small-time dealer, questioned a few times but never cracked. Your friend is right to be concerned. He sounds like a bad guy never got caught."

"But no convictions?"

"Never even got himself arrested."

"Anything else?"

"Yeah. He filed an assault complaint last spring. I got a copy of the report here. Just a second." Rustling papers. "May third. He claimed to have gone to a meeting of this church group, made a few unwelcome comments, been dragged out behind the building and beaten up. The injuries were superficial. Case never went anywhere."

"Why not?"

"Apparently, Hilton had not been invited to the meeting. He was being disruptive. Refused to leave. They threw him out."

"Who were 'they'?"

"Just a second. The name of the place was . . . um . . . ACO Ministries. Rupert Chandra, Polyhymnia DeSimone, Charles Bouchet, and Charles Thickening were named in the complaint."

"I think the first two were Hilton's partners in the health food store," Crow said.

"I see. Apparently, Hilton was totally out of control, screaming threats and obscenities at Chandra and DeSimone. When Bouchet tried to escort Hilton to the door, according to witnesses—there was a whole room full of people—Hilton kicked Bouchet in the shin and took a swing at him . . . 'fists flying,' it says. This is a pretty good. The guy should'a been a writer. Let's see . . . Thickening and Bouchet grab Hilton, hustle him out the back and toss him in a dumpster. After hearing all this, told back to him—listen to this: 'Upon being apprised the opposing point of view, the complainant elected to drop the charges.' Reading between the lines, I'd say the officer taking the complaint told Hilton to get lost."

"I'm getting too old for this kind of work," said Lawrence Bolles, M.D., who had recently celebrated his twenty-eighth birthday. "What have I got next?" He was scrubbing his hands again, the twenty-third time since the beginning of his shift. Having just finished stitching up another rollerblader, he was preparing to minister to his twenty-fourth patient. He hoped that it would be someone unconscious. He'd run out of bedside manner six patients ago.

"You've got an abdominal pain," said the nurse, Ginny Stevens.

"Oh, *man!*" Dr. Bolles preferred the straightforward mechanical jobs: cuts, tears, breaks, punctures, and dismemberments. Things that could be sewn, splinted, taped, or clamped back together. Bellyaches were the worst—they could be anything, but were almost always nothing. "Can't you let Varley handle that one?"

"This one's been waiting for a while. She was making a lot of noise. Deedee says she's faking it."

"Deedee thinks everybody's faking it. That's why we love her." He picked the chart from the wall. "Vitals look good. I guess I'd better have a look. Could be anything. Appendicitis, peritonitis, perforated ulcer—nah, not at her age. She isn't pregnant, is she? Could be something. Probably not. Never know." Dr. Bolles knew he was muttering to himself, thinking out loud as he often did near the end of his shift. "Where'd you put her?"

"She's in six."

"How old? Oh, I see. Twenty-three. Name? Carmen Miranda. Fruit on her head?"

"I didn't notice," said Nurse Stevens. "But she's good looking, if you like the sleepy, big-chested type."

"Oh?" said Dr. Bolles, suddenly interested.

Ginny Stevens, who was about the same age as Dr. Bolles's older sister, gave him a crooked smile. Dr. Bolles chuckled. All the nurses were either hitting on him or trying to get him fixed up. They abhorred a single doctor the way nature abhors a vacuum. He stepped through the curtains into cubicle six wearing his sexiest George Clooney smile.

The supply cabinet doors were standing open, but no one was in the room.

Axel and Sophie stood near the center of the American Legion Post 684's banquet room, a dimly lit, wood-paneled cavern that smelled of wet cardboard and Pine Sol. Folding tables and chairs lined one wall. A battered wooden podium stood forlornly on the small stage at the end of the hall.

"It's hard to find a reception space on such short notice," Sophie said. "But with the table settings and the flowers and the band, this room will look quite elegant."

Axel grunted.

Sophie walked up to the lip of the low stage. "We can have the ceremony right here. Once we get it decorated, it'll be really nice. You'll see."

"I thought they were going to get married in a church."

"I thought so too, but Hy's not Catholic and besides, we couldn't get a nice church for the date we want. We were lucky to get this."

"What about that place where we met that Reverend?"

Sophie said, "This will be a lot easier than everybody going to a church, then getting into their cars and driving over here." She had wanted the church, too, but somehow—she couldn't remember his reasoning, exactly, Hyatt had convinced her that this would be better.

Cap York, the post's manager, bartender, and janitor, came in through the door connecting the banquet room to the bar. York was a large man, about Axel's height with twice his girth. He wore low-slung khakis and a powder-blue American Legion T-shirt. Despite his considerable abdominal amplitude, York maintained a military bearing—feet at shoulder width, shoulders thrown back, head held high on his neck. His gray hair was cropped short, as was his bristled mustache. His beefy arms brandished an assortment of faded blue tattoos.

"Whaddya say, folks?" he barked.

Sophie smiled up at Axel.

Axel said, "What's this going to cost me?"

"Basic rate, four-twenty. Includes set-up and cleaning, within reason. You got your own caterer, right?"

Sophie and Axel both said, "Yes."

"I gotta have two hundred to hold the room. I got somebody else might want it, high school reunion, something. Whaddya say?"

Axel said, "Suppose the wedding is called off?"

He shrugged. "We keep the two hundred. Look, I gotta get back to the bar. I got customers. You want to think about it, fine. I'll be up front." He wheeled and marched out, his frame perfectly erect within his sagging abdomen.

Sophie crossed her arms and put her nose right up to Axel's chin. "What do you mean, 'Suppose it's called off?'"

Axel took a step back. "You just never know what's going to happen," he said.

*Novelty, portability, and good taste. You've got to have all three.*

—*Axel Speeter*

"JOE? HOW'S IT GOING?" Axel's voice boomed over the telephone.

Crow held the receiver out from his ear. "It's going okay," he said. He had no idea how it was going. He'd only been awake for twenty seconds.

"What are you doing? I mean right now!"

"Just . . . ah . . . just getting started here, Ax." Crow shuffled over to the refrigerator, opened the door, stared blearily at its contents. "Not really doing anything."

"Well come on over then! I want you to try something."

"Uh . . . I'm just waking up, Ax. Listen, you want to know what I found out about Hyatt? Can I call you back?"

"C'mon over. Let's talk about it."

"There's not much to talk about. I checked into—"

"You know where the trailer is, don't you, Joe? You know where Landfall is?" Crow heard a sharp voice in the background. Axel said, "Sophie says to tell you it's not a trailer, it's a mobile home. Just look for the place with the yellow metal awning. You'll see my truck parked out front."

Crow took a breath and said, "I hadn't really planned to drive across town, Axel. I haven't even had breakfast yet." Crow was still trying to find something of interest in his refrigerator. He had a collection of aging condiments, some week-old spring rolls from the Saigon Cafe, and a butcher paper package, unopened, that had been there so long he could no longer remember what it contained. Whatever it was, it had cost him six dollars and fifteen cents.

"So come on over. I'll feed you. Come on. I want you to try something."

"Look, Ax, it's not like I've got anything to tell you about Hyatt. He doesn't have any kind of criminal record in Minnesota. And he's not married. That's all

I know." Crow pried the plastic lid off a can of Maxwell House. "That's what you wanted, right?"

"Sure, sure. Come on over, and we can talk about it, okay? What do you say?"

Crow peered into the Maxwell House can. Less than a teaspoon of stale coffee remained. He said, "How are you doing for coffee?"

Crow had driven past the village of Landfall hundreds of times, but he had never entered it. A mobile home community with about six hundred residents, Landfall abutted the north side of I-94, just east of St. Paul. From the freeway, it had an uninviting, run-down, trashy aspect. Up close, that impression was amplified. The small cluster of shops at the village gate showed few signs of life. The beauty salon and convenience store were vacant, their boarded-up windows covered with graffiti. Only the liquor store, which was advertising a special on wine coolers, remained open. Crow drove into Landfall feeling like a tourist in a ghetto. These homes might have once been mobile, but most of them now looked as though they wouldn't survive another move. They would be here until they collapsed or were demolished by a tornado.

As Axel had promised, Sophie Roman's trailer—mobile home—was easy to find. It was one of the few Landfall residences that displayed any pride of ownership. A neatly trimmed lawn with a charming border of hasta and petunias surrounded the aluminum and fiberglass home, separating it from its less-well-groomed neighbors. An oversize aluminum awning, egg-yolk yellow, shaded the front stoop. To the right of the front stood a new eight by six-foot deck with a built-in bench and a Weber grill chained to the railing.

Axel smiled and waved from the bench. Crow crossed the small lawn on a narrow walkway made from cast concrete stepping stones. He climbed the three steps up to the deck.

"Siddown, siddown," Axel said, standing and waving Crow onto the bench. He was wearing his usual outfit—white short-sleeved shirt and black trousers held up by clip-on suspenders. "You want a cup of coffee?"

"Sure."

Axel disappeared inside. Crow stood up and put one foot on the bench. He rested his forearms on his knee and looked out at Landfall from this new perspective. Mid-morning sunlight warmed his face. This was what Axel and Sophie saw every morning. The air smelled of auto exhaust and—despite the early hour—barbecue. Rush hour traffic from I-94 produced a constant background buzz. According to Sam, Axel was practically a millionaire, but until he'd moved in here with Sophie, he'd been living in a Motel 6 near the fairgrounds. For Axel, this was living large.

Axel appeared and handed Crow a mug full to the brim with black coffee, very dark. Crow sniffed, took a sip. "Thank you," he said. He sipped again. "It's very good." He tried not to show his surprise. He had expected the coffee to match the surroundings.

Axel smiled, showing off his full set of blindingly white dentures. "I like it strong."

The two men sipped coffee for a minute without talking, listening to the traffic and the sound of dogs barking. Crow said, "I smell barbecue. Who's barbecuing this time of the day?"

Axel gestured toward the Weber. "She's just getting warmed up," he said, offering no further explanation.

Crow said, "Well, I got the info you wanted on Hyatt Hilton."

"You told me over the phone. He doesn't have a record, and he's not married."

"That's about it," Crow said.

"Joe, let me ask you something. If you were at the state fair and you wanted something really tasty, something good for you, something you could really sink your teeth into . . . what would you want?"

Crow hesitated, sensing that he was being tested. "Uh, look, Axel, I'm sorry I laughed when you suggested I open up a stand, but the fact is, I'm really not interested in that kind of a business."

"That's got nothing to do with what I'm telling you, Joe. Think like a guy just wandering around the fairgrounds. What are you hungry for?"

"That would depend on what I felt like."

"You feel a little hungry. You want something freshly made, with a lot of taste. What was your best meal ever?"

"I don't know. I had a truffled capon in Paris," Crow said.

Axel blinked as though Crow had suddenly flickered in and out of existence. He continued as though Crow had said nothing. "Something you could hold in your hand, the perfect food, a balanced medley of flavors. Spicy, but not too. Unusual, but not fancy."

Crow shrugged. "I give up, Ax."

"Think Mexican."

"A taco?"

Axel shook his head. "Close, but not special enough."

Crow tried to remember what Axel called his deluxe burrito. "A Super Burrito?"

"That's *Bueno* Burrito—and no, that's not it. Listen. You just sit tight." Axel went back inside, came out with a platter covered with strips of marinated meat, peppers, onions, and tomatoes. He lifted the top off the Weber, releasing a cloud of blue smoke. "It's good and hot," Axel said, talking more to himself than to Crow. "Gotta be hot." Moving quickly, Axel covered the grill with items from the platter. "Gotta be fast," he said. "People want fast; people want good."

He stood before the smoking Weber, smiling and blinking in the smoke. "Smell that. That's what'll bring 'em round, is the smell." Axel began humming a tune from *Evita*. After a minute he unfolded a paper-thin tortilla a foot and a half across, draped it over the platter, and shoveled the grilled meat and vegetables onto it. He folded and rolled the tortilla expertly, producing an item that looked a lot like an oversized ice-cream cone—but with a crown of grilled meats instead of a ball of ice cream. Wrapping the point of the cone in a napkin, Axel offered the creation to Crow. "*This* is what you want." Crow accepted it uncertainly. He might have been able to handle a bowl of corn flakes, or even a couple of fried eggs, but the object he now held in his hand, weighing in at more than half a pound, did not look like breakfast.

He said, "This is really something, Ax."

"Try it," Axel said.

Crow braced himself and took a bite, getting a bit of tortilla, some of the meat, and a strip of green pepper that flopped down over his chin. He sucked in the pepper and chewed carefully.

"It's really good," he said.

Axel clapped his hands together. "It's the marinade. My own recipe."

Crow took another, larger bite. It *was* really good. Spicy, but not overwhelming. Unusual, but not fancy. Easy to eat. "Is this a new product you're working on?"

"I call it the *Conita*. What do you think?"

Crow nodded. "I like it."

"It's like a fajita in the shape of a cone."

"I get it." Crow took another bite.

Axel watched Crow eat. He said, "So you think he's okay?"

"I think it's great. Good product."

"Not the Conita. Hyatt Hilton."

"Oh!" Crow swallowed. "I didn't say he was okay. I just said he doesn't have a record."

"And he's not married."

"Right."

Axel nodded. "Then that's that. She's gonna marry him."

"There's probably not much you can do about it."

"I can't believe I'm paying for it."

Feeling emboldened by the Conita, Crow asked, "How come you're doing that, anyway?"

Axel said, "I have to, Joe. When you get to be my age you'll understand. You have to give it back somehow, and you don't always get to pick who gets it."

That made no sense to Crow, but he let it go and returned to work on his Conita.

Axel continued. "Between the food and the booze and the photographer and the hall and Carmen's dress, this thing's going to cost me six or seven grand. She even wants a limousine—can you believe that? Five lousy miles to the American Legion, then another couple miles to the goddamn hotel—what do they need a hotel room for? They've been shackin' up for God-knows-how-long—and she wants to ride it in a limo. You know what a limo costs? And So-phie—you know what she's doing right now? She and Carmen went to Bachman's to order flowers. I like flowers, hell, but when I told her to go ahead and get a hundred bucks worth—that's a lot of flowers, isn't it?—she laughed. Boy, do I know what that means. You know how many Conitas I'm gonna have to sell to pay for this thing? I wouldn't mind it so much if she was marrying a stand-up guy, but this Hyatt Hilton—if I found something that would make Carmen not want to marry him, that would be great. But I've got a feeling that's not going to happen. I can feel it coming, Joe. She's heading down the aisle, and there's not a goddamn thing I can do about it."

Crow, chewing on the tip of the Conita, heard himself say, "Do you want me to keep checking on Hyatt?"

"Sure. Let me know if you find anything. Only don't tell me anything unless it's a wedding stopper. If the guy's going to be my son-in-law, I don't want to know any more than I have to."

"I'll ask around," Crow said. "Listen, if they do get married, you mentioned a limo. I know a guy that rents limos. You want me to talk to him?"

"You think he'd give me a deal?"

"I can ask."

"You know, Joe, there's only one thing about this whole wedding thing that's any goddamn good at all."

"What's that?"

"It'll be the perfect time to introduce people to the Conita. I'm going to serve 'em at the reception."

"Really?" That sounded good to Crow.

"Yeah. Carmen doesn't know about it yet. I'm going to surprise her."


With all the time he'd been spending on this wedding business, Hyatt Hilton had fallen behind on his water deliveries. His phone machine held a half dozen messages from retailers demanding their Evian shipments. He'd been in his garage filling cases since six o'clock that morning, and he'd have to spend the rest of the day driving all over south Minneapolis, filling orders, all by himself, no help from Carmen. He still considered himself to be a Player, but this water business was definitely Sucker work.

Another month or so, and he could sell his franchise. Or, more likely, just sell the van, buy himself a Cadillac, and let the Range Boys fill their own god-damn Evian bottles.

He heard the side garage door open. Thinking it was Carmen, he said, "How did the fitting go?"

When she did not reply, he looked up to see a stocky, expressionless man, with a military haircut and two large nostrils, standing in the doorway.

Hyatt grinned. "Hey, Chip, what's going on?"

Chip said, "Here, catch." With choppy underhand motion, Chip tossed him a brown glass jar. Hyatt, taken by surprise, reached for it a moment too late. The jar fell between his hands and shattered on the cement floor, its liquid contents quickly spreading. Chip frowned, did an about-face, and walked out, slamming the door. For a moment Hyatt stood there with an uncertain grin on his face, then the fumes hit him, filling his sinuses with a stench so vile and penetrating that his tongue withdrew into his throat and his teeth jellied in their sockets. Hyatt felt his stomach begin to twist. He ran for the door, but his breakfast got there first.

*Advice is like snow; the softer it falls the longer it dwells upon,
and the deeper it sinks into the mind.*

—*Samuel Taylor Coleridge*

**Z**INK FITTERMAN'S FILLET OF WALLEYE DELUXE—or as his regular customers came to call it, fish-on-a-bun—went for $4.95, or $5.95 for the Fillet of Wall-eye Deluxe-in-a-Basket, which was the same thing with fries and a paper cup full of watery cole slaw. The weekday lunch crowd went through a couple dozen of the things on a good day, and maybe twice that on Fridays. He bought the frozen fillets for a buck a pound from a pair of Native American entrepreneurs off the Leech Lake Reservation—they dropped off four cartons every Thursday. Zink didn't ask a lot of questions—what they did on their own land was none of his business. He wasn't even 100 percent sure it was walleye, but his customers weren't complaining, so neither did Zink.

Joe Crow usually ordered the basket, but today, his appetite dulled by the breakfast Conita, he asked Zink for a plain fish-on-a-bun with an Evian to wash it down.

"How about a Coke, Joe? I'm all out of the Evian."

"Coke is fine," said Crow. He reached across the bar and grabbed a pickle spear from the garnish tray.

Zink lit a cigarette and watched Crow eat the pickle, then said, "You know how long those pickles have been sitting in there?"

"How long?" It did taste a bit peculiar.

"Long."

It was a quiet afternoon at Club 34. Three hours till happy hour, twelve hours till closing. Zink scribbled Crow's order on a bar slip and waddled it back to the six- by eight-foot kitchen, where this week's cook was sitting on the narrow prep table smoking a cigarette.

Crow had known Zink Fitterman for more than a decade. In his drinking days, he'd been one of Zink's best customers. He was still a good customer, albeit of the nonalcoholic and therefore less-profitable variety. Both Crow and Zink were in their middle thirties, but the years had been harder on Zink. His legs had gotten shorter, his waist larger, and his once thick, curly black hair had thinned on top and was beginning to form a reverse Mohawk. Purple pouches sagged beneath his dark brown eyes. Creases deep enough to hide a dime framed his wide lips, which opened only when he was talking or eating, and then only a little. One did not have to know him well to discern a deeply cynical nature. Crow liked him.

Twice a month, Zink would close off his back room and host a poker game, five-dollar ante, table stakes. It was a good game, and Crow played in it when he could.

Zink placed a Coke on a used Grain Belt coaster. "You playing tonight?" he asked.

"I don't know," Crow said. "I've been sort of tapped since I got back from Vegas."

"All the more reason to play. How much you drop?"

Crow produced an embarrassed smile. "Thirty," he mumbled.

"Ouch. What happened?"

"I think the games were too big for me. They play with ten or eleven players at a table out there, what they call a ring game. Too damn many personalities for a midwestern boy like Joe Crow."

"Well, I seen you win a lot more than I seen you lose."

"This time I lost. I might have to get a job. You need a bartender?"

"If I could afford another bartender, you think I'd be pouring your Coke myself?"

"Maybe I'll start buying pulltabs. Get lucky."

"I got 'em for sale right here," Zink said.

Crow chuckled. Matching wits with a slip of paper did not appeal to him. There was no percentage in it. "What would it cost me to buy a joint like this?"

"A bar? You might could prob'ly find something around a hundred, hundred fifty. Fifty if you want a wino bar. You want to buy this place? I'd give you a hell of a deal."

"I was just wondering. I've been thinking about getting into some sort of business. You know. A flower shop or a used-record store or a coffee bar."

Zink snorted and carefully scratched the top of his head. "What do you know about flowers?"

"What do you know about distilling? Anyway, I was just thinking."

"That's where it starts. Next thing you know you'll be bald and losing sleep over this huge monthly nut. How come you're thinking about this now? Midlife crisis? You ain't old enough for that."

"I feel old enough. So how's that kid of yours doing?" Crow asked. Zink had a nine-year-old boy he liked to talk about. Crow always made it a point to ask about him, especially when he wanted to change the subject.

"He's doing great. He stayed with me four days running last week. Wendy's more inclined to let loose of him these days. I think he's driving her nuts. The kid gets into everything. I walk in his room, and he's got my *Playboys* all over his bed. Wendy's never told him a goddamn think about sex—can you believe it?"

"Maybe she thinks it's your job. He's a boy, right?"

"What the hell do I know about sex? It's all on TV anyway. The kid watches it constantly. At least he does when he's not into my adult literature. He's like a sponge. You want to know what else he did? He got into my Rogaine. Rubbed it all over his chest. He wants to have a hairy chest like his old man. You know what that shit costs?"

Crow was laughing. "Did it work?"

"I sure as hell hope not. Wendy would kill me."

"Is it working on you?"

Zink thrust the top of his head toward Crow. "You tell me."

Crow examined the balding crown. "I think I see some fuzz."

"That's three hundred dollars worth of fuzz you're looking at, man." He straightened up. "It doesn't start coming in better, I'm just going to buy myself a hat. Listen, I got four guys want to play. What do you say?"

"I'm thinking. You remember that game out at Bigg Biggle's place? Any of those guys coming?"

"I don't know those guys. Except for Bigg."

"No. You know Hyatt Hilton, don't you?"

"Oh yeah, I know Hy."

"I hear he's got the good price on bottled water."

"Yeah, when he shows up. I haven't seen him lately."

"What do you know about him?"

"Not much. He's kind of a doofus, isn't he? Why?"

"You know my dad?"

"Sam? Sure I do."

"Well he's got this buddy named Axel, who has a daughter—she's not really his daughter, but *he* thinks she is—engaged to marry Hy. So he, meaning Axel, asks me to ask around about the guy Carmen, the girl he thinks is his daughter, is engaged to. Meaning Hyatt. Except I don't know if he really wants me to find anything because he wants to use the wedding to launch his new product. I mean Axel."

Zink massaged his nose with two fingers. "You want to run that by me again?"

"No. What else do you know about Hy?"

Zink shrugged. "He sells water and likes to draw to flushes. He used to be involved in some sort of church, until they kicked him out. He was pretty pissed about that."

"How'd you meet him?"

"I knew him from way back. Hy the Guy."

Crow sipped his Coke. "Hy introduced you to Bigg?"

"Yeah, about a year ago. Bigg was promoting some sort of bodybuilding contest, looking for sponsors. I gave him a hundred bucks to get my name on the program."

"Who's playing tonight?"

"Me, Kirk, Ozzie, Levin. You, I hope."

"Why don't you give Bigg a call?"

"You think so? After that last game, I thought maybe he'd given it up."

"He'd probably jump at the chance to get even."

"I'll call him. Does that mean you'll play?"

"Let me know about Bigg. If he's there, I'll play."

"Okay. Listen, seriously, what do you think about this Rogaine? You think I'm wasting my money or what?"

"It all depends on how important it is to you to have a kid with a hairy chest."

"Goddamn it, Joe, you know what I mean."

"Let me have another look."

Zink leaned over the bar. As far as Crow could tell, it looked the same as ever. He said, "I'd give it another couple months, Zink."

"You think so?"

"Absolutely."

♠

People whose lives were in turmoil, Crow had observed, had a way of sucking in anybody who got too close to them. Crazy people make people crazy. He could feel it happening to him already. Two days ago, the wedding of Carmen Roman and Hyatt Hilton had meant no more to him than a fart in a hurricane, and now he could think of little else. He had become infected by Axel's anxiety. Not only was he thinking far too much about Hyatt and Carmen, he was worrying over the fact that he was spending so much time thinking about them. Crow was not unconscious of his condition. He knew that once anxiety itself became a source of anxiety, his only choices were to bail out, or seek counsel.

A guy like Zink Fitterman, when he had a problem, would ask everybody he knew what he should do. For instance, Zink would ask two dozen or more people whether or not he should continue the Rogaine treatment. How he applied such widespread and varied advice was a mystery to Crow, whose advisers, at this point in his life, numbered two: Laura Debrowski and Sam O'Gara.

Crow missed Debrowski for many reasons. He missed the feeling of having her near him, he missed the heat and sensation of her body pressing against him in the night. He missed the idle banter, her sudden sideways smile, and the jangle of chains as she shrugged off her motorcycle jacket. Right now, he missed her talent for listening carefully and, with a few words, massaging cramped thoughts into a state of relaxed lucidity. Debrowski was the only woman Crow had ever met who seemed comfortable navigating his mind. She knew him, yet she loved him—a fact that astonished him. But Debrowski was on the other side of the world, and he didn't even have a telephone number to call and thinking about it just made him more anxious than ever.

His other adviser, Sam O'Gara, provided guidance in the form of long, tedious, cautionary tales from his youth. His recommendations were rarely practical or useful, but after listening to them Crow usually came away with greater clarity and focus, if only in knowing what *not* to do.

Crow found Sam's legs hanging out of the engine compartment of a 1969 Dodge Dart. The car was one of a dozen assorted non- or semifunctioning vehicles parked in the backyard of Sam's East St. Paul home. Crow closed the gate behind him and waited for Chester and Festus to lumber over and give his crotch a sniff. Crow was one of the few humans who did not arouse a cacophony of bays, howls, growls, and snarls from the aging hounds. He walked up behind Sam and tried to see what he was doing.

"Sam?"

Sam's body jerked in surprise. "Son? That you?" His voice echoed from the engine compartment off the sprung hood, which was held up by a thin, precariously balanced wooden yardstick.

"What are you doing in there?"

"I'm tryin' t' get my goddamn 'spender loose a this goddamn thing is what!"

Crow leaned in for a better look. One of Sam's bib overall suspenders was snagged on the alternator mount, and both his arms were caught down near the oil filter. He couldn't raise his arms without lifting his body, and he couldn't lift his body because of the snagged suspender—a remarkable posture. Crow could not quite see how it had happened.

"How did you do this?" he asked.

"Never mind that, goddamn it! Just get me loose."

Crow reached down and unsnapped Sam's right suspender, then helped him out of the compartment. As soon as he was back on his feet, Sam gave the Dodge a vicious kick in the front quarter panel. The yardstick snapped and the hood crashed down.

Sam jumped a good six inches, then shook his fist at the Dodge. "Goddamn fuckin' Mopar. Tried to eat me."

"How long were you stuck in there?"

"Long enough!" Sam produced a slightly bent pack of Pall Malls, lit one with a stick match and puffed furiously. As the nicotine penetrated his blood-brain barrier, he visibly relaxed. "No more'n five minutes. I could've ripped 'er loose, but these bibs are practically brand new."

Sam's overalls looked about ten years old to Crow, but it was all relative, he supposed. "You're lucky that hood didn't crash down while you were in there."

"I lead a charmed fucking existence."

"You told me Axel was lucky. I think you're the lucky one."

Sam snorted a jet of smoke through his nose. "Not by half. How you doing on monkey-wrenching that wedding?"

"I'm not trying to monkey-wrench it, Sam. Axel just asked me to check the guy out. Make sure he's not a psycho skinhead like the last one. I didn't find anything, though."

"All's that means is you didn't look. Everybody's got something nasty in their closet."

"Even you?"

" 'Specially me."

"You think I ought to keep looking?"

Sam's wrinkles rearranged themselves.

"I'm not talking about you, Sam. How hard should I look at Hyatt Hilton?"

"How hard's Ax want you to look?"

"That's what I don't know. He's sort of ambivalent."

"That mean he can talk out of either side of his mouth?"

"Yes. He's talking like the wedding is going to happen, and he says he doesn't want to know anything half-nasty about his future son-in-law. Unless it's something so nasty that Carmen would back out of the deal."

"Sounds like Ax. I ever tell you about the time him and me got robbed in Brownsville? We was playin' Bourre with a bunch of Cajuns—sharks, every last one of 'em—losin' so fast I was about to just hand 'em the rest of my money and go home. Then Ax got hot, had a run of luck the like of which those Cajuns hadn't seen since Huey Long. We quit winners, then drove out to this little ol' roadhouse to celebrate." Sam took a massive drag on his cigarette, flicked it at the Dodge, and peered up at Crow through a cloud of smoke. "Your old man was a real cock-a-the-walk back then."

"I never doubted it."

"But it was Ax got the girl that night. Little Mex gal, pretty as a pair a aces, charmed ol' Ax like he was hit over the head with a sock full of lead shot. And that's just what she done. Those two went down the road to the joint we was stayin' at and the next thing Ax knew she'd knocked him silly and took all his money. Woulda took our Lincoln, too, only she flooded 'er. That thing always was a little tricky on the start."

Crow waited while Sam lit another cigarette.

"Next night we was in Houston, playing stud poker."

"What's that got to do with Hyatt Hilton?"

"Got nothin' to do with him. I'm tryin' to tell you, son, how when it comes to a certain kind of woman, Ax don't got the sense God gave 'im. You just got to take 'er as she comes."

Crow said, "Interesting."

"I didn't tell you the interesting part. That little Mex gal? He couldn't get her off his mind. Talked about her for weeks. And it wasn't like he was mad at her, either. He just wanted to see her again. So there you go."

"There I go where?"

"That Mex gal, I just seen her that once, but I remember what she looked like. She looked just like that Carmen. He's still got a crush on her. He's shackin' up with the mama, but it's the daughter's ass that's got his bone in a twist. Reason he don't want her to get married don't have jack-shit to do with Hyatt Hilton, and he knows it, too. That's why he's paying for the whole she-bang."

"Now I'm totally confused."

"So's Ax, son. He don't know what the fuck he wants."

*Advice is like a dead fish. It stinks or it don't.*

—Sam O'Gara

**C**ARMEN NOTICED THE SMELL AS soon as she got out of her car in front of Hy's house. At first it smelled good—like hot butter. As she turned her key in the front door lock, the odor became more powerful, reminding her of stale popcorn. Carmen pushed the door open. The smell hit her full force, sending her staggering backward. She put a few yards between herself and the open door, then stood there, breathing deeply, trying to quiet her heaving stomach. What *was* that? The odor reminded her of vomit. Even more vividly, it reminded her of an old boyfriend, a keyboard player named Crustola, who had earned his nickname by his casual approach to personal hygiene. Cautiously, Carmen again approached the front door. The smell seemed slightly less potent—either it was dissipating, or her nose had gone numb. She stepped inside and called Hy's name.

"In here," came his voice.

"Where?"

"In the bathroom," he shouted. "And don't worry, it's only V-8."

V-8? Was that what he'd said? Leaving the front door ajar, she walked through the living room, examining her surroundings suspiciously, breathing shallowly through her mouth. She could hear Hy's low voice. "Yeah, no, that's Carmen. Listen, I understand what you're saying. A job is a job. But couldn't you have just handed it to me? I mean, I've got the neighbors calling me up here, complaining about the smell. Not to mention you've wrecked my water business."

Carmen stopped outside the bathroom door. "Who are you talking to?"

"Hold on a sec—" he raised his voice. "I'm on the phone!"

"It stinks in here, Hy."

"I'll call you later, okay? What's that? Oh no you're not. No way. I don't care what she told you, *Eduardo,* you aren't gonna break anything. You hear me? Not a foot, not a finger—nothing!"

Carmen heard a splashing noise and the beep of the phone being turned off. She said, "What's that horrible stink?"

"You can still smell it?"

"I could smell it from the street. What is it?"

"Butyric acid," Hyatt said.

"Bee-you-*what*?" Carmen opened the bathroom door, took one look at her fiancé, and fainted dead away.


Arling Biggle peeled the wrapper from his Casa Blanca Jeroboam. He crumbled the cellophane, making sure everyone noticed, then placed the enormous cigar dead center in his mouth.

Levin said, "Jesus Christ, are you going to light that horse dick?"

In answer, Bigg bit the end off the cigar and spat it onto the floor. He gave Zink, who was sitting on his left, a nudge.

"What?" Zink muttered, giving the cigar a bland look.

"You got a light?"

"Uh-uh. No friggin' way."

Bigg looked around the table, spotted a book of matches in front of Ozzie, bobbled his eyebrows. Ozzie sighed and tossed the matches across the table. The four men watched wordlessly as Bigg used three matches to ignite the cigar, creating a cloud of smoke that rose slowly toward the ceiling, mushroomed, then slowly settled to hover at head height over the table.

"Looks like you're giving the invisible man a blowjob," Levin said, the corners of his mouth pulled down around his chin.

Bigg grinned and sank his teeth into the cigar. "We here to play cards or whine about a little smoke? Whose deal is it?"

"Mine," said Ken Kirk. He offered the cut to Zink, then dealt each player two cards.

Bigg leaned toward Zink, eyeing his stacked chips. "How are you doing?"

"I'm doing okay." Zink drummed his fingers on his two cards.

"I'm down three hundred already," Bigg said.

"That's rough," Zink said. He knocked on the table, passing the bet to Kirk, who bet twenty. Ozzie called; Levin folded.

Bigg frowned at his cards. The game was "hold 'em," two cards to each player, with five community cards dealt face-up in the middle of the table. Bigg had a deuce of hearts and an eight of clubs in his hand. If the next three cards were three eights, or three deuces, or two eights and a deuce, or vice versa, he could win a big spot. Or if the flop came up five, six, seven of clubs, he'd have a shot at a straight flush. There were all kinds of possibilities.

"You in or out?" Kirk demanded.

"I'm thinking," Bigg said.

Zink folded out of turn. "Let's see what you got." He leaned over to look at Bigg's cards.

"What d'you think?" Bigg asked, his left hand hovering over his chips.

"Get out," said Zink.

Bigg wanted to bet. They would never suspect him of staying in with a deuce, eight. If the cards fell perfect he could win big. On the other hand, if Zink was right, and he lost another three bills, he'd feel like a jerk. With considerable effort, Bigg dropped his cards. "Fold," he muttered.

The first three cards came up deuce, eight, ace.

Bigg said, "I'd a had two pair." He put his cigar between his teeth and bit down. The cigar served two purposes, he believed. First, it irritated the other players. Second, it kept him from grinding his teeth together. According to Bigg's dentist, he'd been losing about a millimeter a year. Another five years and he'd be gumming his cigars.

"You'd a had shit," said Zink. "Wait and see."

The last two cards came up king, nine. Kirk took the pot with three aces over Ozzie's aces and kings. Zink said, "See what I mean?"

Earlier in the evening, Zink had taken Bigg aside and told him straight out how he saw it. "I'm telling you this once, Bigg. Every time I've played with you, you've lost. Since I'm hosting this particular game, I feel it's my obligation to tell you why. Your problem is, you think you got a hand when you got shit. You know what I mean?"

In an intellectual sort of way, Bigg believed that what Zink had told him was true. But the cards were unpredictable, and it all came down to luck in the end. He was counting on the cigar to change his luck. He picked up his fresh cards and squinted at them. Queen, four, off suit. Bigg squeezed his eyes closed, then looked again. Queen, four. He concentrated, trying to make them into something good. You never knew what would win. If the flop came up three queens, or three fours, that would be something! Even a pair of queens would be good. He had seen guys win with less. His left hand moved toward his chips.

By the time Crow showed up, a dense strata of gray smoke hovered a foot above the surface of the table, blurring the features of the five players. Arling Biggle, a huge cigar gripped in his stumpy teeth, clutched his cards and glared across the table at Ken Kirk. Crow knew instantly, without seeing any of the cards in play, that Bigg was about to lose. Kirk was the tightest player at the table, betting only when he had the best hand. Al Levin, Ozzie LaRose, and Zink Fitterman watched as Bigg called Kirk's fifty-dollar raise, then lost to the inevitable nut straight. Bigg flexed his jaw, causing a walnut-sized ash to fall into his remaining chips. He stared balefully as Kirk gathered the pot.

Crow picked up a chair and wedged it in between Bigg and Zink.

"Mind if I squeeze in?" he said.

Bigg rolled his eyes and moved about half an inch to his right. Zink skidded his chair over to make room for Crow.

Crow sat down and said, "Evening, Bigg. How's it going?"

"Screw you, Crow. I got no more free memberships."

Crow smiled. The best way to beat a guy like Bigg at the card table was to make him want to beat you. *Don't play against your opponents. Let them play against you.* The harder Bigg tried to get a piece of Crow's stack, the more money would flow Crow's way.

Al Levin dealt. The bet was checked to Bigg, who bet twenty. Crow looked at his cards. Queen, four. He threw them away. *Wait for the cards.* He sat back and watched the hand play out.

Two hours later, Crow was up a thousand, and Bigg was down two. Zink, who played his cards almost as tight as Kirk, was also a winner. The other players were all within a hundred bucks of even. At Bigg's request, they had switched from hold 'em to seven stud high-low, which had the effect of increasing the number of bad hands Bigg could play.

At one point, Bigg shifted strategies and began to make enormous bets at the beginning of the hand. He picked up several antes by betting two hundred dollars on the strength of his first three cards. Finally, with a pair of aces in the hole and a five up top, Crow called and raised a hundred. Bigg, who was showing an ace, looked startled, then called the raise. Everyone else folded.

Crow picked up the case ace on the fourth card. Bigg was showing ace, ten. To Crow's surprise, Bigg bet five hundred. Crow raised an equal amount. Once again, Bigg called.

The fifth card gave Crow a deuce and Bigg a nine. Bigg bet another five. Crow gazed at Bigg's cards, chewing thoughtfully on his lower lip. Little danger of a flush. The best thing Bigg could have would be three tens, or four cards to a straight, or three cards to a good low hand. Crow called the bet. Ozzie tossed out two more cards, a ten for Bigg and a seven for Crow. Bigg pushed the last of his cash into the pot—three hundred forty dollars.

Because the game was table stakes, players could only bet the amount of money they had on the table. However, according to Zink's house rules, if only two players were involved in the pot, they were free to negotiate additional bets—I.O.U.s, cars, houses, whatever—so long as it was understood that such arrangements were agreeable to both players.

At this point, against anybody else, Crow would simply have called the bet and let the cards fall. But remembering the dent in his GTO, he said, "You want to dig deeper, Bigg?"

"That's all I got," Bigg growled.

"Maybe you got something else you want to bet."

"I already told you, no more free memberships."

"I was thinking more along the lines of a limo rental." It would make a great wedding gift. Crow pushed a small stack of chips toward the pot. "Another two hundred against a limo rental. What do you say?"

Bigg's tongue darted across his lips. "I get six hundred a day," he said. "That's the limo and driver."

Crow added another stack. "I'll go four against a free ride."

Bigg nodded. "Done."

Carmen had a large lump on her head where it had struck the bathroom door. She was treating it with a bag full of crushed ice and a triple vodka tonic. The combination was remarkably effective. Not only did her head not hurt anymore, but she could hardly smell the butyric acid, which, according to Hyatt, was the worst smelling substance on the planet. Carmen believed it. Hy's Evian business was ruined. It would take months for the odor in the garage to go away. Maybe longer. Carmen didn't mind that so much—the water business was small potatoes—but she did not appreciate the fact that her fiancé smelled like aged vomit. Taking another sip of her drink, Carmen watched Hyatt sitting in his red silk boxers on his black Naugahyde sofa watching an infomercial.

She said, "You know what was the first thing I thought?"

The corner of Hyatt's mouth twitched, but he kept his eyes on the television. Carmen fished a piece of ice from her drink and flicked it onto his bare belly.

Hyatt's body snapped to attention; he brushed away the ice and said, "Hey!"

"You know what was the first thing I thought?" Carmen said again.

"You thought I'd killed myself. You already told me that." When Carmen had opened the bathroom door, she had discovered Hyatt sitting in the bathtub four inches deep in V-8 juice.

"That was actually the second thing I thought. The first thing I thought was that you were having one hell of a period." Carmen pulled the ice bag away from her head.

Hyatt processed that for about a nanosecond, then returned his attention to the infomercial. "This is interesting," he said. "You can get rich on 900 numbers. You get a 900 number, put a few ads in the paper, and let some other jerk field the calls. Every time somebody calls in for their horoscope you get a piece of it. That would be perfect. Just sit back and wait for the checks to come in."

"I thought, well, at least we know he's not preggers."

Hyatt gave her a sardonic look. "Which thought was that? Number two or three?"

Carmen rattled the ice in her glass. "That was number one and a half, asshole."

"Hey, I tried to warn you. I told you it was just tomato juice."

"'It's only V-8,' you said. What the hell was I supposed to do with that?"

"I wasn't trying to scare you. I thought it might kill the smell. It works if you got a skunked-up dog."

"Yeah, well it didn't work on you. It still reeks in here. I probably reek, too, just from being here. It's a good thing we aren't getting married tomorrow."

"It'll wear off. What do you think about us getting a 900 number? Wouldn't that be cool? You got a pen?"

Carmen shook her head. Hyatt jumped up from the sofa and ran into the kitchen.

"We're gonna have to move, that's all there is to it," Carmen said.

Hyatt returned holding a stubby pencil. "We're going to move anyway, Carm. We can live wherever you want, once the money starts rolling in."

"What are we going to do for money until then? I don't care what kind of label you slap on it, nobody's going to buy water that smells like puke."

"I've got a little money." Hyatt copied the number on the screen onto the back of a magazine. "You believe this? To find out how to get rich by owning 900 numbers, they have you call this 900 number. That's what I call *perfect*."

"You think everything is *perfect*."

Hyatt jabbed the air between them with the pencil. "Not true," he said. "A wedding reception with Swedish meatballs is not perfect. Sometimes you have to compromise."

*When your mind is elsewhere, go there.*

—*Crow's rules*

**C**ROW FELL ASLEEP FULLY DRESSED on the sofa. He dreamed himself back to Paris where, amazingly, he found that he could speak French after all. He was looking for Debrowski. Everyone he asked remembered her, but wherever he looked, she had just left.

Shortly after sunrise he woke up with a headache and a tongue that tasted like a bad oyster. Two cups of instant coffee did not help, nor did three. Milo made an attempt at being sociable, butting his head repeatedly against Crow's shins, but received no encouraging response. Crow stared out the window, morning light pouring into his eyes but leaving no impression on his mind. He felt as if his head was full of sludge, the tailings of too much second-hand tobacco smoke and adrenaline. It didn't seem to matter whether he won or lost at cards—either way, his body exacted a price. He stared out the window, replaying last night's big hands in his memory.

After an unmeasured period of time—it may have been only a few seconds, or as long as half an hour—he got up and packed his gym bag. He wasn't looking forward to seeing Bigg.

On the other hand, he could hardly wait.

Crow found a parking space beside one of Bigg's limos. He parked in close and pulled the door latch back, paused for a self-conscious moment, and threw his weight against the door, slamming it into the side of the limo. Crow climbed out and examined the resulting dent. Satisfied, he locked his car. When he looked up, he saw Flowrean Peeche sitting in her red Miata, looking at him, wearing a bemused smile. She quickly turned her head away and pulled her car into a parking space at the other side of the lot.

Bigg Bodies was crowded with reasonably normal-looking men and women getting in a workout before going to their jobs—a slightly more ambitious version of the after-work crowd. It was still too early for the gym rats and serious bodybuilders. Arling Biggle sat behind the front counter, filing his nails with an emery stick. Neither man spoke.

Crow went through his routine with robotic precision. At one point, after a set of deadlifts, he looked at the mirrored wall and found Flowrean Peeche's reflection watching him, still with that smile. Embarrassed, Crow finished his workout with six brutal sets of leg extensions. On the way out, he knocked on Bigg's office door and stepped in. Bigg was sitting behind his desk reading *Muscle and Fitness*.

"What the hell do you want?" He looked pale. His eyes were bloodshot and yellow.

"I just wanted to see if you were hiding in your closet."

"Screw you."

"And to make sure you got that date. It's August ninth."

Bigg glared. "I got it."

"Good." Crow felt an unexpected knot of sympathy for the man. Bigg had lost a nice chunk of cash, he was suffering from a hangover, and he owed a debt to someone he despised. Crow had been there. "I'll see you," he said.

Bigg made a grating noise in his throat and returned his attention to his magazine.

The Latin Quarter bistro, half a kilometer from the Louvre, was packed with tourists. Most of them had chosen to sit outside in the hot sun, drinking Heinekens and waving flies away from their *croque-monsieurs*. Even in July, in Paris, the tourists found charm in al fresco dining.

Laura Debrowski sat inside behind a small round table near the air conditioner and lit a Gitane. She no longer minded the tourists, no longer felt self-conscious to be recognized as one of them. After two months, she had made a kind of peace with this city. It was doomed to be neither more nor less than what it was, and so was she.

During her first weeks in Paris, Debrowski had worked hard to merge with the city, observing its residents with fierce concentration, forcing her tongue to mimic their words and accents, training her body to move the way the Parisians moved, memorizing their hand and facial gestures, and buying herself a pair of the odd-looking canvas shoes that were popular with the Latin Quarter students. Three years of French classes percolated through her brain. She challenged herself to speak only the native tongue and proudly proved her ability to blunder her way through the basic communications necessary to get from one end of the day to the other. She was embarrassed by her Americanism, unable to forgive herself for being herself, and angry with herself for giving a damn. During those early weeks she had attempted to embed herself upon the city like a virus attaching itself to a cell, mimicking its proteins, hoping to become a part of it.

A narrow-featured, bearded garçon approached, flipped open a tiny pad, mumbled, "*Pour vous, mademoiselle?*"

"*Un grand noir, s'il vous plait,*" Debrowski rattled off. Her accent was nearly perfect—she had listened to the words dozens of times, practiced them endlessly, even going so far as to tape herself at SuperSon, the recording studio where *Les Hommes Magnifiques* had been laying down tracks for their CD. She knew the waiter understood exactly what she had said, and what she wanted: a large, black espresso. She had ordered it as would a Parisian: one large black, please. An efficient, elegant use of the language.

The waiter frowned at his pad. "Espresso double?" he asked, feigning confusion.

Debrowski sighed and tapped the ash off her cigarette. "*Oui,*" she said. "*Un double.*" This waiter—and every other waiter in this city—knew she was no Parisian. At best, they would think her some other variety of European. She would never be permitted to order her morning coffee in the Parisian manner, but would now and forever be required to order her coffee as would a tourist— in clumsy guidebook French or, should she prefer, in English, German, Spanish, or Italian.

The garçon gave a sharp nod, whirled, and headed for the bar, where the only locals in the bistro, a group of working men, stood sipping pastises and *grand noirs,* their short, broad backs turned on the seated tourists.

Any one of the men could have been Crow, with his French laborer-type body. But Crow was gone, back in the states.

Debrowski fastened her lips on the Gitane and inhaled the powerful blue-brown smoke, bringing it down deep. That goddamn Crow. She'd known he was going home as soon as he'd started talking about his cat.

During Crow's three weeks in Paris he had not uttered a word in French, which had irritated the hell out of Debrowski. She'd worked so hard to fit in, yet had found herself in the company of this—this unrepentant American. What really got to her was that Crow, who refused to take on even the faintest tint of local color, was repeatedly mistaken for a native. People on the street would approach him speaking rapid French, to which he would reply in English. Worse yet, despite his blatant refusal to even attempt to speak their language, the French seemed to like him. She remembered one conversation that had begun when a short man with a wide nose had stopped them on the street and asked Crow—in French—for directions to the nearest RER depot.

"Sorry," said Crow. "I don't know what you're saying."

The man cocked his head. "You are American?" he said, switching effortlessly into English.

"That's right," Crow said.

"Your family, you must be from France, no?"

"My family's mostly Irish, actually."

"Ah!" the man grinned, showing much gold in his teeth. "I love the Irish!"

Nettled, Debrowski had said, "He wants to know where the RER depot is, Crow."

The man had ignored her completely, apparently having lost interest in catching his train, and proceeded to recite his favorite lines from William Butler Yeats.

Crow had left Paris nearly two months ago. At first, she'd felt a sense of relief, as if shrugging off a heavy pack. Then she'd become angry at him for leaving her there. And now? Now she missed him. She wished he was there to see her learning to relax. Making the transition from wannabe Frenchwoman to American tourist. She hoped to get to the point when she could walk into any restaurant in town and blithely order a burger and fries in English, giving the words the full nasal force of her Midwestern twang. One day she might even dare to order a cup of "American coffee"—espresso diluted with hot water—or, better yet, a hot dog for breakfast as she had once seen a Japanese tourist do. A hot dog and a Coke.

The waiter's hand appeared and disappeared, leaving behind an espresso double. Debrowski unwrapped a sugar cube, dipped it into the coffee, sucked on it—a Parisian habit she had picked up. She frowned at her affectation, dropped the cube into the cup, took a large drag from the Gitane, let the smoke drift from her mouth and nose. For a moment, her head swam in a warm nicotine fog. A cool tentacle of air reached out from the air conditioner and exploded the cloud.

It was hard for her, to be an American in Paris. But it was possible, at least. Laura Debrowski considered her options as she absorbed the remainder of her cigarette and coffee. Leaving twelve francs beside her coffee cup, she walked out into the midday heat, located a credit card phone, and entered in a long sequence of numbers.

Known to certain of her coworkers as "Princess Peach," the Flowrean Peeche who worked at Solid Sam's Real Food Restaurant was a different person from the Flowrean Peeche who worked out at Bigg Bodies. Flo the waitress was neat, she was clean, and she smelled good. Her wild mop of hair was pulled back and woven into a precise braid. She wore the same black-and-gold polyester outfit as the other waitresses and, except for her well-defined forearms and callused palms, she did not look like a bodybuilder. When she spoke to her customers she came across as pleasant and even friendly, and if one of them copped a feel, she refrained from breaking his arm.

Flo recognized that holding a good job required certain sacrifices and compromises. She did not mind being called "Princess," but the treatment of her surname—more properly pronounced "Puh-*shay*"—disturbed her. Nevertheless, for the sake of the job, she tolerated the title. The hours were flexible. She never had to miss a workout. And the tips were excellent. On a good night she could take home an easy hundred and twenty dollars, money she needed. Payments on her condo downtown ran nine hundred a month. Protein supplements, amino acids, organic vegetables, and vitamins cost another six hundred. She'd paid off her Miata, but it was four years old and might break down at any time. Money was important. Self-respect was important. The respect of others, that was optional.

Flo understood that she was loathed by the other waitresses. They hated her because she was the best damn waitress Solid Sam Champlin, former Minnesota Viking, had ever hired. They hated her because she was always on time, because she got the best tips, and because she treated the rest of the waitstaff as if they did not exist. And they hated her because Solid Sam, who was by all accounts the nicest three hundred forty-pound ex-linebacker on the planet, was clearly and desperately in love with her. Flo understood all that, but she didn't let it bother her. She showed up and did her job. She flirted with the cooks, ignored the dining room staff, fended off Sam's advances, and provided her customers with flawless table service. Lately, while she did all that, she devoted a significant portion of her thoughts to Joe Crow.

Three images came back to her repeatedly. First, she thought of Crow facing down Beaut Miller, that dreamy expression on his face. That had been a beautiful thing, a moment that made her heart jump in her chest. Second, she remembered looking up one time after screaming her way through a particularly painful set of squats, three hundred sixty-five pounds on the bar, to find Crow staring at her with frank admiration. When she remembered that moment she grew little shivery bumps all over her arms. Her third picture of Crow was of him slamming his car door into one of Bigg's limos. That one got her right between the legs.

She was playing that memory, waiting for a chili fries appetizer to come up, when Solid Sam glided past her—amazing how smooth and quiet he could move for such a big guy—and let his ringed fingers drag lightly across her left glute. The synergy of having Crow in her mind and Solid Sam's fingers on her ass made her knees buckle.

Quickly recovering, she snapped, "Next time you do that I break a finger."

Sam, moving away, chuckled, saying over his shoulder, "I wear you down, baby. I wear you down."

"In your dreams, niggah," Flo muttered, hiding a smile. Her chili fries appeared under the lights; she grabbed the plate and walked them out to the waiting four-top. Sam was a nice guy. She even liked him, most of the time. But he reminded her too much of her mother's boyfriends. Also, he was not so solid as he had been during his gridiron days. The thought of his rubbery embrace frightened her. She might be absorbed and digested.

Crow, by contrast, was small, hard, stoic, and impenetrable. He was separate. His otherness tugged at her with the force of gravity. The more she thought about him, the more she wanted to get inside that shell.

Crow had once asked Debrowski whether she ever astonished herself.

"Every day, Crow."

"No. I mean, do you ever do something and it's like you're watching yourself, and you just can't believe that you are doing it?"

"Yes."

"Like what?"

Debrowski's eyes lost focus for a moment. She said, "One day last week I was getting dressed. I had my jacket, and I was putting on this—" She fingered a thin silver chain that hung from her earlobe to the epaulet of her scarred-up leather jacket, where it was fastened by an antique brass padlock, one of several that adorned her person. "—And I thought, what the *hell* do you think you're *doing*? All of a sudden I saw myself as this weirdo, this poseur, this silly little twit in black leather and chains trying to make a fashion statement. A fashion statement, I mean, what the hell is that? Am I telling people, hey, look out for this chick because she is obviously a dangerously self-involved, tasteless idiot? I felt like a complete fool. Do I ever astonish myself? Hell yes."

Crow said, "You mean you were astonished at the way you were dressed?"

Debrowski gave him an injured look. "It was the thoughts that astonished me, Crow. I dress how I want."

Crow was rarely astonished by his own thoughts. His acts, however, were a continual source of amazement. Every time he remembered putting that dent in Bigg's limo, he became confused. Vandalism was not and had never been his style. The weirdest thing was that it had felt so *good*. It had put his relationship with Arling Biggle back in balance. A dent for a dent.

Such were his thoughts as he climbed the stairs to his apartment door. He had just inserted his key into the lock when he heard the tinny sound of an incoming message on his answering machine. He pushed the door open and strode quickly through the apartment, trying to reach the phone before she hung up. Milo materialized between his feet and wrapped his body around Crow's ankle. Crow lost his balance trying not to crush the cat, whacked his knee on an endtable, and fell headlong on the hardwood floor.

His cheek pressing against the somewhat gritty floorboards, Crow heard, "au revoir, cheri." The machine gave forth a squawk and clicked off, leaving behind only the sound of Milo purring somewhere in the dark.

"Goddamn cat," he muttered as he climbed painfully to his feet. This was not turning out to be one of his better days. He limped to the phone and played back the message.

"Allo allo, Crow, you must be out playing cards, you rascal. What time is it there? You aren't still in bed, are you? Did you get my postcard? You better not be out chasing women, Crow. I think we're getting close to wrapping things up here, but René is being a jerk—*ça me fait shier.* It'll be good to get back. I'll call you tomorrow, same time, same station. Au revoir, cheri!"

Once again, she didn't leave a number where he could call her back. At least the message had been upbeat. Crow rewound the tape and listened to it again. He liked that she didn't want him out chasing women. He liked her calling him "cheri."

*It is the test of a good religion whether you can joke about it.*

—*Gilbert K. Chesterton*

"You still reek off that shit, man." Charles "Chuckles" Thickening rolled down his window and turned up the air conditioning.

Charles "Chip" Bouchet turned his head and glared. The two men were sitting in Chuckles's yellow Corvette, watching the front door of a Dunkin' Donuts.

"You ever hear of *bathing?*" Chuckles asked.

"I took a shower."

"Yeah, well you still stink."

Chip Bouchet crossed his arms and scowled. Smaller, denser, and more rigid than Chuckles, Chip's blocky body moved with robotic precision and inflexibility. He wore his sandy hair in a military buzz cut, carried his chin thrust up and forward, and spoke with minimal lip and jaw movement, which made him difficult to understand. Chip might have been considered a handsome man, in a squinty-eyed Aryan sort of way, were it not for the fact that his nostrils pointed forward rather than down, a feature which, during his brief stint in the Marines, had earned him the nickname "Rooter."

Chip had been with the ACO almost since the beginning. Hyatt Hilton had originally hired him to work the early Extraction Events. Back then, Rupe and Polly and Hy had formed a triumvirate, each of them exerting more-or-less equal power. Those were, in Chip's mind, the good old days. He had seen himself as the Archangel Gabriel, carrying out the wishes of the trinity. His devotion to the church had been boundless. Recently, however, certain church practices had begun to erode his faith. He had found Hyatt's excommunication disturbing, and the recent hiring of Chuckles was a very bad sign.

Chip's job title was "Security Chief." Chuckles, who had come on board just three months ago, had been given the title "Head of Security." No one had yet told Chip who worked for whom. He was afraid to ask. So far, they had managed to work together without confronting the issue, but it weighed on Chip's mind.

Chip and Chuckles were waiting for Hyatt Hilton to emerge from the Dunkin' Donuts. They had been following him since he'd left his house that morning, waiting for a chance to talk to him up close and private. Chip was not looking forward to doing this job. The butyric acid thing had been bad enough, and now this.

So far, Hyatt had visited a health food store, an espresso shop, and now Dunkin' Donuts, all of which were too public for their purposes.

"The man's diet get worse every stop he make."

"They said he abused his temple," Chip said.

"Say what?"

"That's why Polly and Rupe had to shun him."

"Shun? I thought he got his ass kicked out. I heard he was skimmin'."

"They said he was abusing his body."

Chuckles laughed. "You mean I eat a longjohn I lose my job?"

"Hyatt Hilton was an elder. You're only a deacon. Higher offices demand higher standards of behavior."

"Good. I like them longjohns."

Hyatt Hilton pushed open the glass door and ambled over to his Beamer. He wore a loose white collarless shirt, a pair of baggy trousers with vertical red-and-gold stripes and a pair of slip-on huaraches. He climbed into his car and pulled a pastry out of the bag without seeming to notice the yellow Corvette parked across the street.

"What's that he got? A fritter?"

Chip did not reply. Hyatt began to eat.

Chuckles licked his lips. "It look *good.* They really kick him out for eating donuts?"

Chip said, "Abusing his temple." He didn't like talking about this. The whole situation with the Elders was very unstable, very need-to-know. Chuckles didn't need to know, even if he was Head of Security. "There he goes," Chip said.

The Beamer pulled out into traffic. Chuckles let it get a half block away, then followed.

Chip said, "It was not strategic."

"Say what?"

"The butyric acid. We should have planted it in his garage with a small explosive device, then triggered it from a safe distance. That would have been strategic."

Chuckles said, "You ask me, the whole idea sucked. I mean, Rupe, he just don't have Polly's cojones. She bad." Chuckles accelerated to catch a light, staying two cars behind the Beamer. "Sometime she scare me."

"The concept was sound," said Chip. The butyric acid had been his idea. "The execution was not strategic."

"Whatever. I still like Polly's approach a whole lot better. You want to make a point, you break a bone."

Chip wished, not for the first time, that his bosses, Rupe and Polly, would sing in harmony. Ever since Hyatt's excommunication, he'd been getting conflicting sets of instructions. Rupe would tell him to do something, and then Polly would tell him what he was *really* supposed to do. In this case, Rupe had asked him to suggest a nonviolent way of making an impression on Hyatt Hilton, and Chip had suggested the butyric acid. He was familiar with butyric acid from his years working with Operation Rescue. A few ounces of butyric down the roof vents could shut down an abortion factory for weeks. Rupe had approved the action. Rupert Chandra abhorred violence, but had no qualms about using aromatherapy to alter human behavior.

Polly suffered under no such strictures. After Rupe had issued his instructions to Chip and Chuckles, Polly had invited Chip into her office for a private talk. "I want you to go ahead with the butyric acid plan," she said, locking the office door. "But tomorrow, after Hy's had a chance to get himself smelling good again—just about the time he starts thinking we've done all we're going to do—that's when I want you and Chuckles to go talk to him. Make sure he gets the point." She planted a long pink fingernail at the top of Chip's sternum, raked it slowly down his chest until it caught at the first button. "But don't say anything to Rupe, understand?"

Chip understood that Rupert Chandra was to be shielded from such things. Rupe was the holy man. Polly was the hands-on Elder, the one who gave the difficult orders, the one who got things done. "How long you want us to talk to him?" Chip asked, standing at attention, his arms at his sides, the way Polly liked it.

Polly began to unbutton Chip's shirt. "Until you hear something break." She tugged his shirttails out of his khakis.

"What should we break?" Chip asked as Polly unbuckled his belt.

"How about a foot?" She unbuttoned and unzipped his jeans. "Is that easy to do?" She had his erect penis in her hand.

Chip's left knee was shaking. "Sure," he croaked. His hands wanted to be on her, but Polly had made it clear to him on previous occasions that he was not to touch her. He had to simply stand there, gritting his teeth as she milked him, slowly stroking, staring into the flared nacelles of his nostrils. It took him about fifteen gasping seconds to come.

"Good," Polly said as she squeezed the last drops of semen from his softening penis. "Break his foot." She wiped her hands with a Kleenex, took a seat behind her desk, and turned on her computer. Chip tucked and zipped and buckled and got the hell out of there. It was always the same. This was the fourth time Polly had jerked him off while asking him to perform a task—usually something with which she did not want to bother Rupe. Chip wasn't sure how he felt about it, but it was part of the job.

Later, when Polly had left for the day, he returned to her office and retrieved the inseminated Kleenex from her wastebasket. Chip did not like to leave his genetic code where anybody could walk off with it.

Chip did not tell Chuckles about his private encounters with the First Eldress. It was embarrassing, and besides, Chuckles was black. Chip did not consider himself to be a racist, but it would never have occurred to him to talk about white sex with a black man. All he'd said to Chuckles was that Polly had given them another job to do.

Chuckles hadn't acted surprised. In fact, he'd seemed to know all about it. Behind the Corvette seats lay an eighteen-inch pipe wrench, which Chuckles had purchased that morning at Menard's.

"Polly understands strategy," said Chip.

The BMW turned east on Lake Street. Chuckles followed.

Chip said, "You think he knows we're here?"

"You shittin' me? Man, I didn't go with this paint so's I could fade in the trees. Course he knows. Give him time to think on it, repent his sins. Let him get scareder. Sooner or later, he know we gonna be educatin' him. The scareder he is, the better it'll take."

That morning Crow had begun his day with a renewed sense of purpose.

Instead of brooding over whether he should pursue his investigation of Hyatt Hilton, he would simply dive into it, find out what he could, report back to Axel, and be home in time to receive Debrowski's promised call. He decided that the most direct approach would yield the most productive vein, so after pouring a few cups of coffee into his stomach he hopped in the Goat and drove over to Hyatt Hilton's place of residence. He would get his information direct from the horse's mouth. It might work—a guy like Hy, once you got him going, couldn't help but yammer on about himself. It would be worth a try.

He turned onto Hy's block just as Hy was climbing into his BMW. Crow accelerated, thinking to flag him down, but as Hy pulled away, a yellow Corvette pulled out between Hy and Crow.

Crow followed, keeping the Beamer in sight. Hy turned left on 24th Street. The Corvette also turned left. At Hennepin, Hyatt turned right, followed by the vette and by Crow. Hyatt stopped his car in front of Tao Foods. The Corvette passed him, then pulled over to the curb. Crow rumbled by the vette, glancing at its occupants as he passed. Two men, a pepper and salt combo. Crow circled the block, then took up a position on the far side of Hennepin and waited. What would it cost to open a health food store? Crow was attracted by the idea of a retail store. He saw himself sitting behind a counter, people waking in the front door and giving him money. Health food was a growth market, wasn't it? Crow let the fantasy take shape, then rejected it. Too many weirdo customers. Hy came out of Tao Foods with a small bag, got into his car, and drove off, followed by the Corvette.

After a quick stop at Caribou Coffee, Hyatt proceeded to Dunkin' Donuts. The vette parked across the street, and Crow found a spot just up the block. He was becoming increasingly curious about the men in the Corvette. Could Axel have hired someone else to investigate Hilton? It seemed highly unlikely. Were they cops? Not in a yellow Corvette. Bill collectors? That was possible. Maybe they were looking to repo Hyatt's BMW.

By the time Hyatt reached Caribou Coffee, he had become convinced that the Corvette was, in fact, following him. Once inside the coffee shop he was able to get a closer look as the car drove past. He recognized Chip Bouchet's pug-nosed profile through the tinted glass. Just seeing him brought the smell of butyric acid flooding into his olfactory memory. Hyatt couldn't see the driver clearly, but he guessed it was the one they called Chuckles, the same guy who had hoisted him into the dumpster a few weeks back. Hyatt's face assumed a rigid smile, and his jaw began to pulse. He ordered a triple cappuccino to go. As his milk was being foamed, Hyatt noticed the yellow GTO.

At Dunkin' Donuts he became certain that both the Corvette and the GTO were tailing him. Were they both from the ACO? Hyatt couldn't get a good look at the guy in the GTO. In any case, it didn't look like the sort of vehicle of which Polly would approve. And what was with these yellow cars? Hyatt considered his options as he devoured his apple fritter. He thought about pulling up in front of a police station, going inside, and making a complaint. That would solve his immediate problem, but since no one was breaking any laws, it wouldn't prevent them from turning up on his back bumper the next day to continue their program, whatever that might be.

He needed a plan that would not only make them go away today, but would convince them to stay away. Hyatt imagined various scenarios, some of which gave him great satisfaction, but all of which ultimately turned out to be implausible due to the fact that he lacked heavy weaponry, martial arts training, or super powers. He imagined a brace of rockets erupting from his exhaust pipes, taking out both yellow cars, sending up twin columns of fire and smoke. That would be cool.

Hyatt's eyes dropped to the gas gauge. He would have to figure out something soon. He wished he had a car phone. When the money started to flow, he would have cell phones in all his cars. Thinking about cell phones made him think about radio waves, and thinking of radio waves made him think of Jimmy Swann, and thinking about Jimmy Swann made Hyatt Hilton smile.

"What's he doing *here?*"

"Maybe he tryin' to score."

Chip frowned and lowered his chin. "Crack street. Everything boarded up. Looks like Beirut."

"When you in Beirut?"

"I saw it on TV."

A row of neglected Victorians lined the west side of the street, each one competing with its neighbor in a race toward disintegration. Several of them had plywood panels instead of windows, and fluorescent orange notices tacked to their front doors. The opposite side of the street contained a handful of less distinguished but similarly neglected homes; three vacant lots; and a cheaply constructed, two-story, cedar-sided apartment building decorated by a multicolored skirt of spray-painted squiggles along its length. Five young men lounged on its front steps, working their way through a case of malt liquor. Other than the men on the stoop, the street was abandoned.

Hyatt Hilton pulled over across the street from the apartment building, in front of a sagging gray Victorian, one of the few houses on the block with glass in the windows. Chuckles stopped a hundred feet behind him. For several seconds, nothing happened. Hyatt sat in his car. The men on the stoop continued to laugh and talk and drink. After half a minute, one of the young men, a lanky, tea-colored youth wearing a sleeveless white, red, and black Chicago Bulls shirt that hung nearly to his knees, stood up and ambled down the steps to the curb. He leaned forward, shading his eyes, and peered across the street at the BMW. Hyatt's hand appeared, waving him away. The kid turned back to his friends and gave a theatrical shrug. One of them said something, and the kid turned toward the Corvette.

"Here he comes," said Chuckles.

"Tell him to get lost," Chip said.

The kid slowly approached the car, his head ducking and weaving as he tried to see through the glass.

Chuckles lowered his window. "Sa'n'?" he said.

Chip didn't know how these black guys did it, made a whole sentence—What's Happening?—into a single grunt.

The kid bobbed his head, checking out the interior of the car, grinning to give them a look at the gold cap on his front tooth. He looked even younger up close, maybe fourteen or fifteen, with an advanced case of acne.

Chip leaned over and said, "Hey! We don't want any of your crack, Piz-zaface."

The kid took a step back, a stony expression on his cratered features.

Chuckles said, "Never mind him. He disrespec' his own momma."

The kid rolled his thin shoulders. "'Scoo'." He turned and glided back across the street to his place on the stoop.

Chuckles raised his window. "Man, don't you want people to like you?"

"Goddamn crackheads," Chip growled.

"They just tryin' to get by. Hey, there he go!"

Hyatt had left his car and was walking quickly up the walk toward the gray Victorian.

"What do you think? We go in after him?" Chip said.

"I don't go in no place blind. Uh-uh."

"I've got to urinate."

"Just hold it. I'll piss my pants 'fore I walk in on some thing I don't know who it is or what it is about, situation like to get me capped."

Chip crossed his arms. "Death doesn't scare me," he said.

"I know. You fucking immortal."

"You better watch your mouth."

"Hey, man, I believe, all right? I regenerate *my* cells till kingdom come. Only I don't think I'm so advanced that I can regenerate 'em fast enough to close up a bullet hole 'fore it kills me. You know what I'm saying?"

*I teach that all men are mad.*

*—Horace*

Hyatt hadn't seen Jimmy Swann in two years. For a long time they'd had a successful partnership going, a little piece of the local cocaine trade. Hyatt had been retailing grams out of Ambrosia Foods while Jimmy dealt out of his at-tache case, making the rounds of the downtown brokerages, law offices, and night clubs on Friday afternoons. They weren't exactly heavyweights. A couple ounces a week, that was plenty. Every few weeks Jimmy would phone his sec-ond cousin down in Florida and have him ship up another quarter kilo inside a bundle of Tampa-made coronas. Hyatt would foot half the bill, they'd spend an evening around Jimmy's scale weighing out grams and quarter ounces and smoking the cigars, which were not bad, and then they'd go their separate ways until their inventory once again ran low. The arrangement suited Hyatt, since Jimmy took all the risk of bringing the cocaine into his home. Hyatt didn't have to put out a dime until the product was in his hands. He'd never been sure what Jimmy got out of their arrangement. Maybe he just liked the company.

In time, the increasing popularity of freebase and crack had slowly shifted the bulk of the local coke trade from a circle of disaffected, disorganized anglo hipsters—which included Jimmy and Hy—to a more comprehensive and better-organized network of black and Latino gangs. Hyatt quit dealing and focused his energies on trying to get the ACO—at that time little more than an idea—off the ground. Jimmy had continued to buy and sell coke until his cousin got cracked down in Tampa. Hyatt hadn't heard from Jimmy since then. He'd meant to call, but what with one thing and another he'd just never got around to it.

Jimmy had always been peculiar. He'd never had much to say, except when he was high, at which times he talked continually, but even then he didn't say much worth hearing. Toward the end of their partnership, Jimmy had devel-oped an interest in radio waves, which had led to his wearing a headband wo-ven from copper wire. When asked about it, Jimmy would say only that it protected him from the transmissions of "unfriendly entities."

Jimmy had also acquired a shotgun during that period, a Browning twelve-gauge auto, for which he had traded a half ounce of coke. He had wrapped the entire gun in Reynolds Wrap to prevent the unfriendly entities from "fucking with it" and kept the foil-clad weapon by his side at all times.

Jimmy's preoccupation with radio waves had caused Hyatt to think of him that morning, but it was the shotgun that had inspired him to visit. He was rea-sonably sure that Jimmy would be happy to see him.

Hy leaned on the front doorbell. "C'mon c'mon c'mon," he muttered, grind-ing his thumb into the button.

A muffled voice came from the other side of the door. "What do you want?"

"It's me, Jimmy. Hy. Hyatt Hilton."

"What do you want?"

"I want you to let me in!" Hy looked down the block. He saw the yellow GTO parked at the far end of the block. The Corvette had drifted right up be-hind his BMW. The passenger window rolled down to reveal Chip Bouchet's swinish visage.

"I'm busy," Jimmy said.

Hyatt said, "I got a situation here, Jimmy. Let me in!"

Three long seconds passed.

"You come to pay me my money?" Jimmy asked.

Hyatt thought, What money? He said, "Yeah. Whatever. Just open the door."

"You can come in, but your friends stay outside."

"They aren't my friends!"

Hyatt heard a series of locks being opened. The front door swung open, and Hyatt stepped inside. The door closed. Hyatt blinked, waiting for his eyes to adjust to the dim light. The first thing he saw was a crinkled aluminum foil log about six inches in diameter and four feet long. The log had three pair of antennae jutting out at odd angles, with foil flags at the tip of each antenna. The fact that it was approximately the right length and that Jimmy Swann was pointing it at his groin led Hyatt to conclude that this was the latest stage in the evolution of Jimmy Swann's shotgun.

"Let's see it," Jimmy Swann said. His voice, which Hyatt remembered as being on the light side, had taken on a shredded quality.

Jimmy Swann had evolved as well. Hyatt remembered him as a short, fidgety, and slightly plump young man with ruddy cheeks and an immaculate white smile. In short, a reasonably normal-looking human being, once you got past the woven copper headband.

Apparently, radio waves had become a larger part of Jimmy's reality in the past couple years. The copper headband had evolved into a complex appurtenance, which now included brass tubing, bits of colored foil, and a fulgurite that Jimmy had found on the beach during his Boy Scout days. The last time Hyatt had seen the fulgurite—a root-shaped piece of fused silica formed by the action of lightning on sand—it had been displayed on Jimmy's dresser. It now formed the centerpiece to the metal sculpture on his head. Shanks of long, matted hair threaded through the apparatus and spilled down over his bony shoulders.

The new Jimmy—copper, brass, foil, and fulgurite included—could not have weighed more than one hundred twenty pounds. Other than the headpiece, he wore nothing but a pair of oversized Levis that rode so low on his emaciated hips that a tuft of pubic hair showed above the waistband. His pasty skin looked as if it hadn't seen the sun in years.

"It's me, Jimmy. Hy."

"I know who you are. Where's the money?"

"Uh, let's just talk about that." Hyatt still did not know what money Jimmy was talking about. "How about you put the gun down?"

"You owe me, man."

"I understand that. Uh, how much was it again?"

"You know how much it is. Three hundred forty-six dollars. Let's have it!"

Hyatt tried to remember. Did he owe Jimmy Swann three hundred forty-six dollars? It was certainly possible. When Hyatt owed someone money, he made it a policy to put it out of his mind until payment was demanded.

He said, "I didn't pay you that? Hey, no problem. I've got the money—" Hy slapped his wallet, which contained about fourteen dollars. "—and I'll pay you. Aren't you going to invite me in? Offer me a beer or something?"

Jimmy's posture softened. He let the shotgun barrel dip—now it was pointing at Hyatt's knees. "Who's in the vette?"

Hyatt shrugged. "Just some assholes."

"They pissed off my neighbors, man. I don't need that shit."

"Like I said, they're assholes."

Jimmy grinned. Everything else had changed, but the smile was exactly as Hyatt remembered. He shifted his grip on the shotgun, letting it dangle from one hand, the barrel now aimed in the vicinity of Hyatt's right foot, giving him a better look at the weapon. Despite all the tinfoil, the gun appeared to be operational. The trigger was clear of obstructions as was the ejection port. The last two inches of barrel jutted ominously from the tinfoil casing.

"Come on in," Jimmy said, backing down the hallway, which was lined on either side with stacks of magazines, books, and newspapers. Jimmy had always been a sucker for ordering subscriptions every year during the Publisher's Clearinghouse Sweepstakes, but the situation had gotten way out of hand in the two years since Hyatt had last been there. Access to the upstairs was completely blocked by stacks of magazines chest high on the steps, and to get to the kitchen required climbing over a pile of furniture chinked with periodicals. Jimmy led him into the sitting room where, it seemed, he now spent nearly all of his time.

The center of the room was filled with an unfolded sofabed piled with books and magazines. A full-size refrigerator, a microwave oven on a stand, and a large-screen television set stood around the bed like relatives visiting a dying uncle. A collection of empty pizza boxes filled the fireplace. The room reeked of stale beer and sweat and aging deep-dish pizzas.

"I just love what you've done with the place," Hyatt said.

"I don't get out much. Fact, I don't get out at all." Jimmy opened the refrigerator. "You want a beer?"

"You know what I really want? I want you to loan me that shotgun." In the old days, Jimmy had always responded positively to bullying.

Jimmy closed the refrigerator door and faced Hyatt, renewing his grip on the shotgun. "Why should I?" he said, his tone of voice suddenly that of a child. "It's mine!"

"I just need it for a minute, Jimmy." Hyatt took a step toward him. "Then I'll pay you."

"Three hundred forty-six dollars?" Jimmy's tongue crawled out of his mouth and explored his upper lip.

"That's right."

For a few seconds, it looked as if Jimmy, confronted by Hyatt's superior intellect, would simply hand over the gun. Then his expression changed. He seemed to be listening to something—possibly an emanation from his headgear. After a moment he nodded, smiled triumphantly, raised the gun, and aimed it at Hyatt's chest. "Pay me now."

Hyatt did not like the way things were going. In the past, he had usually been able to tell Jimmy Swann what to do, but even then he had sometimes encountered interference from the local radio wave gods. Once Jimmy got a message from "certain interested parties," he could become quite stubborn.

Hyatt said, "I'm going to pay you, Jimmy. But tell me something. Why do I owe you three hundred forty-six dollars?"

Jimmy glared. "You owe everybody money."

"I know that. But why three hundred forty-six dollars?"

Jimmy's eyes rolled up into his head, then snapped back into focus as the message came through. "That's how much I owe the gas company," he said.

Hyatt had thought it might be something like that. Unfortunately, in Jimmy's mind, admitting the spurious assignation of debt did nothing to cancel it. The shotgun was still there, and Jimmy still wanted his money, and Hyatt didn't have it. He was starting to wish that he'd taken his chances with Chip.

Hyatt squinted and stared at the cone-shaped coil of copper tubing that crowned Jimmy's headpiece. He said, "That's odd."

Jimmy tried to look up. "What's odd?"

Hyatt said, "Look what it's doing."

"What? What what's doing?"

"That." Hyatt pointed. "There's a huge cockroach on your wires, Jimmy." He wasn't sure where he was going with this, but when all else failed, it paid to improvise.

Jimmy took a step back, as if trying to get out from under his headpiece. "Where is it? What's it doing?"

"It's chewing on the wires. Have you been experiencing any degradation of signal quality?"

Jimmy's jaw dropped. He reached up with one hand.

"Don't touch it!" Hyatt warned.

Jimmy jerked his arm down. "Where is it?"

"It's on the coil now. It's moving down the coil. Oh my god!"

Jimmy dropped the shotgun and grabbed the assemblage of wires and tubing and tried to tear it from his head, shrieking as shanks of hair, tangled in amongst the wires, refused to let go. Suddenly, he noticed that his shotgun had appeared in Hyatt's hands.

Hyatt said, "Hold still." He aimed the shotgun at the copper coil.

Jimmy dropped his hands and screamed, "No!"

Hyatt fired. Lead pellets ripped through copper, rattled off of steel and fulgurite. The force of the blast jerked Jimmy's head back, sending him staggering onto the sofabed. He fell across the mattress, sending several dozen magazines sliding off onto the floor. Hyatt pumped a new shell into the chamber.

"I think I got it," he said. His ears were ringing.

Jimmy, his eyes showing white all the way around his irises, reached up and explored his shredded headset with shaking fingers. "I can't hear you, man. I'm not receiving."

"That's okay," Hyatt said. "I didn't have anything more to say."

A five-year-old, beige four-door Plymouth Reliant, Crow had once read, was the least likely of all vehicles to be noticed or remembered, thus making it the perfect surveillance vehicle. That being the case, a three-decade-old, lemon-yellow, hood-scooped, gas-guzzling muscle car had to fall somewhere near the other end of the conspicuousness spectrum, right up there with the Oscar Meyer Weinermobile.

The two kids eyeing the GTO looked to be about twelve. They stood a few yards away on the sidewalk, talking and pointing at Crow and his car as though they were discussing a museum display: White man in automobile, circa 1969. Crow rolled down his window and beckoned them with a crooked finger. The taller kid, who had been doing most of the talking, fell silent. After a moment he took a cautious step forward and said, "Wuzapp'n."

"Not much," Crow said.

"That your car?"

"That's right," Crow said.

"You with thems?" He looked toward the Corvette parked beside Hyatt's BMW.

"Nope. I'm a good guy."

"How 'bout you take us for a drive?"

Crow laughed. The kids laughed, too. They edged closer. Crow said, pointing at the gated Victorian, "You know who lives in that house over there?"

The shorter kid said, "The scary dude."

The other kid said, "He ain't so scary. He just mess up in the head."

"He scare me. He got a magic gun."

"A what?" Crow asked.

The kids looked at each other. The tall kid licked his lips and turned away.

"You a cop?" the short one asked.

"Nope. Are you a gangster?"

The kid shook his head, taking Crow's inquiry very seriously. "He got wires coming out his head."

"Wires?"

"Uh-huh. And he gots this big silver gun. He shot Scoopy's ass for going in his yard."

"Who's Scoopy?"

"Scoopy don't live here no more."

Crow heard a muffled report. "What was that?"

"Sometimes he just like to shoot."

Crow saw the front door to the Victorian open. Hyatt Hilton emerged and started toward the gate. He had something long and silver in his hands. Crow lost sight of him behind a lilac bush, then the gate swung open and Hyatt stepped out onto the sidewalk and shouldered the silver object, pointing it at the front of the Corvette. Crow saw a puff appear at the end of the silver object and heard the blast. Blue smoke erupted from the Corvette's rear tires and the car rocketed backward, in Crow's direction. Hyatt fired again. The vette, still smoking its tires, suddenly slued around in a one-eighty. Hyatt's third shot was drowned out by the sound of clashing gears and the roaring engine. The vette screeched past Crow's position, its windshield shattered to opacity but still intact, the driver hanging his head out the window to see. Within two seconds it was out of sight, leaving behind a dissipating cloud of smoke and the reek of burnt rubber.

Crow sat with his mouth hanging open, his brain unable to accept what he was seeing as real. Hyatt had run out into the street, still holding the bizarre-looking gun against his shoulder. Crow suddenly remembered the two kids he'd been talking to, but when he looked for them they had disappeared. He returned his attention to Hyatt and found himself looking at the end of Hyatt's weapon. The fact that it was more than half a block away did little to make him feel more comfortable. Crow jammed the Hurst shifter into first gear just as Hyatt let fly. The sound of pellets rattling his hood and windshield was distinctive—a hundred micro-impacts, all in the space of a millisecond. Crow cranked the wheel and stomped on the gas pedal, spinning the car, leaving a pair of hook-shaped rubber marks on the street. He made it all the way to third gear without ever taking his right foot off the floor.

Chuckles and Chip each had their own way of dealing with their recent near-death experience. Chip became uncharacteristically voluble, dissecting the confrontation in military terms.

"His mistake was to carry his weapon in full view, giving his opponents time to analyze the situation and neutralize the attack. We could have pre-empted his strike with our own firefight. A surgical strike." Chip subscribed to *Soldier of Fortune* magazine.

Chuckles, staring at the crumbled remains of his windshield, grunted. "I'm just happy to be *alive*," he said. He rubbed the grinning skull tattoo on his forearm with his thumb, an unconscious habit. Polly was always complaining about his tattoo. Said the skull was a holdover from his Death Program days, but Chuckles liked it. He called it Good Luck Charlie.

"You're suffering from post-traumatic stress. You should increase your vitamin C intake."

"Hey, screw you, man. You see what he done to my *ride?* Polly didn't say *nothin'* about the dude havin' no *shotgun.* Fucked up my *glass,* fucked up my *paint.* Coulda been my *face,* man."

"It's all part of the job."

"All I know is, next time that bitch go down on me, I gonna be looking out both eyes and that ain't no lie."

Chip said, "She . . . what did you say?"

*Play to behavior, not personalities.*

*—Crow's rules*

**T**HE MORE CROW THOUGHT ABOUT it, the madder he got. By the time he got home and got out and looked at the side of his car and saw the hundreds of tiny gray scuff marks on the hood and the right quarter panel, he was mad enough to turn around and drive over to Hyatt's house to wait for him. So he did. He parked his car around the corner where Hyatt wouldn't see it and walked up to the front door and leaned on the bell. Carmen answered the door wordlessly, blinking at him with sleepy eyes, containing not a scintilla of recognition. Crow told himself that he shouldn't care, but it still irritated him that Carmen never seemed to recognize him.

Crow said, "Mind if I come in?"

"I don't think so," Carmen said. She tried to close the door, but Crow blocked it with his arm. "I really need to see Hy," Crow said.

"He's not here."

"I know that."

Carmen glared at him for a moment, then released the door. Crow followed her into the living room. She flopped onto the sofa, lit a cigarette. The apartment smelled like vomit. A cheerful man on the television was demonstrating a mop. Carmen regarded Crow through a haze of smoke.

"What's your name again?" she asked.

"Howard Holiday," Crow said. "I'm Hy's brother."

Carmen snorted smoke. "Yeah, right."

"When do you expect him back?"

"About an hour ago. He went out for coffee."

Crow sniffed. "What's that smell?"

Carmen shrugged and turned her attention to the television. Crow watched her watching the infomercial. She was attractive enough, he supposed. Regular features; full lips; big, heavy-lidded, brown eyes. Auburn hair worn long and loose. A pair of jeans, faded almost to white, all holes and frayed edges, and a black T-shirt that had been chopped off between her navel and her ample breasts. Crow did not think of himself as a "breast man," but Carmen's set drew his eyes mercilessly. The rest of her body was nicely proportionate. Not an athletic body, but she had the curves.

What turned Crow off was the slack, sleepy quality that imbued her posture, her movements, her facial expression. It was similar to the narcotic contentment of a drug addict, but deeper, more a part of her core personality. Even her skin looked sleepy. Crow had the sense that she was in a transition phase, waiting out the metamorphosis from adolescent to adult, from baby fat to cellulite, from careless innocence to jaded cynicism. Or maybe she was more like overripe fruit: sweet, soft, and loose on its stem, beginning to ferment. Some men would find that attractive. Necrophiliacs, for instance.

He tried to see her as the reincarnation of the Brownsville chicana who, thirty years ago, had cold-cocked Axel Speeter. He couldn't see it. Where would she get the energy?

Crow was rescued from his thoughts by the sound of a slamming car door. He looked out the window. Hyatt was locking the door of his BMW, holding the silver gun in one hand. Crow took up position near the front door and waited.

Hyatt entered the apartment with the bright-eyed look of a man who had just survived a traffic accident. Crow snatched the gun from his limp grasp, felt his fingers sink into loosely wrapped foil. A visible tremor ran up Hyatt's body. He backed down the short hall into the living room, holding his hands in front of him. "Joe! Jesus! Watch where you're pointing that thing!"

"I am. Whatever it is." There appeared to be a shotgun beneath all the decoration. "How come you shot my car, Hy?"

"Shot . . . what? I don't know what you're talking about. Wait a second—Jesus!—that was you?"

"You telling me you shoot a car, you don't even know who's in it?"

"I thought you were with them!"

"With who?"

"The guys in the vette!"

"What made you think that?"

"Jesus, Joe, I don't know. You were both on my ass. Both cars yellow?"

Crow let the gun barrel drop. "Remind me never to buy another yellow car."

Hyatt laughed.

"It's not funny yet, Hy."

"I'm sorry, man. Really. Those guys were gonna hurt me. I was scared."

"Scared of who?"

"The church."

"What church?"

"The Amaranthines. My former partners. Polly and Rupe and their crew. You remember them, don't you? From Ambrosia Foods? They're out to get me, Joe. I swear to God, I thought you were with them. I didn't know it was you."

"You're lucky nobody got killed."

"It was me or them. They would've killed me. You saw. You're my witness, Joe."

"Witness? I saw you shoot at a couple of guys in a Corvette who weren't doing anything."

"They were following me."

"I was following you, too."

"I'm not afraid of *you,* Joe."

Crow wasn't sure how to take that. "Then you shouldn't be shooting at me."

Hyatt asked, "How come you were following me, anyway?"

Carmen said, "I remember you now. You're a friend of Axel's."

"Let's take a walk, Hy," Crow said.


Polly floated deep in the zone, feeling Obo's probing fingers as globes of warmth moving in and out of her body. Obo was the best. He was the one person she could count on to bring pleasure into her life on a daily basis. Obo had magic hands, zero sexuality, and absolutely nothing to say. He was the perfect masseur. She felt a little sad when he gave her spine that final flat-palmed stroke.

Polly heard the soft click of the door closing behind him. In precisely six minutes, he would return for his massage table, folding it with his efficient, short-fingered hands, never meeting her eyes, in and out in seconds. Polly gave herself four of those minutes to lay still, letting her body remember the massage, then she rolled off the table and dressed. She sat behind her desk, turned on her computer, and began reviewing the weekly cash-flow statement. It had been a negative period—a lot of money going out to Stonecrop. One shipment of limestone had cost them over forty thousand dollars.

Stonecrop, the future world headquarters of the Amaranthine Church of the One, had been under construction for more than a year. It had been part of Rupert Chandra's vision since his awakening—a permanent haven for the first immortals, a retreat where church members could insulate themselves from the madness of the Death Program and the coming collapse of the twentieth-century military-industrial construct.

Three years ago Rupe had signed a purchase agreement for a 236-acre tract of land in western Wisconsin, sixty miles southeast of Minneapolis. It was a beautiful site located on the bluffs high above the Mississippi River, and a bargain at nine hundred dollars an acre. He had named it Stonecrop, and had declared it to be the future sanctuary of the Amaranthines as foretold by Zhang Daoling.

Polly thought her Eternal Companion had lost his ever-loving mind. Back then, the Amaranthine Church had been little more than a small-time New Age workshop, a protoreligion with fewer than three dozen adherents who met once a week in the back room of Ambrosia Foods. They could hardly make the monthly rent on their store, let alone take on a two hundred thousand-dollar debt. Polly had been furious. When she found out her husband had taken out a second mortgage on their condo for a down payment, their marriage had nearly imploded.

Hyatt Hilton, she remembered, had thought it all quite amusing. When they incorporated the Amaranthine Church of the One, Rupe insisted on transferring the Stonecrop mortgage to the corporation. Hyatt had refused to sign the papers, saying that he wouldn't accept any ownership of an entity with negative value. That, at least, had worked out for the best. It had made it a lot easier to get rid of him.

Somehow, they had survived those difficult years. Driven by Rupe's faith, optimism, and refusal to entertain the possibility of failure, ACO membership grew exponentially. When they needed money, it seemed, new members would appear, or old members would add to their Life Accounts, or the bank would prove to be uncharacteristically receptive to Rupe's promises. For several months, Rupe and Benjy Hiss, a young architect and one of their charter members, spent their evenings building a scale model of Stonecrop, a utopian community designed to last for millenniums. Benjy quit his job and came to work full time for the ACO, and a year ago last May, ground was broken.

The chapel and the main cottage were nearly complete, but at least another year and another six million dollars would be required to complete the parsonage, the cottages, the auditorium and the three-mile long, twelve-foot-tall limestone wall that was to surround the entire compound. The expense weighed heavily upon Polly, who was responsible for church finances, but so far they had been able to attract enough new members, and extract enough donations from existing members, to keep the work moving forward. When Stonecrop was completed, it would be a fortress. As Rupe liked to point out, "It must stand for ten thousand years."

One small problem was that the plans called for only nine cottages, but Rupe had promised private quarters to twenty-three of the Faithful. Numbers never seemed to bother Rupe.

"Eternity will provide," he would say.

It had been a particularly expensive week with the limestone shipment, plus more graft to the local township officials to have some code violations overlooked, and an astonishing nineteen thousand dollar-bill from the electricians. Perhaps eternity would provide, but Polly was counting more on Friday's Anti-Aging Clinic.

Some time later Polly heard a knock on her office door. She looked up from the computer monitor and found that the massage table had disappeared—Obo had come and gone without her noticing.

"Come in," she said.

It was Chip, followed by Chuckles. Polly sat back in her chair and smiled, anticipating good news. The two men arranged themselves in front of her desk.

"Well?" she finally asked, "How did it go?"

Chip said, "Not bad." His eyes were somewhere behind her.

Chuckles made a sound with his lips.

Polly said, "Chuckles?"

"Yeah," Chuckles said. "It went *real* good. He's taking us serious now, and that's no lie. And we still alive."

"We've got him scared," Chip added quickly.

"Yeah, he scared all right."

A whiff of butyric acid extinguished the last glowing remnants of Polly's massage. "Tell me what happened," she said.

Frowning, Hyatt examined the GTO's hood, his nose almost touching the marred finish. He said, "It was only birdshot, Joe. It just marked up the paint is all." He licked a finger and rubbed one of the gray spots to no effect. "That'll buff right out."

"Fine, if it buffs out it'll save you some money."

"You were way out of range. I was just trying to scare you." He dropped his eyes to the foliated shotgun in Crow's hands and hastily added, "I didn't know it was you at the time, of course. And I want to make things right by you."

"I'll get an estimate."

"One nice thing about a gun like that, you can carry it down the street and nobody knows what you've got."

"Is that why all the foil?"

"Nah, that was my crazy buddy Jimmy. It's his gun."

"What are these things sticking out?"

"Antennae."

"Very nice. I'm sure Jimmy won't mind if I keep his magic gun."

Hyatt shrugged, apparently bored with the topic. He drummed his long fingers on the GTO's roof. "When I was a kid, this was the hottest thing going. What's it got in it?"

"Four hundred cubes. Three hundred sixty-six horses."

"Huh. A real gas hog, I bet."

"Not too bad," Crow lied. "Tell me something, Hy. What did you do to get those guys so pissed at you?"

"I didn't do anything. Not really. Not yet. I mean, it's not what I did, it's what I know."

Crow waited for more.

"I mean, I know everything about the ACO, Joe. I know all their secrets."

"Like how to live forever?"

Hyatt nodded. "Physical immortality is a real possibility, Joe."

"You just take your vitamins and avoid getting shot, right?"

"It was my idea, you know."

"What was? Immortality?"

Hyatt answered seriously, "No. Rupe was the first. But I *founded* the Amaranthine Church. If it wasn't for me, Polly and Rupe would still be hawking vitamins. They'd be immortal, but what would be the point?"

"I heard they kicked you out."

"They did."

"How could they kick you out of your own church?"

Hyatt shrugged. "Legally speaking, you can't own a religion. We'd incorporated as a nonprofit and copyrighted our name and materials under the name. Rupe and Polly had their names on the lease and the bank account. I was a silent partner. Actually, legally speaking, I wasn't a partner at all. But we had an understanding. Where I come from, a man's word is his bond."

"I thought you came from up on the Range. Biwabik, wasn't it?"

"I told you that?" Hyatt looked surprised. "Anyway, the point is that I trusted them, and they cut me out. Let me tell you, Joe, you ever own your own business, you better *own* it. You can't believe what anybody tells you. I talked to a lawyer. There was nothing I could do."

"Is that why you broke up that meeting last month?"

Hyatt tipped his head. "You heard about that? Jesus Christ, I'm talking to Mr. Moto here. I was upset. I lost my head, and they threw me out." Hyatt crossed his arms and produced a flat smile. "What else do you know about me? You're checking me out, aren't you? Did Sophie ask you to check me out?"

"I'm just trying to find out why my car has all these marks on it."

"Seems to me the question is, why were you following me in the first place?"

Crow did not reply. He was still trying to work that one out himself.

"You know, pointing that gun at me, Joe, that really scared Carmen."

"Oh? I was trying to scare *you.*"

"I knew you weren't going to shoot me. How long have we known each other? I wasn't worried. But Carmen, she doesn't know you like I do."

Crow thought back to the scene in Hyatt's living room. "She didn't look scared to me," he said. "In fact, she didn't look like she gave a damn, one way or the other."

"You're wrong about that." Hyatt pushed his hands into the pockets of his red-and-gold striped pants.

"How come you're marrying her, Hy?"

Hy raised his eyebrows and spread his pocketed hands, which caused the sides of his trousers to spread like a pair of bloomers. "What do you mean? I love her." He frowned. "I don't understand how my marriage is any of your damn business."

Suddenly, Crow wasn't sure either. "I'm your fiance's pseudofather's best friend's illegitimate son," he said.

Hyatt smirked and gazed out over Crow's head. "Then I guess that makes us family," he said. "In which case, *brother,* I'm sure you'll forgive me if I tell you to fuck off."

"Just tell me one thing."

Hy lowered his eyes to a focal point in the vicinity of Crow's forehead.

"What did you do that got the Amaranthines so upset they'd want to hurt you? I mean, really."

Hyatt considered for a moment, then said, "I don't like to see innocent people ripped off."

"Meaning yourself?"

"Meaning the Pilgrims."

"What does it cost to become immortal these days?"

"That depends on how much you've got." He winked, spun on one heel, and walked back down the sidewalk, striped pants fluttering, huaraches slapping his soles.

*Every man has two countries, his own and France.*

—*Henri de Bornier*

LAURA DEBROWSKI HUNG UP THE phone and walked out onto the shallow balcony. She had been counting on hearing Crow's voice. She lit a cigarette and leaned out over the railing. On the sidewalk below a man with a green plastic broom was sweeping. A woman in high heels walking a toy poodle picked up her pace to walk quickly past the sweeping man. He said something as she passed, and the woman made a face that may have been a smile. Observing such uneventful encounters had occupied much of Debrowski's time during her first weeks alone in Paris, but lately the street life had come to seem pedestrian. The fact that the people here spoke French could no longer camouflage the fact that their daily lives were as trivial and mundane as those of people elsewhere.

She would wait a few more minutes, then try Crow again.

The afternoon session at SuperSon had not gone well. René Missett, the vocalist and leader of *Les Hommes Magnifiques,* had shown up at the studio forty minutes late with an ugly hangover. He said he was too sick to make any decisions, he was tired of being the leader, and they should all fuck off and die. He deposited himself on a plastic bench and fell into a fitful sleep.

"He'll be okay in an hour or so," Debrowski said to the engineer. She'd seen René in this condition before. "Maybe we can get some work done before he wakes up."

The other members of the band laughed uncomfortably. In the absence of René's guiding hand, Bobo, Vincent, and Antoine were lost.

Vincent and Bobo wanted to do a song Bobo had written called "American Friend." Antoine, the drummer, maintained that the song was too "Paris." He was unable to explain what he meant by that, but refused to be swayed. He tried to wake René for support, but René simply glared at him, looking as if he might throw up at any moment.

Debrowski, still hoping that they might get some work done, suggested that they run through Bobo's song once, just to see how it sounded. Vincent, Bobo, and Antoine all looked at René, who roused himself enough to sit up and say, "I've got a better idea for the title. We call it 'The American Cunt.' How do you like that, eh?"

Debrowski quickly said, "I like it." She didn't care any more, as long as they got something on tape. Her relationship with *Les Hommes* had been increasingly difficult lately. When they'd first started working together, the band had treated her like a goddess. She was the producer from America, their ticket to the big time. She would deliver them to the promised land of concert halls and rivers of cash and groupies by the bedful. For a few weeks, they had devoted several hours of every day to writing and rehearsing, trying to come up with enough songs to fill a disc. Debrowski's suggestions had been taken as gospel.

"You only need one great tune and two okay ones to make *Billboard*," she told them. "The rest of the CD can suck." *Les Hommes* had started out with a unique, hard-core sound and one great tune—a three-minute tour de force called "*Ça me fait shier*," which would translate on the American disc as "It Makes Me Shit." They'd laid down that track in their first afternoon at Super-Son. The rest of the album had not gone so smoothly. As the band members, and René in particular, had become more familiar with Debrowski, her pedestal sank slowly into the earth.

One week ago as they all stood in the Metro waiting for the Mairie D'Ivry train, René had felt familiar enough to give Debrowski's ass a rather aggressive squeeze, to which she had responded by bringing her boot heel down on his instep. Vincent, Bobo, and Antoine had derived great merriment from watching René hopping about on one foot, cursing wildly.

That might have been the end of it, but René's character was such that he chose to regard Debrowski's foot-stomping as a form of flirtation. The next night, his inhibitions eclipsed by several glasses of marc, he had shown up at her hotel saying he wanted to go over some new song ideas, but as soon as he got inside her room he'd made it clear that his ideas were of another sort. Debrowski gave him fair warning, and when that didn't work she clubbed him between the legs with a one-litre bottle of Perrier.

Thereafter, René had discontinued his physical advances, but he was unable to restrain himself from taking frequent verbal shots at her femininity, at what he perceived as her dubious sexual orientation, and at her American origins. Debrowski tried to ignore him and focus on completing the album. The other band members seemed embarrassed by René's behavior at times, but because René was male, French, and their leader, they let it go.

"Okay then," René stood up and shuffled over to the microphone. "Hey

Jules!" he shouted at the man in the sound booth. "You ready for us, Jules? We're gonna lay this one down the first try."

Jules, who had been patiently waiting at 140 francs per hour, gave the thumbs up.

Going into this supposedly final session they had, in addition to "*Ça me fait shier,*" a half dozen mediocre tunes, one that was marginally good, and three stinkers that needed serious remixing, at the least. *Les Hommes Magnifiques'* debut album would not be what Debrowski had hoped, but if they could come up with one decent B-side rocker, it might play in the states. She'd heard them do "American Friend" live. It had potential. *Les Hommes,* for all their problems, had their moments of creative brilliance.

Despite Antoine's objections to the tune, he laid down a powerful backbeat, and René launched into an entirely new and apparently ad-libbed set of lyrics, which described, Debrowski quickly realized, the rape, beating, murder, mutilation, and dismemberment of an American woman in Paris. His bloodshot eyes never left her face as he screamed into the microphone.

Laura Debrowski had once believed herself to be unshockable. She had thought she had heard, seen, or done just about everything. But she had never heard anything like this, at this volume, aimed with such malice directly at her. It was a tremendous performance, *Les Hommes* at their rocking best. She knew she was hearing *Les Hommes'* first hit single, and it frightened and disgusted her beyond anything she had ever heard in a recording studio—or anywhere else. She looked back at Jules in the sound booth, but instead of finding shocked indignance on his face, found herself facing a delighted leer. Wooden-faced, Debrowski left the studio. She walked for four kilometers back to her hotel, feeling utterly alone for the first time since she had arrived in Paris. She forced her mind away from *Les Hommes* and imagined herself in her room with the phone in her hand and Joe Crow on the other end.

Now she was here and the son-of-a-bitch wasn't home.

She picked up the phone and dialed again. His answering machine picked up, again. She said, "You bastard! Where the hell are you?"

She heard a click. "I'm here," Crow said, sounding breathless.

Debrowski began to cry.


Crow's mind had become so cluttered with the morning's events that he'd forgotten about Debrowski's promised phone call. It hadn't hit him until the phone started ringing, just as he entered his apartment. He tossed the foil-wrapped shotgun on his sofa and picked up the phone.

"Men are scum," Debrowski said. Her voice sounded wrong. Was she crying? Impossible.

"I completely agree with you," he said, playing a safety.

"Why haven't you called me?"

Crow thought quickly. He hadn't called her, of course, because he didn't know how to reach her. But this was not the time to make that argument.

"I'm sorry," he said. "Where are you?"

"I'm in France! Where the hell do you think I am?"

"I mean, are you at your hotel?"

For a moment, Crow thought he'd lost the connection, then he heard her say, "Yes, I'm in my room."

"Are you sitting?"

"I'm standing at the window."

"How's the weather?"

"It's warm. The sun is setting."

"How are you?"

"Not great."

"What happened?"

"Nothing." She cleared her throat. "Nothing I can't handle."

Crow did not doubt that. Laura Debrowski always *handled* things. He said, "You sure?"

"I'm sure." Her voice was stronger now. Sometimes Crow wished she was less capable. Sometimes he wanted to be able to open pickle jars and kill spiders and slay dragons for her. But most of the time he liked Laura Debrowski straight up.

"How's the recording coming?"

"I don't want to talk about it. How's Milo?"

"He's fine."

"How are you?"

"I'm okay." Crow looked at the foil-wrapped shotgun he'd thrown on his sofa and reconsidered his answer. "I mean, I got shot at this morning," he said. "But they missed."

The telephone was ringing when Hyatt emerged from the shower. He walked out into the living room, screwing the corner of a towel into his ear. Carmen sat on the sofa, inert, staring at the television.

"You gonna answer that?" he asked.

"Why? It's probably Sophie."

Hyatt frowned, draped the towel over his shoulder, and picked up the phone. "Hello?"

"It's me."

"Oh. Hi, Chip."

"This is *Eduardo!*"

"Oh. Sorry, *Eduardo,* I forgot."

"Those men you shot at could have been hurt. It was not strategic."

"Yeah, well it was either that or wait for you guys to do whatever it was you were going to do."

"Polly said to break your foot."

"Yes." Hyatt shuddered. "'Break my foot.' He was sure that Chip would have gone through with it despite their special relationship. Chip took his job very seriously.

"Just one. Our strategy would not have been affected. It was not necessary to shoot.'

"Yeah? Well I don't plan to walk down the aisle on crutches, *Eduardo*."

"Chip was doing his job. We agreed that he could continue to do his job."

Hyatt looked down at his bare feet, still pink from the hot shower, whole and unbroken. "You could have at least warned me."

"I was under surveillance not to. My cover might have been broken."

"You—what? Never mind. Look, are you—are *they* going to try again?"

"Polly has issued no further instructions respective to the matter of the subject."

"But you'll let me know?"

"Unknown. Circumstances might endeavor alternate strategies."

"Let me rephrase that, *Eduardo*. It is essential and *strategic* that you keep me informed as to any and all plans, proposals, or efforts to damage my immortal ass. This is absolutely essential and highly strategic. Understood?"

There were a few seconds of silence, during which Hyatt imagined Chip's cranial pressure increasing. He half expected to hear a pop.

"I understand," Chip said.

"Good. Are Polly and Rupe still planning their sabbatical?"

"They will be leaving for Stonecrop on the eighth, as per my earlier intelligence to you."

"Good. Report to me if anything changes." Hyatt hung up. "You subhuman Nazi," he added.

Carmen asked, "Who was that?"

"That was Chip the troglodyte."

"Who's Eduardo?"

"Same troglodyte." The phone rang again; Hyatt answered. A shriek of anxious chatter hurtled from the receiver, causing him to jerk the phone away from his ear. He waited for it to subside, then cautiously brought the phone closer to his mouth. "Sophie? That you?" He frowned, listening, then handed the phone to Carmen. "It's for you."

"Thanks a hell of a lot." She took the phone. "Hi Mom."

Hyatt worked on drying the nooks and crannies of his lanky body as he watched Carmen. She was not a good phone talker. She muttered, let her sentences trail off, and often neglected to speak into the mouthpiece. Instead of saying "yes" or "no," she would nod or shake her head. Hyatt could hear Sophie's voice more clearly than he could Carmen's. She was screaming about somebody named "Conita." Whoever Conita was, and whatever she'd done, she had Sophie ready to pop a vessel.

After listening to Crow describe his day, and the events that had led up to it, Debrowski said, "Forget about it, Crow. Walk away from those people. Play it the way you'd play a bad poker hand."

"It's easier with cards," Crow said. "But this is a family thing." His hand was cramping from gripping the phone, and his ear was getting sore. He switched sides.

"Family? My god, Crow, you've said yourself you aren't one hundred percent sure that Sam is really your father. And we're not even talking about Sam. We're talking a friend of his that has a girlfriend with an idiot daughter who happens to be getting married. That's not exactly what you'd call 'family.'"

"You take what you can get." Crow was surprised to hear Debrowski telling him to back off. He thought of her as more the act-first-regret-later type. He said, "Besides, Hyatt Hilton has me sort of curious. I can't figure out what he's up to."

"Do me a favor, Crow. Forget about it. I don't want to come home and find you full of buckshot."

"It was birdshot. And by the way, when *are* you coming home?"

"Listen, you did what Axel asked. Just tell him what happened and let him sort it out."

"I'm not sure I even want to mention it to him at this point. I was thinking I might pay a visit to that church, see what the immortal nuts have to say about him. Just to bring some closure."

"Closure? Why? For who? Axel? You know that every time you try to do somebody a favor you get screwed. They taught us that in AA, remember? You can't fix other people. All you can do is fix yourself."

"Tell me about it."

"I am telling you. Walk."

"Tell me when you're coming back."

Debrowski let a moment go by. "Maybe pretty soon. I've got a situation I might need to walk away from myself."

"Who are *you* trying to fix?"

Crow thought her laugh sounded a bit hollow, but perhaps it was the distance.

*You get old or you die. Take your pick.*

—*Sam O'Gara*

Back when he had lived by himself in the Motel 6, Axel had led a more disciplined life, allowing himself one twenty-minute nap every afternoon, setting his clock-radio to make sure he didn't oversleep. Since he had moved into Sophie's mobile home, all that had changed. Most days, he didn't get his nap at all. Sophie would be puttering around making noise, or she would have him out driving around doing errands, or the phone would be ringing; or Harvel, the guy in the trailer behind them, would decide to mow his twelve by thirty-foot lawn with his four hundred-dollar, self-propelled, mulching LawnBoy. Then he'd start with his weed-whacker, an oversized, gasoline-powered trimmer that produced a whine even more annoying than the roar of his mower.

As a result of these disruptive influences, Axel took his naps when and where and for however long he could. Whenever he found himself home alone, and Harvel wasn't mowing, and the phone wasn't ringing, he would hit the sack without so much as looking at his clock-radio. Usually something would wake him up within the hour, but if nothing did, he could dream on for hours.

The depth of Sophie's feelings about his plans to serve Conitas at the wedding reception had taken him completely by surprise. Of course, she got her way. She always did. In the face of Sophie's offensive, Axel had crumpled like a shot dove. They would be serving vegetable timbales and stuffed mushrooms and a bunch of other stuff nobody would eat if they weren't stuck at a wedding reception and had nothing else to do with their hands. At least there'd be some Swedish meatballs. He'd agreed to give up his Conita plan, then gone into a sulk, drinking multiple Coca-Colas and reading back issues of *Fair Times* until Sophie finally left, saying something about going to Dayton's with Carmen. Axel didn't care where she was going. He just needed to be left alone.

Axel had planned to spend the afternoon working on some variations on the Conita, but as soon as the door closed behind Sophie, the narcotic lure of an afternoon nap proved irresistible. Within five minutes he was deep into a dream about the state fair, selling tacos at the top of the Ferris wheel. He had been asleep for nearly three hours when a slamming door brought him back to consciousness. He heard the crackle of Sophie's voice, then Carmen's low mutter. The shaft of sun grazing the curtains told him it was late in the day. Maybe they would leave him alone for a while, let him wake up slowly.

Almost the moment he had that thought, the bedroom door opened.

"What are you *doing?*" Sophie demanded.

"What does it look like I'm doing?"

"Are you *sleeping?*"

Axel struggled to sit up, but his body refused to bend. He twisted to the side, swung his legs over the edge of the mattress, and let their weight pull him up into a sitting position.

"How can you *sleep?* It's almost seven o'clock at *night!*"

He could tell that Sophie had had a few drinks.

"Did you already eat *dinner?*"

"No." Axel rolled his shoulders, feeling the blood start to move again.

"You were in bed with your *shoes?*"

Axel looked down. He was fully dressed. "I just laid down for a minute. I fell asleep." He scratched his head and was surprised to find that he was bald on top. He'd been bald a good thirty years, but it still took him by surprise sometimes. Sophie was giving him her look, the one she gave him when she felt she'd been wronged—arms crossed, jaw set, nostrils flared.

Axel licked his lips, fighting off remnants of sleep. "What's going on?" he asked.

"We have to *talk.*"

Axel groaned. He had no idea what she wanted to talk about, but he could tell he wasn't going to like it. "Now? I'm half awake. I need a Coke." He stood up, hoping his knee wouldn't lock up on him again. "What do you want to talk about?"

Sophie looked back through the doorway at Carmen, who was sitting in the kitchenette drinking a beer. Returning her attention to Axel, she said, "We have to talk about Joe Crow."

The dinner menu that evening at Chez Crow included Grape Nuts with milk, one egg lightly scrambled, and a pint of chocolate Haagen Daz. As he worked his way through the tub of ice cream, Crow let his eyes rest on the red notebook lying open at his elbow. The items listed on the page were numbered nineteen through twenty six, the latest in the list of poker rules he had begun recording several months earlier. The most recent entry, number twenty-six had occurred to him during the first course of the evening's meal: *If you don't know the rules, don't play.*

After an indefinite period of blank thought, Crow drew a picture of Mickey Mouse's head next to the numeral 27. He had learned to draw Mickey in the fourth grade and had never forgotten. He could also draw Yogi Bear, Donald Duck, and Spiderman's hands. Unfortunately, he had failed to fulfill his early promise as a cartoonist, and by the time he turned ten years old, the other artists at Cedar Manor Elementary School had surpassed him. Now he revisited his talent only when he happened to have a pencil in his hand and nothing whatsoever in his head. He drew spikes around the circumference of Mickey's ears, and a little lightning bolt at the end of each spike. Mickey on LSD.

"Well, shit," he finally said, stabbing the pencil into the lone grapefruit in the fruit bowl. So much for personal goal setting. He'd been living in a motivational limbo for most of his thirty-five years. Maybe it was time he got used to it.

Seconds later, when the phone rang, he went for it like a drowning man lunging for a lifesaver.

"Joe?" It was Axel, the closest thing he had to a taskmaster.

"Axel! How's it going?"

"It's going fine, Joe." He sounded tired. "I just called to tell you, you know what we were talking about before? About Hyatt?"

"Yeah. I, uh, I talked to him today." He hadn't yet figured out what to tell Axel, if anything.

"I heard."

"You did? You talked to him, too?"

"No. I talked to Carmen." Axel cleared his throat. "She said you were pretty rough on him."

"Did she tell you he took a shot at me?"

He heard Axel say something to someone, then a sharp squawk that could only be Sophie Roman. "Listen, Joe, I'm not saying you did anything wrong—"

"That's good, 'cause I didn't."

"But I want you to leave him alone now, okay?"

"You sure?"

"Yeah. I had no business asking you to investigate him. So let's just forget about it, okay?"

"Sure. Whatever you say. By the way, I've arranged for your limo."

"You did? What's it going to cost?"

"It's my wedding gift to the bride and groom."

"Oh! Well, okay then. Thanks."

"Yeah, you're welcome."

"Uh, look, I gotta go, Joe. Talk to you later." Axel hung up.

Crow looked at the phone, set it back in its cradle, and returned his attention to his list. He retrieved his pencil from the grapefruit and drew a speech balloon coming from Mickey Mouse's mouth: *Don't try to make people like you.*

*Once you fold a hand, you are better off never knowing what you would have got.*

—Crow's rules

"**Y**OU OUGHTA GO FISHING," Sam said. "Ax ain't worried about you, no reason you oughta be worrying about him."

"I'm not worried about him, Sam," Crow said. He leaned against the battered grill of a thirty-year-old Ford flatbed, one of the many unfinished restoration projects filling Sam's backyard.

"You wanna hold this here?" Sam held out a thick, black extension cord. Two one-inch-long twists of bare copper wire protruded from the end.

Crow accepted the wire without thinking. "I was just saying that if I was Axel I'd go with my first instinct and take a closer look at Hyatt Hilton. The guy's up to something. Why do you think Ax told me to lay off? It's not like I was costing him anything."

Sam lowered himself to his hands and knees, rolled onto his back, and pulled himself under the faded red truck. "Maybe it was the shotgun," he said, his voice filtering up through the engine compartment and echoing from the open hood. "Ax don't like guns."

"I don't know," Crow said. "It feels wrong is all. I've been thinking about it all week."

"You a hundred percent sure he don't want you to keep doing what you was doing?"

"I hadn't thought about that."

"On account of Ax don't al'ys say what he wants a guy to hear."

"You think he wants me to keep investigating Hyatt?"

"Could be. You want to feed me that cord? Just run 'er under the truck here, and don't let it touch nothin.' She's hot."

Crow looked at the bare copper wires, then followed the extension cord with his eyes across the lawn, up the steps, and into the back door. He returned his eyes to the bare copper with new respect.

"This is plugged in?"

"Just slide 'er in here, son."

"Jesus, Sam, how come you didn't tell me? I could've killed myself."

"Just feed her to me slow, son."

Crow crouched and peered under the truck. Sam had somehow managed to light a cigarette. Smoke curled around the starter motor.

"What are you doing, Sam?"

"Got a jammed-up starter."

"What's the juice for?"

"Gotta break 'er loose, son." He reached out with a grease-rimed hand. "Give 'er here, son."

With some misgivings, Crow slid the end on the cord across the dirt toward Sam.

"Thing you got to remember is Ax has got what you call your infernal conflicts." Sam grasped the cord. "He's got his own private thoughts, and then he's got Sophie's thoughts mixed in there. That's the problem with living with a gal. A guy spends half his day trying to figure out if what he done on his other half the day is gonna get him in trouble." Sam brushed the wire against the frame, producing a miniature flash of lightning.

Crow jerked his hand away from the bumper. "You sure you know what you're doing?"

"Son, I been fixin' starters since hand crankers." He squinted his eyes down to slits and jammed the bare wires against the starter connections. Instinctively, Crow jumped up and backed away from the truck. The engine roared and turned over once, followed by a metallic scream of protest, a loud popping sound, and a flurry of sparks. A cloud of smoke rose up through the engine compartment.

Crow crouched down and peered under the truck.

"Sam? You okay?"

As the smoke dissipated he could see his father's soot-blackened face. Sam's eyes were open wider than usual, and his cigarette terminated in a frayed mass of tobacco shreds.

"Way-ell," he said, "she's cooked now!"

♠

For the past two weeks, Crow had been working out afternoons, in part because he'd been having trouble getting out of bed, and partly because he wished to avoid Beaut Miller, whose latest intimidation technique was to wear a pair of dark wraparound sunglasses and stare at Crow from across the room while lifting some outrageously heavy weight. Beaut's workouts had become alarmingly vigorous, and his overall size seemed to be increasing on a daily basis. Crow had considered confronting him again, but his more rational self decided that avoidance was a better long-term strategy.

Bigg Bodies, at two o'clock in the afternoon, was nearly deserted. Only one other person was using the facilities—a desperately pedaling woman on the recumbent stationary bike. Bigg had shut himself away in his office. The heavy metal tapes that blasted from the sound system mornings and evenings had been replaced by a talk radio station. Afternoons lacked the energy of mornings and early evenings, but Crow liked it. He'd been doing less lifting and putting more time in on the aerobic equipment, reading *Sports Illustrated* or *Vogue* or whatever he found in the box near the door. Today he'd lucked onto a nearly complete copy of the *Star Tribune,* only two days old.

Another week or so, he told himself, and he'd get back into the heavy lifting. For now, he was happy to be climbing the stair machines, reading the classifieds.

Crow checked the listings under Sports & Hi Performance Cars, looking for a '69 GTO. Every now and then he saw one for sale, which made him feel good. Given his uncertain finances, he felt compelled to stay on top of the local GTO market. He never knew when he'd have to sell his. Crow squinted, trying to climb the Stairmaster while keeping his head still enough to read the classifieds. Very few GTOs for sale. A 1968 model with the notation "Eng. nds wrk.," and a 1972 convertible which, in Crow's view, didn't really count, since GM had, by that time, abandoned their efforts to dominate the muscle car market. Main Street had been ceded to MoPar: Chargers, Road Runners, and Barracudas had ruled the strip from 1970 until the onset of the gas crisis.

He closed the classified section and was about to drop it on the floor when an ad surrounded by a heavy black box caught his eye.

For the past couple weeks, ever since Hyatt Hilton had fired the shotgun at him, Crow had been feeling particularly mortal. But his interest in the ad had nothing to do with any hopes he might have of retarding the aging process. He couldn't seem to get Hyatt Hilton off his mind. Maybe it was getting shot at, or maybe it was the sense that Hyatt, through the medium of Carmen and her mother, had influenced Axel to call off the investigation. Sam might be right—maybe Axel secretly wanted the investigation to continue. Crow wasn't sure about what Axel wanted, but as soon as he saw the ad he knew he was going to follow up, if only to satisfy his own curiosity about Hyatt Hilton and the Amaranthines. The "Free Anti-Aging Clinic" looked like a good way to get in the door, get a close-up look at these immortals. Besides, with Debrowski still in Paris and no card games scheduled, he had nothing else to do.


Some nights Flo liked to get dressed up real nice and go out on the town. Walk over to the Luxe, sit at a table by herself, order a ginger ale, listen to some jazz, pretend she was waiting for somebody. See if some guy had the balls to move on her, get shot down. Or go eat at a restaurant, some place nicer than Solid Sam's. One of those places with cloth napkins and free bread and a wine list with more than three kinds of wine on it where she could watch the waitresses without having to be one herself. Some nights she went to see a movie. Some nights she just got in her Miata and drove around with the top down, all dressed up and no place she had to go.

Joe Crow lived on the second floor of a duplex on First Avenue just south of downtown Minneapolis. Sometimes she drove past his place, looking up at the windows, wondering what was inside. She tried to imagine what his life could be like. Did he sit inside reading books? Did he have friends? Did he watch TV, or listen to music, or fold his legs in the lotus position and do meditation? Maybe he had a family up there, a wife and kids that no one knew about. Maybe he was gay. Maybe he was an illegal alien, or a criminal mastermind, or a secret agent. She had seen cat hairs on his sweatshirt. Maybe he had forty cats.

Sometimes Flo parked her car down the street from Joe Crow's apartment and sat there for an hour or so. Once or twice she had seen him come out and get in his car. She had followed him, thinking that maybe he would go to some public place—a mall, or a nightclub. Something like that. A place where she could just run into him, a coincidence, dressed up and looking good, let him get a look at her without her goldfish necklace.

It hadn't happened yet, but Flo was hopeful. Friday night. Maybe he would go someplace tonight. Maybe he would go to the Luxe to listen to some jazz, and she would just walk in and sit at her usual table and order a ginger ale, and they would see what happened next.

*To grow is to live, to live is to grow.*

*—Second Maxim of the Amaranthine Church*

**P**OLLY DESIMONE WAS JITTERY, as always, before going on. Once she got out there and started talking she'd be fine, but the waiting was always hard on her. She wished she had a cigarette. Beside her, Chip Bouchet stood at attention beside a large urn decorated with gold leaf. He was wearing his toga. Chip was nervous, too, shifting his weight from one leg to the other, his jaw muscles pulsing. It was his own damn fault. Ever since Chuckles had begun working the stage, Chip had insisted on doing something, too. The toga and urn routine had been Chuckles's idea. Polly had mixed feelings about it, but as long as it kept her security force happy she was willing to go with it.

Chuckles had been warming up the audience for ten minutes. He wore a rose-colored suit over a black silk shirt. Polly had frowned at the black shirt—she disliked all things black—but she said nothing. Chuckles had his own style. As long as he kept that tattoo of his covered up, she would make no complaint.

The turnout was their best ever. The ads had attracted an unprecedented number of Pilgrims, 90 percent of them women between the ages of forty and sixty, the perfect demographic. Every seat in the auditorium was occupied; a few latecomers stood against the walls. They'd never had a full house before, at least not since they'd moved into their new headquarters with this nice big auditorium, two hundred sixteen seats.

A few weeks back, when Chuckles had first asked to participate in the program, Polly had resisted. She'd feared that the very large, very black head of security would alarm her largely suburban, white, female audience. Rupe, however, had loved the idea, and Rupe had been right. Chuckles was a natural. His soft but powerful voice soothed the Pilgrims while his imposing physical presence commanded their respect from the moment he took the stage. They had used him to open the last two Anti-Aging Clinics, and were thinking of enlarging his role, perhaps one day letting him conduct his own Extraction Events.

Chuckles's story was compelling. He spoke of his impoverished Alabama childhood, dropping out of school to support his mother, getting mixed up with a bad crowd, getting in trouble with the law, hopping a train up north, more bad companions, drugs, crimes, landing in the penitentiary at Stillwater, and nearly dying in a cafeteria knife fight. He told it all in a liquid, rumbling voice, sorrowful and soulful, with occasional touches of humor. He spoke of himself as a man who'd had nothing—no prospects, no hope, no friends—a man who expected to die before his thirtieth birthday. But then he had discovered the Amaranthine Principles. By the time Chuckles concluded his tale of hope and redemption, the Pilgrims were tender as pounded veal.

Rupe took the stage next, starting out with a few jokes, telling them about his early life, about how he had used drugs and abused his body with red meat, alcohol, stress, and self-destructive belief systems—a sort of a middle-class version of Chuckles's story. He painted a picture of himself as a man in search of death, which was not, Polly recalled, far from the truth.

"I believed in death," he confessed. "My life was a toilet, a toxic spinning whirlpool draining all its energy into a bottomless pit, creating nothing but my own doorway into oblivion, rushing toward it with my arms spread wide as if death and destiny were one and the same. I was a hundred fifty pounds overweight, I had ulcers, a chronic cough, blurred vision, and gout. My hair was falling out by the handful. Fifty-six years old and I was ready to die like an animal, ready to give up my life force and let my body rot like a three hundred-pound sack of garbage. I was all but compost, my friends. Fifty-six years and I was ready to throw it all away. Today, three years later, you see me at fifty-nine. Do I look like a dead man?"

Led by the handful of Faithful scattered amongst them, the audience applauded. Polly, watching from the wing, felt a pang of concern. The last time they'd done a clinic, Rupe had claimed to be fifty-six—also not true, but at least it had been in agreement with their literature.

Rupert Chandra had, in fact, been born forty-six years ago. The liberties he and Polly took with their claimed ages were a bit of stage fiction designed to make a point, but consistency was important. Rupe was not a detail guy. That was Polly's job. She'd have a talk with him later.

Rupe raised his right hand. "Let's see a show of hands. How many of you expect to be alive and in good health five years from now?"

Nearly every hand in the audience came up.

"How many of you expect to be alive in twenty years?"

Most of the hands stayed in the air, a few dropped out.

"Fifty years?"

About two-thirds of the audience dropped their hands. Rupe's remained pointed toward the lights.

"One hundred years?"

All hands but Rupe's fell.

"That's what I thought." He dropped his hand. "It is a very sad thing, this belief in the Death Program. Let me ask you something else. How many of you would like to halt or even reverse the aging process? Yes, of course you would. Well, ladies and gentlemen, age reversal is more than a theoretical possibility. This evening you will witness proof that the fountain of youth has been found. Too late for Ponce de Leon, I'm afraid, but not too late for you! This evening you are going to take your first step outside the tautological murk of the Death Program and into the clean, clear light of the soul. Aging is not an inevitable process, but rather an outmoded evolutionary device. This evening, you will witness incontrovertible proof of this simple fact. There was a time in human history when the gradual disintegration of the human form served the greater purposes of our race. That time is past.

"I'd like to introduce to you now a person without whom I might never have discovered the anti-aging secrets, which are about to be revealed to you. My wife and Eternal Partner, Polyhymnia DeSimone."

Polly took a breath, thrust her chest forward and bounced out onto the stage. She greeted Rupe with a kiss, flashed her teeth at the audience, and took the microphone. Rupe sat in a canvas-backed chair at stage right. Polly glided forward to the lip of the stage and leaned out over the audience.

"Can anyone here tell me what cellulite is?"

One of the Faithful raised his hand and shouted, "Fat!"

Polly shook her head. "Wrong. It may look like fat, but it's a scientific fact that doctors do not actually know what cellulite is, where it comes from, and why it appears. Let's try another question. Who knows what causes wrinkles? The sun? Then why do dolphins, who have skin as smooth as a baby's bottom, and whose lifespans have yet to be measured by modern science, spend hours on the surface of the sea basking in the sun's rays?" She scanned the audience, letting her point sink home. "How about liver spots? Osteoporosis? Cataracts? Arthritis?

"The fact is, every one of these are symptoms of the disease we call aging, a disease that until recently was thought to be inevitable, incurable, and unavoidable. Well tonight, ladies and gentlemen, you are going to witness the literal, actual, genuine reversal of the aging process. One of your names will be drawn, and that individual will literally have twenty years stripped from his or her age. This is no trick. This is no illusion. The results will be immediately apparent and, if our lucky subject follows the Amaranthine Principles, the changes to his or her appearance will be permanent.

"Before we proceed, I want to be completely honest with you. The process is not easy. It is not free. And it will not work for everyone. It requires commitment, faith, and a lot of hard work. The miracle you are about to witness—and it is indeed a miracle—shall be performed at great personal cost to Mr. Chandra." Polly turned to look at Rupe, who was sitting hunched forward in his chair, hands steepled in front of his mouth, his face stony with concentration. A blue spotlight highlighted the beads of sweat on his knitted brow.

"He is able to do this once or twice a year only. If, in the process, he should lose consciousness, do not be alarmed." Polly crossed the stage and whispered in Rupe's ear, "You ready, big boy?"

The weirdest part of the show so far, Crow decided, was the swinish drill sergeant with the toga. The last time he'd seen him he'd been riding in a yellow Corvette, along with the big black guy in the pink suit. Why a toga? Why all of a sudden introduce this Greco-Roman flavor to the proceedings? Crow looked around. No one else seemed surprised by the fact that a crew-cut Roman senator had just carried a golden urn onto the stage.

There is no understanding any of this, Crow thought. There is only watching it unfold, the way one might watch fish in an aquarium. The whole experience had a psychedelic quality.

Dialing LLL–LIFE had provided instructions—spoken over a background recording of *Thus Spake Zarathustra*—on how to get to the Anti-Aging Clinic. The address had sounded familiar to Crow. He had thrown on a pair of jeans and an old, striped referee shirt—the only two clean articles of clothing in his closet—and headed out. When he pulled his GTO into the parking lot, he had realized that the Amaranthines occupied the same gray brick structure that had once been known as Fitzgerald Elementary School, where he had attended the third and fourth grades. Filing into the small auditorium had brought a flood of disjointed memories. The last time he'd been there he had watched a film titled *Donald Duck in Mathmagic Land.*

The drill sergeant in the toga knelt and presented the open mouth of the urn to the woman with the platinum wig, Polyhymnia DeSimone. Polly. Crow remembered her from Ambrosia Foods, before she'd gone with the big hair.

Tonight she wore solid white, from her jutting, low-cut bodice to her four-inch heels. Her dress clung to her upper body like paint. From her hips down it became a diaphanous, veillike structure that clung to her long legs, or floated free, depending on how she moved. Crow found the effect to be stimulating and far more interesting to watch than the twenty-minute rant he had just endured from Rupert Chandra, a.k.a. Rupe.

Polly reached deep into the urn and extracted a slip of paper. She read it, smiled, rested a hand atop the kneeling man's bristly head, and faced the audience.

"Mrs. Veronica Frank?"

An ear-piercing squeal came from a few rows behind Crow.

"Would you like to join us on the stage?"

Crow turned to see, two rows behind him, a woman erupt from her seat. She made her way clumsily toward the aisle, holding her voluminous purse high, creating an eddy of commotion as she stepped on feet, tripped on purse straps, and grabbed at people's shoulders and arms for support.

Leaving behind a row of excited, disheveled women, Mrs. Veronica Frank reached the aisle. She was a woman in her sixties with uniformly grey hair, excited eyes, and too much makeup. Her baggy cotton print dress, featuring multicolored overlapping tulip outlines on a navy field, fluttered around her ample waist as she jogged toward the stage.

The toga man lifted her up onto the stage, producing another delighted squeal. Polyhymnia embraced the woman and led her to the microphone.

"Congratulations, Veronica. One God."

The woman nodded vigorously. "One Way!" she squeaked.

"One Life. Before we begin, perhaps you could tell us a little bit about yourself, starting with your age, please. How old are you?"

Mrs. Frank leaned in close to the microphone. "Sixty-four!" she shouted, spontaneously breaking into applause for herself.

"And you live here in the Twin Cities?"

Mrs. Frank nodded eagerly.

The interview went on for a few minutes longer. Crow shifted in his seat, feeling trapped. The novelty of the event was wearing thin. This wasn't his idea of what a Friday night should be, but he was determined to stick it out. He told himself that, if nothing else, he would be exposing himself to a reality he had never before sampled. Maybe it would make a funny story to tell Debrowski, or to fill the time between hands at the next poker game.

Having given her vital statistics, a compendium of her physical ailments, and the names of her six grandchildren, Mrs. Frank was led by Polly to a padded stool, which the toga man had placed at center stage. The lights dimmed, and a low-wattage spotlight waxed directly above her grey head. Rupert Chandra rose from his seat and approached the woman, his dark suit shimmering. He stood behind her, his face in shadow, placed his hands on either side of her neck and began to massage her shoulders as he chanted in a low voice. The chant sounded like "Wonga wanna wolf, wonga wanna wolf." The tulip dress bunched and wrinkled under his fingers, the woman's expression went from excited and eager to uncomfortable and concerned. Her hands came up from her lap; Rupert Chandra grabbed them and gently forced them back down, whispering something in her ear. He continued his massage, moving out to the points of her shoulders, then down her back, then up her neck. Mrs. Frank's expression changed every time he moved his hands—her face went from agonized to orgasmic to grieving to joyful.

The massaging and chanting continued. Crow did not know what was supposed to be happening and, after watching closely for the first few minutes, his attention drifted. He noticed that the majority of the people around him were deeply absorbed in the process. A few appeared to be excited, as if they were seeing some change in the woman on stage. A distinct minority looked, like Crow, bored. He amused himself by picking out individual faces in the crowd and trying to guess their religious background, ancestry, and socioeconomic class. Most were easily placed as protestant, Germanic, and upper-middle class. The faces that drew his attention were those that contrasted with the waspish majority. He saw signs of Irish here and there, and a significant number of bejeweled, Jewish-looking women. He saw no Africans, Asians, or Hispanics, but one woman, sitting a few seats to his left, defied categorization. Perhaps she had come from the West Indies, or Polynesia. Whatever her ancestry, it had produced a remarkable-looking woman. She had strong but regular features, olive-gold skin tone, golden-brown eyes, and thick slabs of long, rippling, jet black hair framing her forehead and her firm, square jaw. Her lips were full and prominent and painted an odd shade of maroon, matching her long nails. She wore a metallic gold, faux-snakeskin jacket with cartoonishly exaggerated shoulders. Ribbed black capri pants clung to muscular thighs. Her lime green pumps displayed exceptionally high, sharp heels.

Crow had the impression that he'd seen her somewhere before. As he stared at her, trying not to be too obvious about it, sorting through his memories, she turned her head in his direction and smiled. Recognition hit him low and hard.

Flowrean Peeche. His immediate reaction was to stop breathing. In his experience, that was what one did when one got this close to Flowrean. But he'd been sitting within a few feet of her for several minutes now and had smelled nothing other than the crowd's melange of perfume and breath fresheners. How had he not recognized her? It had to be that he'd never seen her without her dead-goldfish necklace, or in any setting other than Bigg's gym.

A room-wide rustling and muttering sent Crow's eyes back to center stage. Rupert Chandra had been working on Mrs. Frank's face, pulling and prodding and squeezing her wrinkled features. The audience's reaction was to a visible change in the color of her flesh. It had taken on a glow, as if her dermis had begun to fluoresce, and the sagging skin beneath her jaw had visibly tightened. Rupert Chandra himself, whose head appeared and disappeared from the light as he moved around Mrs. Frank, appeared to be changing as well. Perspiration rolled freely down his forehead and cheeks, and the front of his silk shirt was plastered to his chest, soaking wet. His eyes, which had glittered with vitality not ten minutes earlier, now sagged in bruised-looking pouches. Deep lines bracketed his mouth. He seemed to have aged decades.

Chandra's hands continued to flutter over the woman's face and neck. His chanting had become hoarse, and now sounded like "Wagga omma oof." His fingers darted and stroked her as if she was a harp. Mrs. Frank had settled into a vacant, mesmerized gape, seemingly oblivious to the fact that she was sitting on a stage with hundreds of people watching, being massaged by a sweaty man in an iridescent black silk suit.

Once he caught the drift of the anti-aging demonstration, Crow had expected an illusion of some sort. He thought that Chandra might be able to knock a few years off the woman's apparent age, maybe by inducing some mild swelling, bringing the blood to the surface to give her that flush of youth, but mostly by creating a state of total relaxation, a hypnotic effect, making her believe that the years were falling away. Creating anticipation and desire on the part of the audience would also be an important part of the package. They would see what they wanted to see. It would be no great trick for a charismatic and clever conjurer to produce the flush of youth in the old woman's timeworn features. The same techniques were used again and again by evangelical preachers who regularly convinced wheelchair-bound believers to stand and take a few tottering steps.

But Mrs. Frank's transformation went far beyond such psychological trickery. He watched as Chandra's manipulations caused lines and wrinkles to fall away from the old woman's entranced features. Her lips grew fuller, her eyes larger, her cheeks became smooth and unblemished. The effect was utterly convincing. For all his self-imposed, fortified skepticism, Crow felt a part of himself wanting to believe. He had seen lesser examples of reverse aging in middle-aged people who had fallen suddenly in love, for example, or who had undergone cosmetic surgery, or spent a month at a remote health spa, but he had never witnessed so rapid and extreme a reversal of aging as this. Mrs. Frank looked younger than Liz Taylor had at forty, fifty, or even sixty.

Without warning, Veronica Frank slumped forward, Rupert Chandra's hands flew out to the side and his chanting abruptly ended. Giving forth a loud moan, he took four shaky steps backward, then collapsed. The stage lights flared to full brightness. The toga man and Chuckles, the big man who had opened the program, lifted their unconscious leader and carried him off the stage. The audience began to seethe, people rising half out of their seats, talking to one another, all asking the same questions—is he all right? Is *she* all right? What happened? Did someone call 911? The voices rose in pitch and volume. The woman on the stage appeared dazed, her upper body resting on her thighs, head hanging, arms dangling, hands flopping like dying fish on the stage floor. The sound from the audience rose to a hysterical drone. Polly rushed out onto the stage and embraced Mrs. Frank. She whispered something, then helped her up. The two women faced the auditorium.

The panicky buzzing subsided into slack-jawed wonder as the people got their first look at Mrs. Veronica Frank since the lights had brightened. Except for her gray hair and her baggy, boomerang-print dress, she now appeared in every respect to be a woman in her early thirties.

Flo was thrilled and fascinated by what she had seen on stage, but not surprised, amazed, or frightened. After all, she had performed much greater metamorphoses on her own self. As a teenager she had gone from black virgin, to whore, to white virgin in a matter of minutes. Later in life, she had used weight training to transform herself from a fearful, scrawny young woman into a broad-shouldered, rock-hard Amazon. And by working at Solid Sam's, she had lifted herself from the trash-heap of her old neighborhood to her own condo on the twenty-third floor of the Greensward, with downtown Minneapolis laid out like a gameboard below her.

Flo understood that the process of becoming someone new begins and ends between the ears. Even changing clothes, getting ready for work, or putting on a dressy outfit like the one she was wearing, began with a vision. Believing it and seeing it, that was the first and most difficult step. Once you can see, you can believe, and once you believe, you can slide into the attitude; once you own the attitude, then you got your shot at it, whatever it is. Once you got your shot, then you've got to believe you can make it. And once you make it, you've got to believe it was you that made it happen. The process was ongoing.

With Joe Crow, for instance, she had the belief and she had the attitude, and now she was waiting for her shot. Funny how these things worked out. She'd been watching Crow, driving past his house a few times a day. Sometimes his car was there, sometimes it wasn't. She had seen him once through his window, talking on the phone. She had been parked across the street from his place earlier that evening, fantasizing, and when Crow drove off in his yellow car, Flo had followed. Now here they were, sitting in the same room, witnessing a miracle together.

She looked at Crow, who was staring intently at Mrs. Frank. What was he thinking? His face betrayed nothing, so Flo simply assumed that his thoughts reflected her own. She was sure he did not like being in this unfamiliar room crowded with strangers. They had that in common, she and Joe Crow. So why was he here? Was he, too, struggling to believe? Not an easy thing, Flo thought, despite having witnessed it. Some things were simply too incredible. For instance, Flo could not believe that if she flapped her arms fast enough she could fly, or that money would materialize in her purse of its own accord, or that she possessed the strength to bench press five hundred pounds. But she had *seen* the woman transformed. She *wanted* to believe. Flo began to alter her version of reality to make room for the possibility of age reversal. Maybe she had been wrong in some of her lifelong assumptions. Maybe she should be more flexible. Another ten or fifteen or one hundred years, it might come in handy.

The woman with the platinum wig, Polyhymnia something, was talking again. Flo did not like her much, but she admired the way she came off as both intimate and untouchable. Flo had noticed this quality in other public figures, an ability to be inside you and on the other side of the universe, all at the same time.

Polyhymnia was inviting those who wanted to learn more to join her in the reception area. She also promised an up-close look at the new Mrs. Veronica Frank. She led Mrs. Frank off the stage and down the hallway.

Buzzing and scuffling, the gathering rose unevenly, many of the women having trouble untangling their purses and bags from the chair legs. The rows emptied into the aisles and headed for the exit. Flo tried to keep Crow in sight, but was blocked by a cluster of chattering matrons who had stopped in the middle of the aisle to give one another verbal recaps of what they had seen. She jumped up onto one of the seats and surveyed the exiting crowd. Crow's dark hair did not appear in the sea of gray, white, silver, and blond. Had he already made it out of the room? Flo scanned the crowd again, and this time she saw him—not heading for the exit, but climbing onto the empty stage. He looked back over the crowd, his eyes pausing briefly on Flo, then walked quickly into the wings.

*During the Second Age of Mankind, which began with the dis-
covery of the cell in 1665, the average human lifespan increased from thirty-six to over seventy years. The collapse of
the Western military-industrial complex and the decimation of
the human race by AIDS, ebola, influenza, and Lyme disease
will mark the end of the Second Age. This process will begin
with the dawning of the millennium and will continue throughout the twenty-first century. On January 1, 2100, the mantle of
world leadership will be assumed by a new race of Immortals:
the Amaranthines.*

*—The Amaranthine Book of Truths*

THE OFFICIAL TEACHINGS OF THE Amaranthine Church of the One forbade the
use of alcoholic beverages, tobacco, or caffeine. The ACO also counseled the
Faithful to avoid red meat, refined sugar, and saturated fats. The Faithful expected to live a very long time and were therefore expected to take good care
of their bodies. This was common sense. Why spend eternity in a wheezing, alcoholic haze? Or waddle through the next millennium with thighs swishing, or
a belly hanging out over your belt?

No one would want that—especially not Rupert Chandra who, before his
extraction, had smoked three packs of Winstons a day, weighed in excess of
300 pounds, and whose idea of healthy eating had been to swallow a handful of
vitamins and herbal medicines with a Bloody Mary for breakfast. That was the
old Rupe, the mortal Rupe. The new Rupe was a clean machine.

Nevertheless, Rupe felt he deserved a good stiff drink after making it
through another anti-aging demonstration. About four ounces of Glenfiddich
would release the tension he felt in his chest. And a small cigar, one of the slim
Havanas he'd brought back from his last trip to England, would help quell the
mild nausea he'd been experiencing the past few days. That was his reward to

himself, both for having achieved immortality and for shouldering the burden of leadership.

Rupe propped his feet atop his desk blotter and reclined in his high-backed leather chair. The sun's last tangential rays sliced across his office, illuminating golden dust motes and blue curls of cigar smoke. He sent a series of smoke rings toward the sunbeam, watched them catch the light, waver, then disintegrate. He swirled the scotch in his glass. Yes, this was a well-deserved reward. He had done his job and done it well. He had created the perfect illusion, had opened the door, had shown the Pilgrims a way to believe. Now it was up to Polly and the rest of the Faithful.

The fact that the demonstration had been staged bothered him, but only a little. It was a clear case of the ends justifying the means. Regretably, it was necessary to deceive the Pilgrims in order to give them the gift of immortality. In the early days Rupe had questioned the need for such deception but, as Polly argued so convincingly, it had advantages. Nothing else they had tried had brought so many new Pilgrims into the fold so quickly.

Rupe took a large swallow of scotch. One day soon, the church would become rich enough and powerful enough that such crude recruitment techniques would become unnecessary. Soon, Stonecrop would be completed. He and Polly and a select handful of the Faithful would be residing happily within its twelve-foot-high limestone walls, safe from the collapse of the twentieth-century military-industrial complex, safe from the ravages of the Death Program, ready to reemerge after one hundred years of solitude into the Third Age, the age of enlightenment.

Rupe puffed on his cigar and imagined himself at the completed Stonecrop, deer and rabbits scampering alongside him through the parklike landscape. In the meantime, he was looking forward to his and Polly's sabbatical at Stonecrop. Most of the building remained unfinished. For four weeks, Rupe and Polly would have Stonecrop to themselves, a taste of utopia to come. Free from the day-to-day aggravations of ACO business. Free to let their bodies heal.

The door opened and a compact, dark-haired man stepped into the office. Rupe felt a twinge of fear. He did not know this man, and this part of the building was supposed to be off limits.

"Can I help you?" Rupe asked. He set his drink on the leather blotter. The man appeared to be harmless enough, just a guy in blue jeans and a striped, short-sleeved shirt. He looked like a referee. Probably a Pilgrim looking for the restrooms, but it paid to be careful. The church had a way of attracting some fringe elements.

The man said, "How's it going, Rupe?"

Rupe frowned. Only Polly called him Rupe to his face. He pulled his feet off the desk and sat forward. "I'm sorry," he said. "Do I know you?"

The man smiled. "My name is Joe Crow."

"How do you do?" Rupe said automatically. The name meant nothing to him.

Joe Crow looked around the office. "This used to be Mr. Bongard's office," he said. "I used to spend a lot of time in here."

"Who is Mr. Bongard?"

"He was the vice principal."

"This is no longer Mr. Bongard's office," said Rupe. "Might I ask what you are doing here?"

"You don't remember me? I used to be one of your customers at Ambrosia Foods. Didn't you used to be heavier?"

Rupe made a strained smile. He was supposed to remember every customer from the old store? "Are you here for the clinic?" he asked.

"Yes. It was quite a show. That smells like a good cigar."

"It's quite good. May I ask what you are doing here? This is not a public part of the building."

"That's all right." Crow sat down in one of the two chairs in front of the desk. "I just wanted to talk."

"Look, Mr. Crow, I am very tired. If you want to talk, I'd like to ask you to call tomorrow and make an appointment with my secretary."

Crow showed no sign of departure. He laced his fingers behind his neck and leaned back. "That a Cuban?"

Rupe looked at the cigar. "Yes. I'm afraid I'm going to have to ask you to leave."

"I enjoyed the show. How often do you perform?"

"Are you referring to the age regression?"

"Yes."

"It was no show."

Crow laughed. "Sure it was. I can see the makeup on your hands. It's all over your sleeves. You should have cleaned up better. You never know who's going to come walking in on you."

Rupe stood up. "That's enough. Get out."

"Is the woman a regular, or do you use a different one each time?"

Rupe wanted to leap across the desk and throw the guy out, but the man was so confident and relaxed that Rupe wasn't sure he could handle him alone.

Crow said, "Relax, Rupe. I'm not here to bust your act."

"What is it you want?" Rupe asked.

"I want to talk to you about Hyatt Hilton."


Rupert Chandra had a remarkably flexible and mobile mouth. When he spoke, his dark lips massaged and softened the words, giving them a warm velvet buzz with an inviting lilt at the end of every sentence. Even when he said "Get out," his lips oiled and caressed the words to make it sound like a polite, slightly regretful request.

Rupe had changed a great deal since Crow had last seen him behind the counter at Ambrosia Foods, when Rupe's aspect had been that of a wheezy sumo wrestler. His claim to have lost a hundred fifty pounds, at least, appeared to be true. The new Rupe had a slim, roll-free neck, a single chin, and nicely concave cheeks. His eyes were large, clear, dark, and long-lashed, and his once pudgy hands had become slim and elegant. His lips were still full, but had lost their pouty aspect. Rupe had transformed himself into an attractive, sleek man, radiating the smug but sincere solicitousness of your typical guru.

When Crow mentioned Hyatt Hilton's name, Rupe's mouth contracted into a large maroon asterisk. Crow almost laughed, but restrained himself. If he wanted to learn anything, it wouldn't be a good idea to totally alienate the man. Still, he found it difficult to take Rupert Chandra seriously. The man was covered with makeup. It showed between his fingers, on the sleeves of his shirt, and under the arms of his blue silk shirt. He had smudged it under his eyes and deepened the lines that bracketed his mouth, trying to make himself look aged and tired. At close range, with the sunset pouring in through the window, the makeup on his face appeared crude, like something a four-year-old might do. But Rupe had applied it to himself surreptitiously, without a mirror, in front of a live audience—after removing it with his bare hands from the face of "Veronica Frank." As he had stripped away her illusion of age, he had applied her years to himself. On stage, under controlled lighting, it had been utterly convincing.

Rupe said, "Why would you want to do that?"

"Talk about Hy?" Crow shrugged. "Is there some reason you don't want to talk about him? Would you rather talk about how you pulled off that fountain of youth trick out there?"

"You are an extremely offensive man," Rupe said, pointing his cigar.

"Sorry," Crow said. "It's just that I have this reaction when I see somebody running a game on innocent people."

"You have no idea what you are talking about."

"Possibly, but it doesn't matter. I came here to talk about Hy."

Rupe frowned. "What does he want? Is it money?"

"What makes you think he wants something?"

"Why else would he have sent you?"

That surprised Crow. "Hyatt didn't send me. I'm investigating him for a client. A third party."

Rupe relaxed visibly, his shoulders dropping a full two inches. "You are a private investigator?"

"That's right."

Rupe drew on his cigar, frowned, examined it critically.

"Your cigar went out," Crow observed.

"I am aware of that." Rupe set the dead smoke on the edge of his desk blotter and sat down. He rested his elbows on the desk and laced his fingers. "Who is this third party?" he asked.

"That's the private part."

"I see. In any case, I can't help you. I haven't spoken with Mr. Hilton since he left our organization last year."

"You mean, since you kicked him out."

"Mr. Hilton left of his own accord."

"Really? Why did he do that?"

Rupe picked up his glass, rattled the ice cubes, and took a large swallow. Crow felt a twinge of envy come and go, like a bird's shadow.

"It's quite simple," Rupe said. "Hyatt lost the faith."

The reception area had once been a gymnasium. The basketball hoops were gone, but the painted lines still showed on the hardwood floor. The room now held two dozen large, round tables, ten chairs per table, and a long buffet table at each end. Nearly everyone who had witnessed the demonstration had stayed for the reception, many of them jockeying for position to meet the miraculous Mrs. Veronica Frank, who stood beside the platinum wig lady near the freethrow line. Flo was curious, too, but she decided to wait for the crowd to thin. Heading for the food, she picked her way through the tables and clusters of chattering women, keeping an eye out for Joe Crow. She'd missed eating dinner that night. Flo loaded up a paper plate with cauliflower and carrot sticks.

Several green-jacketed men and women carrying armfuls of literature were working the crowd. One of them, a bright-eyed young man with carefully groomed blond hair, spotted Flo standing alone. He flashed a white grin and marched up to her with his right hand extended.

"One God," he said.

Flo ignored his hand. "One what?" she asked, biting into a carrot stick.

"One God, One Way, One Life," he recited. "Our first maxim. Are you familiar with the Amaranthine precepts?"

Flo, who was not, awaited enlightenment. The Amaranthine handed her a thin booklet. The cover read, in flowery script, *The Seven Steps to Physical Immortality.*

"My name is Ted. I'll be your ACO representative. What did you think of the demonstration?"

"Could you not stand so close?" Flo asked.

Ted took a step back and hugged his armful of booklets against his green jacket.

"Thank you," said Flo. She opened the book and flipped through the pages.

After a moment, Ted spotted another lost soul and took off across the room. Flo relaxed and began to read the introduction.

> *Since the dawn of Mankind, human beings have sought to improve their lives. Many have found brief periods of health and happiness, but only recently have a chosen few succeeded in the greatest human endeavor of all time: the quest for Eternal Life.*
>
> *The Amaranthine Church of the One was founded by Dr. Rupert Chandra, one of the world's foremost authorities in the fields of Herbal Geriatrics, Shiatsu Regenerative Therapy, Extraction Psychology, and the teachings of the immortal Zhang Daoling. Dr. Chandra has multiple degrees from the Institute of Vedic Pharmatechnology in Rawalpindi, Pakistan; the Gahniv University Medical School in New Delhi, India; and the Vortex Herbal Institute of Sedona, Arizona. He sits on the editorial boards of several major medical journals including the* New Herbal Reporter, *the* Journal of the Alternative Medicine Association (JAMA), *and* Metropolitan Homeopathy.

Flo raised her head and scanned the room. The miracle lady was still out of sight behind a press of bodies. The tables were beginning to fill, with the seated groups listening to one or another of the green-jackets deliver an earnest pitch. Flo saw no sign of Joe Crow. She returned to her reading.

> *At the age of fifty-one, while performing an experiment with an infusion of amaranth petals and stonecrop rhizomes, Dr. Chandra became so involved in his work that he did not sleep for several days. It was during this period of sleeplessness that he experienced a spontaneous series of spiritual, psychophysiological and microbiological events, which led to a remarkable and unprecedented alteration of his body's neuroelectrical balance.*

Flo did not understand a word of what she had just read, but she was impressed. It was a lot like reading *MuscleMag International*. Nothing made sense, but the physical evidence was overwhelming.

> *Dr. Chandra immediately undertook the writing of what has become known as the Amaranthine Principles. For two days and three nights, he wrote, without stopping, a single, unending sentence, compelled and guided by the voice of Zhang Daoling, the immortal founder of the Taoistic sect of Right Unity, until, after completing four hundred pages, Dr. Chandra collapsed at his desk, falling into a coma which persisted for twenty-nine days.*
>
> *At the end of the twenty-ninth day, Dr. Chandra awakened in a hospital room. To the amazement of the doctors, he knew exactly where he was and how long he had been there. He knew all the doctors and*

*nurses by name. Furthermore, during his month-long coma he had lost
134 pounds, yet had retained all of his physical strength and was able
to walk immediately upon awakening.*

*Before releasing him, the doctors insisted on performing a bat-
tery of tests. When they compared the results of these tests with the
tests they had administered upon admitting him to the hospital, the
doctors were stunned. For all intents and purposes, Dr. Chandra had
gone from being a 300-pound, fifty-one-year-old diabetic asthmatic
with a cholesterol reading of 379, to a strong, healthy, 166-pound man
who appeared to be in his early thirties. His blood glucose levels were
normal, his lungs clear, and his cholesterol reading had dropped to an
incredible 138.*

*None of these facts seemed to surprise Dr. Chandra, for during
his coma he had in fact been redesigning his own cellular structure
under the guidance of Zhang Daoling, who informed him that the time
had come to take humanity to the next step in their evolution, the step
beyond the Death Program.*

*Since that day, Dr. Chandra has devoted his life to bringing
these cellular regeneration techniques to the rest of mankind. Through
the bimonthly ACO Extraction Events, he and his Eternal Companion,
Polyhymnia DeSimone, have successfully taught thousands to reverse
or halt the degenerative process known as "aging."*

Flo flipped through the rest of the booklet, searching for the "Seven Steps to
Physical Immortality" promised in the title. She liked numbered processes. Articles titled "Three Steps to Bigger Biceps," or "Five Guaranteed Techniques
for Expanding Your Ribcage" always caught her eye. But the "Seven Steps"
were nowhere revealed in the booklet, only a mealy-mouthed invitation at the
very end:

*Is physical immortality a reality? Without question. Is it possible for
you? Dr. Chandra would like to invite you to find out.*

*There are Seven Steps to Physical Immortality. Each step must
be undertaken in the proper order, with the proper guidance. The Elders of the Amaranthine Church of the One have created a series of
programs designed to guide you easily and swiftly through each step.*

*For more information, please consult your ACO representative.*

Flo closed the booklet and pushed away from the wall. The crowd around
the miracle lady had shrunk considerably. The green-jacketed Amaranthines
were herding groups to the tables. One of them, a beaming, fluff-haired young
woman, approached Flo.

"My name is Pam! One Life!"

Flo nodded, looked down at the three feet of space that separated them, took a step back.

"Are you here by yourself?" Pam asked.

Flo shook her head, thinking of Crow. "I don't know where my friend went," she said.

"Well, I'm sure she's here someplace. Would you like to join us?" She indicated one of the tables where a few seats remained empty.

"Maybe later," Flo said, edging away. She wound her way through the tables toward the miracle lady, spotted a rift in the crowd, and slipped through. Her view was blocked by the platinum wig lady. Flo sidled around and finally got her first close-up look at Mrs. Veronica Frank.

Flo experienced a crushing, instantaneous disappointment. The woman looked perfectly ordinary—a smiling, attractive, healthy-looking woman of thirty. Except for her tulip dress and old-fashioned clip-on earrings, she showed no evidence of her former self, nothing to help Flo believe what she had seen.

"How old are you really?" Flo demanded, interrupting another woman's question.

"I'm sixty-four, dear," said Mrs. Frank.

Flo squinted at the woman's smooth features and was reminded of those bodybuilding ads, before and after shots of scrawny little guys who supposedly gained forty pounds of solid muscle in six weeks. Flo didn't believe those ads, and she didn't believe this. This woman was a fake.

"You want to know what I think?" Flo asked.

Mrs. Frank blinked and smiled glassily.

"I think you're full of shit," Flo said.

She felt a pair of large hands grasp her upper arms. She heard a deep voice near her ear telling her to be cool. Be cool? Flo snapped her head back, hit something, heard an intake of breath, felt the grip on her arms tighten painfully.

"Be nice now," said the voice.

Flo kicked, but only brushed her abductor's legs. He dragged her backward through the door into the hallway. Tense with anger and the beginnings of panic, she kicked again, this time hitting his knee with the back of her heel. Suddenly she was free and falling, stumbling forward into the tile wall, hitting it with her shoulder as she twisted to see the man who had been holding her.

He wasn't as tall as Bubby Roode had been, but his arms and chest were thicker, and he was just as black. He wore a rose-colored suit, a black silk shirt, a bolo tie with a huge hunk of turquoise at its clasp, and he was gripping his knee with both hands. She remembered watching him on the stage. She'd liked him then.

"Jus' go easy now, sister," he said, grinning through his pain.

Sister? Who was he calling "sister?" Flo could feel more adrenaline, gallons of it, squirting into her arteries.

The man spread his hands and gave her a pained smile. "Look, all's I want is for you to take yourself on out of here, you understand? Nobody wants to hurt you. Just you go on out the door, and no harm done. You understand?"

Flo heard the man's words, but they weren't making sense. She felt the wall pushing against her back. She saw the man, pink-jacketed shoulders from here to there, five feet away. Her eyes were glued to him, the periphery of her vision obscured by dark bubbles. She tightened the muscles in her back and chest, trying to hold back the twin volcanoes of anger and panic. The man seemed to be growing larger and blacker. His grin became wider and intensely sinister, sharp white teeth protruding from blood-red gums. He wasn't moving, but he wasn't getting out of the way either. She dropped into a crouch and lowered her chin and felt a vibration from deep in her gut rise up through her lungs and throat and gush from her lips.

She screamed, and she leaped.

Seventeen years ago, back home in Burnt Corn, Alabama, Charles Luther Thickening's mama had sent him out to the old shed at the back of their quarter acre to fetch a weed hoe. Young Charles, at that time nine and a half years old and better known as Cubbie, had not liked to go anywhere near that rickety old shed, for he believed that it was haunted or, if not haunted, then at the very least teeming with black widow spiders and copperheads and other malevolent and venomous beasts. Cubbie attempted to explain his position to his mother, but she was intent on getting her hands on that weed hoe, a fact that she made abundantly clear to her son. Being marginally more afraid of his mother than he was of venomous beasts, young Cubbie proceeded to the shed and, using a broken broom handle, pushed the door open.

He'd been right about the spider. A big, fat black widow had filled one corner of the doorway with her chaotic weaving. Cubbie could see her shiny black back up near the top of the torn cobweb. He used the broom handle to crush the widow and clear away the web, then peered carefully into the dim interior of the shed, looking for copperhead snakes, which were common in the area. He did not spot any copperheads, but he did see the weed hoe his mother wanted, propped up against the far wall of the shed, less than eight feet away. Cubbie considered simply running in, grabbing the hoe, and running out again, but being a cautious lad, he first gathered a handful of pebbles and hurled them into the shed, hoping to stir up or frighten away whatever other beasts might be lurking within.

The pebbles produced no apparent effect. No clouds of hornets or rabid skunks or armies of fire ants appeared. Cubbie began to feel resigned to his mission. He had been hoping that the shed would produce something so terrible that he could safely report back to his mother that her request was impossible to fulfill. Taking a deep breath, which he hoped would not be his last, he stepped into the shed and grabbed the hoe and immediately had his worst fears realized when an angry mother possum dropped from the rafters onto his head, all hisses and teeth and claws and horror.

Chuckles was reminded of that day.

The gold-jacketed woman with the incredible legs landed pretty much everywhere at once, but Chuckles mostly felt the sensation of sharp acrylic nails penetrating his scalp. For perhaps seven-eighths of one second, he was too stunned to defend himself. That was enough time for him to sustain several blows, rips, slashes, and a bite to the forehead. By the time the message reached his muscles to respond, the insane possum woman had sprung free and was running down the hall. Chuckles started after her, but was stopped by a sickening pain in his left leg. He looked down and saw one of her lime green shoes hanging there, slick with blood, its spike heel embedded in his inner thigh.

*But from the hoop's bewitching round,*
*Her very shoe has power to wound.*

*—Edward Moore*

CROW SAID, "LOST THE FAITH? What do you mean?"

"Precisely what I said," said Rupert Chandra, folding his arms across his chest. "Hyatt Hilton was unable to believe. I am afraid that we failed him."

"So you kicked him out, just like that?"

"Not at all. But when we discovered that Hyatt was only involved in the church for personal materialistic gain, we asked him to give up his leadership responsibilities. He has always been welcome to remain as one of the Faithful, should he choose to embrace our principles—as is required of any member of the church. Hyatt left of his own volition."

Crow puzzled over that for a second, then understood. "You cut him out of the money."

Rupe shrugged. "Money is of no importance," he murmured.

Crow laughed.

Rupe picked up his cigar and relit it. He puffed several times, building up a good-sized cloud. "What did you say your name was?" he asked.

"Crow."

"Yes. You don't know me, Mr. Crow. I don't know why I should care what you think, but in the unlikely event that you have an open mind, I tell you that I am motivated by two desires only. To live forever, and to show others how they can do so, too. Do you believe in science, Mr. Crow?"

Crow tipped his head a noncommittal five degrees.

"For the past two centuries, human beings have been successfully increasing their lifespans. If you had been born in 1800, you would likely have been dead by the age of forty-eight. If you had been born in 1900, you'd have died at age fifty-nine, on average. Tell me, Mr. Crow, how old are you? Forty?"

Crow frowned. "I'm thirty-six."

"So you've lived half your life, according to the current mortality tables. You are middle-aged."

Crow had never thought of himself as middle-aged before. He didn't like it. "What's your point?"

"You don't like that, do you? The idea that your life is half over?"

"I prefer to think of it as half yet to live."

Rupe grinned and sat back in his chair. "I've got some good news for you. In the first place, since you've already made it to thirty-six, your *statistical* lifespan expectation is somewhere around eighty-five. But it gets even better. By applying logarithms to the acceleration of human lifespans over the past two centuries, science tells us that you will probably make it to one hundred nine. Science has been increasing our statistically expected lifespan at an ever increasing rate. The discovery of antibiotics gave the average human being an extra eight years of life. The invention of the airbag increased it by twenty-seven minutes. The Heimlich maneuver gave us all another fourteen seconds of life—statistically and collectively speaking. Every time one individual lives longer, the average lifespan of the collective increases proportionately. Now let me ask you this, Mr. Crow. If science increases our expected lifespan by more than one year for every year that passes, what do you have?"

"I give up."

"You have eternity. According to our computers, that day is rapidly approaching. We believe that mankind will become statistically immortal in the year 2078."

"Too late," Crow said, "since according to your figures I'm dead at one-o-nine."

"Not for the Amaranthines," said Rupe. "Have you ever heard of telomeres? No? Every strand of DNA in one's body is capped by a tiny strand of protein

called a telomere. These telomeres act as the software that controls cell reproduction. As one grows older, one's telomeres shorten and lose their ability to
replace damaged cells. The body's systems slowly break down. This is what we
call the Death Program. We Amaranthines have extracted the Death Program
from our bodies. We have learned to rejuvenate our telomeres through both
lifestyle changes and highly focused mental exercises. Most important, we believe in what we are doing. You see, Mr. Crow, we are not here for *money*. We
are here for*ever.* The fact that Hyatt Hilton was primarily motivated by mone-
tary forces was precisely the reason he lost his status as church elder. The ACO
is a nonprofit organization. What modest funds we are able to raise go toward
sharing our knowledge, and toward the construction of Stonecrop."

"What is Stonecrop? Some sort of super telomere?"

"Stonecrop is our retreat for the coming millennium, a sanctuary for the
Faithful." The rhythm of Rupe's voice changed. "One limestone brick at a time,
high on the bluffs above the Mississippi River, Stonecrop grows. Like the
mighty white oak, it sends roots deep into the earth, knowing it must stand for
millennia. Like the pyramid of Cheops, it shrugs off wind and rain. Like the
Garden of Eden, it offers peace and perfection. Stonecrop. One Dream, One
Way, One Reality."

Crow said, "You should put that in your annual report."

Rupe drew on his cigar. "We did," he said.

"You really believe this stuff, don't you?"

Rupe spread his arms. "You say you used to know me at Ambrosia Foods.
Three hundred pounds, borderline diabetes, three-pack-a-day cigarette habit.
Look at me now. Of course I believe. If I didn't believe I'd be dead. Believing
is what got me here. Believing is what enabled me to access my cells, to destroy the Death Program. Tell me something, Mr. Crow, do you want to die?"

"I've had my moments," said Crow.

"That's the Death Program." Rupe's nostrils flared. "I can smell it on you.
Beware your desires, Mr. Crow."

Crow said, "So, then, since Hyatt is out of the church, does that mean he's
mortal now?"

"I suspect so. You know, Mr. Crow, it is not necessary to believe in something today in order to believe in it tomorrow. One need only wish for belief."

A response stirred in Crow's sinuses but was preempted by a sound from
outside the office, a sound that began low, like the distant roar of traffic, and
ended high as a dying cat's final shriek of anguish and fury. Rupe stood up so
quickly his thighs hit the front of his desk.

A prickling sensation rose from the back of Crow's neck.

"What was that?" Rupe asked.

"I don't know." Crow walked to the door and opened it, and put his head
cautiously out into the hall. He saw Flowrean Peeche rounding the corner, com-

ing toward him with legs churning, bare feet slapping the tile floor, the whites of her eyes showing as she blew past. Crow expected something or someone to come flying after her—an army of ninjas, perhaps, or a pair of Doberman pinschers. Two seconds passed, but no one seemed to be chasing her.

Behind him, he heard Rupe say, "What was that?"

"That," Crow replied, "was Flowrean Peeche."

It was a law of nature: There would always be one troublemaker at every meeting, whether it was a simple Anti-Aging Clinic, or an actual Extraction Event. Last time it had been Hyatt, spreading his leaflets all over the parking lot. This time, it was a wild woman in a metallic gold faux-snakeskin jacket. Polly made a mental note to reward Chuckles for being so on top of it, for recognizing what was happening and ushering the woman out of the reception before she could do any serious damage.

Other than that, the clinic was going splendidly. Val Frankel had been completely convincing as the aged Mrs. Veronica Frank, and she was perfect playing the part of a thirty-year-old woman which, of course, she was. The Faithful were herding everyone to the tables, laying out the ACO program. If all went well, a solid 20 percent of the Pilgrims would sign up for the next Extraction Event series. Polly was about to invite the few women who seemed unable to tear themselves away from the miraculous Mrs. Frank to join her at the reserved center table when a sound—a horrid, gut-twisting shriek from the hallway—brought all conversation to an abrupt halt. For a moment, two seconds at most, Polly thought that the chatter might resume, as if interrupted by a mere crash of thunder, or a flicker of the lights, but the scream had been too—the word actually occurred to her—*bloodcurdling* to be easily forgotten.

Polly said, in as firm a voice as she could summon, "Excuse me." She gave Val's arm a reassuring squeeze and headed for the door. She motioned to Chip, who had changed out of his toga, to accompany her.

They found Chuckles sitting on the floor in the hallway, looking ashen, holding a bloody, spike-heeled, lime-green pump in his hand. His rose-colored pant leg was dark with blood. Chip turned his head and swallowed.

"Where did she go?" Polly demanded.

Chuckles pointed down the hallway with the bloodied heel.

Blood, especially fresh, warm, wet blood, had a dizzying effect on Chip Bouchet. He could not have said whether it was a good or a bad feeling, but it was certainly intense. He trotted down the hallway after Polly, his stomach rolling, his mouth filled with saliva, black UFOs crowding his vision. He did not understand what had happened, and he was frightened. He saw Polly stop in front of Rupe's open office door. A dark-haired man in a black-and-white-striped referee shirt stepped out into the hall, along with Rupe. Was this a hostage situation? Chip slowed down, forced himself to swallow his mouthful of spit just as a figure in a metallic gold jacket came flying around the corner at the far end of the hallway, a black-haired woman with a wild, trapped expression. Rupe ducked back into his office; Polly stepped in front of the woman, blocking her. Chip couldn't see exactly what happened next, but Polly was suddenly on the floor, and the wild woman was charging directly at him. Chip stepped aside and clotheslined her with one arm as she tried to pass, catching her neck in the crook of his elbow, swinging her into the tile wall. As she bounced off the wall he bore down on her arm, forcing her to fall face-first to the floor. He grabbed her other hand, dropped his knee onto the small of her back and pushed her arm up toward her neck. The rapid sequence of actions occurred without a conscious thought on Chip's part. He did his best work that way.

Polly had risen to her hands and knees. Rupe emerged from his office and tried to help her stand up. The woman beneath Chip was writhing and growling, trying to buck him off. "Get off me you goddamn ape!"

Chip wasn't going to let go until he received orders from his superiors. The man in the referee shirt, who had stood by and watched Polly get bowled over, walked up to Chip, put his hands on his knees and bent forward, getting his face a few inches from Chip's nostrils.

"Let her up, Sarge," he said.

Chip tried to see past him to Polly and Rupe, but the referee blocked his view.

"Get off her," the man said.

The woman growled, "You heard him. Get off me before I break that ugly nose of yours."

"Stand back," Chip said to the referee. "The situation is contained."

The man reached out and inserted one finger into each of Chips nostrils and lifted. Chip's head followed his nose. The weight came off his knee. The woman exploded beneath him, was on her feet and running down the hall in an instant. Chip jerked his head back, disengaging the fingers, and struck out with his fist, hitting nothing—the referee had jumped back out of range.

Chip spread his arms wide and advanced on the striped shirt, his nose throbbing. He heard Rupe shouting something, but his anger garbled the words. The referee held his palms out, backing away. Chip lunged forward. The guy tried to dodge, but Chip caught one of the striped sleeves in his left hand and came around hard with his right fist, grinding it into the guy's kidney, swinging again and hitting him on top of the head, grabbing the shirt with both hands and slamming him against the wall, then getting in two more shots, right under the ribcage, each punch producing a satisfying gasp from the referee. Chip let go and stepped back; the guy slid down the wall, arms hugging his midsection.

Rupe's voice came into focus. "That's enough, Chip, okay?" He had his hands on Chip's arm, pulling him back.

Polly asked Rupe, "Who is he?"

"He says his name is Crow. He knows Hyatt. Do you think we should call an ambulance?"

Crow, breathing shallowly, began to get up.

"Hit him again," Polly said to Chip.


Chuckles wondered when he'd had his last tetanus shot. Did being immortal mean he didn't have to worry about tetanus? He believed in the Amaranthine principles. He truly did. But he also believed that if the spike heel had gone in a little deeper and crushed his femoral artery, he'd be one dead immortal. He decided right then and there to get a tetanus booster. Chuckles believed in many things, but most of all he believed in covering his ass.

He heard shouting from down the hall. Apparently they'd caught her. Putting all his weight on his good leg, Chuckles stood up and hopped toward the sounds. He wanted to see her again, see if she was as scary and as beautiful as he remembered. He was almost to the intersection of the two hallways when she appeared, shoeless now, charging at him. Chuckles spread his arms to intercept her. She slid to a halt, gasping for breath, her eyes darting from side to side, seeking a way around him.

Chuckles said, "Hey, just take it easy, okay? Nobody wants to do nothing."

She was on her toes, chiseled calves quivering.

"How about I walk you to your car? How that be?" He lowered his arms. "Then you just go, okay? That's all."

She took a step toward him. He backed away, giving her all the space she needed.

"My name's Charles," he said, moving to one side of the narrow hallway. He heard what sounded like blows and angry voices from back by the offices.

"What's happening back there?" he asked.

The woman licked her lips and edged closer to the opposite wall.

"I guess it don't matter," he said.

They moved slowly down the hallway, six feet between them, Chuckles limping from his wound, leaving a trail of red droplets, the woman tense as a drawn bow.

"What's your name?" he asked.

She said something that sounded like "Flow Reen." Her voice was low, with a sexy buzz to it.

"That's a nice name," Chuckles said, meaning it, but not trusting himself to repeat it accurately. They passed the gymnasium and were within sight of the exit.

She picked up her pace slightly. "I gotta go," she said. Suddenly she was running again, her phenomenal legs pumping, bare feet slapping the linoleum. Chuckles smiled and watched, making no attempt to pursue her, simply enjoying the feeling he was getting in his chest. It had been a while, but he remembered the sensation clearly. It was the feeling of falling in love.

*A trash container is but a repository for unrealized opportunities.*

*—Harley Johnson*

**A**RNOLD SCHWARZENEGGER: BLACK LEATHER JACKET, wraparound shades, and fifty pounds of Hollywood artillery gazed out across Beaut Miller's cluttered bedroom. Beaut licked his lips and looked from the Terminator to the disposable syringe, from the syringe to the image of his own pimpled ass in the mirror.

"Aw, shit," he said through gritted teeth as he punched the needle into his left glute. "Shit, shit, shit," he said, squeezing his eyes shut and ramming the plunger home. The solution of testosterone propionate spiked with five units of Humulin entered his gluteus maximus at fifty-eight degrees below body temperature, producing a starburst of pain. Beaut jerked the needle free with a gasp. He blinked tearily at the poster of Arnold, who did not know the meaning of the word "pain," and recapped the syringe. He'd been using the same needle for a couple weeks now. It was getting dull.

But the stuff was working. He massaged his ass gingerly, then tugged up his shorts and limped back to the kitchen to finish his Mass Driver 4000 Hi-Protein, Pre-anabolic Power Shake, his fourth one that day. That was the thing about stacking insulin with testosterone. Hungry all the time. But man, was he growing. In five weeks he'd added fifty-two pounds, a good third of it solid muscle. Little Leslie Miller was a big boy now.

He thought, as he often did these days, about Joe Crow.

♠

Arling Biggle, sitting in his massage chair in front of the TV, looked up as Beaut lumbered into the living room carrying the blender bowl. Bigg hit the mute button on the TV remote and switched the chair control to a gentle lumbar stroking. He watched Beaut dig into the blender with a tablespoon and shovel a mound of yellow goo into his mouth. Beaut liked his Mass Driver shakes thick, the consistency of wet cement. The denser the shake, according to Beaut, the harder the resulting muscle. Beaut's science may have been suspect but, Bigg had to admit, his recent gains had been impressive. The guy was growing like a tumor.

Bigg asked, "What are you sticking in your ass this week?"

Beaut, his mouth overloaded with Mass Driver, could only shake his head.

"More testosterone?" Bigg guessed.

Beaut nodded.

"You still mixing in the insulin?"

Beaut shrugged.

Bigg said, "You're gonna get fat."

Beaut swallowed, his powerful neck muscles forcing the glob of wet protein powder down his esophagus. "Muhgugage*ggig*," he said.

"Say what?"

Beaut held up a hand, went back into the kitchen and swallowed a pint of water from the faucet. He returned to the living room and repeated, "I'm gonna get *big*."

"Yeah, right. You're gonna be this huge motherfucker." Bigg made an adjustment to the chair control, getting some of that side-to-side action.

For the past three months, Bigg had been letting Beaut stay at his house. He had plenty of room. Besides, he enjoyed having the younger man around. Beaut reminded Bigg of himself, twenty years ago. Only maybe not so bright. Bigg had been living alone for too long—three years since Toanie had left him for a former Mr. Iowa, then moved to Santa Barbara, the bitch. Yeah, it was good to have company, although he was somewhat concerned about Beaut's increased steroid intake. The 'roids were basically safe and effective drugs, Bigg believed. If he didn't believe that, he wouldn't have used them himself for twenty years. But like any other drug—heroin, caffeine, cough medicine—it was possible to overdo it. The way Beaut was growing these past few weeks, something had to give. Either the guy was going to blow a vessel, or fly into a 'roid rage and get himself in more trouble than Bigg could get him out of. Either way, Bigg would lose an employee.

"You can't just keep shooting the same shit in your ass every day, weeks and weeks. Especially the testosterone. You got to cycle. Take a couple weeks off, then go back on the Deca. And bag the insulin. You don't need it."

"The Deca didn't work."

"It works. You just have to give it time. You can't get bigger every day, Leslie. Give it a rest."

"I'm benching four twenty."

"Yeah, and you got zits all over your ass and bitch tits comin' off your pecs and in another couple weeks your 'nads are gonna be the size of Tic-Tacs."

"Screw my 'nads," Beaut said, "I'll get implants."

"Can I tell you something?" Bigg asked. "I mean, as a friend."

Beaut shrugged. "Sure."

"You're an idiot."

"Screw you."

"And you gotta open up in six hours."

That was part of the deal. As long as he stayed in Bigg's house, Beaut had to open the gym every morning.


Beaut finished spooning the Mass Driver into his mouth. Maybe he'd get lucky tomorrow. Maybe Joe Crow would show up at the gym and give him some shit, make some wise-ass crack, bump into him or something. Beaut imagined his fist driving into Crow's chest, shattering ribs, punching his heart out through his spine. But Crow hadn't shown his smarmy little face at the gym all week. Maybe he was scared. Beaut had caught him staring a couple times, gawking at Beaut's increasing mass. Maybe he was scared off for good.

Deep beneath slabs of muscle and fat, Little Leslie Miller breathed a sigh of relief.


Axel lay beside Sophie in their bed, flat on his back, doing a mental inventory of his abdomen. He visualized each of his major organs—heart, lungs, liver, kidneys, pancreas—attempting to imagine its precise shape, location, and condition. He added in his gastrointestinal tract, bladder, and spleen. Was that everything? He raised his head and looked toward his feet. In the faint light filtering through the window, his naked belly formed a pale horizon.

Something was in there. He was sure of it. For over a month now, ever since he'd accepted the fact that the wedding would be going forward, Axel had felt wrong inside, as if all his cares had taken up physical residence in the vicinity of his stomach. For some reason, it sent him back about thirty years.

A friend of his, Grace Lee, one of the last of the old-time fan dancers, had got herself knocked up. She and her carny husband, a ride boy twenty years her junior, had been terrifically proud of her delicate condition, but five months into her pregnancy the ride boy had jumped the train in Des Moines, and a week later the fetus had died, still inside her. Axel remembered seeing her that year, working the Minnesota State Fair midway. He'd stopped by her trailer to pay his respects, and she'd told him all about it. He remembered the way he'd felt when she'd told him she had a dead baby inside her, and he remembered asking her why she didn't go to the hospital and have them take it out, and her telling him, standing there in her feather boa, face covered with glitter and paint, that it wasn't natural, that the doctors said the dead child would come out of its own accord when it was good and ready and, besides, she didn't have no insurance. She'd carried that dead fetus inside her for another four weeks, doing her fan dance from Omaha to Minneapolis to Ohio and never missing a call, before it let loose.

Whatever Axel was carrying inside him, it was sure as hell no dead fetus. It was the wedding. Carmen wanted money for her wedding gown? Axel would write the check and keep his misgivings inside. If Sophie wanted to tell him in excruciating detail about the nuts and bolts of the imminent ceremony, Axel would listen, let her words pour into his ears, and drain right down into his gut. When he thought of things to say back to her, or to Carmen, he put those away, too. They were all there, someplace inside him.

Sophie muttered and rolled onto her side. Axel closed his eyes and renewed his efforts to visualize his insides. He saw something, a long dark serpentine form, twining around his liver, disappearing into a snarl of intestine. One day it would slither out, probably the moment the wedding was over, and he would be free. He thought then he might understand how Grace Lee had felt letting loose of that ride boy's dead baby.

After that whole thing with Joe Crow, Axel had simply given up. He had asked Joe to *discreetly* check out Hyatt Hilton. Or something like that. Whatever he'd said to Crow, he had clearly intended it to be low key. He hadn't asked Crow to threaten Hyatt with a shotgun. He hadn't planned for Sophie to get wind of the investigation. The whole thing had blown up in his face, and now everybody was mad at him, including his best friend, Sam, who thought his kid walked on water.

Well, hell. All he could do now was hunker down and let matters take their own course. Maybe Hyatt Hilton wasn't such a bad guy. Maybe he should consider letting the kid in on the concession business, introduce him to the space rental guy at the fair. Maybe help him set up a concession to sell that fancy French water of his.

Axel ground his teeth together and buried those thoughts, feeding them to the snake along with the rest of the garbage that had been infecting his mind. All he wanted was for it to be done and over with so he could get back to running his business. He had ordered a custom Conita grill for the back of the Taco Shop. He'd lined up his new suppliers, ordered the new signage, and convinced space rental to approve the menu addition. One more week and the whole wedding thing would be out of the way. He felt like a convict with seven days left on a ten-year bid, unable to sleep for worrying over all the things that might happen before he walked out those gates.

It had taken Vince Mudge years to figure out what to tell people who asked him what he did. For a while, back in the seventies, he had called himself a garbage man. He had liked the uncomplicatedness of it, and the way people blinked and tried not to recoil. During the boom years of the eighties, however, Vince became self-conscious about his profession. The guys he had grown up with had all turned into suits—doctors, lawyers, accountants, stockbrokers—real jobs. Vince was just a garbage man. He tried calling himself a sanitation engineer, but most people were smart enough to figure that one out, so he had taken to simply telling people he worked for Browning-Ferris Industries and leaving it at that.

Within the last year, after twenty-two years of tipping dumpsters, Vince had finally settled into a Zen-like acceptance of his lot in life. With acceptance came new levels of skill, and with skill came pride. He began to think of himself as a recycling specialist and would tell anyone within earshot exactly what he did five days a week, seven and a half hours per day.

Vince's most popular stories were those involving curious things that he had found in dumpsters. He had once found a computer, brand new, still in its box, which he had later sold for twelve hundred dollars. Empty purses and wallets were common. By his own calculation, Vince had emptied more than sixty thousand dumpsters. Sometimes, he thought he had seen it all.

He had found cats, dogs, raccoons, and opossums, both dead and alive. He had found human body parts, including a hand and a complete set of male genitalia. He had found sleeping winos and bag ladies, and he had once found a bride and groom in the act of consummating their marriage.

But he had never before found a referee.

Crow heard his alarm clock go off: screee, screee, screee. It sounded like a dump truck backing up. He flailed at the snooze button, but could not find it. Suddenly his bed was grabbed by a giant, convulsing lobster. Crow grabbed his pillow. The foot of the bed began to rise, accompanied by a grinding, scraping, howling sound.

Crow opened his eyes. For one full second, he remained completely disoriented. He was half-buried in plastic bags, and the sky was moving. Then the smell penetrated his awakening consciousness. He experienced a small but crucial epiphany: stink, garbage, dumpster, dumping! He fought his way free of the bags, caught the rusty metal lip of the dumpster, pulled himself over the edge, and tumbled to the ground. The impact of his shoulder hitting concrete nearly caused him to pass out. He rolled out from the shadow of the rising dumpster, got to his feet, staggered a few yards, and collapsed. The grinding, whining noise ceased. Crow heard a voice.

"You okay?"

Crow pushed up with his arms, felt hands under his shoulders, lifting. He stood up and turned to face the dumpster and the man who had been operating the lift arms.

"Jeez, mister, what were you doing in there?" The dumpster operator was a solid, compact, middle-aged man with a concerned demeanor. His brown baseball cap read: "BFI."

Crow shook his head, but stopped immediately when he felt his brain banging off the walls of his skull. "I don't know," he said.

"You look sorta beat up, mister. Some softball team didn't like the way you called 'em?"

"Where am I?" Crow asked.

"Behind the old Fitzgerald school. You want I should call an ambulance?"

"No, that's okay." It was coming back to him. Crow felt his pockets for his keys. "I think my car's still out front." He remembered pretty much all of it now, right up to the moment the guy called Chip had hit him the third or fourth time. "What time is it?"

"About five."

"In the *morning?*"

"That's right."

He had spent the entire night in the dumpster. He thought about asking the garbageman what day it was, but then thought of a better question.

"How old do you think I am?"

The garbageman squinted at him. "I dunno. Forty? Forty-five?"

Crow winced. "Thanks a lot."

"You sure you're okay?"

"For a middle-aged guy who just spent the night in a dumpster? Yeah, I'm feeling great." He walked away, feeling far older than anyone would have guessed.

One meets his destiny often in the road he takes to avoid it.

—French Proverb

"WHAT ABOUT NAMES, HY?" Carmen said.

Hyatt looked up from the paper. "What?"

Carmen cracked an egg into the batter and stirred. "Do you want blueberries? I bought some blueberries."

Hyatt said, "Sure. I like blueberries." He was worried about Carmen. She'd been spacier than usual lately. And she was actually cooking, making pancakes from scratch. He couldn't remember her ever making anything more challenging than macaroni-and-cheese from a box, and here she was, first thing in the morning, making blueberry pancakes. Getting all domestic on him. "What are you talking about, 'names'?"

"For the baby. What should we name it?"

Hyatt scratched his nose with a long forefinger. "What baby is that?"

"*My* baby."

"Carmen, doll, you aren't having a baby."

"I mean, what if I was? What would we name it?"

Hyatt folded the newspaper. He said, thinking to humor her, "How about 'Rasputin'?"

Carmen made a face and shook her head. A small chunk of pillow foam fell from her hair, which was still mussed from sleeping, and landed on her cotton nightgown. She looked, Hyatt thought, like a young mother-to-be, letting herself go now that she'd captured her hubby's seed.

"I was thinking, if it's a girl, we could name her Courtney. Or if it's a boy we could name him Sterling."

The scene was giving Hyatt flashbacks to a life he'd never led. Sitting in a kitchen with his pancake-cooking fiancée, reading the funnies, talking about baby names. He decided it would be safest to say nothing further. Carmen dumped a pint of blueberries into the batter. "Are you excited about the wedding?" she asked, stirring with a dreamy smile.

This was a time to stay focused on business, and here she was drifting off into la-la land, Hyatt thought. He had seen it before, the salesman believing his own pitch, the actor caught in a role, the politician making promises he actually intended to keep. Maybe he should just let her be there—wherever the hell she was.

"Sure," he said. "I'm excited."

"You're going to love my dress."

"I'm sure. How's your mom doing?"

"She's totally into it." She poured a ladle full of batter into the frying pan. "Damn!"

"What's wrong?"

"I forgot to turn the pan on." She poured the batter from the pan to the bowl, rinsed the pan, put it back on the stove, this time firing up the burner. "I never really learned to cook."

"Carm, when the money starts rolling in, you'll never have to crack another egg. We'll hire a cook."

"We can get a nanny, too."

"Don't space out on me, Carm."

"Don't you worry about me." A minute later she tried pouring another pancake, and this time was rewarded by a sizzle and the sweet smell of hot blueberries.

"I'm not worried," Hyatt lied.

"Good." Carmen lifted a corner of the pancake with a spatula. "Suppose we have twins," she said. "What would we name the twins?"

Hyatt sighed. "Beavis and Butt-head?"

"No, I mean if they were girls."


Crow woke up in his own bed, again. After finding himself in that dumpster last Saturday, each morning had arrived with a note of fear and uncertainty. He wasn't sure until he opened his eyes that his pillow was not a Hefty bag. He might find himself in another bed, or another dumpster, or tied to railroad tracks, or in free fall, or in the wrong body. Could be anywhere. But this morning, once again, he found himself in his own rumpled bed with a cat sleeping between his knees.

He sat up and worked his tongue around in his mouth. The sensation was revolting. He stood up carefully and made his way to the bathroom, where he brushed his teeth and threw handfuls of cool water on his face.

The cuts on his unshaven cheek and lower lip had nearly healed. Maybe he could shave today. The sclera of his left eye, with its broken blood vessel, was clearing up nicely, the red giving way to streaky yellow. Bending forward no longer produced shooting pains in his torso, and the ache in his right shoulder had taken on a distant quality.

He fed Milo and made a cup of coffee for himself, then went to sit on his porch swing to watch the rush hour traffic hurtling along First Avenue toward downtown Minneapolis. He'd been watching the traffic a lot lately.

Sometime during the past week, Crow had rounded a bend in his quest for self-improvement. Rather than adding new items to his compendium of poker wisdom, he had been reading and rereading his rules, searching for enlightenment, and had discovered that he had broken no fewer than five of his promises to himself, which had led directly to his dumpster adventure.

*If you don't know the rules, don't play.*

He had gone to the Anti-Aging Clinic blind, without knowing who or what to expect. He had learned nothing much other than that he had somehow entered middle age, that Hyatt Hilton had been excommunicated for lack of faith, and that Flowrean Peeche did not always reek.

*Don't try to play someone else's hand.*

Without a clue as to why Flowrean Peeche had been at the Anti-Aging Clinic, Crow had taken her side in an altercation. For all he knew, she had deserved to be knocked down by the toga man. Maybe she had stolen something, or committed some other transgression. Crow had acted impulsively, siding with the underdog.

*Never play uninvited.*

Axel had clearly asked him to leave the game, yet he had continued to play.

*Play to win, or don't play.*

With nothing at stake, there was nothing to win.

*Do not play in wild card games.*

As near as he could tell, all the cards in this game were wild.

Crow felt the weight of his own foolishness pressing in on his chest. He had let himself be drawn to the Amaranthine Church because, like the other Pilgrims at the Anti-Aging Clinic, he'd been trying to fill a hole in his life. Like a child misbehaving, he had sought out punishment as an alternative to boredom. Now he had sentenced himself to the ultimate boredom of being with his own middle-aged self for days on end.

His body was healing. He was not so sure about his other parts.

*When you have the nuts, squeeze.*

—*Crow's rules*

**F**ORGET ABOUT IT, CROW. WALK *away from those people.*

Debrowski heard the echo of her own wise words. Easy advice to give.

She speared a cold *frite* with her fork, raised it to her lips, and bit off the tip. She had been working her way through the mound of deep-fried potato sticks for nearly an hour. The waiter had been stopping by every four or five minutes to pick up her unpaid check, examine it with a portentous frown, then slip it back beneath her coffee cup.

Debrowski didn't care. She had the perfect table, the weather was flawless, and she was well on her way to not giving a shit what anybody on this side of the Atlantic thought about anything whatsoever.

*Walk away from those people.*

The *Les Hommes* project was doomed. Even if they were able to complete the CD, René would make the process hell for her. She might never earn a franc and, if she did, it would be money hard won. When the mix sours, it is best to walk. The financial rewards were never worth it.

But she had never walked away before.

The waiter again approached her table, said something in French. Debrowski let the words roll off her, not bothering to translate, and lit a cigarette. If only she could maintain such insouciance, perhaps she could work with *Les Hommes.*

Impossible. Unacceptable.

The thought of two, or three, or four more weeks dealing with René was unbearable. But to simply board the RER for Orly, to fly back home defeated . . . that would be equally intolerable.

She stood, dropped two twenty-franc notes on the table, and walked out onto the boulevard. Only one person could help with her decision, and that was René himself. She might as well get it done.

René Missett lived above a small bakery on Casimir-Delavigne. He answered his door wearing nothing but a pair of cotton briefs.

"Ah," he said. "The American Cunt." He stepped back, inviting her to enter with a smile and a sweep of the arm. Debrowski stepped into the small one-room apartment. She had never visited René at home before and was surprised to find a neat and orderly space. His meager collection of books was neatly shelved as were his CDs and record albums. His furniture consisted of three plastic chairs, a small folding table, and a neatly made bed. The room smelled of yeast and baking bread. René stood very close to her. His breath smelled like cheese.

Debrowski said, "I thought we should talk."

"I agree!" said René. He gestured toward the bed. "Would you like to sit down?"

Debrowski remained standing. René shrugged and dropped onto the edge of the bed. Debrowski let her eyes examine his body. Unclothed, it was much as she had expected. René Missett was an extremely attractive man. At twenty-six years old, a good age for a man to be, he showed no signs of fat. His muscles were taut, his skin free from blemishes. He would make a beautiful pop icon.

With a twinge of regret, and of relief, Debrowski realized that she had made her decision.

"I'm walking," she said.

René wrinkled his brow, not sure he understood.

"I wanted to say it to you in person. I'm leaving the project."

René's eyes widened. "Ah!"

Debrowski started for the door.

René stepped in front of her. "Wait."

Debrowski waited.

"A goodbye kiss," said René.

Debrowski said, "Do not touch me." She wanted him to touch her.

René's eyes dropped to her hands, checking to make sure she wasn't wielding another Perrier bottle. Seeing nothing resembling a weapon, he reached out with his long arms and placed his hands on her cheeks.

"Take your hands off me," said Debrowski. Her voice, level and calm, detached itself from her body and filled the space between their faces. René's hands pressed in on her face, forcing her mouth open. Debrowski stepped into his embrace, slipping one hand into the front of his briefs. Her hand slid past the base of his hardening penis, located a testicle. She squeezed, digging in with her nails, draining all of her strength into the fingers of her right hand.

René gasped and shoved her head back, hard. Debrowski felt a sharp burning sensation in her neck, but she hung on as René pounded her body with one fist while grabbing her wrist with the other. She held on for what seemed like minutes, though it could not have been more than a few seconds until René's flailing fists found a spot on her arm that caused her hand to go slack, releasing him. Debrowski remained standing. René dropped to his knees, moaning, one hand cupping his groin. Debrowski took a step back, then walked around him and let herself out of the apartment.

Everything hurt. How many times had he hit her? Spikes of pain traveled up her neck into the base of her skull. Her chest, shoulder, and arm throbbed, and every finger in her hand pulsed painfully. Had she hurt him enough? Had she made her point? She stepped out of the building into the evening light. A man stood outside the bakery cleaning the sidewalk with a hose. Debrowski looked at her hand. Her palm was slick with blood. Bits of flesh were embedded beneath her fingernails, and coils of dark pubic hair had caught between her fingers. She suppressed a wave of revulsion, walked over to the man with the hose, and plunged her hands into the stream of water. The man held the hose steady, saying nothing, and let her finish washing.

"Merci," said Debrowski.

The baker shrugged. "You're welcome," he said.

*Remember, people are not cards.*

—*Crow's rules*

JOE CROW SAT UP, DISORIENTED, groping for the ringing phone. He found it, pressed the talk button, put it to his ear. "Hello?" He was home, in his own bed. He cleared his throat. "Hello?" he said again, more clearly this time.

An extended moment of silence followed. Another sales call. He could see some guy in a cubicle searching his call list, trying to remember which number he'd dialed. Crow got tired of waiting and said, "No thank you." He turned off the phone and set it on his bedstand. Where had he been? Asleep, someplace interesting. He closed his eyes, hoping to reenter the dream he'd been having.

The phone began to ring again. He let it go a few times, then answered.

"Is this Joe Crow?" A woman's voice, deeper than Debrowski's.

"Yes," he said.

"Are you okay?"

"Who is this?"

"This is Flowrean. Flo."

Crow sat up. "Flowrean?"

"I work out at Bigg's?"

"I know."

"I saw you at that meeting. Are you okay? I haven't seen you at the gym. I wondered if you were okay."

"I'm fine."

"You haven't gone out all week. I wanted to make sure you were okay."

Crow said, "How do you know I haven't gone out all week?"

"I mean, I haven't seen you at Bigg's," Flowrean said quickly. "I just thought, you helped me, I just—I wanted to make sure you were okay."

"Like I said, I'm fine. What was that all about, anyway?"

"At that meeting?"

"Yes."

"You know the lady that got younger?"

Crow nodded. His whiskers scraped the mouthpiece of the phone. "Uh-huh."

"It wasn't real."

"I know that."

"A man grabbed me. I had to get away."

"What were you doing there in the first place?"

Flowrean took a moment to reply. "Nothing," she said.

"You were doing nothing?"

"I'll tell you. Would you like to go to dinner with me?"

Crow imagined himself sitting in a restaurant, very elegant, watching the flies buzzing about Flowrean's rotting goldfish. He said, "I'm flattered, but—"

"Lunch," Flowrean interrupted. "Have *lunch* with me."

"Lunch?"

"We have to *talk*," said Flowrean.

Crow found Flowrean Peeche already seated at one of Figlio's sidewalk tables, sipping an ice tea. He had suggested the outdoor restaurant hoping for a breeze, but his precaution turned out to be unnecessary. Flo's dead-fish necklace was nowhere in evidence. She looked clean and strong and beautiful in a sleeveless chocolate-colored silk top, jeans, and multicolored high-heeled sandals. The midday sun brought out red and blue reflections in her thick black hair. Her eyes were hidden by a pair of dark sunglasses with small octagonal lenses.

Crow sat down across from her.

"Sorry I'm late," he said.

"I just got here myself."

The waiter appeared with menus. Flowrean ordered a salad. Crow scanned the menu, found nothing that interested him, and ordered a Coke and a club sandwich.

"The Figlio Club?" the waiter asked.

"But of course," sighed Crow. He asked Flowrean how her workouts had been going.

"I'm working on my arms," she said, squeezing her fists and looking down at her left biceps. "Every other day now." She looked at her other biceps.

"Your arms are sensational," said Crow. On most women, arms that size would look freakish, but on Flowrean they looked good. "You ever compete?"

Flowrean shook her head and relaxed. "I do it just for me."

"That's best."

"It's good to be strong."

"I know what you mean."

"I think you're very strong."

Crow laughed and shook his head. "Not like some of those guys. Not like Beaut Miller."

"Beaut is weak."

"I mean physically. Last time I saw him he looked like his skin was going to burst. He's got to be on the 'roids."

"Steroids are for the weak. Beaut is every way weak." Flowrean leaned forward, hooked a forefinger over the bridge of her sunglasses and pulled them down toward the tip of her nose. "You are strong. That's why I like you."

Crow held her eyes for a moment, then looked away. He had made a mistake, coming here. "Tell me," he said, "how did you happen to be at that anti-aging thing?"

"I followed you," said Flowrean Peeche.

"You did?"

"Yes. I've been stalking you."

*N.W. Flt 222 Arr 6:05 p Friday.*

Crow drew a box around the note, then made a decorative border for the box. The phone message from Debrowski had made him lightheaded with pleasure and fear—an erotic stirring combined with breathlessness. How long?

Three months? Would it be the same? Would *she* be the same? His thoughts drifted, settled on the last time he'd seen her, standing on the sidewalk as his cab pulled away. He remembered the sick feeling in his belly. Had she wanted him to stay? No, she was the one who had told him to leave. He had simply suggested the possibility. Wasn't that how it had happened? Maybe he should have stayed another week, learned a few words of French to please her.

He noticed that he was drawing little croissants. What was this scrap of paper? He turned it over. His invitation to Carmen and Hyatt's wedding. Saturday. Would Debrowski want to go to a wedding? Would that be too strange? A wedding with jet lag?

Crow stood abruptly and went into the bathroom to look at himself in the mirror.

*The man sitting in your seat is the one to watch out for.*

His body had changed since he had seen her last. Would she like it? He flexed his biceps, then pictured Flowrean Peeche standing beside him, comparing arms. Hers were bigger. Maybe in the morning he'd get over to the gym, get back into his routine.

Flowrean had taken rejection well. He had been as gentle as possible, explaining to her that he was involved in a long-term relationship with another woman. He had told her a few things about Debrowski.

Flowrean listened, eating her salad, her gold eyes moving quickly, scanning him, pausing for an instant on each of his parts. Crow felt them hot on his forehead, his cheek, his neck, his lips. He spoke rapidly, repeating himself, watching the romaine lettuce disappear into her wide mouth, waiting for a sign that she understood, or for her to interrupt him, but Flowrean simply ate and watched him talking.

When he finally ran out of things to say, she dabbed her dark lips with her napkin. "You are very attractive."

"Well . . . thank you. You aren't going to keep following me, are you?"

Flowrean shrugged. "This Debrowski, you really like her?"

"Yeah, I do."

"What if it doesn't work out?"

"I don't think that's going to happen."

Flowrean pursed her lips and leaned forward. "She makes you more attractive. She is like a fence around you."

Crow thought he understood, but he was surprised to hear it coming from this young bodybuilder. He bit into his "Figlio Club." It was pretty good.

"Or maybe she is like a silk tie," Flowrean continued. "You could take her off for a while."

Crow shook his head and swallowed. "No, I couldn't. I'm sorry."

Flowrean said, "Okay then." Her shoulders relaxed. She sat back and smiled. "I'm happy for you. I won't follow you no more."

Crow believed her. He didn't know why he believed her, but he did. She seemed relieved that he was not available, as if now she could devote herself to other, more important pursuits. He was slightly miffed. As much as Flowrean's unwanted attention had disturbed him, he hated to think that her feelings toward him could so easily dissolve.

He said, "You're a very attractive woman. Under different circumstances, things would be different."

Flowrean wrinkled her brow. "That sounds like something Beaut would say. If things were different, of course they'd be different."

Embarrassed, Crow searched his mind for a way out. "Tell me something," he said. "In the women's locker room, on the wall that faces Bigg's office. What's there?"

Flowrean thought for a moment. "Lockers?"

"You sure?"

She thought some more. "No. That's where the mirror is."

Crow nodded. "I thought maybe."

"Why?"

"It's just an idea I had. I was wondering why every time you use the locker room Bigg locks himself in his office, that's all."

"Oh," Flowrean said. *"Oh!"* To Crow's surprise, she laughed delightedly. "Really? Bigg's been *watching* me?"

"That's what I think."

"That's funny."

"It is?"

"I've been spying on you, and Bigg's been spying on me. Are you spying on anybody, Joe Crow?"

Crow shook his head. "Not anymore."

It had been awkward, both of them trying to pay the bill, but Crow had walked away feeling as though he'd done right. He had been honest, kind, and had not allowed himself to think of Flowrean Peeche as a potential lover. He could meet Debrowski at the airport without feeling guilty. He imagined himself putting his arms around her, letting her feel his newly hardened body. It would be great to see her again. Really great.

He did not completely understand why the thought of it made him feel a little sick inside. Maybe he was afraid that she had changed, too.


Buck Manelli's favorite time of day was about 3:15 in the afternoon. His favorite place was the second booth from the back at the Courthouse Bar and Grill, and his favorite level of intoxication arrived midway through his fourth martini. That was when he felt closest to God, adrift in a heavenly fog, floating from one truth to another as a pilgrim visits shrines in the Holy Land, or something like that. He should write some of these things down, use them in a wedding sometime. Or use them in his book *The Marriage Maker.* He'd thought up the title a few years back. All he needed was to marry a few celebrities, or marry some couple who would get famous somehow, so his name would get picked up by the media. If it ever happened, he would write that book.

Buck waved to Hal, the bartender. He pointed at his depleted martini glass and laughed. "Ha ha ha ha ha!" Hal nodded and set about constructing Buck's number-four martini, his daily ticket to Nirvana.

Half an hour later Buck found himself on the downslope, trying to level off with a few beers, when Hy the Guy slipped into the seat across from him holding a tall drink with a straw in it and a cherry on top.

Buck said, "What the hell do you call that?" He had become surly during his number-five martini.

"John Collins," Hyatt said.

"*Tom* Collins," Buck corrected, adding, "you fucking idiot."

That made Hyatt sit back, startled. Buck laughed, "*Ha ha ha ha ha ha ha ha,*" an extended version of his usual outburst. Saying the word "fuck" out loud always made him a little giddy, like a bottle of champagne uncorked.

"Actually," Hyatt said, looking hurt, "it's a *John* Collins. They make it with ginger ale." He bent over the drink and sipped through the straw.

Buck blinked, not sure what to do with that bit of information. "How the *fuck* did you know to find me here?"

Hyatt tipped his head, looking amused and puzzled. He said, "When I called you this morning, you said I could meet you here."

"Oh." He watched Hyatt eat his cherry, the bright red orb leaving blue-green afterimages on his retinas. "Where the *fuck* is Maraschino, anyway?" The problem with the "f" word was that it lost power as fast as a sputtering party balloon.

"It's in California," Hyatt said. He worked the cherry stem over to the corner of his mouth. "So listen, Buck, I don't want to take up too much of your time. What I wanted to ask you is—man to man—when you marry us, me and Carmen, is there something you can do? Forget to file some papers, or say the wrong words during the ceremony, you know, so that we aren't really legally married?"

Buck was offended. "I won't screw it up," he said, trading in the "f" word for its more acceptable alternative.

"You don't understand. I mean, what would it *take* for you to screw it up? Could you—for instance, if you forget to say 'I now pronounce you husband and wife?' Would the marriage be illegal then?"

Buck gaped. Was this guy for real?

"You don't want to get married?" he asked, staring at the cherry stem sticking out from between Hy's lips.

"I want to *get* married," Hyatt said. "I just don't want to *be* married."

*Raise or fold.*

*—Crow's rules*

**S**OPHIE LIT ONE OF HER long brown cigarettes and watched her daughter open-ing envelopes, the last of the RSVPs before they had to let the caterer know how many guests to expect. As each envelope revealed its contents, she could see by the expression on Carmen's face whether it was a yes or a regrets.

Mostly, the returns had been running in favor of regrets, much to Sophie's relief.

They had mailed nearly five hundred invitations. Three dozen to Sophie's friends and relatives, half as many to Axel's acquaintances, including his bitchy sister in California, another thirty-four to high school friends of Carmen's, and the remaining four hundred to a list provided by Hyatt Hilton. Sophie had balked when Hyatt had presented his original list, which had contained close to six hundred names.

"I didn't know you had so many friends," Sophie had remarked.

"Don't worry," he had told her, "most of them won't be able to come. We probably won't have to feed more than a couple hundred."

"Two *hundred*? There's no way Axel will pay for that!"

Hyatt had agreed to cut back, but they had still ended up with four hundred names for Hyatt's side of the aisle.

Later, while addressing the envelopes, she noticed that Hyatt had invited the governor, both Minnesota senators, a horde of local television and radio per-sonalities, and Conrad Hilton who, she thought, had been dead for years. Hyatt had also invited the entire Minnesota Twins baseball team and the CEOs of 3M, General Mills, Cargill, Dayton Hudson, and Honeywell. She almost de-cided to cull the list herself without saying anything to Hyatt, but the possibil-ity, however slim, that Hyatt actually *knew* some of those people seduced her into completing her task. The idea of the governor coming to her daughter's wedding, no matter how unlikely, made the cost and effort worthwhile.

Thus far, the only public figure to have accepted the invitation was Billy Budd, a pro wrestler who was familiar to TV viewers as the spokesperson for Wally Wenger's Truck Country, a Roseville GMC dealer. Wally Wenger himself had declined. Most of Hyatt's other invitees had simply not responded.

"How many do we have so far?" Sophie asked.

Carmen consulted a sheet of paper. "About eighty all together. Hy's going to be real disappointed."

"It'll be big enough. There were only about eighteen people at mine."

"Yeah, and look what happened."

"The wedding had nothing to do with it. Your father turned out to be a jerk."

"That won't happen with Hy." She laughed. "He's a jerk already."

"That's not funny. Axel's spending a fortune on this."

"Axel has money."

"You're even getting a limousine. I don't know why you need a limousine."

"Trust me, Mom. We need the limo."


Beaut Miller felt like a six-foot-four-inch hard-on, pumped from his bulging traps to the tip of his half-hard salami, busting out of his black AC/DC T-shirt. A month ago, the shirt had fit him, but that morning, before he'd even started his routine, the shirt had split down the back and the armholes had parted at the seams. He loved it. A hard-on so hard it was busting out of its skin.

Beaut understood that pumping anabolic steroids into his body might have certain undesirable side effects, including liver damage, blood clotting, hypertension, swollen breast tissue, reduced sperm count and shrinkage of the testicles and, most obviously, severe acne. The acne was the only part of it that bothered him, and that would go away. The positive effects from the testosterone—increased strength and endurance, increased muscular hypertrophy, faster recovery time, increased aggressiveness, and enhanced sex drive—were so immediate and profound, why worry about things he could not see?

Recently, he had added a new exercise to his routine. He called it "slamming." Grasping a fifty-pound dumbbell in each hand, he swung his arms up over his head and slammed the dumbbells together, producing a loud clang. He then brought the dumbbells down, clanged them again in front of his thighs, and repeated the motion until he could no longer lift them, or until one of the weights went sailing off across the room. He had done as many as twenty-four of them in one set. The exercise gave him an awesome pump, and the feeling of the crashing iron, felt from his wrists to his flared lats, was orgasmic. Afterward, he could almost feel his quivering arms growing.

Because of the occasionally airborne dumbbells, slams could be performed only when Bigg was not on the premises. Beaut liked to do them first thing in the morning, before Bigg showed up. It was a good way to wake up the pencil-necks. He liked the way they watched him, giving him plenty of room. Even the serious bodybuilders found something to do on the far side of the gym when Beaut was slamming. Lately, a lot of them had been waiting till after-noon to visit the gym. This morning, Beaut had the place to himself.

He was on his second set of slams when Joe Crow walked into the gym.

The prudent course of action, Crow knew, would be to stay as far as possible from the pumped-up gym rat with the shredded shirt and the flailing dumb-bells. Looking around, he noticed that, except for Beaut, Bigg Bodies was un-populated—unusual for 7:30 A.M. on a weekday morning. It made him doubly uncomfortable to be around Beaut with no witnesses. While Crow had been re-covering from his beating, Beaut had continued to grow at an astonishing rate. He had stretch marks across his chest and shoulders, his back was spattered with pimples, his arms were ropy with enlarged veins, and the way he was slamming those dumbbells together was insane. And dangerous.

Crow decided to add another rule to his ever growing list: *Avoid insane, dangerous bodybuilders.*

On the other hand, Crow had come to the gym for his first workout in a week. It just wouldn't feel right to let Beaut scare him off. He had a right to be there, and he needed to get back into his routine. That was the key to getting in shape: no excuses. He waited until Beaut finished his set, then walked over to the rack and picked up a pair of fifteen-pound dumbbells. Beaut, slick with per-spiration, gasping for breath, glared red-faced from the other end of the twenty-foot-long rack. Crow turned his back, put Beaut out of his mind, and began a series of slow lateral raises to warm up his shoulders.

Something about the way Crow held his dumbbells had an intensely irritating effect on Beaut. Maybe it was the slow, deliberate way he performed his lifts. Or that he had turned away, showing Beaut his back.

Beaut aimed his eyes at Crow's neck. Laser vision. If he stared hard enough, he might produce a puff of smoke. Set the son-of-a-bitch's hair on fire.

Crow continued his exercise, showing no signs of discomfort. Beaut kept his eyes focused, methodically flexing his traps, his lats, and his biceps. A few more threads parted on the left sleeve of his shirt. Whatever uncertainties Little Leslie might have been feeling were lost in the soup of steroids and adrenaline flooding his arteries.

Crow finished his set and replaced the dumbbells. He looked at Beaut, then turned away as if there had been nothing for him to see and picked up a pair of sixties. Beaut stood up and lumbered past him, his swollen arms held well out from his body in the official bodybuilder's swagger. He let his left arm brush against Crow, knocking him aside.

Crow's hip slammed into the dumbbell rack, bringing a surprised curse from his throat.

Beaut stopped and swung his shoulders toward him. "What did you say?" he demanded.

Crow stood up in the narrow space between the rack and Beaut, still gripping the dumbbells. Beaut looked down into Crow's impassive face, inches away. A droplet of sweat fell from the pimple at the tip of Beaut's nose, leaving a dark streak on Crow's T-shirt. Beaut imagined what would happen if *he* tried to put on a shirt that size. It would disintegrate into cotton dust. He lifted his right hand and pressed his palm against Crow's chest, then slowly closed his hand, gathering a fist full of cotton.

"What did you say to me?" he said again.

Arling Biggle had been hanging around bodybuilders and gym rats for most of his adult life. He'd been performing seven hundred–pound squats back when Arnold Schwarzenegger was no more than an Austrian rumor, and he had opened Bigg Bodies years before the days of spandex and Nautilus and chrome-plated barbells. He had, he felt, a unique understanding of the subrace that looked upon each new hypertrophied muscle fiber as another riser on the stairway to heaven.

He was starting to worry about his assistant manager. Since Beaut had taken over the morning shift, the number of members signing in before noon had declined precipitously. In time, he knew, this would be reflected by a decline in membership renewals. Whatever his 'roided-out assistant manager was doing to scare people off, it would have to stop.

Bigg could see, the moment he stepped through the front door into the gym, that Beaut was about to erupt. He had seen his share of 'roid rages. He had experienced them himself, back in his competition days.

Being on a steroid cycle, he recalled, was to be an angry god in human guise. To walk the streets among mere mortals, holding back the power, filled with joy and fury. Holding it in for days or weeks. Seeing every slight, real or imagined, as a personal insult to one's dignity. That was the hardest part. Holding it in when challenged by a rude waiter, or when cut off on the freeway, or when some pencilneck wanted to work in between sets. Thinking about calling up the power, but doing nothing. It took both iron discipline and strength of character, two qualities lacking in Beaut Miller.

Bigg also remembered what it felt like to let go, to give in to the wrath and damn the consequences, a feeling of orgasmic intensity. He could see it happening for Beaut. He almost felt sorry for Joe Crow, who appeared to be the focus of Beaut's swelling rage, but not sorry enough to do anything about it. In fact, he thought, he might just enjoy it.

Joe Crow did not want to get hurt again. His feelings on the matter were quite definite. At this point, with the memory of his last beating painfully fresh in his mind, he would have done almost anything to avoid it—confess to crimes he had not committed, pay extortion money, run like a scared rabbit—whatever it took to remain pain-free. But in this situation, no words or promises, not even out-and-out groveling, would blunt Beaut's rage.

Only one course of action suggested itself. Crow opened his hands and let the two sixty-pound dumbbells fall toward Beaut's size-twelve Nikes.

Arling Biggle did not see Crow release the dumbbells, but he heard a soft snap and, simultaneously, the familiar thud of iron striking the rubber mat. Beaut's mouth fell open. He folded at the waist and took a clumsy step back, letting go of Crow's shirt. Crow leapt quickly aside. Beaut seemed to recover, starting toward Crow, but as he took his first step he collapsed with a groan and lay on the mat, clutching his right foot. The entire incident took no more than two seconds.

Bigg sighed and shook his head. He'd liked to have seen Crow take the worst of it, but this was not all bad. Beaut had needed taking down, too. One thing Bigg had learned in his forty-eight years, you take what you can get. He walked over to Beaut, a faint smile on his lips, and asked him if he was all right.

Beaut said, through gritted teeth, "Fuck you."

"That's what I thought," said Bigg.

Crow had backed a few yards away. He was breathing heavily, keeping his eyes on Beaut, his body tensed.

"I wouldn't worry," Bigg said. "I think you made your point."

Crow said, "Was that your idea?"

"Me? Hell no. Beaut's his own man, Crow."

"Yeah, right."

Bigg shrugged. Why should he care what Crow thought? Squatting beside Beaut, he asked him again if he was all right. "You gonna be able to walk, you think?"

Beaut tried to put weight on his foot and gasped.

"I believe you might have a fracture there, old buddy."

Beaut, tears streaming from his eyes, did not reply.

Bigg stood up. Crow was walking toward the door. "Where you going?"

"I'm out of here," Crow said over his shoulder.

Bigg smiled. "Congratulations," he said to Beaut. "You finally scared him off."

Crow stopped and turned back. "Don't forget to have that limo ready. You've got the time and place, right?"

Bigg laughed. "Sure I do. I got the time and place. But there's one thing I don't have. At least not anymore."

Crow waited, giving him that flat look.

Bigg said, pointing toward the agonized Beaut, "You've just taken out your chauffeur."

*Human beings are able to alter their own cell structures through pure mental effort. It is a proven fact that many practitioners of Zen Buddhism have, through extensive meditation, reversed the "handedness" of their own DNA, becoming mirror images of their former selves. In this respect, human cells are fundamentally different from those of all other living creatures. Except Cetaceans, of course.*

*— "Amaranthine Reflections" by Dr. Rupert Chandra*

RUPERT CHANDRA WAS AT HOME sitting cross-legged on the bed applying his highly focused mental energy to the red mole on his abdomen when he heard the downstairs door open. He looked up, frowned, then refocused his mind on the mole. He was sure that it was a melanoma. A small thing, but something that needed to be dealt with. He had been working on it for several days now but the mole had, if anything, grown slightly larger.

He relaxed his neck muscles, lowering his head to bring his mind closer to the mole. It was an ugly little thing, a tiny red cauliflower, about the size of a baby pea. He explored its perimeter with his mind, willing power into the surrounding cells, creating a psychic barrier to contain the growth. He looked for the shimmering that was a sign of cellular activation.

Over the preceding weeks he had attempted to use negative energy to destroy the growth. That, he now realized, had been a mistake. The negative energy had spilled over onto the healthy cells surrounding the cancer cells, effectively eliminating their power to resist the unwanted tumor. All that negative energy might also explain the nausea that had been bothering him lately, and the tight feeling he'd noticed in his chest. He had ignored his own teachings. The key to cellular regeneration was positive thoughts. Amaranthine theory was not about destroying the old, it was about creating healthy new tissue.

There. He could see it now. The edges of the mole were beginning to shimmer. It seemed to be rising up off the surface. He could sense the power flooding into his cells, surrounding and lifting the mole, creating a shield between his healthy body and the red cauliflower.

The bedroom door opened, breaking his concentration. The mole settled back into place.

Rupe said, "Damn!"

Polly set her bag on a chair near the door. "Contemplating your navel again, Rupe?"

"I almost had it," he said. "You broke my concentration."

"Sorry. Let's have a look." Polly knelt down beside the bed and examined the spot on her husband's stomach. "It doesn't look any smaller," she said.

"I know that."

"Maybe you should just have Dr. Bell cut it out while we're in Rochester."

Rupe shook his head and stood up. He closed his bathrobe and tied the belt. "That's Death Program thinking," he said.

"I call it being practical. He's going to have to knock you out to do your eyelids anyway."

Rupe shuddered. "Don't remind me."

"How many hours have you spent worrying about that little old mole?"

"I'm not worrying. I'm extracting."

"Whatever you're doing, it's sure taking a lot of your time. I could've used you at the meeting today." She sat down on the edge of the mattress and pulled off her shoes.

"How did it go?" Rupe asked.

"Good." Polly flashed a smile and rubbed her foot. "Actually, it went great. We've got forty-seven new members."

"Forty-seven!"

"The hair was the kicker. Valerie did a nice job. I gave her a bonus. You should have seen them, Rupe. They took one look at those black roots growing in on her head, and they couldn't open their checkbooks fast enough."

The free, heavily advertised Anti-Aging Clinics were what attracted newcomers to the ACO. It was relatively easy to fill seats in the auditorium by offering a free show with refreshments, but turning Pilgrims into Faithful, that was a more difficult undertaking. It was the follow-up meeting, the "Forever Tea," that truly separated the wheat from the chaff.

Everyone who had attended the post-clinic reception was told that a small percentage of them would be receiving invitations to the Sunday tea, based on recommendations from the ACO staff. Names and phone numbers were gathered, and a few days later the ACO staff phoned every last one of them and invited them to attend the very exclusive Forever Tea, where they would have the opportunity to meet with First Eldress Polyhymnia. They were also promised a free computer-generated personalized "Life Expectancy Report" based on questionnaires they had filled out at the reception.

Typically, about 10 percent of those who witnessed an Anti-Aging demonstration were sufficiently impressed to return to the church to learn more about the Amaranthines, and to find out how long they could expect to live.

The Forever Tea took place in the more intimate setting of the ACO chapel, an octagonal room with one hundred chairs arranged in five concentric circles around a low platform. After a brief welcome by Polly, the Life Expectancy Reports were handed out.

Each twenty-six-inch-long computer printout showed the Pilgrim's name at the top, followed by columns of numbers, two complicated-looking graphs, a boilerplate disclaimer and, at the very bottom, in purposefully small print, subject's projected date of death. It was not unusual for a Pilgrim, upon receiving his or her LER, to become hysterical, or to simply faint dead away.

Although the effect of the LERs was always gratifying, the most powerful element of that morning's Forever Tea turned out to be the subject of Rupe's age reversal, Mrs. Veronica Frank. Past seminars had netted from six to ten new paying members, but this time forty-seven of the fifty-three attendees, convinced by Val Frankel's dark roots, agreed to sign up for the autumn Extraction Event for a minimum donation of four hundred ninety-nine dollars a head.

Later, once they began to enjoy the life-extending benefits of the events, they would be privately encouraged to contribute additional funds to their Life Account to demonstrate their commitment to the Amaranthine Way. Life Account contributions made up the bulk of overall ACO receipts.

Gaining forty-seven new members was unprecedented in ACO history.

"I really think it was the dark roots," Polly said. "The hair was the one thing they could not deny. It was like watching forty-seven Thomases touching Christ's wounds."

Rupe shook his head, smiling sadly. "They reject the truth and embrace the illusion," he said.

"We've always known that. Either way, we bring them life. It's a case of the ends justifying the means."

"Only if their commitment is real."

"It's no less real to them, and that's what matters." Polly walked over to her husband and embraced him. "You gave them reality," she said. "You showed them what was possible. That's why they came back."

"I don't know. I think I'm getting burnt out. I'm tired all the time. I feel like I'm being squeezed by giants."

Polly touched the corner of his left eye, traced the crowsfeet with a long pink nail. "The stress is showing on both of us. But not for long."

Rupe grasped her hand in his. "Age is an illusion, my sweet."

Polly used her other hand to smooth his forehead. "The wrinkles are real," she said.

"Four weeks," Rupe said. "The time might be enough all by itself. Maybe we should go straight to Stonecrop, let nature and the powers of our minds sculpt our bodies."

Polly laughed.

"I'm serious," said Rupe. "Your Dr. Bell, with his knives and his lasers, I do not like him."

"Rupe, we talked about this. It's just part of the sizzle, a thing we do to make it easier for the Pilgrims to believe. You said it yourself. They embrace the illusion. We have to give them what they want."

"Perhaps." Rupe smiled sadly. Polly was right as usual. Cosmetic surgery violated certain of the Amaranthine teachings, but it served to advance a greater Amaranthine principle, which embraced any and all means to achieving the seven steps of the Amaranth. He had moments when the larger picture escaped him, when he experienced doubts or anxieties over little things, like their scheduled visit to Youthmark, Dr. Bell's private hospital. Polly always brought him back to ground zero.

Polly said, "I talked to Benjy this morning." Benjy Hiss, one of the ACO's charter members, had been placed in charge of building Stonecrop. "They finished the chapel yesterday."

"Good! What about the house?"

"The house was done last week. All of the furniture is in and the refrigerator is stocked. We had to pay for some overtime." Polly frowned. "It put us over budget."

Rupe kissed her frowning lips. "Eternity will provide. Just think, my dear. After tonight's meeting there'll be no seminars, no workshops, no teas, no phone calls for four lovely weeks. Just you and me and Stonecrop." He looked down into his robe at the spot on his belly. "Time to focus on the important things."

"You know, it's probably not too soon to see an obstetrician," Sophie said, leaning forward over the steering wheel to see past a parked minivan.

"Why would I do that?"

Sophie let the Hyundai creep forward a few feet, nosing out of the Litten Paper Company parking lot. "I can't see," she muttered. A green pickup truck flashed by, missing her front bumper by inches. Sophie let the car roll out a little farther, then tromped on the gas. The Hyundai's tires spun on a patch of sand, chirped, and propelled the car out onto Washington Avenue, cutting off an MTC bus.

The back seat of Sophie's car was filled with paper cups and plates, plastic utensils, and assorted decorations, including expandable crepe wedding bells, large plastic bows, and a twenty-foot-long banner spelling out "Congratulations" in silver glitter letters. Sophie said, "Because you're pregnant, that's why."

"Oh." Carmen had momentarily forgotten that she was supposed to be pregnant. "I'm not *that* pregnant."

Sophie reached over and poked Carmen's belly with her forefinger. "You're not showing, but you look like you're holding water."

"I might've gained a pound or two."

"I hope your dress still fits."

"It'll fit."

"It had better." Sophie drove for a few blocks, thinking about all the things that could go wrong—in other words about everything from Carmen falling asleep at the altar to Hyatt not showing up at the church to a tornado interrupting the wedding ceremony to the untimely rapture of Reverend Buck Manelli.

Carmen said, "You worry too much."

"I know that." Sophie looked over at her daughter. "Tell me again, Carmen. How pregnant *are* you?"

Carmen shrugged.

"When was your last period?"

Carmen thought for a moment, trying to remember what she had told Sophie the last time they'd had this conversation.

"April?"

"Last time we talked you said March."

"Well I don't remember." In fact, she didn't. It was now August seventh. When had she had her last period? It seemed like a long time, now that she was thinking about it.

Sophie was giving her this frowning look. "Are you really pregnant?"

Carmen was still trying to remember when she'd bought her last box of tampons. She thought it had been just before Memorial Day. Could that be right? Maybe the stress of all this wedding preparation—not to mention worrying over Hyatt's plan, which seemed crazier every time she thought about it—had thrown off her cycle.

Sophie said, "You just made it up, didn't you? You're not pregnant at all, are you?"

Carmen put a hand on her belly and rubbed in a slow circle. A missed period would not be that unusual. But that wouldn't explain why her breasts had
been feeling so full lately, or why she'd puked up her breakfast that morning.

"As a matter of fact," she said, "I think that maybe I might be."

*There seems to be some disagreement about the exact origins of
the Judge, but basically the option began life as a low cost
GTO. By the time everyone had had their say, it had become a
rather expensive option on top of the GTO package. The Judge
became a parody of the entire musclecar movement.*

—*Web site devoted to GTOs*

THE WORST PART OF TRAVELING outside the country was coming home to the
Hubert H. Humphrey International Airport in Minneapolis. Debrowski shuffled
forward a few steps, dragging her two suitcases, waiting for her turn with the
customs officer, waiting for him to direct her off into one of the inspection
rooms so that one of them could paw through her belongings and hammer her
with accusatory questions. They might even do a body search. It had happened
to her before.

Debrowski had been in and out of the United States more than a dozen
times in the past five years and, without exception, her return had excited the
interest of the customs inspectors. The first time it had happened she had been
flying in from Peru, where she'd gone to spend a few weeks with a group of
coca leaf–chewing Indians. That had been during the last months of her druggie days, when she was still trying to convince herself that there was something
hip and noble and natural about cocaine. She had gone in search of Native
American wisdom and spirituality, but had found only a lot of drug dealers,
guns, bad teeth, and poverty. She had returned to the states thoroughly depressed, only to be subjected to a ninety-minute inspection at the airport. She
hadn't been surprised or particularly offended. She figured it must have been

the motorcycle jacket that made her stand out. Or the marijuana-leaf design stitched across its back. Besides, it was reasonable that they should suspect her. She might have been transporting a balloon full of coke in her rectum, as had been proposed to her by one of the coked-up Americans she'd met in Lima. Fortunately she had declined, and the customs officers had found nothing.

Her second trip out of the country had been a vacation in the Caymans. She had quit using by that time and had left her leather jacket at home, but was once again subjected to a search. She had thought, I must still look like a druggie. Maybe it was the multiple earrings.

For the return from her third journey, a business trip to Barcelona, she had disguised herself in a lady executive ensemble—a soft gray suit, low-heeled pumps, and a single set of pearl earrings. The customs guy took one look at her and directed her to the inspections table. Since then, she had tried a number of guises, but the customs experience was always the same. There was something about her that punched their buttons. She figured that she could wear a nun's habit and they'd still search every fold.

This time, she decided not to fight it. If it was her fate to be searched by customs, then so be it. She would wear what she wanted. Little black sunglasses so dark they made it hard to see colors. Left ear heavy with metal and stone. Her hair, hacked short and dyed jet black this month, jutted from her scalp in asymmetrical spikes. Big bad black boots. Leather choker. Well-worn black jeans. Motorcycle jacket, decorated with chains and pins and graffiti, over a black T-shirt bearing a scrawled red circle "A," for anarchy. Debrowski was no anarchist, but she liked the logo.

As she moved up in the line, she told herself to relax. It would do no good to antagonize them. One flip remark could turn a twenty-minute ordeal into hours. She was tired, her back hurt from hours of sitting, and the sandwich she had been served on the plane was performing gymnastics in her gut. She had to keep her feelings bottled, at least for a little while. Closing her eyes, she searched for her center but saw only phosphenes dancing across her retina. She opened her eyes. The man in front of her hand moved on, and the customs officer, a slack-faced man in his fifties, regarded her through the bottoms of his bifocals.

Debrowski read the officer's name tag: "B. Monk." She handed him her passport, saying nothing. Officer Monk's eyes flickered from the photo to Debrowski.

"Anything to declare?" he said.

Debrowski gave him her signed declaration slip, which officer Monk inspected.

"You're declaring nothing at all?"

"That's what it says."

"No alcoholic beverages? Fresh fruits or vegetables? Cuban cigars?"

"No," said Debrowski. "No and no."

"Okay then. Thank you." He motioned her toward the exit and turned his bifocal gaze onto the man behind her.

Debrowski said, "Wait a minute. You aren't going to search my bags?"

Officer Monk frowned. "Do you want us to search your bags?"

"No. But why aren't you doing it?"

"What do you mean, Miss?"

"It's *Ms.* I just mean, why did you decide not to search me this time? You guys always search me. Did I do something different? How do you decide these things?"

Officer Monk seemed to consider his answer. He said, "Are you sure you want to do this?"

"Do? I don't want you to do anything, I just want to know how come all of a sudden I'm getting a pass."

Officer Monk tipped his head back. The fluorescent lights turned his spectacle lenses into featureless white discs. "I believed you when you told me you had nothing to declare. Do you?"

"No."

"Then I don't see the problem."

"Look, I have *never* gotten through customs without getting searched. I just want to know what I did right this time."

"You didn't do anything. You seemed to me to be a nice girl. That's all."

Debrowski said, "Nice?" She looked down at her leathers. "You think I look *nice*?"

"You remind me of my daughter."

"Your daughter? You're passing me because I look like your *daughter*?"

Officer Monk sighed. "Perhaps I made a mistake," he said.

According to the sidebar in *USA Today,* 78 percent of American males believed themselves to be better-looking than average. Twelve percent described themselves as "extremely handsome." Only 3 percent confessed to being "extremely unattractive." Crow raised his head from the paper and looked around the waiting area. Of the dozen men in sight, at least half of them had to be among the "extremely unattractive." This did not support the poll results. Crow wondered whether there was any relation at all between a man's actual appearance and his self image. It seemed to him that a guy on the extreme ugly end of the scale—say with a grotesquely oversize nose and cheeks covered with suppurating sores—would be hard pressed to see himself as an Adonis. But what about a guy like the guy sitting across from him—pasty skin, sagging jowls, protruding eyes, and crooked, yellowish teeth. How did that guy see himself?

Could go either way, Crow thought.

The clock on the wall read 6:32. He had been waiting for Debrowski for nearly an hour. Her flight had arrived late, but not that late. Apparently she was having trouble getting through customs.

Crow stood up and went into the restroom to look at himself in the mirror. Better than average looking? He had always thought so. Not great looking. Not movie star good-looking, but on a scale of one to ten he'd always considered himself at least a seven or eight. But then, so did eight out of ten other guys.

The numbers were disturbing. Crow leaned into the mirror. Was it even possible to see one's self? He stared at the reflection of his nose. The harder he looked, the broader it became. His pores enlarged into gaping pits. His eyes became small and piglike; his lips grew swollen and ropey. Better than average looking? For an unemployed middle-aged gambler, perhaps. He returned to the waiting area to find Debrowski standing between her two huge suitcases looking lost and tired and pissed off, looking at all the ugly men, looking for Joe Crow.

"So they searched your bags?"

"They sure did. Can you believe it? The guy was going to let me through, I ask him a simple goddamn question, next thing you know they're going through my underwear. Jesus, Crow, where'd you park? Canada?"

"Why don't you let me take that?"

"I got it, I got it." Debrowski had consented to let him carry only one of her suitcases. "So this guy says I remind him of his daughter. You know what his daughter does? She teaches second grade."

"I could see you doing that."

"Yeah, right."

"You've got nice handwriting, and you can spell."

"Thanks a lot. Are we there yet? My arm is numb."

"I think it's up about three more rows. Tell me something, do you think I'm good-looking?"

Debrowski stopped and dropped her suitcase. "Compared to what?" She massaged her right arm.

"Compared to, say, the average guy."

"Sure."

"On a scale of one to ten, where would you put me?"

Debrowski squinted at him. "Nine point two," she said.

Crow grabbed both suitcases. "Thank you," he said.

Debrowski followed. "Feeling a little insecure these days?"

"I was just checking."

"Never hurts. Listen, you don't have to carry both of those. Hey! Good-lookin'! What about me? Aren't you gonna tell me how gorgeous I am?"

Crow stopped and set the suitcases down. "You know you look great. I like your new hair. Do it yourself?"

"As a matter of fact, yeah. Come on, Crow. One to ten. Lay it on me." She lifted her sunglasses onto her forehead, revealing startling blue eyes and an even, white smile.

Crow held up two imaginary scorecards and said, "Nine point nine."

Debrowski arched an eyebrow. "Not a ten? What, have I got something in my teeth?"

"If I said ten you'd think I was flattering you."

"Flattery I can handle. Now, where the hell's the car."

"We're here," he said. They were standing beside the GTO.

Debrowski took a step back, blinking in the yellow glare. She tipped her sunglasses back over her eyes. "Crow? What the hell do you call this?"

"Sixty-nine GTO," Crow said, grinning. "The Judge. Three hundred sixty-six horses."

Debrowski shook her head. "Jesus, Crow, I leave you alone for a couple months . . ." She gave him a searching look. "You aren't having your midlife crisis, are you?"

*Never, believe me,*
*Appear the Immortals,*
*Never Alone*

—*Samuel Taylor Coleridge*

THE SPANDEX-CLAD BLOND AT Bally's knew of no one named Florian, or Flo Rain, or Florie, or any woman who matched the description of the green-shoed beauty. Chuckles thanked the woman and limped out to his Corvette.

For the past week Chuckles had been using his spare time to search for the woman whose heel had penetrated his thigh. She'd said her name was Florian, or something close to that, and he knew from the quality of her physique that she worked out. He also believed that wherever the woman did her workouts, she would be noticed and remembered.

He wasn't surprised to have struck out at Bally's. A body like Florian's came from lifting tons of raw iron, not from dressing up in spandex and playing with brightly painted Nautilus and Cybex machines.

A copy of the Minneapolis/St. Paul Yellow Pages lay open on the passenger seat beside the pair of lime-green high-heeled pumps. Chuckles uncapped a felt-tip pen and crossed off Bally's. There were only about forty health clubs and gyms in town, so unless she had her own private workout facility, or unless she was from out of town, he would find her. He ran his finger up the listings. He had to be back at the church by six for the elders' address to the Faithful, so he was looking for a gym he could check out on the way there. Minnesota Muscle? Too far north. Gold's Gym? He looked at his watch. Three fifteen. Not enough time. His finger stopped at the listing for Bigg Bodies. Just a few blocks out of his way. Chuckles started the vette and pulled out onto Nicollet Avenue, driving with one thick-fingered hand resting atop the steering wheel, the other one idly fondling the smooth patent leather surfaces of Florian's green shoes.

Drew Chance reclined in his BackSaver Executive and looked at the three Alan Orlich originals taped to his office wall. Alan's mother, Gert, had dropped them off that morning.

The first painting, a composition in red and brown, depicted a large hairy creature—possibly a bear—impaled on a spike. Drew thought it might have something to do with Russia, or Wall Street. Or maybe it was simply a bear on a spike. The second painting showed a burning boat sinking into a black ocean. That could be about an oil tanker accident, or a terrorist attack, or something going on in the Black Sea. The third painting showed a mushroom cloud rising over a burning city. That one seemed pretty straightforward.

Little Alan Orlich, the six-year-old clairvoyant fingerpainter, had first attracted media attention a week ago when his third-grade teacher noticed that his fingerpaintings had clearly anticipated major disasters, including the crash of a Northwest Airlines 737, the eruption of a volcano in the Philippines, and a drive-by shooting in south Minneapolis that killed two children. Each of these three paintings, according to the teacher, had been completed approximately 72 hours before the actual events occurred. The teacher had called a local radio station and gone public with her discovery.

After hearing about the ominous fingerpaintings, Drew had contacted the boy's parents and convinced them to sign an exclusive television deal with *Hard Camera* in exchange for a quick five hundred dollars. Drew was now trying to decide whether he should show all three of the kid's paintings, or leave out the nuclear holocaust. If any one of the predicted events came to pass, he'd have a monster story. But if it was the nuclear bomb one, well, maybe nobody would be left to give a damn. He was trying to figure out which painting he should use for the opening shot when Annie buzzed him. Drew snatched up the phone.

"I'm busy," he snapped.

"Sorry, Mr. Chance," Annie said. "It's Mr. Hilton on line one. He insists on talking to you."

Drew drew a blank. "Who?"

"Mr. Hilton. He says he's one of our reporters. Isn't he the man who brought you the Evian?"

"Oh. Hy the guy." Drew hadn't thought about Hy in over a month, not since he'd run out of Evian. "What does he want?"

"He's on line one."

"Okay, okay, okay." Drew turned his irritated sneer into a wide smile and punched the lighted button. "Hy! Sorry to keep you waiting! What can I do you for?"

"Just checking in, Andy. Saturday's the big day. You're coming, aren't you?"

"Sure, sure." Big day? Drew couldn't remember what he was supposed to be remembering. He remembered Hyatt's idea, sort of. Something about getting married, but that was weeks and weeks ago. Drew had sort of put it out of his mind. Lots of other stuff had been coming down the pipe. Big stories, like the clairvoyant fingerpainter. He'd put Hy's story in his "If it happens, I'll be there" mental file.

Hyatt said, "You got an invite, didn't you?"

"Ahhhh . . ." Drew remembered, now, the invitation to Hyatt's wedding. Junk mail. He said, "You know, Hy, I don't believe I did."

"Andy, you're just as full of shit as ever."

Drew blinked and his smile fell.

"Listen, you're going to thank me for this one, Andy. You gotta be there. This story has network written all over it."

Drew opened his mouth to make an excuse, say his mother had died or something, but the word *network* rang in his ears. "Uh, when did you say it was? Saturday?"

"Andy, don't flake out on me. I'm counting on you. Be there. And bring a cameraman."

"You want me to tape your wedding?"

"Just have a guy there. I want *you* at the wedding because we're *friends.*"

Drew said, "Oh." He frowned. "So, I suppose that means I have to buy a gift."

"We're registered at Dayton's. Look, if you don't want in on this, tell me now and I'll talk to the guys over at WCCO."

"Did I say I didn't want in?"

"You aren't exactly coming across gangbusters."

"Yeah, well, if you've got a story—that's what we're talking, right? This isn't just Hy the Guy gets hitched, right?"

"Jesus, Drew, you ever listen to me? This is gonna be *huge!*"

"Right. You got a story, then I'm your man."

"We're gonna have a story, Drew, remember?"

"Uh, this is the thing with that cult, right?" It was coming back now.

"That's right. The Amaranthine Church."

"The vampire thing, right?"

"That's right. What the hell is wrong with you? Did we not discuss this in detail right there in your office?"

"I talk to a lot of clients, Hy. I got stuff coming at me every which way. I got a kid that draws pictures of the future."

"You want a picture of the future, Drew? I got two of them. One, you're sitting on a pile of cash. Two, you got your head up your butt. Which one you want on your wall?"

"Okay, okay. Look, you want to run through it again for me, Hy? I mean, just the high points."

Hyatt turned off the phone and set it on the coffee table. He looked through the archway into the kitchen. Carmen stood at the stove wearing a red apron over her white bra and blue panties, stirring something in a big saucepan. He said, "Shit!" Carmen did not look up. Hyatt raised his voice and slammed his fist on the table. "Shit!"

That time Carmen turned her head toward him, smiled, then went back to stirring. Hyatt flopped back into the sofa. He didn't understand how she could be so utterly incurious. Anybody else would have asked him what was wrong, and who he'd been talking to, but Carmen showed no interest whatsoever. All she seemed to care about lately was this stupid wedding. At least it was keeping her busy. But it would have been nice if she worried about Hy Hilton now and then.

That son-of-a-bitch Drew. All the time and effort to prep the guy, to bring him on board, and he spaces. Good thing he called.

Hy rocked forward and stood up. A whiff of butyric acid followed him. There were little pockets of it throughout the apartment, like aromatic mines, waiting to be triggered. The garage was still unapproachable. He walked into the kitchen and looked over Carmen's shoulder into the saucepan.

"Spaghetti sauce?"

"Sophie gave me the recipe. It's ready. You hungry?"

"Starving. Drew Chance is coming to the wedding."

"Who?"

"Drew Chance. The guy on *Hard Camera*."

"Oh. Did he RSVP?"

"I doubt it. You know, the presents alone are going to make this whole thing worthwhile."

"Sophie's gonna be pissed, he doesn't RSVP."

Hyatt shrugged. "You want to know something funny? Did you know that in Minnesota you can get married by a dog?"

Carmen set the spoon on the edge of the pan. "Forget about it, Hy. I'm not getting married by a dog, I don't care how it will look on TV."

Hyatt laughed. "No, I'm just saying it's the *law*. If two people say their vows in public, and if they *think* they just got married, then they're married. Doesn't matter if the minister is licensed or anything. Doesn't matter what they say. It still counts! They're married! The minister doesn't even have to be human!"

"Tell me we're not gonna be married by a dog."

"No. I just thought it was interesting. I mean, everybody makes such a big deal about weddings, and in the end it comes down to 'bow-wow-wow,' you're married."

"You're a weird guy."

"Yeah, I know that."

"You want to set the table?"

"Hey, we're not married yet!" Hyatt looked around the kitchen. "What kind of pasta are we having?"

Carmen stopped stirring. "Oh," she said.

"You're kidding, right? You forgot the spaghetti?"

"Do we have some?"

"Jesus, Carm, you scare me sometimes."

Carmen nodded. "Me, too."

The man behind the counter at Bigg Bodies sat with his thick arms crossed over his bulging chest, staring bleakly at his right foot, which was wrapped in a thick cocoon of white gauze and resting atop a stool. He did not look up when Chuckles limped in and leaned his elbows on the counter.

Chuckles said, "You drop a plate?"

The man turned his head slowly and stared. He reminded Chuckles of Chip. Squinty little redneck eyes. "Something I can do for you?"

Chuckles leaned across the counter, offering his hand. "Name's Chuckles. You the owner?"

"I'm the manager. If you're selling something, we're not interested."

Chuckles kept his hand out. "I'm not selling. I'm buying."

The man with the foot seemed disappointed, but he took the proffered hand and pumped it once. "Beaut Miller. What are you buying?"

"I'm looking to join a gym."

"Yeah? Well, you found one. We got it all. I'd give you the tour, but—" he gestured toward his bandaged foot.

"'s cool." Chuckles looked out across the room. "I see what you got." Only a few guys were working out. He did not see Florian.

"We're running a special promotion, this week only. Join for six months, you get one month free. One forty-nine ninety-nine."

"What if I can't decide till next week?"

Beaut shrugged. "I could extend the offer."

"You got any lady members?"

"Sure. Mostly they come in evenings."

"Got one named Florian?"

"Florian?"

"Yeah. Good looking woman. Got a kick like a mule."

Beaut laughed. "I got a Flow-REEN, only she just *smells* like a mule."

"Say what?"

"Actually, our Flowrean smells more like dead fish. That the bitch you looking for?"


Many thousands of Pilgrims had come to the Amaranthine Church of the One seeking to lengthen their pitifully brief lifespans. The majority, confronted with the rigors and costs of the Amaranthine way, chose to remain mortal. They came for the free clinic, and they left. Fewer than a thousand had gone on to attend an Extraction Event and, of those, only forty-four had completed the first five of the seven steps required to achieve true physical immortality. The sixth and seventh steps were held to be among the greatest secrets of the Amaranth. Thus far, only Rupe and Polly had achieved them.

The forty-two people now seated in the meeting room were all fifth-steppers and had reached a state known as "proto-immortality." Rupert Chandra, seated on a swivel chair in the precise center of the small octagonal room, felt his chest swell with pride. He hoped that he could contain his emotions—but he also felt that these were his people, and that he could be himself.

"Thank you all for coming," he said, placing one hand over his heart. He pushed off with one foot, spinning slowly, watching the sea of friendly faces swirl around him. "I never expected so many of you—" He stopped the spinning chair. "—Would come to say good-bye." He smiled and blinked; a tear spilled from his left eye. "But of course, this isn't good-bye. Polly and I will return from Stonecrop. What is four weeks? A moment. A blip. A fragment of eternity." He shook his head. "As you all know, the ACO has been our life, our dream. To have led you all into this unending future has been a great privilege and an even greater joy, but leadership has its price. The things we have to do to bring new Pilgrims into the fold, the Anti-Aging Clinics . . . you have seen me perform age-reversals. We do these things to overcome the natural doubts of the Pilgrim, but there is a price. My cells suffer, draining energy from my system. Electron microscopic analysis has shown that my telomeres actually grow shorter during an age reversal. And Polly, my Eternal Companion, as much a part of me as this hand you see in front of my face, is drained as well. The age reversal demonstrations are necessary, but they are not healthy, and we have suffered; and that is why we are taking this sabbatical and leaving the church in your hands." Rupe paused. "I asked you all here not only to say good-bye, but to make you a promise. In four weeks, Polly and I will be back, younger and stronger than ever. We will return with new energy, new spirit, and new ideas. We will have moved far beyond the Rupe and Polly you see standing here before you. We will be better than ever."

Falsehood and deception, betrayal and treachery. The words spilling from Rupert Chandra's mouth went straight to Chip's soul, staining it with the putrefying reek of the Death Program. In the old days such deceit would have been rewarded with a shower of stones, or fire, or a simple defenestration. But modern-day politics were more complex, more strategic. There were too many laws. The direct approach didn't work anymore, not since the Jews and the Japs had taken over the government.

Rupe was talking about step four again—Give More—telling them they had to give and give and give to reap the rewards of eternity. But Chip knew where that giving was going. It was going to the Doctors of Deception, to the architects of the Death Program. Not to building the future, but to concealing the past.

The door opened and Chuckles slipped into the meeting room, late again, and winked at Chip. Chip the Security Chief nodded to the Head of Security, carefully expressionless. Another symptom of decadence. Chip permitted himself a grim smile. Once he became Director of Strategic Operations as Hyatt had promised, the first thing he'd do, he'd fire Chuckles's black ass.

*A coward is incapable of exhibiting love; it is the prerogative of the brave.*

—Mahatma Gandhi

DEBROWSKI ROLLED ONTO HER SIDE and fingered a Gauloise from the pack on the bedstand. "Let me see if I'm understanding this." She fitted the cigarette to her lips. "You want me to go to this wedding with you." She snapped a farmer's match to life with her thumbnail.

"That's right," said Crow.

Debrowski sucked flame into the cigarette, blew smoke at the ceiling. "Only we go in separate cars."

"I'll have to meet you there," Crow admitted.

"And we don't even go home together."

Crow closed his eyes. Sunlight angled in from the window opposite the bed. He could feel it on his feet. "You make it sound worse than it is."

"Months I'm gone, I come back and this is our big date? We hop into the sack, then arrange to meet at an American Legion Post?"

"It's not like I planned it that way."

"What kind of wedding present is it, you give the bride's father—not *even* her father—you give him a free limo rental? Something you won in a card game? Jesus, Crow, sometimes you amaze me."

Crow opened his eyes a millimeter and watched her smoke.

"I don't see why you have to be the one to drive it," she said.

"I told you why."

"I wish you hadn't agreed to it."

"I wouldn't've if I'd known you were coming home."

"Yeah, well I'm home now."

"Tell me about it."

Debrowski raised her eyebrows and fired twin jets of smoke through her nostrils. "I am telling you."

Crow grinned. Debrowski took another drag and tried to hold a scowl, but her face broke up and she started laughing, then coughing. Crow waited for the hacking to subside.

"You ought to quit those," he said with all the self-righteous confidence of one who had quit—again—just a few months ago.

Debrowski shrugged and swung her legs off the mattress. She walked to the window and looked out. Sunlight silhouetted her body. "You've got a nice view here."

"I sure do," said Crow. He especially liked the bright line where the sun grazed her hip, and the shadows that fell across the backs of her thighs.

"You can see the sky. Downstairs, I can't see anything."

"You know what I don't get?"

"What?"

"How come you don't have any tattoos?"

"I like to keep my options open."

"When we met, I was sure you'd have a lightning bolt or something on your butt."

"You disappointed?" She turned to face him.

Crow smiled. "Not really. Look, I'm sorry about this wedding thing. You don't have to go, you know."

"Not go? Not go to little Carmen's wedding? I wouldn't miss it. The only question is, who am I going to go *with?*"


Debrowski balanced a slab of paté de foie gras on a slice of baguette and bit into it. The heady aroma of chopped black truffles filled her sinuses, raised goose bumps on her bare belly. They were sitting on Crow's porch, looking down at First Avenue. Debrowski had on a pair of Crow's jeans and her motorcycle jacket and nothing else.

"What have you been doing with yourself? I mean, besides playing cards and pumping iron."

Crow followed her example with the paté. "I went fishing with Sam," he said. "And I did that thing for Axel." He tasted the paté, chewed slowly. "This is really good."

"It had better be. It costs about five dollars a bite. We're lucky the customs officer didn't crack it open to look for contraband."

"What else you bring back?"

Debrowski looked in her bag from the duty free and pulled out six more tinned patés.

"More paté? That's all? No cheeses?"

"What were you expecting? What did you bring when you flew back?"

"Nothing," Crow admitted.

"You know, for an unemployed muscle car–driving poker-player, you've got some pretty high standards." Debrowski glared.

Crow helped himself to more paté. "I thought you missed me," he said.

"I did miss you." She reached over and rubbed her knuckles lightly on his scalp. "I was afraid you'd changed."

"I have changed. I'm stronger, and I have less money."

"Me, too. Maybe it's not a bad tradeoff. But you know what the other half of it is? I was afraid you'd changed, and I was afraid you hadn't. You know what I mean?"

"No."

"I was hoping you'd found something to be passionate about, Crow."

"I'm passionate about you."

"Remember when you used to talk about opening a fishing camp?"

"I don't know anything about fishing."

"That's not the point. The point is, you had something going in your head. I mean, is this where you want to be in ten years? Sitting here eating foie gras and waiting for the next card game?"

Crow looked thoughtful. "The paté is not bad," he said.


"I'm sorry," Debrowski said.

Crow looked over but her face was in shadow. He waited until they reached the next streetlight to reply. "Sorry about what?"

"I've been sniping at you ever since I got back." She looked tired. A few more steps and her face returned to shadow.

"You're tired," he said. He was tired, too. Two thirty in the morning, and they'd been wandering for more than an hour, periods of intense conversation interspersed with wordless walking, the soft scuff of his running shoes and the clop of Debrowski's boots, a rhythm like that of a distant train passing. Crow wasn't sure, but he thought maybe they were having a fight. Not a fight exactly. More like a renegotiation.

Debrowski said, "I'm not tired. In Paris, it's time for coffee. I think I had this fantasy I'd come back and you'd have become a marine biologist or something, and you'd grab me and say, 'Let's go to Aruba.'"

"You want to go to Aruba?"

"No. I'm just having this girl fantasy. A handsome man appears and carries me away on his big white horse. That old thing. Don't worry. It'll pass."

"You saying you want to go riding?"

Debrowski's pace faltered, then picked up. "You're being obtuse."

"Not a good quality in a marine biologist slash equestrian."

♠

The Buzz coffee bar never closed. Debrowski added four cubes of jaggery to her espresso, poked at them with a wooden stirrer until they crumbled. A red neon lightning bolt illuminated their window table.

"I think what it is, I think you make me look at myself more than I want to. It's that Crow stare. You take what I got, and you give it right back to me. I remember one time I was talking to Sam, and he told me that's how you win at cards. The other players look at you, and they don't see you, they see themselves."

"If you haven't figured out by now that Sam is full of shit, you're even more screwed up than you think I am."

"Your old man's hipper than you think, Crow."

"Now there's a scary thought."

"I'm thinking about asking him out."

Crow laughed. "Sam would like that."


"You know when I like you best? When you're in trouble. Is that sick?" Debrowski's head rested on Crow's lap. They were on his porch swing, facing east.

"I think it's normal," Crow said. Orange mist bled onto charcoal sky. A row of pigeon silhouettes crowned the apartment building across the street. He could hear soft cooing.

"It doesn't feel normal."

"Normal never does."

Debrowski didn't say anything for more than a minute. He thought she might have fallen asleep, but when he looked down her eyes were on him. She said, "If I hadn't been awake for thirty-six hours, that would probably have sounded really stupid."

"I can't even remember what I said."

"This is kind of like getting drunk together, isn't it?"

Crow frowned. "I've got an idea."

"What's that?"

"Let's get some sleep. We've got to be at a wedding in ten hours."

Debrowski sat up. "I'm too wired from all that coffee. Maybe I'll go downstairs and unpack."

"You go unpack. I'm going to sleep."

"Good. Stay out of trouble. I don't want to have to start loving you all over again."

"I'll do my best."

*The telomere, that cap at the end of every strand of DNA, controls the rate at which our cells age. This is scientific fact. But what many scientists overlook is the equally compelling fact that the telomere is but a physical manifestation of our essential spirit, a measure of our commitment to the Life Program. Why should one individual outlive another? Put quite simply, it is a function of belief and commitment. Do immortals have longer telomeres? Unquestionably.*

*—"Amaranthine Reflections" by Dr. Rupert Chandra*

Aᴿʟɪɴɢ Bɪɢɢʟᴇ ʀᴏᴀᴍᴇᴅ ᴛʜᴇ ɢʏᴍ with a spray bottle and a towel, wiping down the benches, cleaning handprints off the mirrors, picking up bits of lint, and rearranging misracked weights. The only sounds at Bigg Bodies were the squeaking of the spray bottle, the hum of the air conditioning, and the soft clank of iron.

The first customer showed up at ten minutes after six: a large, cheerful, gimpy black man wearing a navy-blue sweatshirt that read, "Amaranthines Have Longer Telomeres." Bigg's eyes flicked to the man's crotch, but saw nothing beyond a baggy pair of sweats. He'd never heard it called a "Telomere" before. And what the hell was an "Amaranthine"? Must be the new member Beaut had signed up. The Amaranthine—if that was what he was—limped straight back to the chest area and loaded a couple of forty-fives onto a bar, then sat down on the bench. Bigg thought about wandering back to introduce himself, make the newbie feel welcome, but he just didn't feel all that friendly at that time of the morning. He moved down the long dumbbell rack, rotating each dumbbell so that the raised numbers on the ends read right-side-up. When he got to the sixty-pounders he remembered again why he was up at dawn, and how Beaut had annexed his massage recliner to keep his foot elevated. He thought about that goddamned Joe Crow.

Fingerprints and chalk spill were getting scarce. Bigg hung up the towel and spray bottle and retired to his office, where he sorted through the basket of papers on his desk. He ran across the membership application that the new guy had filled out. Charles Thickening. The address he'd given was care of something called ACO Ministries. Funny. The guy didn't look like a preacher. Bigg flipped through his pile of unanswered mail. Most of it was ignorable: catalogs from vitamin supplement manufacturers, solicitations from bodybuilding promoters looking for sponsors, and bills for nonessential services. Bigg threw away everything except the utility bills and the latest issue of *MuscleMag*. He briefly considered the invitation to Hyatt Hilton's wedding, shook his head and threw that away, too.

The cold vinyl on his back and knurled steel against his palms took Chuckles back to the iron pile at Stillwater. He turned his head to look at his surroundings. Infinite rows of red upholstered benches and neatly stacked weight racks. This was no prison weight room. This was the real world, where you could eat a Big Mac and open any door and sit under a tree on the grass. Chuckles gripped the barbell and lifted it off the rack. It felt heavy, but that was to be expected. It had been nearly a year since he'd been granted parole, and he hadn't touched a weight since. Chuckles had never much enjoyed pumping iron, but in prison it was something you had to do just to stay even. In prison, the last thing a guy wanted was to get small. Bigger was safer. Maybe that was true on the outside, too. Maybe he should get back into it. According to Amaranthine theory, he should be able to shape his body without the inconvenience of physical exercise, but lately he had noticed that the cells around his middle had been growing faster than the cells in his arms and chest. A little exercise wouldn't hurt.

According to Beaut, the guy with the broken foot, Flowrean did her workouts in the morning, usually about nine or ten, sometimes earlier. Chuckles had decided to get there early, be there when she showed. He didn't want her to think he was following her. He wanted it to be, like, a coincidence. He'd seen what she was like when she was scared. His thigh was still throbbing, and his arm had stiffened up where the nurse had given him his tetanus shot. He did not want to frighten Flowrean. He just wanted to get acquainted.

During his three-year bid at Stillwater Penitentiary, Chuckles had spent a great many hours quietly constructing his fantasy woman. At first, inspired by magazines, television, and his own memories, he had experimented with different types of women—black, white, passive, domineering, tall, short, young, and old. He imagined women named Mai Lee, Gretchen, Thulani, Starflower, Dorita, Punky, and dozens more. He saw them in bathing suits, leather chaps, business suits, evening gowns, and birthday suits. He directed his mind to consider new combinations of physical features and bizarre behaviors—anything to distract him from the raw, cold fact of his incarceration. He conjured up a woman with four breasts, a woman with the brain of an Irish setter, a woman ten feet tall, and a woman who was turned on by the smell of his feet. As the months passed, he discovered common elements in his fantasy women, certain qualities and traits that felt right and true, and he found himself returning to an ever-shrinking repertory of fantasy players. Experimentation slowly lost its appeal and, about fourteen months into his bid, the women in his dreams had coalesced into a single construct: a female of mixed heritage, both fearless and afraid, large and small, alien and familiar. In short, he had conceived a woman very much like Flowrean Peeche.

Since his release from Stillwater, Chuckles had been with four dozen different women, every one of which had been a disappointment. Even his encounters with the First Eldress left him strangely unsatisfied. He understood this to be his own fault, something to do with a discordance between his expectations and the realities of the physical world. As the First Eldress would say, he was not sharing the fullness of his flesh. Sharing was a big part of the Amaranthine Way. The Sharing of the Flesh was one of the keys to stepping out of the Death Program.

Polly was a smart lady. She scared him, but she was smart.

Polly would answer all concerns by telling Chuckles to follow the Sharing of the Flesh, to let his cells lead him beyond his own physical form.

Rupe would tell him to focus his thoughts on a cellular level, to drive out the cells of self-destruction, to open his flesh to a new, life-affirming cellular structure. It came down to the same thing, Chuckles supposed: You get laid a lot.

Chuckles slowly lowered the barbell to his chest, feeling his pectorals stretch, feeling the cells lengthen and separate. He pushed, raising the weight, straightening his arms, squeezing his pecs, then lowered the bar again, repeating the movement, expanding and contracting his muscles. After sixteen reps he racked the bar and closed his eyes, directing the cells in his chest to divide, to grow, to draw nutrients from his blood. This was one of the more advanced Amaranthine skills, one he had been working on for the past several weeks. The process required absolute concentration. It was difficult with his leg and arm throbbing so, but he gave it a few minutes, imagining his chest swelling with new growth.

All things considered, Chuckles's life was going remarkably well. He was free, immortal, employed, and getting oral sex from his boss. But he was still searching for his soulmate, for the one who would bring the present into phase with his self, a woman who could help him share the fullness of his flesh. He had a feeling about this Flowrean Peeche. He thought that he would like to Share his Flesh with her.

♠

Yesterday, Flo had felt embarrassed and sad over her ill-fated luncheon with Joe Crow. What had she expected? She was a musclebound waitress who reeked of dead fish. Last night she had looked at her image in her bathroom mirror and cried. Who would want such a creature? Flo slept fitfully. She dreamed of being lost in an enormous mall, bigger than the Mall of America, but it wasn't a mall, it was a gym, and all the men were looking at her, and she realized she was naked, and all she could think of to do was to dance, as if it was the most natural thing in the world.

She woke up at dawn, hollow-eyed and irritable. She no longer felt sad, she felt angry. If Joe Crow was a fool, she was lucky to be rid of him, lucky to have kept her options open. There were two billion men on the planet, and no reason whatsoever to waste another moment on a man who refused to appreciate her. She should be glad.

Flo zipped herself into a black nylon coverall and grabbed her gym bag. She let her anger propel her out of her condo and into her Miata. She needed to get to the gym, work it off. Who did he think he was, kissing her off like some damn stalker groupie? She banged through the gears, pushing the little car hard through the early-morning traffic. Treating her like a little teenybopper with her first crush. Telling her about his girlfriend in Paris. Paris? Like hell. Probably didn't even have a girlfriend. Probably gay. She was lucky to be rid of the rat weasel skunk son-of-a-bitch.

Flo pulled into the Bigg Bodies parking lot ten minutes after leaving her apartment, some kind of record. Other than the two limos parked at the back, there were only two cars in the lot: Bigg's Cadillac and a yellow Corvette. Joe Crow's car wasn't there, and that was fine with her, though she really didn't give a damn one way or the other.

Bigg was working on the payroll, trying to decide whether to fire Beaut, when he heard the front door buzzer. He leaned across his desk and looked out of his office, caught a glimpse of Flowrean Peeche as she blew past the counter, not bothering to sign in, and headed for the locker room. He regarded the papers on his desk. The numbers looked like meaningless scribbles. He squeezed his eyes closed, then opened them. Nothing had changed. Bigg got up, closed and locked his office door, turned out the light, and climbed into his viewing closet.

Flowrean was standing directly in front of the mirror, staring at her reflection. She wore a silky nylon coverall, black with gold trim. Her gym bag, unopened, sat on the bench behind her. Bigg waited for her to unzip, to shake loose those breasts and flex those remarkable thighs. He waited for her to open her bag, to dress herself in her reeking sweats, to drape that dead-goldfish necklace around her neck. But Flowrean didn't move. She simply stood staring at the mirror, almost as if she were looking straight through it.

♠

Was he watching her? Flo wasn't sure, but she smiled, aiming her eyes at a spot six inches on the other side of the glass. She gave it half a minute, then turned her back to the mirror. She thought about going into one of the shower stalls to change, but that felt wrong. It would be like hiding. She opened her bag and pulled out her workout sweats. The anger she had felt on the drive over was still with her, but now something else was happening, a hollow feeling in her womb, a shiver at the base of her spine. She tugged down the zipper on the front of the coveralls, took a deep breath, and dropped them. It took her less than five seconds to step into her sweat pants and pull on her sweatshirt. She turned back toward the mirror and lowered the necklace of dead goldfish over her head. Three of them had fallen off, but the other three were still hanging in there.

When she came out of the locker room, Bigg was standing behind the front counter studying the morning newspaper, frowning with concentration. Flo walked past him, going directly to the squat rack where she began her warm-ups, a set of twenty-five deep knee bends followed by some long, slow stretches.

The only other person in the gym was a guy doing bench presses. Flo paid no particular attention to him, except to note that he was big and black. She was thinking more about the way she had felt in the locker room, imagining Bigg on the other side of the glass, there but not there, real but not real, like a creature watching her from another dimension. It reminded her of being a little girl, of the excitement she had felt undressing alone in her room at night, wondering if God was peeking.


Chuckles stared at the woman with the snarled hair and rumpled, dirty-looking gray sweats. He wasn't sure. She was about the right size, but she looked different when she wasn't running and screaming and leaping and dressed in gold snakeskin and lime-green pumps. She was barefooted. If he could get a closer look, maybe he'd recognize her feet. He searched for an excuse to walk past her, spotted a drinking fountain, and headed for it. She was on the floor doing a hurdler's stretch, her face to the mat as he walked by. The feet looked right—long and slim, about a size seven, maroon polish on the nails. Chuckles drank a few ounces of water, then made a second pass. This time she looked up, right into his face, showing him those golden eyes.

"S'app'n," Chuckles rumbled, moving quickly past. It was her all right, but what was that *smell*? It reminded him of something out of his past, something sour and sweet and overwhelming. He sat down on his bench and took a deep breath, inhaling the gaseous fragments that had clung to him in passing, and remembered. The smell came from years ago, from his old apartment in St. Paul, across the alley from a Vietnamese restaurant. That was it. The Vietnamese restaurant's dumpster in August: fish sauce and lemongrass, rotting fruit and maggoty meat. He raised his eyes. Flowrean was on her feet, staring at him. What was that around her neck? It looked like a bunch of dead fish.

Chuckles smiled and gave her a little wave. Did she remember him?

She turned away and began a set of calf stretches, looking back over her shoulder every few seconds, as if she thought he might sneak up on her. Chuckles decided to continue doing his bench presses, give her time to get used to him. He added a pair of ten-pound plates to the bar, bringing the weight up to 245, and managed to squeeze out eight reps. When he sat up, she was gone. No. She was at the other end of the gym talking to the guy at the front counter. They both looked at him. Chuckles returned a friendly smile. The counter man smiled back, but Flowrean looked away.

Chuckles loaded another twenty pounds onto the bar and lay down on the bench. He stared up at the knurled steel, his fingers laced across his chest, thinking about two things. He was imagining Flowrean watching him, and he hoped he could still handle that much weight. Back at Stillwater, two sixty-five would not have presented a problem, but that was a year ago. He'd lost a lot of muscle tone since then. Eaten a lot of longjohns.

"Want a spot?"

Chuckles rolled his eyes up to look at the man standing behind him. It was the counter guy.

"My name's Bigg."

"You the owner, huh?"

"Yup. I haven't seen you here before. You just join?"

"Last night. My name's Chuckles. Your man with the sore foot sign me up."

"That would be Beaut, my assistant manager." Bigg checked the plates, snugging them up against the collar. "You look like you could handle more than this," he said. He added a five-pound plate to each end of the bar. "There you go."

"I don't know," Chuckles said.

"Sure you do," Bigg said. "So, you know Flowrean?" He inclined his head toward the squat rack, where she was performing a set of slow, deep, warm-up squats with the empty bar.

"We met," Chuckles said.

"Yeah, that's what she says."

"I didn't think she'd remember. What's she got 'round her neck?"

"Those are her pet goldfish. They give her that little extra something, you know?"

"Uh huh. She got a boyfriend?"

"Flo?" Bigg laughed. "You gonna do your set or not?"

Chuckles grasped the bar. "Sure," he said. He lifted the weight off the rack and, not giving himself time to think, lowered it to his chest, then heaved, the small of his back coming up off the bench, his chest bunching, his arms slowly straightening. At one point the bar stopped its ascent and began to tip to the left. Bigg's hands appeared, lightening the bar by a pound or two, just enough to let Chuckles complete the lift.

"Again," Bigg said.

"I dunno." Chuckles was breathing hard.

"Go for it."

Chuckles took a breath and lowered the barbell. This time, Bigg kept his hands cupped under the bar the whole way. Chuckles stopped it at his chest, then pushed. The bar didn't move. He focused his mind and pushed harder, to no avail. Bigg's hands were gripping the bar, but they weren't helping.

"Hey," Chuckles gasped. "Come on, man."

"You need a little more lift?" Bigg asked, pulling up on the barbell. It came up an inch, then stopped again. "Or maybe you don't need my help." Bigg leaned on the bar, pressing it down into Chuckles's ribcage. Chuckles's arms quivered with effort, fighting the increased weight.

Bigg said, "Flowrean, she likes to be left alone, you know? She comes here, she doesn't want to be bothered. You bother her. You hear?"

Chuckles gave up a nod. Bigg eased up, giving Chuckles room to take a breath. "We've got three rules here at Bigg Bodies. You rack your weights. You pay your dues on time. And you stay the fuck away from Flowrean. Understand?"

Chuckles nodded. He understood. This wasn't so different from prison after all.

With no apparent effort, Bigg lifted the loaded barbell off Chuckles's chest and racked it. "Any time you need a spot, you just give a wave." He gave Chuckles a friendly grin, and walked away.

Chuckles turned his head and looked over at Flowrean doing her slow squats, smiling to herself, her eyes fixed on someplace far away. Sooner or later, he thought, all things must come to pass. One of the advantages to being an immortal was that whether they happened sooner, or later, he would be there.

Polly stood beside the Range Rover watching, her arms crossed, as Rupe lifted the last suitcase into the back and closed the tailgate. Rupe smiled at her and rubbed his hands together. Polly frowned and looked away. She was still sleepy, and angry about being forced to skip her morning café au lait.

"What's the matter, love?" he asked.

"I'm tired, and I want my coffee."

"It's a beautiful day." Rupe gestured skyward.

"I'm worried. I've got a bad feeling. What does Benjy know about running the church? He's been working full time on Stonecrop. What if something comes up?"

"The Charles's will be here to help him."

"That worries me, too." She yawned. "Chip's been acting strange."

"Chuckles will keep an eye on Chip."

"He's been acting weird, too, ever since that woman stuck her heel in his thigh."

"They'll be fine, love. They can watch each other. And Sandra will help Benjy with the day-to-day details—she knows the computer system inside and out. Everything will be fine."

"I can't believe we're doing this."

"You must let go of your doubts, my love." He held his hands out, palms up. "Give them to me."

"Jesus Christ, Rupe, give it a rest, would you? This isn't a goddamn event."

Rupe pushed his hands closer to her. "Give them to me."

Polly sighed. She knew he wouldn't quit until she did as he asked. She reached out her own hands and let him fold them into his own, let him draw her close.

"Give it all to me," he said again. Polly felt the tendrils of energy reaching out to her, felt the heat of his will. For a few seconds, she resisted, holding back, clinging to the solid comfort of her doubts and fears, but then, as if her psychic arteries had suddenly opened, she felt a stream of energy gush out through her palms into her husband. It lasted less than one second. Her knees buckled. She would have fallen if Rupe had not caught her.

"Are you all right?" she heard him ask.

She nodded shakily. The surface of the parking lot looked bright, the pebbles standing out in painfully sharp focus.

"That was a big one," Rupe said.

Polly took a breath and looked around, reorienting herself. They were leaving for Stonecrop. Going away for four weeks. She had been worried about leaving the business in the hands of the Faithful. What was there to worry about? She couldn't remember. And she didn't need that café au lait anymore—she felt strong and alert, energetic enough to jog the seventy miles to Rochester.

She said, "I don't know how the hell you do that."

Rupe smiled. "Neither do I," he said. He looked at his watch. "We had better go. We're supposed to be in Rochester by ten. Dr. Bell was quite clear on that point."

*How old would you be if you didn't know how old you was?*

—*Satchel Paige*

"IT'S A LITTLE TIGHT," CARMEN SAID.

Sophie picked up Carmen's Marlboros from the nightstand and shook one loose. "I told you it would be."

"Maybe it's supposed to be tight."

"I don't think so. That roll you've got going . . . no, I really don't think so."

Carmen looked down at her bare midriff, where the waistband of the skirt was buried in her flesh. She raised her arms and sucked in her stomach, turned her right hip toward the mirror. "That looks pretty good."

"I'd like to see you hold that pose for the whole ceremony. Have you got a light?"

"There's a lighter in my purse. What am I gonna do?"

Sophie shrugged. "We could make you a sash. You know, like a beauty queen." She found the lighter and lit the cigarette. She'd been off them for three months, but marrying off her only daughter, that was no time to quit. She'd been bumming them off Carmen for the past week. "This is a nice lighter," she said.

"Hy gave it to me. It's a Dunhill."

"It looks expensive."

"Three hundred dollars."

Sophie put the lighter back in Carmen's purse. "That would buy a lot of matches."

Carmen tugged the waistband down an inch, revealing a red stripe where it had dug into her stomach. "You don't think we could let it out in back a little?"

Sophie breathed smoke out through her nose. She sat down on the edge of the bed. "Let's have a look."

Carmen swished over to her mother and presented her derriere. Sophie fixed the cigarette between her lips and examined the seam that began at the small of Carmen's back. "There's no extra material back there. I don't see how we could let it out. Unless you want to walk around with your butt hanging out."

"Better than this thing digging into my belly."

"I suppose we could open up the seam, then cover it up with something."

"Like what?" Carmen asked.

Sophie frowned, then smiled. "How about a nice big bow?"

After their little talk, the long telomere guy had simply walked out of the gym without another word. Bigg figured he wouldn't be back, and that was what he told Flowrean.

"I guess I owe you," she said, looking not at all happy about it.

"Just part of our complete membership services package."

Flowrean returned to her workout. She must've done eighteen sets of squats, going all the way up to three fifty-five for her heaviest lift, then coming back down, a plate at a time, working as hard, in the end, to lift the empty bar as she had at three fifty-five. Bigg loved that about Flowrean. She held nothing back. Every set was done to failure, even if she had to repeat a lift thirty or forty times. Two solid hours of brutal lower body work, as much as Bigg himself had done back in his powerlifting days.

Flowrean had gone from the squat rack to the vertical leg press, then on to leg extensions, curls, and three varieties of calf raises, attacking each new exercise with undiminished intensity, leaving each machine pooled with perspiration. At one point, Bigg could stand it no longer and had wiped down the leg extension machine. Flowrean seemed not to take offense—if she even noticed.

She was on the mats now, finishing up her stretching routine, sweat dripping from the tip of her nose, contorting her body in ways that had Bigg adjusting his briefs every thirty seconds. When she finally gave it up and headed into the locker room, Bigg hurried into his office, locked the door, turned off the light, and opened the door to his viewing chamber.

This time, he was not disappointed.

Flowrean had positioned herself directly in front of the mirror. As Bigg watched, she slowly peeled her sodden top up over her head and dropped it on the floor. Her upper body glistened, striped with rivulets of perspiration. Bigg put his face close to the glass, watching one descending droplet, then another. For several seconds she stood there, her breasts rising and falling with each breath, eyes on her reflection, one hand stroking her belly, her index finger making slow circles around her navel. With her other hand, she pushed her sweatpants down past her hips, let them fall around her ankles. Her legs were pumped and flushed. She stepped out of her puddled sweats and turned slowly around, flexing and relaxing her calves, thighs, glutes. Bigg pressed his face to the glass, breathing heavily as Flowrean Peeche showed him, in narcissistic detail, every square centimeter of her flesh.

When she came out of the locker room, Bigg was waiting at the front counter.

"Hey, Flo? You got a second?"

Refusing to meet his eyes, she headed out the door. He caught up with her outside as she was unlocking her car.

"Can I talk to you for a second?"

"I'm kind of busy," she said, opening the door to put it between them. She was still turned on from her performance in the locker room. Being this close to Bigg, having a conversation, felt weird and wrong, as if he had stepped inside of her body.

"I wanted to ask you something."

Bigg wasn't acting like his usual self. He seemed uncomfortable and embarrassed. Flo waited, suddenly curious.

"I was wondering . . . I have to go to a wedding tonight." He held up a slightly crumpled invitation and gave her a crooked smile. "I was wondering if you'd like to go. With me."

Flo gaped. This was so far from anything she had ever expected of Bigg, she did not know how to respond.

Bigg continued, "I don't mean like on a *date*. It's just that I'd feel funny going to a wedding alone, you know? Think of it as a free dinner. That's all."

Flo said, because she did not know what to say, "Dinner?"

"Yes. Dinner and music and, you know, it might be fun."

Flo peered closely at Bigg. Was she missing something? Was this really Arling Biggle?

"You want me to go to a wedding? With you?" This was all very strange. She said, "I don't think so."

"We could take one of the limos."

"A limo?" Flo had never ridden in a limo before.

"I promise not to touch you." Bigg put his hands in his pockets. "I won't let anyone touch you."

"I don't know."

"I'll drive the limo. You can ride in the back. All by yourself."

Flo lowered herself into the driver's seat of her Miata. She rested her hands on the steering wheel and stared out through the windshield, surprised to find herself actually considering it.

"You don't even have to talk to me," Bigg said. "Just sit at the same table. You don't even have to do that."

Flo looked up at him and asked, "Who's getting married?"

"A friend of mine."

Flo shook her head. "I won't know anybody."

"You know me."

"I mean besides you."

Bigg's face sagged, then tightened. "You know Joe Crow, don't you? Works out here? He'll be there."

"Joe Crow?"

"Yeah. He'll be driving the other limo."

The rental tux fit perfect. Hyatt ran his fingers through his hair a few times, made minor adjustments to his tie and cummerbund. He did a slow pirouette, watching himself in the dressing room's three-way mirror, giving himself a suave, slightly cocked smile. Very elegant.

"I do," he said. "I do, I do, I do."

He cleared his throat and loosened the bow tie. He closed one eye, leaned into the mirror, and twisted his features into an expression of agony. "Oh my god!" he moaned, clutching at his side. "Please help me! Oh my god!" He grabbed his stomach and hunched forward, his reflection only centimeters away. He stared into his own eyes, unblinking, holding them open for ten, fifteen, twenty seconds. When he blinked, the tears came. "Lord God in heaven," he sobbed. "They've taken her!"

Sixty seconds later, Hyatt emerged from the dressing room to find Ted the salesman looking extremely concerned.

"Are you all right, sir?" Ted asked.

"I'm perfect," Hyatt said, giving the guy a reassuring grin. "Everything is perfect."

"I'm not s'posed to work till four," Beaut whined.

Arling Biggle squeezed the telephone handset, feeling the plastic flex. "I don't care," he said. "This is an emergency. I gotta go to a wedding."

"You getting married?"

"No. Hy Hilton is."

"The water boy? That's your big emergency?"

Bigg said, "This isn't the time to argue with your landlord *and* your employer, *Leslie.*" He listened to the sound of Beaut breathing into the phone.

"Okay, but I get double time."

"You'll get your butt down here in double time, is what you'll get." He knew he shouldn't keep pushing Beaut's buttons, but he couldn't help it. He was all jazzed up from talking to Flowrean. Sometimes he amazed himself, the things he would do.

"Okay, okay," Beaut said. "I'll be right over. Only you owe me for this."

Bigg hung up the phone. He looked at the clock on his desk, trying to organize the next few hours in his head. He had to get home to find out if any of his suits still fit. There was the one he'd bought for his mother's funeral, that was only a couple years old. If it didn't fit, he'd have to get an emergency alteration job. He knew a guy. And he had to get some kind of flowers or something. Maybe fill up the back of the limo with them, just in case Flowrean got the idea to wear her organic necklace to the wedding. And some kind of present. Did he have time for a haircut? Bigg rubbed his hand over his wispy scalp. Forget the haircut. What he'd do, he'd leave his car at the gym and take one of the limos home, save himself a trip back. And then—shit, he had to come back anyway to give Joe Crow his goddamn limo. Get him to sign a contract for it. Maybe he could have Beaut take care of that . . . on second thought, he'd best keep Crow away from Beaut. Christ almighty, how had this day gotten so complicated?

Flowrean Peeche's Miata descended into the underground parking garage of the Greensward, one of those big apartment buildings downtown. Chuckles pulled over to the curb and stared at the building, fixing it in his mind, wondering whether she lived there, or was simply visiting someone. He could see a man sitting behind a desk in the lobby. Should he ask? That might not get him anywhere. After a moment's thought, he made a U-turn and drove back to a florist's shop he had noticed earlier. One dozen roses with extra baby's breath—Chuckles liked baby's breath—cost him forty-three dollars. He returned to the Greensward, parked in front of the lobby, and carried the roses inside. The security guard was in the process of taking a huge bite from what looked like a peanut-butter-and-pickle sandwich. He looked up and frowned, one cheek distended.

"Delivery for Ms. Flowrean Peeche," Chuckles said.

The guard flexed his eyebrows and nodded as he chewed. He set the sandwich on his desk and picked up the phone. He was about to punch in a number when he realized that if anyone answered, he would be unable to speak. Returning the phone to its cradle, he began working his jaw furiously, holding up one forefinger, bidding Chuckles to wait.

Chuckles said, "I'll just leave these with you, okay?" He put the bouquet on the desk and backed away. The guard, still chewing, watched him leave.

"That's not acceptable. You are scheduled to be here. I have to leave at o-four hundred." Chip Bouchet pressed the phone against his mouth. "That's four o'-clock." He listened, nodding. "I know you know that. I have an engagement.

You were scheduled. We have a schedule you know—" He blinked, looked at the phone, hung it up. "That was not strategic," he said.

Benjy Hiss, sitting across from Chip in the ACO Security Annex, said, "What's that?"

"That was Chuckles," said Chip. "He says he's sick."

"Oh. Was he supposed to work today?"

"He was scheduled."

Benjy shrugged and returned his attention to the multipage memo on his lap. "Man, they don't want much, do they?"

"Who?"

"Our fearless leaders. Four weeks they'll be gone, and they want miracles. This will take four months."

Chip compressed his thin lips. This scrawny little raghead with his accent and his black eyes was another example of what had gone wrong with the church. How could Polly and Rupe entrust their entire organization to this fast-talking Iranian or Arab Jew or whatever the hell he was? Didn't they ever read the papers? Those people were all insane.

Benjy said, "They want all the rooms on the east wing repainted. Do we have any painters among the Faithful?"

"I have to leave at o-four hundred."

"So leave. I'll be here. Rupe wants new carpet in his office. Polly wants a new *window*. A *window*! What does she think, it's like hanging a picture?"

Chip shook his head. He did not like surprises, especially today. Chuckles calling in sick—more evidence that the church was rotting from within, its foundations weakened by the lies of the elders. Other people had become ill, too. Becky the shipping clerk had caught a cold. And Nan Blagen, one of the ACO's wealthiest members, had recently undergone surgery for breast cancer. Polly and Rupe had concealed Nan's illness from the Faithful, but Chip had overheard them talking about it in Rupe's office, where he had planted one of his microphones. Immortals weren't supposed to get sick. If they got sick, they had done it to themselves. Or the church had failed to protect them. Because the corruption of the elders filtered down to the Faithful. Then there was the crazy woman in the hall, and her friend the referee. More signs of corruption. He kept thinking about what Chuckles had told him a few weeks ago. He imagined Polly, the First Elder, kneeling on the floor, unzipping his pants—

"No!" he barked.

Benjy jumped. The memo fell off his lap onto the floor.

"Whatsamatter?"

"Nothing," said Chip, embarrassed by his outburst.

Benjy picked up the memo and found the page he had been reviewing. "They want to completely redecorate the auditorium and the gymnasium. And look here—" He stabbed the page with his forefinger. "Put up website. Three words. 'Put up website.' Like 'Take out trash.' What are they thinking? I just snap my fingers, and we're on the Net?"

"I have to leave at four," Chip said.

"Fine. I'll lock up. I'll lock the doors, and then I'll 'put up website.'"

"There are procedures. Twelve doors. Windows to check. Surveillance and alarm system protocols."

Benjy smiled and leaned back in his chair. "Cheep, I know all that. Who do you think installed the alarms?"

Chip pinched his nostrils shut with his left hand, clamped his lips shut, and flexed his diaphragm—an exercise he had been performing since he was a kid. The increased internal pressure calmed him and helped him think. He held it in for about ten seconds, then released his nostrils and let the air hiss slowly out through his nose.

Benjy said, "What are you doing? Popping your ears?"

"Polly said that one of us, me or Chuckles, were supposed to be here always."

"What, twenty-four hours a day?"

"During business hours."

"Oh. So, do you take everything she tells you literally?"

"What d'you mean?"

"Polly says we are going to live forever. You believe that literally?"

Chip was shocked. "What?"

"Do you think we are immortal, Cheep?"

"Yes!"

Benjy nodded. "Good. I was just checking. But as far as leaving work early, I wouldn't worry about it. What's a couple of hours when you're going to be around for a few thousand years?"

*I say, beware of all enterprises that require new clothes, and not rather a wearer of new clothes.*

—Henry David Thoreau

"THERE'S NO FOOL LIKE AN OLD FOOL," Axel said as he gave a final tug on Sam's tie.

Sam said, "I heard that before." The two old men stood stiffly in front of Sophie's vanity, awkward in their jackets and ties. Sam had shown up twenty minutes earlier, looking for help with his tie, a four-inch-wide acid trip in orange and bile green polyester.

"That's 'cause it's always been true. You don't believe me, take a look."

Sam was already looking in the mirror, grinning at his reflection. "I may be an old fool, but I damn sure got me a date." His three-piece suit, an iridescent blue polyester relic from the seventies, shimmered luxuriously. "She still fits," he said.

"It's quite a suit, Sam."

"Bought it for my daughter's wedding. Turned out I never got my invite, but I got myself this suit just in case."

"Yeah, you look pretty sharp for an old fool. Sort of like a bluebottle fly."

"You ain't lookin' too bad yourself." Sam gave Axel a poke in the cummerbund.

Axel shrugged, causing his tuxedo jacket to rise and catch under his armpits. He shook out his arms and tugged down on the lapels, returning the jacket to its original shape. "You know, I bet it cost me more to rent this monkey suit than it cost you to *buy* that thing."

"Traded a valve job on a six-banger Camaro for it."

"Like I said," Axel said. He looked at the alarm clock. "I wish Sophie would get back here. We're gonna be late."

"You got time, Ax. They ain't gonna get married without you and your checkbook." Sam leaned toward the mirror, scratching his neck. "Think I oughta shave again?"

"I don't expect it'll make any difference. Once she gets a load of your sartorial splendor, she's not gonna notice anything else."

"I guess you're right. Hey, you got another beer?" Sam headed toward the kitchenette.

Axel followed, walking with the peculiar gait of a seventy-four-year-old man wearing a tuxedo for the first time in half a century. Sam had located a Budweiser and was pouring it into his mouth.

Axel said, "Your first date since nineteen sixty-nine, you don't want to show up drunk."

Sam swallowed and wiped his mouth with an iridescent blue sleeve.

"You got that one dead wrong, Ax. This little gal, I got to do the drinking for both of us."


As soon as Sophie left, Carmen looked again at the bow attached to the back of her dress. Her legs went weak. She sat down on her bed. The window was bright with sunlight, but the room felt dark. The clock on her dresser read 2:09. The red numerals frightened her. For more than two months now she had observed the people around her moving toward this day, carrying her with them, pushing and pulling, and all the while she had on some level thought that it really had nothing to do with her, that she just happened to be traveling in the same direction. Now here she was, still with them, a huge white bow on her ass. She lifted her left hand and looked at the ring. She had never had it appraised. Her hand trembled. She tucked it under her armpit and squeezed until she felt the diamond or whatever it was grinding into her rib. That had been a shock—learning in nursing school anatomy class that men and women had the same number of ribs. She only remembered a few things from the catechism classes her father had made her attend, but one of them was that men had one fewer rib than women because God had taken one out of Adam to make Eve. Which had turned out to be untrue. A sudden visual memory of her father came and went, leaving behind an unwelcome notion. Carmen tried to shake it, but the idea wouldn't go away. She went into the kitchen and opened her purse. In her wallet, between her phone card and an expired student ID, she found a small color photograph of herself, nine years old, holding a giant stuffed Pink Panther, standing beside a tall man with blond hair and an off-center smile. They were standing in front of a sofa she remembered spilling a chocolate milk all over and getting yelled at by Sophie. Their pupils were red from the flash camera.

Carmen's earliest memory of her father, Gerry Roman, was from when he had visited their home the day that picture had been taken. She remembered him as a cheerful man who had burst into their life with flowers and gifts and plans to buy a big house on a lake where they could all live together. He had been living in St. Louis, he told them, making it big in real estate, and now he had a deal going in the Twin Cities and he was about to get rich. After a lot of talking, Sophie had agreed to let him stay with them in Landfall, just for a few weeks while he put his big land deal together. It was a heady time. Carmen remembered going to the zoo, and to fancy restaurants, and to a lot of other places she had never been. Gerry Roman had got religion down in St. Louis, so they all joined St. Mary's Catholic Church and Carmen began to attend catechism classes, where she had learned all about Adam and Eve and the ribs, and that men were made out of mud, and all about the Blessed Virgin Mary and the martyrs. Gerry had stayed with them for most of that summer until his land deal fell apart and he got into a drunken fight with Sophie and hit her and she stabbed him in the face with a paring knife and the cops came—that had been quite a night. A few months later they heard that Gerry Roman had died in an auto accident.

Carmen set the snapshot down on the table and stared at the image of her father. She hadn't looked at the photo for a couple years, but it was true, what she had feared. He did look a lot like Hy Hilton. Not as if they were brothers or anything, but the same general format: tall, blond, and smiley. Carmen had once heard something about women marrying their fathers, meaning they married men who reminded them of their fathers. Maybe it was just something that happened, a fact of life over which she had no control. There were a lot of those things in her life. Usually she avoided thinking about them. Like the pregnancy test kit in the bathroom. Sophie had given it to her a week ago, and she still hadn't got up the nerve to pee on the stick. Carmen let her mind spin off into areas having nothing to do with marriage or fertility. It landed on ice cream.

When Hyatt arrived home wearing his tuxedo, Carmen was sitting at the kitchen table wearing an apron over her wedding dress, drinking a bottle of beer, and eating French vanilla ice cream from a half gallon tub, and reading *Modern Bride.* She looked up at him.

"Look at you," she said.

Hyatt said, "Is that it?"

"Is that what?"

"Is that the dress? That's what you're wearing?"

Carmen looked down at her dress. "This would be the dress," she said. "Only without the apron. You're not supposed to see it, you know." She was feeling a bit more relaxed now, full of beer and ice cream.

"Stand up," Hyatt said.

Carmen stood up. "Actually, we're not even supposed to ride to the church together. We're doing all kinds of stuff wrong, Hy."

"That's the wedding dress?"

"You want to know something? I don't even know why we're getting married."

"That's really the dress?"

Carmen plucked a cigarette from the pack on the table. "I've got a bad feeling about this, Hy." She lit her cigarette. "We're doing everything wrong."

"You look like something out of a rock video. I thought we agreed that this was going to be a traditional wedding."

"Traditional? What's traditional? Getting married at an American Legion? You know what Sophie asked me? She asked me who was my maid of honor. I don't *have* a goddamn maid of honor. I didn't even get a freakin' bridal shower."

Hyatt couldn't stop staring at the dress. It was white, but did not resemble a wedding dress in any other respect. In the first place, there wasn't enough of it. The skirt was all but transparent, a filmy, ghostly dome of fabric sprinkled with small white explosions. Her midriff presented a startling expanse of uncovered flesh. Four thin white fabric chains ran from the waist of the skirt, crisscrossed her back, and ended at a two-inch-wide satin-covered choker. Two more fabric chains attached to the front of the choker provided structural support for a pair of jutting, conical breast cups somewhat reminiscent of a 1956 Cadillac bumper but looking more like a pair of space shuttle nose cones. An enormous white bow was anchored to the region of her tailbone.

Hyatt said, "I was kind of hoping for something more virginal, Carm. Something that would look sweet and innocent on TV." He frowned. "I can see your underwear right through that thing."

"I'll wear pantyhose."

Hyatt tried to imagine Carmen on TV. Maybe it would work. Maybe this outfit would look better on a twenty-six-inch color television screen. He imagined how it would look all torn and bloody. The rock video styling might turn out to be a plus. "I like the bow," he said.

Carmen gave him her arched eyebrow, are-you-out-of-your-mind look.

"I hate the bow," she said, cracking open another beer.

There were times when Crow would not have minded living a shorter life. He wished he could excise certain periods of time, such as most of the years he had spent playing policeman in Big River, or the last six months of his ill-fated marriage, or the times he had been sick with the flu, or hung over . . . or those last few hands in Las Vegas. If he could simply slice out the bad parts he would still be a young man. Maybe even a teenager if he were to cut out all the little dead periods between doing things he enjoyed and doing things he did not want to do. Like now, sitting out on the porch checking the time every five minutes waiting until it was time for him to pick up the limo and do his chauffeur thing for Axel. This was a part of his life he could do without. Milo sat on the railing staring at him, giving his tail a jerky twitch every few seconds.

Crow said, "I suppose you think I should be doing something productive, like feeding you."

Milo's eyes dilated slightly.

"Maybe I should open a pet shop. Sell cats. What do you think? What do you think you'd go for?"

Milo slashed the air with his tail.

"I'm talking to the goddamn cat," said Crow.

Mile dropped softly from the railing to the porch floor and stalked back into the apartment.

"Now I'm talking to myself." Crow heard the sound of clattering lifters. He looked down and saw a scarified blue Plymouth idling at the curb. The last time he'd seen that vehicle, his father's rear end had been hanging out of the engine compartment. His perception was confirmed seconds later when Sam himself stepped out of the car wearing—Crow blinked—iridescent blue coveralls? No, it wasn't coveralls, it was a suit. And what was wrong with his head? Crow experienced a moment of disorientation. Something wrong with his hair. No. No cap. Had he ever seen his father without a cap on his head?

He had now. Crow leaned over the railing. "Hey Sam! What's going on?"

Sam looked up from the sidewalk, shaded his eyes with one hand, and grinned. "Son?"

"I've never seen you dressed up before. What's the occasion?"

"Ax's wedding."

"You mean Carmen and Hyatt's wedding?"

"Same thing."

"It's over on the other side of town. What are you doing here?" Crow asked.

Sam shrugged. He seemed embarrassed. "Got a *date*," he said, setting his jaw in a way that dared Crow to contradict him.

Crow heard Debrowski's door open. "Well, look at you!" he heard her say. "That is one handsome rag you got on there, Sam O'Gara. How am I going to keep the rest of the women away from you?"

It may have been a trick of the afternoon light, but Crow thought he saw his father blush.

♠

Axel had seen Sophie in a tizzy before, but never quite like this. Bouncing from one end of the mobile home to the other, moving in short, sharp jerks like a wind-up doll or a character in a cheap animated cartoon. Her dress, a stiff, royal blue taffeta garment with pointy shoulders, seemed to be a fraction of a second slow—her body would move first, then the dress would have to do a frantic scramble to catch up. She stopped at the sink and washed the two dirty glasses, then zipped a few feet to her left and threw away the empty beer cans Sam had left on the counter. Axel could hardly follow her actual movements. She was doing this, then suddenly doing that, followed instantly by a swish of taffeta. She watered her coleus plant, examined her fingernails, talking the whole time but saying nothing, using her voice like a safety valve on a pressure cooker.

He watched her from his chair, hands clasping his knees, keeping his mouth shut even though he was about to explode himself. Axel looked at his watch, again. They were supposed to be at the church in thirty minutes. It was a ten minute drive, but he liked to leave some extra time for the unexpected. Flat tires could happen anywhere, at any time. There could be a traffic jam. Besides, it never hurt to be early. Sophie knew how he felt about that, but here she was cleaning the kitchen and watering plants. Now she was looking at herself in the mirror. How many times had she done that in the last half hour? About as many times as Axel had looked at his watch. He wanted to say, "Let's go," but he was afraid that if he said it at the wrong moment, or in the wrong tone of voice, she would go *sproing,* and it would be all over.

Best to wait. Sophie wouldn't want to be late for her daughter's wedding. Any second now she would pick up that little beaded purse and look at him expectantly.

Axel had no longer had that thought than Sophie turned the full intensity of her narrow-eyed gaze upon him.

"What are you staring at?"

"Nothing," Axel said.

"Nothing? Do you know how much I paid for this dress?"

"You look great," Axel said. "You've never looked better."

Sophie said, "Huh!" and turned away, but she looked pleased. After another minute or two of nervous puttering, she grabbed her purse.

"What are we waiting for?" she asked.

"Nothing," said Axel. "Not a thing."

*In the future, physical aging will be considered an eccentricity, an embarrassment, a form of pointless self-destructive behavior. Perhaps even an art form.*

—*"Amaranthine Reflections" by Dr. Rupert Chandra*

"I'M NOT WEARING THE HAT," Crow said.

They were standing beside one of Bigg's white limousines. At ten o'clock in the morning the air was already uncomfortably warm and moist. Crow was wearing his only suit, a navy-blue tropical worsted he had bought last summer for Tommy Fabian's funeral. Tommy, one of Sam and Axel's old friends, had been the only other man at that small gathering to be wearing a suit. This was the first time since that dreary day that Crow had worn the thing. A year ago it had fit him perfectly. Now it was tight around the chest and shoulders, but it looked great next to the thing Bigg was sporting—a gray herringbone sport coat with black leather detailing on the lapel points and pocket flaps, buttons made from Mexican coins, and a red carnation pinned to the lapel. It fit him so snugly that his every movement was accompanied by the faint sounds of threads parting.

"You want to drive an Arling Biggle limousine, you wear the hat." Bigg set the navy-blue chauffeur cap on Crow's head. "This is a class operation. I got a reputation." He laughed.

"Yeah, right. Speaking of class, how's Beaut doing?"

"He's limping along. You sure you got a chauffeur's license?"

"I got one," Crow growled. He slid onto the driver's seat.

"Mind if I take a look at it?"

Crow said, "Yes." He slammed the door.

Bigg knocked on the glass; Crow lowered the window and raised his eyebrows.

"Watch those right turns," Bigg said. "I'm holding you responsible for damages to this vehicle."

"Don't worry about it," Crow said. He only had to drive the thing a few miles. Pick up Carmen and Hyatt, deliver them to the American Legion, and then drop them at the Radisson after the reception. What could go wrong?

Driving out of the parking lot, he missed the curb cut with his rear wheels and nearly clipped a utility pole. He heard Bigg shout something.

"Watch those right turns," Crow muttered to himself. He tossed the chauffeur cap out onto the street.

Chuckles laughed. Even from fifty yards away he could see the vein pop out on Bigg's forehead as he shouted at the guy in the limo. The man had no self control—yelling and shaking his fist even after the guy was long gone; nothing much he could do. Chuckles pushed the last of the longjohn into his mouth and smiled as he chewed.

One of the things that had helped him do his bid in Stillwater was the fact that he was slow to anger, especially if he had a full stomach. A guy bumped him in line, or gave him some shit, or looked at him wrong, Chuckles wouldn't lose his cool. He wouldn't even *feel* angry. Not right away. For Chuckles, anger began as a dull ache, barely felt, that would get bigger and hotter until it filled him up, swelling his throat and turning his eyes red at the corners. It sneaked up on him. Sometimes he didn't even know he was mad until he saw himself in a mirror, or noticed that his lips hurt from being squeezed tight together.

That morning, when Bigg had been pressing the barbell down against his chest, Chuckles had felt fear and discomfort, but he had not been angry. He had seen Bigg as a force of nature, a sudden thunderstorm, or an earthquake. It was all about understanding one's own psychology. No point in getting upset.

But that was then. Now, as Chuckles watched Bigg from his Corvette, he let the anger begin to flow. His mind became a flickering catalog of jailhouse revenge: the sharpened spoon handle between the ribs, the hand in the license plate press, the lightbulb up the ass. He allowed himself to imagine each of these acts, like watching TV, and felt the heat in his throat. That was how it had been in prison, coming on slow, giving him time to plan, to channel that sweet, hot energy.

He watch Bigg get into the white limousine, back it out of its parking stall, pull out onto the street. Chuckles dropped the vette into gear and followed.

Rupert Chandra heard a woman's voice: "Now Mister Chandra, you behave yourself." He felt sharp nails digging into his wrists. Everything was black, and he did not know where he was, and his entire body ached. He tried to speak, but his mouth wasn't working. He heard a noise like a moan coming from his throat.

"Don't try to talk, just relax." Hands cupped his shoulders and pushed him down into a chair. He realized that he'd been standing. "Sit here and relax, the doctor will be just a few minutes. Everything went fine, you're just a little muzzy from the anesthetic."

Anesthetic? It came to him then, where he was. At Youthmark, Dr. Niles Bell's private hospital. He raised a hand to his face, felt his fingertips brush fabric before his wrist was grasped and pulled gently away.

"Try not to disturb the dressings, Mr. Chandra."

He cleared his throat and tried again to speak. "Polly?" It came out sounding more like "oll-ee," but the woman seemed to understand.

"Your wife is fine," she said. "She's resting right now. The reason you can't talk is because we have your jaw immobilized. We'll take the brace off in a few minutes as soon as the doctor is free."

"Ah an *ee*!"

"You can't see because of the bandages. Your eyes are fine, Mr. Chandra. Everything is just fine."

Rupe nodded and tried to relax his body.

It was all coming back to him now.

Flo's closet, everything in it, was laid out on her bed or spread on the floor. What does one wear to ride in a limousine to a wedding? She had tried on just about everything.

The outfit she kept going back to was what she thought of as the "pipe," a metallic silver-gray, calf-length, sleeveless sheath with a plunging neckline that reached nearly to her navel. The fabric—she hadn't a clue what it was made of—looked like liquid titanium. She loved the way it shimmered and laid itself close on her body, especially when worn over nothing at all. She'd bought it months ago, but had never worn it. The problem was that it just didn't work with her coloring—or so she'd been told by the makeup lady at Dayton's, who told her that she was an "autumn" and warned her off of blue and gray apparel. But she really loved the pipe. It was so shiny and sleek and beautiful it begged to be touched, but it also possessed a fearsome aspect, as if brushing against it might cause one's bones to shatter.

Flo held the dress up to her naked body and stared fiercely at the mirror, imagining how it would be, all these people around her, men in suits, the bride and groom, Joe Crow. She imagined Bigg on the other side of the mirror.

The makeup lady was right. The silver-gray color was jarring against her warm olive skin, but maybe that was good. Maybe that was what made the dress so powerful. Add some pale silver lipstick to the mix, and her silver spike-heeled sandals . . . Flo smiled and did a dance for the mirror, watching the way the light jumped across the silver fabric.

She would look like a techno-Amazon from the fifth dimension. Was that the look she wanted?

Absolutely.


Although he was not an educated man, Charles Thickening had done a good deal of reading during his bid in Stillwater. His reading had begun as a search for sexually explicit materials in the prison library. He'd found few scantily clad starlets in *People* magazine and, by referencing the most dog-eared back issues of *National Geographic,* he had found some smudged photographs of topless African women with the longest, skinniest tits he'd ever seen, like nylon stockings with shriveled tangerines in their toes. Other than that, his library search had been largely fruitless.

The best reading materials were to be found in the prison black market. Some of the inmates could afford to subscribe to magazines such as *Sports Illustrated, Prison Life,* and the ever popular *Vogue.* These magazines quickly entered the prison economy, trading for cigarettes and other items of interest. Now and then, a copy of *Hustler* or *Penthouse* would somehow make its way into the population. Such a treasure could be purchased or rented for an exorbitant sum, but usually lasted only a week or two before becoming unreadable due to excessive handling.

Like every other inmate, Chuckles would have loved to spend his cell time looking at photographs of naked, pouting eighteen-year-old women, but since he could not afford the best, he contented himself with publications of lesser interest such as *Men's Health, Muscle and Fitness,* and *Newsweek. Muscle and Fitness* was his favorite. Not only were there lots of pictures, but the women had some real meat on them. Even the articles were interesting. It was in the pages of *Muscle and Fitness* that Chuckles had first come to understand the importance of the mind-body connection. He had learned that the body is an extension of the mind, and that understanding psychology is the key to success. Every bodybuilding champion, from Charles Atlas to Arnold Schwarzenegger, said the same thing. With the right mental attitude, anything is possible.

It was during that same period that Chuckles had first heard of the Amaranthine Church of the One. He had come across one of their booklets in the TV room mixed in with a pile of old *Watchtower* and *Christian Life* magazines and had started reading it. Almost at once, Chuckles had recognized the truth and the power of the Amaranthine teachings. It became suddenly clear to him that if the mind of Arnold Schwarzenegger could produce the body of Arnold Schwarzenegger, then it must be equally possible for other minds to sustain eternal life.

The next day, he had written to the church requesting additional information and, when he made parole nine months later, he had attended his first Extraction Event. Shortly thereafter, Charles Thickening became immortal.

Chuckles had to remind himself of this fact every now and then. Like now, as he followed the limousine down Third Avenue. He had no plan. He was simply gathering information, trying to get a feel for the guy.

So far, he had followed the limo to a florist shop on Franklin Avenue, where Bigg and a guy in a green apron had loaded three large flower arrangements into the back. There'd been a minute or two there when Chuckles had almost made his move. But the guy in the flower shop had been looking out the window, and there'd been too many people on the street and besides, it hadn't felt right.

"You got lots a time," he said, half to himself and half to Bigg.

He held on to that concept all the way downtown, right up until the limo slowed and turned into the circular driveway of a familiar-looking high-rise. The Greensward condominiums. Chuckles felt his heart and stomach collide. Bigg and Flowrean? He pulled over to the curb.

"Now you got *no* more time," he muttered.

*Wedlock, indeed, hath oft compared been*
*To public feasts, where meet a public rout,—*
*Where they that are without would fain go in,*
*And they that are within would fain go out.*

—*Sir John Davies*

"ONWARD, JAMES. TO THE CHAPEL."

Crow felt his neck go rigid. He turned around and looked at the couple sitting in the back of the limo. Carmen, looking even sleepier than usual, in her outlandish dress, conical breast cups jutting from above a fluffy, translucent skirt. Hyatt looked as awkward as a prom date in his maroon tuxedo, a goofy smile on his face, his hair nearly brushing the ceiling. The moment they'd climbed into the limo, Carmen had popped open a bottle of Champagne.

Crow said, "Don't push it, Hy. You could end up walking."

Hyatt shrugged, whispered something to Carmen, who giggled.

Crow pressed a button on the dash and a privacy panel emerged from the seat back, separating him from his passengers. He put the limo in drive and pulled away from the curb. The best thing to do, he decided, would be to take whatever shit Hy dealt him and just get the whole stinking afternoon behind him. Ten minutes to the American Legion Post. He turned on Lake Street, heading east. He could hear occasional bursts of laughter interrupting muted conversation. They were about eight blocks from their destination when Crow heard a knocking behind his head. He lowered the privacy panel.

"Could you make a stop for us, Joe?" Hyatt asked.

"What for?" Crow asked.

"There's a Clark station up here. Carmen needs some cigarettes."

Crow tried to think of a good reason to refuse, but could come up with nothing. He pulled into the gas station. Hyatt perched a five-dollar bill on his shoulder.

"Would you mind getting them, Joe? She smokes Marlboros. The box."

Once again, Crow could think of no good reason to refuse. He took the five and went into the small building. Maybe he should buy a gas station, or a little convenience store. Sell cigarettes and Pepsi for a living. The Hispanic kid behind the counter was absorbed in an examination of his fingernails.

Crow said, "Pack of Marlboros, please."

The kid looked up. His eyes found Crow's face, then shifted to something behind him. His mouth fell open. Crow turned and saw a pair of nostrils coming at him. He had less than a quarter of a second to put a face around the nostrils. He never saw the thing that crashed into the base of his skull.


Drew Chance imagined himself telling his wife, Franny, about Hyatt Hilton's wedding.

"It was a really goy deal," he would say. "Red punch in plastic glasses, beer in cans, and a cash bar f'Chrissake."

It was, in short, exactly the sort of affair Franny would hate. She should be happy not to be here.

"Pink paper tablecloths and printed paper napkins," he would say. "They got married in a freaking American *Legion*! There were stuffed fish on the walls."

If he'd brought her along she'd never have let him forget it. At the same time, the fact that he hadn't shown her the invitation, giving her no opportunity to decline, that was turning into a problem. His explanation that the wedding was strictly business had done little to calm her. All she understood was that he was going to a party without her.

"The parents of the bride live in a *trailer* park," he'd told her. "I just have to show my face, shake a few hands, then get out of there. I'm going with a cameraman. It's *work*, Franny!"

His protests hadn't helped. And his last minute offer to bring her along had only made matters worse since, as he should've known, there was no way she was gonna coldcock the thing without a new dress and an afternoon having her hair and nails done. No, what Franny would do, she would hold this one over his head. She'd parlay this perceived slight into another fur coat. Or a week at some Palm Desert spa. Drew shuddered at the imagined expense.

He looked around at the people filling the hall: a preponderance of elderly couples, many of whom looked as though they could not remember why they were there. One of the standouts was a big old guy in a tuxedo who was making hostlike overtures to anyone who passed within range of his considerable reach. Drew overheard him introduce himself as "Axel." That was perfect. No doubt Lars, Sven, and Gunter would likewise be in attendance.

The bride and groom had not yet arrived. Drew hoped they wouldn't be long. He wanted to get through the ceremony, then offer his congratulations, grab Deano, the camera guy, and get the hell out before they started square dancing or whatever the hell it was they did at these things. Where had that Deano gone to, anyway? There, over by the buffet table, drinking a beer, the camera slung over one shoulder. Another half hour and Deano would be shit-faced, but Drew didn't much care. He could be passed out in his van—if there was nothing to shoot, it wouldn't make a rat's ass worth of difference.

Drew sidled toward the entrance, where the wedding gifts were piled on a folding table. An unimpressive haul—a mere three dozen or so gift-wrapped boxes, the largest of which might have contained a bread machine, or a popcorn popper. Drew permitted himself a superior, pitying smile. He'd done better at his Bar Mitzvah, thirty years ago.

He edged close to the gifts and pulled an envelope from his coat pocket. He looked over the stacked gifts until he found a medium-sized one with a nice, reasonably expensive-looking wrapping and a card attached to the outside. A toaster? Maybe one of those pricey European models. He took a quick look around to make sure nobody was watching, then switched cards.

Shopping for the perfect wedding gift had never been easier.

The scene reminded Axel of the state fair, only more intense. People coming in, not quite sure what to do, gathering in clusters looking over at the buffet table. Axel bounced from one group to another, introducing himself to those he didn't recognize, exchanging happy greetings with those he did. Bob the taffy guy was there with his wife and daughter, and so was Pete Carlson the Kiddy Train driver. Axel met some of Sophie's old friends for the first time, and a lot of friends of Hyatt's. None of Hyatt's relatives, though—he said he didn't have any. Weird. Axel still had his doubts about this whole affair, but it was too late now. Nothing to do but try to make sure people had a good time.

A thin young man with a camcorder was moving among the people, shining lights at them and asking questions. Axel didn't know who the guy was, but he liked the idea that the evening was being captured on videotape. Probably one of Sophie's ideas. He'd have to ask her about that.

Axel's natural inclination was to lead everyone he talked to over to the buffet table, but Sophie grabbed him early on and put a stop to that. She said no eating until after the ceremony. He supposed she was right—it wouldn't do to have folks chowing down during the "I do's." The problem for Axel was that feeding people was what he did, and the Swedish meatballs were the best he'd ever had. After Sophie put the kabosh on the prenuptial snacking, Axel had to content himself with just *telling* people about the food. He opened every new conversation with, "I hope you didn't eat before you came!"

Sam O'Gara and his date, Laura Debrowski, showed up a few minutes before six o'clock. Axel thought it incestuous and altogether peculiar that Sam should be dating his own son's girlfriend. He was fairly certain that Laura Debrowski was not thinking of Sam romantically, but what Sam was thinking—that was anybody's guess.

Axel shook Sam's hand and said, "Hope you didn't eat before you came!"

Sam tipped his head back, gave Axel a bleary look of semirecognition, and said, "You better take that back, mister." He raised a fist. "That's my woman you're talkin' 'bout!"

Axel looked at Debrowski, who rolled her eyes and tightened her grip on Sam's arm.

"Sam's having a good time," she said, "Aren't ya, big guy?"

"Firs' date in twenny years!"

"He's snookered," Axel said, his voice filled with wonder.

"I'm not snoogered." Sam pulled a pint bottle of Jim Beam from his suitcoat pocket. He tugged his other arm from Debrowski's grip and uncapped the bottle. "I'm shit-faced," he said proudly, taking a hit of whisky.

"Jeez, Sam, they aren't even married yet."

Debrowski reclaimed her date's arm. "What do you say we find a place to sit, big guy?" She winked at Axel and pulled Sam toward the back of the hall.

A bright light flashed in Axel's eyes.

"Hello there, sir! Are you the father of the bride?"

"Uh . . ." Axel did not know what to say. The light was blinding him.

"We are here with the father of the bride, waiting for the bride and groom to appear. Spirits are running high here at American Legion Post 684." The camera swung toward the retreating Sam O'Gara, then back to Axel. "I understand that the groom is a man of some importance in the community. A water distributor?"

Axel held up a hand, blocking the bright light. "Listen, do you mind turning that thing off?"

"Just doing my job, sir. Do you have anything to say to the *Hard Camera* viewers?"

"Uh . . . I'm on TV?"

"That's right."

"Uh . . . Just having a good time here. You see this buffet? We got a lot of food here!"

Axel felt a breeze, heard the rustle of taffeta and Sophie's flinty voice in his ear.

"Where *are* they?"

"Who?"

"Carmen and Hyatt! Where are they? They were supposed to be here five minutes ago!"

"We seem to have a situation here, folks," said the cameraman. "The mother of the bride senses disaster. Could this be the beginning of something greater? Something newsworthy?"

Sophie snapped her head toward the cameraman, her mascaraed eyelashes trembling like spastic caterpillars. Taffeta swishing, blindingly blue in the glaring light, she advanced on him. "Who the *hell* are *you*?" she demanded, making a swipe at the camera.

The man pulled the camera up out of her reach and backed up a few steps.

"Turn that light off before I bust it over your goddamn head, you little twerp."

The light went out.

Sophie returned her attention to Axel. "That Joe Crow was supposed to pick them up. What if he didn't pick them up? All these people here. What am I going to do?"

Axel clasped her shoulders. "Take it easy, Soph. They probably ran into traffic. They'll be here."

Sophie shook herself loose. "If that girl doesn't show up soon I swear I'm gonna kill her. I need a cigarette." She scanned the room, head swiveling like a high-speed radar dish. Axel wasn't sure whether she was looking for the wedding couple or a plume of cigarette smoke. His question was answered when Sophie zeroed in on Sam O'Gara and Laura Debrowski, who were sitting in the back sending up twin smoke signals. She headed directly for them, cutting through the crowd like a blue taffeta bullet.

Axel looked around, disoriented by Sophie's sudden departure. He spotted the flash of oversize spectacles and the ashen form of Frank Knox, his attorney, standing uncomfortably in the far corner. Axel grinned and started toward him. Frank Knox rarely appeared in public these days. For the most part, he hid out in his cluttered home, avoiding bacteria. Axel felt honored that Frank was exposing himself to this room full of germs and evil vapors. He had almost reached Knox's corner when a babble of excited voices caught his attention. Axel veered toward the noise. Near the doors, several people clustered around something on the floor. He heard someone say, "Should we call 911? Should somebody be calling 911?" Had someone fainted? Axel pushed into the gathering, curious and alarmed.

The Reverend Buck was standing just inside the doors, shaking hands and waiting for the lucky couple when a man staggered into the hall, blood running down his neck, his shirt collar wet and red. The Reverend's first thought was that the guy had been in a fight. He stepped in front of the man and caught him, tried to turn him around, get him out of there before he created a disruption, but the instant his hands touched the man's shoulders, the man collapsed into his arms.

"Are you all right?" Buck asked, even though it was obvious that the man was all wrong.

"They're gone . . ." The man spoke slowly, as if drugged. "They got took." His eyes closed and he slumped to the side. Buck heard others gathering behind him, excited mutters of "Oh my god," and "Who is he?"

Buck knelt beside the man, keeping him upright. He thought he remembered something about people with head wounds—you were supposed to keep them awake. "What happened to you?" he asked.

The man groaned.

Buck heard a woman calling 911 on her cell phone.

Someone said, "Oh my god—is that Joe Crow?"

The injured man roused himself at the mention of his name. "A man . . . took them both . . . Hyatt and Carmen . . . in the limousine."

"Who?" Buck asked. "The bride and groom?"

"All gone," Joe Crow muttered. He sagged to the floor.

Flowrean Peeche gazed in admiration and amazement at the titanium-wrapped Amazon in the mirrored walls of the elevator. Over the past few years she had spent a substantial portion of her earnings on such apparel. Most of her purchases were never worn in public. Workout sweats and her waitress uniform pretty much took care of her day-to-day fashion needs. This wedding thing, this was her chance to do it right, and she had. That Bigg, she'd be hurting him big time. Make him see what she could do with herself. He liked to look? Well, he could look, but he could never, ever touch. Serve him right. Flo touched her belly, felt the texture of the fabric, softer and warmer than it looked.

She wondered, not sure which way she wanted it to go, whether Bigg would keep his promise not to touch her. If he tried, by god, she'd show him why she was lifting all that daily iron. The elevator doors opened. She stepped out into the lobby and saw, through the glass entryway, Bigg's long white Lincoln limousine parked at the curb, the back door standing open. From that sector of her mind where the ancient memories reside, she heard a little girl shrieking, "Cinderella! Cinderella!"

Drawn by the open door, Flo floated across the foyer and out to the circular driveway. The inside of the limo fluttered with kaleidoscopic colors. The smell hit her. Flowers. The back of the limo contained a huge bouquet of flowers. Flowers for Flowrean. White and pink roses, a huge spray of chrysanthemums, even a bird-of-paradise.

She climbed inside, pulled the door closed and settled into the L-shaped white leather seat. The limousine immediately began to roll. Flo looked around the plush carriage, noticing the television set, the bottle of champagne cooling in an ice bucket, the privacy panel separating her from the driver's compartment. They were on the freeway heading south before she noticed the pair of lime green pumps perched neatly on top of the wet bar.

*The Seven Steps of the Amaranth present a formidable flight.*
*Only a few of us have the key to the elevator.*

—*"Amaranthine Reflections" by Dr. Rupert Chandra*

"Would you try to drive smoother, love?" Rupe said, keeping his teeth clamped together. "I'm in agony here."

He had been warned against opening his mouth. "Avoid talking for a few days," the doctor had told him, "and try not to eat anything that requires a lot of chewing." That wasn't so bad, but they hadn't told him that every time the Range Rover hit a little bump an intense bolt of pain would arc from his right ear over the top of his head to his left temple. Rupe had never experienced electroshock therapy, but he imagined that this is how it would feel.

Polly said, "I'm not feeling all that good myself, you know."

"At least you can see what's coming." That was the worst part. With the bandages over his eyes, the jerks and bumps and curves in the road all took him by surprise. He never knew when the next painful explosion would occur.

"I told you we should've stayed overnight in Rochester."

"No." Rupe swallowed. His throat hurt, too. "I wish to be at Stonecrop. I feel horrid."

"Dr. Bell said you'd be uncomfortable. We should've filled that prescription."

"I don't need drugs."

"Then quit complaining."

Rupe tried to relax his shoulders. The discomfort encompassed his entire body. His thighs were throbbing unpleasantly, and his chest hurt. He felt as though his torso was being squeezed by steel bands. Maybe some pain management techniques would help. He began by regulating his breathing, slow and deep. He emptied his mind, visualizing a featureless gray plain. He imagined himself traveling its surface, seeking out inflamed knots of synapses, surrounding each pulsing node, expunging it with a soft mental squeeze. A simple variation on his cell regeneration techniques, and highly effective. He began to feel whole as the nodes of pain disappeared, one by one. He saw the fibers of his mind relaxing and detangling. His spine seemed to loosen, translating the vibration of the tires on the road into a shimmering caress.

The pain management program was working. Maybe they could offer a seminar on it. People with chronic pain might benefit from this new branch of Amaranthine technology. Maybe if they didn't hurt so bad they'd want to live longer. He expanded his visualization exercise, imagining his face as it would appear after the surgery healed. His eyelids tightened and youthful-looking from the blepharoplasty procedure, his chin ever-so-subtly larger and firmer from the implant. Rupe had always hated his weak chin. He could hardly wait to see the results.

Of course, he already knew what he'd look like. He'd seen his face magically transformed on Dr. Bell's computer screen—as amazing to behold as the actual Amaranthine cell regeneration techniques, only much, much faster.

Just then the truck hit a crack in the pavement. A shock wave snaked up his spine; the base of his skull bloomed with agony. Rupe gasped and slumped forward, holding his head in his hands. "I'm going to be ill," he groaned.

He heard Polly's exasperated sputter. "You puke in my Range Rover, I'll hit every pothole from here to Stonecrop."

Rupe swallowed and attempted to reboot his pain supression program, but all he could think about was the next bump in the road. "Just get me there," he said.

The guard-rail posts pounded by faster than her heartbeats, the limo going much too fast to jump, but Flo almost went for it. She still remembered paying seventy-nine dollars for those green pumps, and she remembered where she'd lost them. Flo went into trapped animal mode, everything packed tense, ready to explode at the slightest hint of an escape opportunity. She looked out the window, down at the blurred concrete surface of the freeway. If she threw open the door and jumped with all her pent-up strength she might make it over the guard-rail onto the grassy median.

The more evolved portion of her brain managed to rein in the flight impulse. She saw herself skidding across the road surface, the techno-Amazon instantly becoming a tattered bloody mess. She whispered, "Just be here for a minute, girl. Just think."

A mechanical ringing sound, like a cross between a doorbell and a pager, startled her. On the second ring, she saw that it was coming from a telephone handset above the wet bar. After six rings, she picked it up and put it to her ear.

"Don't be mad." The voice was deep and masculine. It did not belong to Arling Biggle.

Flo said nothing.

"You okay?" the voice inquired.

Flo said, "Are you the driver?"

"Yeah. I'm the driver."

"Pull over the car, please."

She heard a cavernous chuckle. "You okay, I guess. You like the flowers?"

Flo replaced the receiver, opened the door, and kicked the vase of flowers out onto the freeway. The vase shattered. She looked back, saw cars swerving to avoid the sudden floral hazard. The phone began to ring again. This time she let it ring for five minutes before answering.

"I guess you don't like flowers."

"You better let me out, whoever you are, or I'm coming right through the back of your seat. Rip your fucking spine out."

"I let you out, Mizz Peeche, I might never get to know you."

"You better hope you don't get to know me. Who the hell are you?"

"Folks call me Chuckles, on account of I like to laugh sometime. We met at the Amaranthine Church, remember? I brought you your shoes back. You see 'em?"

"I see them."

"I wanted to talk to you."

"Pull over and let me out, then you can talk all you want." She heard the deep chuckle again. Amazing that it could come through so thin a wire. "Why should I talk to you?"

"Mizz Peeche, we are movin' south on I-35 at sixty miles per hour. No stop signs. I just keep the needle steady, no reason to slow down 'cep to fuel up, and there's enough gas in this stretch to roll us clear to Kansas City. What else you gonna do with yourself? You got nobody else to talk to."

Flo hung up the phone. A few seconds later it rang again. Flo picked up the champagne bottle, wrapped the bar towel around its neck and swung it as hard as she could against the privacy panel, right where she figured his head would be. The bottle exploded with a satisfying liquid boom. The limo swerved slightly, but the panel held and the phone continued to ring. Flo ripped the television set from the entertainment console and hurled it at the panel. The picture tube shattered, filling the compartment with some nasty dust. Flo rolled down two windows and let the wind clear the air. The ringing persisted.

After a few face-saving minutes, she picked up the phone again.

"Why are we going to Kansas City?"

"We're not. We just riding. Just makin' conversation. How you doin'?"

"What do you want?" she asked.

"Just to talk. Like I said."

"So talk."


Hyatt and Carmen were arguing again. Chip could hear them right through the privacy panel. The bride was mad, and Hyatt was trying to calm her down. It reminded him of Polly and Rupe, the way they'd go at each other sometimes, only this was worse because they just kept saying the same things over and over.

At least the drive was nice, with plenty of rolling hills and trees and green fields. Chip liked being out in the country. He thought how much nicer it would be on his motorcycle, with the sound of wind in his ears instead of the whining and cajoling going on behind him.

The bride, Carmen, wanted to know why she wasn't married. Chip could've told her that. He would've told her it was because she was a complaining, drunken, cigarette-smoking bitch. Even with the air on and the privacy panel closed, the entire limo reeked from her cigarettes. She was back there drinking champagne and smoking and bitching. He couldn't understand how Hyatt, a founding father of the Amaranthine church, had wound up with this one-note whiner.

"You told me it was gonna be *after* the wedding, Hy! We get married, *then* we get snatched. That's what we talked about. I didn't even get to go to my own reception!"

Here they're making history, in the middle of reforming the Amaranthine Church of the One, and she's worrying about missing her party. Chip, he'd've just popped her one.

Hyatt was more patient. He kept trying to explain strategies to her. About how it was better to get kidnapped before instead of after. This was some real, first-class strategizing, the kind of complex thinking that Hyatt Hilton was so good at. Chip appreciated a strategic mind. Polly, she was strategic, too, but not as strategic as Hyatt.

"This is all about public perception," Hyatt was explaining. "It has to do with the concept of the bride. We were kidnapped *on the way to the altar.* If it happened after, it wouldn't have the *impact.* It's all about what order things happen in. That's what it's about, Carm, is *impact.* Why do you think O.J. Simpson got so much press? It was the *order* that things happened in."

"Sophie's gonna kill us both," Carmen said.

"Look at it this way," Hyatt said. "Once we get on TV, then we can do whatever we want. We can get married on the *Tonight Show,* like Tiny Tim. Would you like that?"

"I want to go to the reception."

Hyatt seemed to run out of patience. "Well," he said, "you can't. Deal with it."

Chip smiled. That was much better. That was strategy.

When had she lost control? A few months ago, Carmen had been in charge of her life. She'd been the one who called the shots. She had decided when they would go out, when they would have sex, and what movies they would see. He would come to her with his ideas, and she would pick and choose. But lately—for a *long* time now, come to think of it—she had been more like a passenger, watching life coming at her, unable to get a grip on the wheel. It reminded her of her experience with her last boyfriend, the skinhead psycho James Dean who had ended up dead and almost got her killed, too. Only Hyatt wasn't scary dangerous like Dean had been. She couldn't imagine Hy actually hurting her. So how and when had she lost control?

She poured herself another glass of champagne, spilling a little when the limo swerved. Or maybe the limo hadn't swerved. They were on their second bottle, so it was hard to tell exactly what had caused the glass to move just as the champagne emerged from the bottle neck. Oddly enough, although she felt a pleasant alcoholic buzz from her toes to her fingertips, her mind remained clear. Memories played one after another as she searched her recent past for clues to her present situation.

The day she had moved into Hyatt's apartment. Was that when she had lost it?

No. By that time, the out-of-control feeling had already arrived.

Hyatt was up front talking to the driver, Chip. Carmen did not like Chip. She didn't like his reptilian eyes and the way she couldn't help but look into his nostrils when he faced her.

She looked further into the past, searching for that moment when she'd blinked and her life had gone off in this strange direction. Was it when she had told Sophie that she was getting married? Or before that? She looked into her champagne flute and saw, through the bubbles, the ring around her finger. She switched the glass from her left hand to her right and looked at her ring. Sunset slanted in through the tinted windows, hit the diamond, and threw sparks into her eyes.

That was it, she thought, blinking. She had lost it the moment he gave her the goddamn ring.


"So what you're saying is that these telomeres get a little shorter every time I do something bad to my body?"

"That's right. You go out in the bright sun, your cells got to fight the light, your skin telomeres shorten up faster. You smoke a cigarette, your lung telomeres get shorter. You eat a Twinkie, you messing with all kinds of 'em."

Flo said, "Huh." It made sense to her. "What about when I work out, breaking down those muscle fibers."

"That different. That not damaging cells, it challenging them." Chuckles held up a clenched fist, saluting the concept. Flo could see his grin in the rearview mirror. They were still cruising down I-35, coming up on the Iowa border. Chuckles had lowered the privacy panel a few miles back. He was not bad looking. He knew how to wear gold. A lot of men didn't. A lot of men, especially black men, had these big yellow watches and rings and such but it was the gold wore them. This Chuckles, he wore the gold.

She couldn't remember exactly what he had said that had got her to listening. Somewhere back around Owatonna, he'd started to make sense. Chuckles—or Charles Thickening, which was his real name—was a very smart man. He knew all kinds of stuff about cells and telomeres and the mind-body interface. He knew things she'd never heard before.

Flo said, "But that lady that got younger, that was fake."

"Rupe, him and Polly have a philosophy. They figure it's cool to fool folks if that's what you got to do to teach 'em the real thing. See, one secret to longer telomeres is you got to believe. Rupe, he says it don't matter if you fooled or not, long's you *believe*."

"You are what you think you are," said Flo, quoting one of her favorite articles from *Muscular Development*.

"You got that right, what Rupe called the first step: *believe*. And there's more. The second step is . . . you know, you not suppose to know this one yet, but I gone tell you anyway. *Live longer.*"

"Sounds sort of obvious."

"A lot of the steps do, until you really think on 'em. See, the longer you live, the more science you got to help you live longer. For instance, a fifty-year-old man in 1950, he could expect to live maybe to fifty-eight. But if he manage to live to seventy, his life expectancy went up to seventy-nine. And if he make it to ninety, he might could expect to live to 100. Every year he live he get another year! According to Rupe, anybody who can make it to the year 2078 is going to live forever."

"I'd be pretty old."

"Yeah, but you'd look and feel young. Those are just two steps I told you. There's five more. Once you do all seven, you there."

"Tell me one more."

Chuckles chuckled. "I don't know you ready, Mizz Peeche."

"Tell me."

"Okay, I tell you. You ready?"

Flo nodded.

*"Be there."*

"That's mine!"

"That number three."

"It's mine. Tell me the rest."

*Kathie: What are you rebelling against?*
*Johnny: What have you got?*

—*Mary Murphy and Marlon Brando,* The Wild One

"Let me ask you something, Crow. How many times have you been hit on the head so hard it knocked you out?"

Crow lifted a hand and felt the back of his head. It was bandaged, and numb. His mouth tasted awful. He had awakened in hospital rooms before, and his mouth always tasted the same.

Debrowski sat back in the beige plastic chair, playing with the zippers on her jacket. "Do you even remember?" She had something on her head. An old 1950s-style motorcycle cap.

"I think four or five . . . or six. What's that on your head?"

"You know, most people go their whole lives without getting knocked out." Zippers opened and closed, making soft metal buzzing sounds. "How many times has it been this month?"

Crow frowned. "Two?"

"That's what I told the doctor. He said you're lucky to be alive."

"Doctors say that all the time."

"Maybe it's true."

"Of course it's true. You're alive, too. Do you feel lucky?"

"Yeah. I'm lucky I'm not you."

Crow turned his head away, taking a break from Debrowski's eyes, which became unbearably rectangular when she was angry. On the other side of the bed, Sam sat slumped in a chair, snoring gently. The zipper noises merged with Sam's snoring, sounding like a slowed-down recording of buzzing insects. Behind Sam, Crow could see a street lamp through the dark window.

"What time is it?" he asked.

Debrowski said, "A little after eleven. Maybe you should get yourself a motorcycle helmet. What would you think about that? Since people keep hitting you upside the head. You know, I'm kinda P.O.ed at you, Crow."

Crow thought, I could get hit by lightning, and she'd get mad at me. She'd say, why didn't you duck? All he'd been doing, he'd been trying to do a favor for Axel. Then something had happened. Something not his fault.

"Are you going to tell me what happened?" he asked, watching a bead of drool form at the corner of his father's mouth.

"What's the last thing you remember?"

Crow explored the scrambled regions of his brain. "I remember going into a place to buy a pack of cigarettes for Carmen." He turned back toward Debrowski.

"The Clark station."

"Right. What's with the biker hat?"

"You don't like it?"

"It looks like somebody else put it there, doing a remake of *The Wild One*."

Debrowski removed the leather cap, gave it a brief inspection, tossed it through the lavatory door into the open toilet.

"Nice shot."

"I never liked that movie."

"You think it'll flush?"

"You never know. So, you were at the Clark station . . ."

"Yeah. Carmen wanted Marlboros in a box. Then the guy behind the counter did something. No. He *saw* something. Somebody." Trying to remember made his head hurt worse.

"You don't remember running a half mile to the American Legion?"

"Uh-uh."

"You made quite an entrance. Blood all over your shirt. You don't remember any of that?"

"I remember the guy at the counter. He saw something. That's it. Look, just tell me what happened, okay?"

"Okay. I talked to one of the cops and he told me that the kid behind the counter said that a man dressed in black followed you into the store, slapped a gun up against the side of your head, then robbed the place of two hundred nineteen dollars and a carton of Snickers.

"So, it was just a robbery?"

"More than a robbery. Apparently, the robber needed wheels, and you'd left the limo idling out front. The guy took the money and his candy bars and jumped in the limo and took off. With Hyatt and Carmen in it."

"No kidding? Then what? They get dropped off some place?"

"Nobody knows. The cops aren't using the word kidnapping yet—my guess is they want to avoid getting the FBI involved—but nobody's heard from Hyatt and Carmen, as far as I know. You're supposed to call this guy—" She unzipped a side pocket and produced a business card. "—When you're able to answer questions."

"Who is he?"

She frowned at the card. "Wes Larson. Some cop." She tossed the card on his bedside table.

"As far as he's concerned, I'm still unconscious." Crow found the bed control and pressed buttons until he found one that raised the back. "Am I supposed to stay here overnight?"

"I think so. They want you to be here in case your brain swells up and your head explodes."

"They know I don't have health insurance?"

"They've got my American Express card."

"Ouch. Maybe we should just go home while you've still got your fortune."

"Forget it, Crow. You die tonight, you do it here."

That was fine with Crow. He wasn't sure he could stand up, and he didn't want to put it to the test.

Debrowski said, "The wedding has been postponed, of course."

"Axel should be happy about that."

"To tell the truth, he's pretty upset."

A liquid rumble exploded from Sam, a laugh turning into a wet cough. Crow and Debrowski looked at him, waited for the hacking and throat-clearing to subside. Sam pushed the suit coat off his chest, sat up straight, and thumped his chest with a fist.

"You okay?" Crow asked.

Sam cleared his throat and wiped his mouth with the back of his hand. "It's the food's got his bone in a knot," he said. "All these people goin' nuts, you on the floor bleeding off your head, waiting for the ambulance, that one guy runnin' around with his camera, Sophie screamin' at the cops. All this and Ax says to me, he says, 'What am I gonna do with all this food?'"

"You see this?" Chuckles plucked a thin orange carrot stick from his salad and held it between his thick dark fingers.

Flo nodded. She watched Chuckles insert the carrot stick into his wide mouth and chew. She noticed for the first time that he had a gold canine tooth to match his earring.

Chuckles said, "Eat life."

They were sitting in a Union 76 truck stop just north of Des Moines having a late supper.

"Eat life?" She dropped her eyes from his mouth to his black silk warm-ups, some kind of design on the chest, black on black embroidery, two segmented worms swirling around each other, the same design as he had shaved onto his close-cropped temples. She pointed at his chest. "What is that, anyway?"

"The Amaranthine coil. It's like the double helix, you know, like DNA. Cell software. The heart of the cell, where regeneration take place." He pointed at the twists of black thread. "You got your genes, which are the secret code. And these lumps on the end here, they're the telomeres, what tell the cell to keep on keepin' on. You got to make your telomeres longer. The longer telomeres you got, the more years you got. What the seven steps do is they stretch 'em out."

Flo blinked. Chuckles are another carrot. "*Eat life.* That step number five. You suppose to eat things were alive within the last twenty-four hours."

"How do you know that carrot was alive?"

"Fresh vegetables always alive. They maybe not growing, but they alive."

Flo looked down at her chicken sandwich with fries. "How long you think this chicken's been dead?"

"No more'n a month."

Flo pushed her plate aside. "How come you let me order it?"

"I don't tell you what to do. You want to stop and eat, I pull over. Your wish is my command."

"Say what? You didn't pull over the first time I axed."

"That's cause I had some things to tell to you."

"Tell me what? I can't have chicken no more?" Flo noticed that she was talking the language of her teenage years. Slipping into jive. *Get hold, girl,* she said to herself.

"You eat what you want. I'm just telling you how it is."

"I like chicken."

"You want to know the steps, I'm just telling you. Number six, now, that a tough one. *Be rich.* The more money you got, the longer you gonna live."

"That makes sense. Poor people die."

"Rich folk they die, too, only not so soon. You don't hear about no rich folk havin' no heart attack from shoveling snow, or getting lung cancer from no coal dust. Money is life. People got money they got the good air, the good food, the good doctors. They drive the big safe cars."

"Like your big car?"

"That not my car. I borrow it."

"From Bigg?"

"Yeah. I axed him could I use it. He say no, but we work it out."

"Oh. Okay. So what's number seven?"

"You know how many folk know number seven? Only three."

"You don't know it?"

"I'm number three. Rupe and Polly are the only other."

"How come they told you?"

"They didn't. Got me a look at Rupe's secret book, where he put it *all.* Far as they know, I'm still on step four."

*"Give more."*

"You got it. Most of the Faithful, they still on step four. Rupe and Polly, they like them there."

"What's number seven?"

"My favorite. All them first steps are nothin' compare to number seven." Chuckles grinned, making her wait.

"You don't say something quick, I'm gonna plant another heel in your ham." Chuckles moistened his lips.

*"Be God,"* he said.

"Be God?"

"Like Rupe and Polly done." Chuckles winked, took a handful of fries from Flo's plate, and put them into his mouth.


Shortly before ten o'clock, Zink Fitterman looked into the room.

"Hey there, it's Laura Debrowski, back from wherever-the-fuck you were. And my man Sam O'Gara." Debrowski and Zink embraced. Sam roused himself sufficiently to wave a hand and belch. Zink regarded Crow, who was asleep.

"How's he doing?"

"He's going to be fine," said Debrowski.

"I see he's getting the V.I.P. treatment. Got his own room and everything."

Sam cleared his throat. "That one nurse got a little testy about the hat in the shitter, but mostly they been waitin' on him foot and mouth."

Zink blinked, then looked to Debrowski. "If what he just said made sense, flash me a sign."

Crow said, "It makes perfect sense."

"My god, the dead man speaketh. You look like hell, man."

Crow opened his eyes. "Thanks for coming, Zink."

"You're welcome, but I can't stay long. I left my kid downstairs. You know they got a game room here? This visit's gonna cost me a goddamn fortune in quarters." He looked at his watch. "Anyways, visiting hours are over. Fuckin' bureaucrats."

Crow produced a weak smile. "Zink, I know damn well you showed up late so you wouldn't get stuck talking to an invalid for more'n five minutes, so cut the crap."

Zink shrugged. "Hey, I showed up, didn't I? And you ain't gonna believe who I ran into in the emergency room. Your friend Biggle. Looking like he got hit by the same truck ran over you."

*Even the basest of creatures are ennobled by their young.*

—*H.M.S. Johnson*

CARMEN WOKE UP TO THE sound of men talking. She tried to make them into voices on her clock radio, but it was Hyatt and Chip.

"You sure? This doesn't look like it goes anywhere."

"There's a back gate. I been here before."

"Then how come we've been driving around lost for the last half hour?"

"The roads must've changed."

Carmen opened her eyes. She was on the back seat in the limo. They weren't moving. The headlights illuminated a narrow dirt road. Tree branches touched the windows on both sides. Hyatt was sitting up front with Chip, arguing.

"I don't want to be driving around here all night, Chip. We've got work to do."

"There *is* a back gate. Someplace. And call me Eduardo."

"Let's get off this cowpath and go back to the highway, Eduardo. Come at it from the front."

"The plan was to infiltrate the compound through the rear entrance."

"I know what the *plan* was, Chipster. It's not working. Now we go to plan B."

Carmen sat up. Her head was not good. She groped around on the seat, found her cigarettes and her lighter, and lit up.

The limo started forward down the narrow dirt road. A few seconds later Hy said, "I thought we agreed to go back to the highway."

"I gotta find a place to turn this thing around."

They drove another hundred yards, tree branches scraping the sides.

"There's a pullout," Hyatt said, pointing at an aneurysm in the road. "Turn around there."

Chip swung the front end of the limo into the wide spot and stopped. They were looking at a short, rutted lane ending about thirty yards away at an iron gate built into a stone arch. Carved into the top of the arch was the word STONECROP.

"Told you so," said Chip.

"So you did."

"So we're back to the original strategy?"

"Roger wilco, Chipmeister." Hyatt turned toward Carmen. "How you doing back there? Waking up?"

"I'm okay," Carmen said.

"You better grab onto something, okay?"

"What for?" Carmen asked.

The limo suddenly lurched forward, dirt and rocks spewing from the rear tires. The gate rushed toward them. Carmen heard herself scream in reverse—sucking the air in instead of forcing it out—then they hit the gate, broke through, and skidded to a stop. One of the limo's headlamps now pointed up, illuminating the top branches of a pine tree.

Carmen picked herself up off the floor.

"You okay?" Hyatt asked.

Carmen touched her forehead. "I bumped my head." She looked at her fingers. "Am I bleeding?"

Hyatt said something to Chip, who turned off the headlights and turned on the interior lights. Hyatt got out of the limo and reentered through the rear door. He turned Carmen's face toward the overhead light. "You've got a little cut there. But that's good. It'll make the whole thing look more real."

"Real?" As far as Carmen was concerned, it *was* real.

"The realer the better," Hyatt laughed and turned to Chip. "Onward, Eduardo. To the chapel. The forces of darkness await us."

"What was that?" Rupe sat up and swung his head back and forth, but could see nothing due to the bandages over his eyes.

"What was what?"

"That sound."

"What sound?"

"You didn't hear it? A crunching, screeching sound, far away."

"I didn't hear anything. Why don't you go to sleep?"

Rupe laid his head back on the pillow. He heard Polly turn a page in her book. A minute or so later, he heard her turn another page. After three pages he said, "It's too quiet here."

"Do you want me to put some music on?"

"No." Rupe lay still for another few minutes, tuning out the noise of turning pages, the thumping of his pulse, waiting for the distant crunchy-screechy sound to repeat itself. The sound did not come again, but he heard something else, faintly. "I can hear my cells talking," he said.

"What are they saying?"

"They're healing my incisions. By morning I'll be whole again."

"Good."

"The scars will be invisible."

"Uh-huh."

"Or nearly so," he added.

He heard Polly breathing through her nose the way she did when she was feeling irritable.

"I wonder what that noise was," he said. "An animal, maybe."

"I'm sure that's what it was," Polly said. "A rabbit or something. I understand they have those out here. In the woods."

"You know what would be justice?" Chip said. "Justice would be if the surgery made them look older." He was guiding the limo slowly along the dirt road, seeing by moonlight.

"Justice will be served when their sins are made public," Hyatt said. "Where are we?"

"The main house is to our left. You see that bunch of trees there? The house is on the other side of that, about three hundred yards."

"You're sure they won't see us?"

"The security system isn't on-line yet. I warned Rupe that it was not strategic for he and Polly to be here before the area was secured, but he chose to ignore me."

"You warned him not to come here? What did you do that for?"

"It was my *job*," Chip said. He had tried to explain this to Hyatt Hilton several times already. Even though he was working with Hyatt to expose the sins of the Elders, he still had to perform his duties as Head of Security. It was one thing to stage a coup—sometimes drastic measures were necessary. But it was another thing to fail to do one's job. The job came first.

"What if Rupe had listened to you?"

"Then we would have had to establish new parameters for our strategy."

"Chip, you're a piece of work."

"Thank you."

"Where's the chapel?"

"Right up here." Chip slowed the limo from walking speed to a crawl as they topped a low rise. "They call it the Telomere Chapel, on account of the double helix design in the stained glass." The silhouette of a low building appeared against the backdrop of a starry sky. "It's very inspiring."

"Does it have a bathroom?" Carmen asked.

Chip said, "I don't know."

"I'm sure it does," Hyatt said.

"It had better," said Carmen.

Chip bit his upper lip and held it. The thought of this cigarette-smoking whore pissing her used champagne in the Telomere Chapel offended him greatly. In fact, there were many things about this situation that made him uncomfortable, but there were times when the ends *did* justify the means. Being immortal had taught him to look at things from a long-term perspective.

"They can't see the chapel from the house, right?" Hyatt asked.

"That vector is blocked," Chip said.

He stopped the limo in front of the chapel.

"Here we are," he said.

Carmen was already out of the car, trotting toward the door in her white gown, looking phantasmic in the light of the full moon.

"She's in a hurry," Chip said.

"She's got a whole bottle of bubbly inside her."

Carmen pulled the door open and disappeared into the chapel.

"How's she gonna find the bathroom in the dark?"

"She'll figure it out. Where'd you put my bag?"

"It's in the trunk."

"Good. How about you open the trunk, then make a run over to the house, make sure Rupe and Polly are here. See if their car is there."

Chip reached under the dash and popped the trunk. "You want me to reconnoiter the perimeter."

"That's right. I'll take care of Carmen, you reconnoiter the perimeter."

"Gotcha." Chip pulled a black watch cap from his pocket, pulled it down over his head and ears. He'd been hoping for the opportunity to do some surveillance. Taking his mark by lining up a tall pine tree with the moon, he chose his vector and took off cross-country.

Using her Dunhill lighter, Carmen quickly located the restroom, found the light switch, and took care of her immediate problem. Sitting on the toilet, surrounded by the stiff folds of her skirt under the glare of the overhead fluorescence, Carmen considered her situation.

A few months ago, Hyatt had made it sound easy, and exciting, and glamorous. Her ticket to fame and fortune. But now? Now it just sounded damned uncomfortable. Not to mention dangerous. In fact, it reminded her of nothing more than the situation with her last boyfriend, Dean, which had ended with a bunch of people dead and no money. Axel and Sophie had been pretty upset about that whole deal.

She could take a stand. Refuse to go along with Hy's plan. Demand to be taken home. Insist on going ahead with the wedding.

Maybe not the wedding part. Maybe it wasn't time to get married, despite her delicate condition. They could talk about it, though. She tried to imagine the conversation with Hy, but failed. She kept seeing her mother's face. Sophie would never let her forget this one, no matter what happened. But she could deal with her mom when the time came. All she knew for sure was that she did not want to be here in this weird little church with Hyatt Hilton and his swine-faced chauffeur. It was too much like some movies she'd seen, movies that had scared hell out of her when she was a little kid.

Carmen took a deep breath. The building smelled new. The smell of new paint and construction materials. That reassured her. She might be the first person ever to have peed in this particular toilet, and almost certainly the first woman. Deriving a modicum of personal power from that thought, Carmen stood up and dragged the skirt back down over her hips. She needed a cigarette.

She found Hyatt in the main room of the chapel, holding a canvas bag. He was standing at the head of the chapel on a low stage, silhouetted against a ceiling-to-floor stained-glass window. The design in the glass, illuminated by the full moon, looked like a pair of intertwined, multicolored snakes. Hyatt was muttering quietly to himself.

"What's the matter?" she asked.

"I was hoping for a real, you know, altar," Hyatt said. "A big stone altar." The raised area at the head of the chapel was an expanse of wooden flooring, about twenty feet wide by ten feet deep and bare of furnishings. It looked like a stage. "I don't see where we're going to tie you up."

"Maybe we should just skip that part." Carmen sat down on one of the low, backless wooden benches that filled the rest of the chapel.

Hyatt said, "Ha-ha." He set the bag on the floor and removed a camcorder.

Carmen lit a cigarette and watched.

"Where's Chip?" she asked.

"He's reconnoitering the perimeter. Keep him out of trouble for a while."

"Oh." She blew a lungful of smoke out through her nostrils. "Hy, I've been thinking."

"This is no time to think, Carm. We're in action mode here. What are we gonna do for an altar?"

"I was thinking we might want to, you know, change the plan a little."

"Maybe we could use one of those benches. Spread a blanket over it or something. Are they bolted down?"

Carmen gave the bench in front of her a kick. It moved a few inches. "This one's not," she said.

"Bring it on up here."

"Listen, Hy, I'm serious. I don't really feel like doing this. I just don't think it'll work. I've been thinking. Even if we go ahead with the plan, who's gonna believe us? Why would they believe anything we tell them?"

Hyatt hopped down, lifted one end of a bench onto the lip of the stage. "Carmen," he said in his serious voice, "believe me, they'll believe. They'll believe because they'll want to believe. Same reason they believe what politicians tell them." He climbed back up and dragged the bench up after him. "They'll believe for the same reason they believe that Nike shoes will make them better athletes, and that Coca-Cola tastes like a cigarette should. We're talking something bigger than the truth here, Carm. We're talking about a story that people want desperately to hear. They've been waiting for this one. We're going to give them the story they've been waiting for, the one they're all desperate to see in real life. Or on TV." He positioned the bench in the exact center of the stage. "What do you think? Does this look like an altar?"

"It looks like a bench. We better change the plan, Hy. How about if we *both* escape?"

"Won't work. Gotta have the visuals. Seeing is believing, and they want to see it. Pretty girl in distress, evil cults with super powers, violence . . . they want to see the big white dress with blood on it. They want to believe in immortality, and they want to see it fail. Why do you think vampires are so popular?"

"Vampires?"

"Sure. We've created the perfect real-life vampire story. We've got you, the pretty bride. We've got me, the brave hero. We've got the evil cult of blood drinking vampires. People want to be scared shitless. Why do you think people buy snuff films? The want love and death."

"What d'you mean, love and *death*?"

"The *idea* of death. The *symbol* of death." Hyatt rubbed his thumb against his fingers. "That's why they pay the big money, Carm."

"I don't know, Hy. The more I think about it, I don't think anybody's gonna buy it."

"Hey, Carm, gimme a break. What about Woodstock? You think anybody believed in Woodstock?"

"What? That concert?"

"What concert? It was a movie, Carm. You really think a million people sat in the mud to hear Sha-Na-Na? It was a concept, something some ad agency made up. Woodstock never happened, Carm. It's all about image. We're creating an icon here, Carm. Like the Beatles or the moon landing. Or when President Kennedy got shot. It's all about creating an unforgettable image in people's minds. Doesn't have to make sense, it just has to stick. That's where the money is. Once you're an icon, they throw the stuff at you. Look at Michael Jordan. Look at Joey Buttafuco."

"Who?"

"Never mind. Look, this is some pretty advanced psychological thinking. I don't want to bore you. You don't have to understand it, you just have to trust me."

"Suppose I don't."

"It's a little late now."

"Suppose I say 'Forget it!' Then what do we do?"

"That would be a huge mistake."

"I just don't get it."

"You don't have to get it. C'mere, lay down on the bench. I want to see how it looks."

Carmen threw her cigarette on the floor and ground it out. "Hy, I've got something to tell you."

"Uh-huh. Come on, Carm. Lay down her a sec." He picked up the camcorder. "I want to do some visualization, find my angles."

Carmen climbed up onto the stage and sat on the bench. "Listen to me, Hy."

Hyatt aimed the camera at her. Moonlight filtered through the stained glass turned him purple and green with a glowing red eye. "Lay down, Carm. Let's see what you look like laying down."

"Hy, I'm pregnant."

Hyatt lowered the camcorder. His face performed a rapid sequence of multicolored expressions, from stunned to joyful to fearful to calculating to witless. He said, after settling into slack-jawed stasis, "You mean, like, with a baby?"

"I *hope* so. Jesus, Hy, what do you think? I'm pregnant with a *dog*?"

Hyatt shook his head, slowly. "I think that's great, Carm. Really great."

"You think so?" Carmen felt something proud and maternal swelling her breasts.

"They'll eat it up, Carm." His mouth widened into a smile. "I should've thought of it myself."

*Insured by Smith & Wesson—Policy # 357*

*—T-shirt collection of Charles Bouchet*

THE PERIMETER LOOKED SECURE.

Chip slowly approached the sprawling, single-story stone house, slapping mosquitoes and slipping in the muck. Benjy and his crew hadn't had time to finish the landscaping—the area around the house was crisscrossed by muddy ruts left behind by the builders' trucks. Chip's mud-caked boots weighed about five pounds each. The house was dark. It might have been unoccupied. But they were in there. Chip could sense their presence. He had a sixth sense about such things. As Security Chief, such perceptiveness came in handy. The fact that Polly's Range Rover was parked out front only served as additional proof. Chip moved through the muck, lifting his feet slowly to minimize the sucking sound, and moved in closer.

All the money they'd spent on the place, they could've come up with a more strategic design. Could've built it higher, giving them a better view of the surrounding landscape. If it was him, he'd've at least built a lookout tower into the place, or an electronic perimeter. As Security Chief, Chip had recommended the electronic perimeter but Rupe and Benjy had overruled him saying that the deer and rabbits would be setting it off every night and, besides, Rupe had said, the entire compound was going to be surrounded by a twelve-foot-high stone wall.

Chip set his face in a grim smile. He'd have built the house up on the rise, not down here in this shallow depression. He began to circle the house, peering into each window. Too many low windows. If they turned a light on, anybody could look right inside. But with the lights out, there wasn't much to see.

Just as he was having that thought, a light came on—one of the windows ahead of him—spilling out of the house, a faint rectangle of light settling on the muddy landscape. Chip froze. He must have known that was going to happen, his extra sense talking to him. He stole closer to the lit-up window, keeping his back to the wall, his heart beating rapidly. This was the real thing. Nothing he liked better than this kind of surveillance, watching subjects who were totally unaware. Maybe it would be Polly, naked. He'd never seen her without clothes. He reached the window, saw it was covered on the inside with a miniblind. Chip liked miniblinds. You could always find a crack. The bottom vanes of this one weren't quite closed. He looked in upon a bedroom. The bed was rumpled, someone in it. Rupe, with bandages over his eyes and on his chin, mouth hanging open. He seemed to be snoring.

Chip crouched low and moved to the other side of the window to see the room from the other angle. The bedroom door was open. No Polly. Probably woke up and went to use the bathroom. Where would the bathroom be? Or should he wait here, wait for her to return? Wait. Wait for her to step into the bedroom, naked. That would be strategic.

"See anything?"

Chip experienced a moment—it may have been as long as two seconds—when he thought that the voice had come from inside his head. Then his sixth sense kicked in, and he turned to see Polly DeSimone, wearing a very short nightie and rubber boots, pointing a large handgun at his belly. Chip's mind seized. He felt his body straighten and stand at attention. This was not strategic. In fact, it was decidedly unstrategic.

Chip stood very still in the moonlight, waiting for her to tell him what to do.


Hyatt made an adjustment to the drapery and stepped back. Not bad. Now that they were covered with fabric, the four benches, two stacked on top of two, actually looked like an altar.

"What do you think?" he asked.

"It looks like a buffet table," Carmen said. She was sitting near the back of the chapel, a ghostly pale blur in the half-light.

"You getting hungry? We've got a whole box of Snickers bars in the limo."

"I just want to go home, Hy."

Hyatt laughed. "Quit kidding around, Carm. Where'd that tubing go? Is it in the bag?"

Carmen said, "I told you, Hy, I'm not gonna do it."

"Sure you are." Hyatt opened the canvas bag and pulled out a flat plastic bag containing the phlebotomy tubing setup Carmen had stolen from the emergency room at Our Lady of Mercy hospital. He looked at his watch. "I wonder what's keeping Chip?"

"Probably got lost."

"Well I'm not gonna wait for him. If I have to, I'll videotape it myself."

"You don't know how to run a camera."

"What's to know? Everybody with a kid has one of the things. You ever see *America's Funniest Home Videos?* Come on up here, Carm." He waved the phlebotomy setup. "I can run the camera, but you've got to show me how this thing plugs in."

"I'm not gonna do it, Hy. I told you, I'm pregnant."

"Carm, don't give me a hard time here. Don't you want to be on TV?"

Carmen stood up. "Forget it, Hy. I want you to take me home now."

It felt good to make a stand, Carmen thought. Let him know where things were at. And really, it was the first time. Before, she'd made demands, thrown a few tantrums, wheedled and cajoled and got him to do what she wanted. But she'd never before stood right up to him and said no, I don't want to, I won't, you can't make me. She'd be tough, like Sophie. She would walk right out to the limo and sit in it and not budge until they drove her home.

Picking her way through the half-dark of the chapel, she heard him behind her, calling her name. Carmen ignored the voice. If he wanted to say something to her he could talk to her on the way home. She felt the weight sloughing off her, the burden of the wedding, of Hyatt's plan to get them on TV, the whole mass of worry that had been building up in her for the past few months. She was at the door, stepping out into full moonlight when she felt his hand gripping her shoulder.

"Carm . . ." His voice had gotten louder.

"Let go of me, Hy," she said. She turned to face him. His face was shadowed; she could see only a faint Cheshire cat grin where the moonlight struck his teeth.

"Come on, Carm." He tried to pull her back into the chapel. Carmen swung at his arm, knocking it away. That was when he slapped her.

It was not a hard slap, just a little cuff on the cheek, but it surprised her. What surprised her more was her instant response. She swung her sharp fist high and hard and hit him perfectly on the tip of his pointed nose. Hyatt squeaked and staggered back, clapping a hand to his face.

"Jesus, Carm, what are you doing?" He looked at his hand. "I'm bleeding."

Carmen had backed away and was standing near the limo now. "I want to go home."

"Carm, I—Jesus, I'm bleeding all over my goddamn tux—Carm, you don't understand. It's not an option. I've put too much into this deal. It's my big score. My window of opportunity. Yours, too."

"How about if *you* stay here and *I* go."

Hyatt seemed to consider that. "I don't know . . . do you know how to get there from here? Do you know where the police station is? Do you even know how to get to Prescott?"

"Chip can drive me."

Hyatt shook his head. "I wouldn't count on Chip. He should've been back here by now. Look, let's go back inside and talk about it."

Carmen hesitated.

"Come on, Carm. Let's put our heads together. We can figure something out. You don't want to be the victim, we'll do something else. Come on."

Carmen felt the tension in her shoulders ease. She had won. She walked toward Hy. When he reached out a hand to her, she took it.

The blow came as a complete and utter shock to Carmen, as if the air had exploded under her chin. She heard a sound like the crack of a bat. Her head snapped back, the stars wheeled, the full moon doubled. She hit the ground flat on her back, driving the air from her lungs. As she lay there with her mouth open, waiting for her collapsed lungs to start working again, watching Hy hopping around and cursing, holding his right hand, all she could think was that she had forgotten what it felt like to get hit, and it had only been, like, a year. She'd forgotten how much it hurt.


Chip was able to tie himself to the kitchen chair with little difficulty. He knew all the knots. He tied each of his legs to the chair legs, and he bound his hands with a locking slip-knot, which he pulled tight with his teeth. It was very efficient.

He could tell from the expression on Polly's face that she was impressed.

"How long do you think that will hold you?" she asked.

"I could get out," Chip said. "I could get out in five minutes." He was proud of both the fact that he had tied himself up so neatly, and the fact that he could escape. But he wished he'd held onto his Smith. Not that she'd given him much choice. It sat on the kitchen counter now, on the other side of the stove.

Polly placed her revolver, a seven-inch Ruger that Chip himself had taught her to shoot, beside Chip's Smith & Wesson. "Would you like some tea?" She turned on one of the stove burners.

"How did you detect me? Infrared motion detectors?"

Polly laughed. She filled a teapot from the tap and placed it on the burner. "I just happened to be up," she said. "I looked out and saw you. You know what I thought? I thought maybe you were Hyatt Hilton." She laughed again. "Isn't that funny?"

Chip did not think that was funny. It was a very unfunny situation altogether. Polly was dressed in a silky nightie—more of a nightshirt, really—and nothing else. She had left her rubber boots by the door. Her legs were extremely naked. Chip had never seen Polly without stockings. He could see little squiggly veins on her thighs and behind her knees, and a painful-looking corn on her little toe. Her hair was short, thin, and close to her head. The fact that Polly wore wigs was no secret, but he had never before seen her without one.

The most startling difference between this Polly and the Polly he knew was the color of her face—bright pink—so pink and puffy he could almost feel the heat coming off it.

He'd thought at first she was furious, red with anger, but she didn't seem to be angry at all. Then he remembered the reason she and Rupe were here. The big lie. The plastic surgery. The pink face must be from that.

Polly took a mug from the cupboard and set it beside the stove. It was one of the official ACO mugs with the double helix printed on one side and a stylized picture of Rupe and Polly on the other. "Would you like a cup of tea?"

Chip shook his head.

"Are you going to tell me what you're doing here?"

Chip clamped his teeth together and lowered his eyes to Polly's knees. Even with the veins she looked good for a woman of her age. She moved closer to him. Her hand settled on his head and rubbed gently, the short, stiff hairs holding her palm away from his scalp. She smelled like soap, but with a sourness behind it.

"Do the girls ever rub your head for luck, Chip?" She moved around behind him. He felt something soft, a breast, briefly touch the back of his head.

"What girls?" Chip's shorts were getting crowded. He squirmed, shifting his hips to a new position.

"All the girls. What are you doing here, Chip?"

"I came to tell you something," he ventured.

"Oh?" Her fingernails were touching the sides of his head, stroking his temples.

"Came to warn you."

"Warn us about what?"

"Um. People."

"What people, Chip?" She moved back in front of him, crouched to bring her glowing pink face down to his level

"What happened to your face?" he asked.

"Just a little sunburn." The teakettle began to whistle. "What people?"

"I know where you were," Chip said.

"Oh? And where was that?"

"The water's boiling."

"Where is it you think we were?"

"You and Mr. Chandra went to a plastic surgeon."

"Yes? So?"

Chip glowered.

"Do you think there is something wrong with that, Chip? With trying to look good?"

"It's a lie."

"So? How is it different from you sneaking up on us, looking into my bedroom window? Spying on us. Who are you spying for, Chip?"

"I wasn't spying."

"What were you doing?"

"I was reconnoitering."

"For who?"

Chip said nothing.

"Chip, if you were me, and someone wouldn't answer your questions, what would you do to get them to answer? Think about that." Polly stood up, put a teabag in the ACO mug, and filled it with boiling water from the teapot. "Are you sure you don't want a cup?"

"What kind of tea is it?" Chip asked.

"Earl Grey. You scare me, Chip. Looking in my window. Keeping secrets. I've been watching you. I know you liked Hyatt. You always liked him. Are you working for Hyatt, Chip?" She had come in close to him again; the sharp aroma of the brewing tea swirling into the sour, soapy smell of her body.

"Chip?"

She reached down. He thought for a moment that she was going to unbuckle his belt. Instead, she dumped the mug of hot Earl Grey onto his crotch.

*The blood of the martyrs is the seed of the church.*

*—Tertullian*

THE SOUND OF BLOOD DROPLETS falling changed as the fluid level rose. Now that there was an inch or two in the champagne bottle, the sound was more of a *ker-plop,* about two every second. Before, it had been more like *plip, plip, plip.*

Hy had been quite apologetic after hitting her.

"Look, Carm," he'd said, leading her back toward the makeshift altar. "You gotta understand, I've been working on this for a long time. This is my shot, Carm. I gotta take my shot. And it's your shot, too. It's our shot."

She'd said, "I know it, Hy. I understand," not wanting him to hit her again.

"This is where we've gotta pull together, trust each other. We go forward, follow the plan as best as we can and believe in it all the way. You start having doubts, that's when things fall apart. You gotta trust me on this one, Carm."

She'd said, "Don't hit me anymore, Hy."

"I said I'm sorry. Here, sit down. Are you okay? Okay. Look, you got a little cut on your chin. That'll look good, like you put up a fight. Trust me."

"I do trust you, Hy. But doesn't it matter I'm pregnant?"

"Yeah, it matters. It matters a lot. It's good. It's a good thing. I mean, the whole virgin bride thing takes on a whole 'nother slant. *Pregnant* virgin bride. They gotta love it. You know how far a guy like Drew Chance can run with something like that? We'll probably get invited to the White House."

That was when Carmen had decided that Hy was not simply a stupid fucking asshole. He was an *insane* stupid fucking asshole.

She'd said, "If we're gonna do it we ought to make it look really good."

"It's gotta look good."

That was when she'd swung the champagne bottle and hit him on the nose and took off running. She'd have got away, too, if she hadn't been half drunk and fallen down before she even got out of the chapel. Hy had been genuinely pissed after that, but at least he didn't hit her again, not right away. He'd just dragged her back in and tied her up, and this time she didn't resist. He tore open the bag containing the phlebotomy setup, a piece of clear plastic tubing with needles at both ends.

"Which needle goes in your arm?"

"Neither one."

"One of 'em's going in, Carm."

"Okay then. The small one."

"They're both the same."

"So what are you asking?"

When Hy finally found a vein, the blood had squirted out quickly, all over his shirt. Carmen had laughed. He must've hit her a good one then, because she didn't remember him taping the phlebotomy tubing to her arm. Next thing she knew he was shaking her awake.

"Carm? Listen to me, Carm. I gotta go. You listening?"

She was listening.

"If Chip shows up, tell him to get lost, okay? Tell him I had to leave."

"Take this tube out of my arm, Hy, or I'll kill you."

"Just hang in there, Carm. And remember our story. Remember all that money we're gonna make. You're gonna be on TV, Carm."

"Hy, I could bleed to death here."

"Don't be silly. It's coming out a drop at a time."

"I'm serious, Hy."

And then he was gone. She heard the limo start and roll away, and the only sound left was the *plip, plip, plip* of blood droplets falling from the other end of the phlebotomy tubing into the Freixnet bottle.

Carmen strained against the ropes. Hy had done a good job. She tried to twist her arm, to dislodge the needle, but it was securely taped in place—*ker-plop, ker-plop, ker-plop*—the sound was almost soothing. She wondered how long it would take for her to lose consciousness. A part of her—a rather large part, she realized—was looking forward to it.

She dreamed she opened her eyes and saw two nostrils, headlights in negative, coming at her, and behind them she saw a beautiful woman with a glowing pink face; the angel of death.

Officer Rob Grunseth, three-year veteran of the Prescott Police Department, had been working the dogwatch three months now, and it was killing him. The gallons of sugary coffee and the half dozen or so Hostess Fruit Pies he consumed during each eleven-to-seven shift had pretty much ruined his digestive system, not to mention his waistline. A few days back, at his wife's insistence, he'd gone to see a chiropractor. The guy had cracked his spine a couple times and told him that, in time, his biological clock would reset itself; his body would adjust to working nights. The chiropractor had told him to quit drinking coffee, quit smoking, and avoid snacks, especially sugary snacks. He had prescribed a sour-tasting Korean ginseng tea—Grunseth was on his fourth cup—and a one hundred fifty-watt full-spectrum light bulb, which was now shining directly in his face from the desk lamp. The visit had cost him a hundred and six bucks, including the light bulb, and he still felt like shit, like he was gonna fall asleep sitting at the desk.

The chiropractor had told him to listen to his body. At three-thirty in the morning, way past the time anything interesting was likely to happen in Prescott, Grunseth's body was making a powerful case for a fruit pie, a Winston, and a cup of something that didn't taste like wet grass clippings. His body was saying screw this Korean tea. And screw this job, too. His wife's brother, up there in St. Paul, making a clean forty a year at the Ford plant, building pickups. No kids calling him Barney Fife. No listening to that fart-ridden Amundson's theories about crime in small-town America—where the hell was Amundson, anyways? The guy says, an hour ago, says he's got to run home for five minutes to pick up some prescription pills. Probably givin' it to the wife, what he was probably doing. Leaving Rob Grunseth, Mr. Reliable, chained to the goddamn phone, all alone with his goddamn ginseng tea. And then his wife calls, crying about their eighteen-year-old niece Daphne who apparently got herself impregnated by a guy works stocking produce over at the IGA. Like he needed one more thing to think about with this ulcer or hiatal hernia or stomach cancer or whatever the hell it was he had. What the hell. He'd smoke a goddamn cigarette is what he'd do, and that chiropractor and that Chief Becker could just stick their antismoking talk right up their self-righteous butts. Becker was the worst. He had his way, smoking would be a capital offense. He liked to brag that not one Prescott cop smoked. Most of them did, of course—just not around Becker.

Grunseth walked out the back doors, leaving one of them cocked open so he could hear the phone. It had started to rain. He ran out to his patrol car, the only car in the quarter-acre parking lot, and got the half pack of Winstons out of the glove box. Nothing he hated more than rain. He ran back to the entryway and lit a match. He was about to touch it to the tip of the cigarette when a pair of headlights rounded the end of the long building and some big white thing, a goddamn limousine, came sliding around the corner, the back tires skidding on the rain-slick pavement. The driver locked up the brakes, causing the rear end to slue around and smash into the grill of the only car in the quarter-acre lot, which happened to be Grunseth's patrol car.

Grunseth felt a burning sensation and noticed that the match he had lit was broiling the tip of his thumb. He blew it out and dropped the smoking match, shaking the pain out of his hand.

A man in a maroon tuxedo jumped out of the driver's seat of the limo and ran up the steps. He fell to his knees and grabbed Grunseth's trousers. "Please help me! Oh my God! They've taken her!"

"Just you take it easy now," Grunseth said, stepping back from the man's clutches. A drunk, an escapee from some wedding reception or class reunion. Blood on his face, his nose all swollen. Maybe got himself beat up.

"You gotta help me," the man said. "We have to save her. Please!"

"Save who? Was there an accident?"

"Yes! I mean, no! We were kidnapped. I got away. The have my fiancée. They kidnapped us. The Amaranthines!"

"Amaranthines?" That sounded familiar. There was a bunch called themselves something like that, building a big place up on the bluffs, a few miles down river. But something about this guy was wrong. He was bleeding and his tux was torn up, but he didn't have that stunned look. He looked nervous and excited, but that was it. Like a kid doing a fraternity prank, only this one was too old for that.

"You have to come with me. We have to save her!"

Grunseth said, "Mister, nobody's going anywhere until you start making some sense. Now just you come on inside out of the rain and sit down and tell me what happened, okay? Meantime, I got to fill out a report on that police car you just punched in the front of."

The man followed Grunseth into the police station, looking at the empty desks.

"Hey," he said. "Where is everybody?"

"You're looking at him," Grunseth said.

The next time Crow woke up he was alone; his thoughts ran clear and cold. Staring up at the acoustical tiles. They looked close, as if he could reach up and touch them, feel their texture. But he didn't want to move. His thoughts flicked from one memory to another, clicking like a slide projector. Sam. Sam and Axel. For one frightening moment, he thought he understood his father. Sam, Axel, Sophie—the whole social dynamic suddenly made sense, including his own place in it. He moved to the next thought quickly, not wanting to get stuck there, and clicked on—Carmen and Hyatt? The limousine. The Clark station. Asking for Marlboros. That was all.

He heard feet in the hallway, two people walking, and voices. Getting louder, then fading as they moved past his room.

He closed his eyes and watched a parade of faces. Debrowski. He realized with a silent jolt that she was angry at him. Not pretending to be angry. Really angry. She was furious, and not just because he'd hurt himself. She'd been mad before that. Ever since he'd picked her up at the airport. Maybe even before that. Ever since Paris.

Well, he was mad at her, too. What had she been thinking, staying in Paris for three months? Treating him like the Ugly American and then, waiting for the Metro, when he wondered out loud how his cat was doing, just making small talk, she jumps on him, telling him maybe he should go home and check. Fly four thousand miles to make sure his cat didn't have a damn hairball? Was she trying to get rid of him?

How could she be angry at him? He hadn't done anything. He was the one that should be mad at her. *He* was the injured party.

Crow rolled onto his side, hoping the movement would reroute his thinking. It didn't work. He was still back in Paris, still fuming. That whole thing with that band had got to him worse than anything. They were supposed to be taking a vacation, spending money, and getting to know each other, eating cheese and visiting museums and taking walks along the Seine. It wasn't supposed to be a business trip. All of a sudden she's spending half her time with a bunch of French generation Xers, hanging out in bars listening to a parade of godawful postpunk Johnny Rotten wanna-bes. Crow had met René. The guy was a prick. He tried to tell that to Debrowski but all she wanted to talk about was the way the guy looked on stage, how he had the makings of a rock and roll idol.

Crow wondered if she'd—no! He heard himself groan and felt the sheets dragging across his hip as he turned over again. He wasn't ready for the image of Debrowski with that scrawny, cocky little frog-eater. The concept was too disgusting to bring into focus. Crow pushed it down, pushed it out, buried it in a storm of mental static.

How could she be mad at him?

*It is a bad plan that admits of no modification.*

—*Publius Syrus*

THE PLAN HAD BEEN TO arrive at Stonecrop with the entire Prescott police force. To storm the chapel, guns drawn. Rush to the altar to save the virgin bride. The *pregnant* virgin bride. The image was powerful and magical and would make great TV. Hyatt had spent many hours fantasizing the climactic scenario. He saw himself striking a dramatic pose, sweeping his bleeding bride into his arms, rushing her to the hospital escorted by a phalanx of blue-jackets.

The reality did not quite measure up. The rain had not been a part of Hyatt's vision, nor had the phlegmatic Officer Rob Grunseth. It had never occurred to Hyatt that there would be only two cops on duty at night in this small town, and that one of them would happen to be gone, and that the other one would refuse to leave the station unattended. It was almost as though Grunseth didn't believe his story.

Grunseth had kept him sitting there for an hour, asking questions, even making him touch his nose and recite the alphabet. The harder Hyatt worked to convince the cop that they had a genuine emergency, the stupider the cop became. Grunseth kept repeating Hyatt's story back to him.

"So, you say you and your fiancée got kidnapped on the way to your wedding, right?"

"That's right," Hyatt said.

"And you say it was those folks building that place up top, on the bluff, right?"

"The Amaranthines."

"And they hauled you up there and tied your girlfriend to an altar and proceeded to drain the blood out of her."

"That's right."

"You say that these Am-ran-*theens* are violating your girlfriend . . . why?"

"How many times do I have to tell you this? Carmen could be dying!"

"I just like to hear you say it, son."

Hyatt sighed. A hundred thousand cops in the country and he gets the densest one of the crop. "They want to be immortal," he explained for the third or fourth time. "They think if they drink her blood, the blood of a virgin, they'll live forever."

"That's what I was thinking," Grunseth said. "They're like—"

"Vampires," Hyatt said.

"Vampires! That's what I thought you said. You see any of 'em turn into bats?"

"They aren't that kind of vampire."

"Uh-huh. And these vampires, they were going to drink your blood, too?"

"I don't know what they had planned."

"You a virgin?"

"Look, we really don't have time for this. Can you call somebody? We have to get up there and save her. I'm not kidding around here."

"I'm just trying to get this straight. So then you escape from the vampires' clutches, jump in your limousine, and come barreling down the bluff road and smash into my car. Have I got that right?"

Hyatt nodded. Hearing his own story told back to him—he had to admit, it *was* a little far-fetched. But wasn't that what made it sexy? Wasn't that what made it powerful? What about Moses hearing voices from a burning bush? What about God saying to Abraham, "Kill me a son?" Did anyone believe them at first? Hyatt didn't think so.

He said, "You know, you could call up to Minneapolis. The kidnapping must've been reported. Can't you call up there?"

"Well now, I could. But if I call there and no such thing ever happened, I'm going to be very upset, son. So let me make sure I got this straight. You and your fiancée were on your way to the church—"

"American Legion Post."

"Right! I knew I had something wrong. So you're riding along in your big white limousine . . ."

The other night-shift cop showed up then, a tall, lanky young man with a lot of pink in his face.

"'Bout time you got back," Grunseth said. "You feelin' better now?"

"I feel great," said the cop, looking curiously at Hyatt. "What happened out there? Where'd that limo come from?"

"This here is Mr. Hyatt Hilltop, vampire fighter."

"Hilton," said Hyatt.

"Vampire fighter?"

"Mr. Hilltop is going to take us to his missing bride, aren't you, son?" said

Grunseth. He grinned at Amundson. "What do you say, Vince? Want to take a ride up the bluff?"

"Sure," said Amundson uncertainly.

"Let's go, Mister Hilltop. On the way there you can tell Officer Amundson all what you told me."


The rain was coming down thick and hard. They had pulled in as close to the chapel as they could get, which still left fifty feet of downpour to negotiate. Officer Grunseth did not look happy. "All I got to say, son, if I'm gonna get soaked, there better be a bleeding bride in there."

"She's in there," Hyatt said. "Let me out."

"You keep your ass on that seat, mister," Amundson said. He turned to Grunseth. "What do you think, Rob? We just go knock on the door?"

"You sure you can't get us any closer?"

"It don't look so good. There's some kind of rock garden in the way. You want to wait for the rain to let up a little?"

Grunseth growled, flung open his door, and ran for the chapel. He opened the chapel door and disappeared inside. Amundson hopped out of the car and followed.

Hyatt took a long, deep breath. This was it: the turning point of his life. The point where instead of Hyatt Hilton going to the world, the world would come to Hyatt Hilton. From now on, it was out of his hands. His only concern, at the moment, was that Chip would show up at some inconvenient moment. What had happened to him? Most likely, he had simply gotten lost, or become so involved in his reconnoitering that he'd lost track of time. Would he have sense enough to simply disappear?

Ten minutes passed before Amundson and Grunseth returned, walking slowly through the rain, arguing. Amundson got behind the wheel and started the car.

Grunseth said, "It's a damn tragedy is what it is."

Hyatt felt a chill rise up through his body to settle in a pool around his heart. His throat tightened. Something was very wrong.

"Is she . . . is she okay?"

Amundson put the car in gear and said to Grunseth, "I don't see what's so terrible. She's eighteen, isn't she?"

"She's twenty-three," Hyatt said.

Grunseth said to Hyatt, "Shut up."

Amundson said, "They'll get married, the guy'll get a better job. Daphne's not the first kid to start a family that way."

Hyatt said, "Hey! What are you talking about? What did you find in there?"

"Shut up. We're taking you back to town."

"Oh my god." Hyatt slumped back in the seat. "She's dead, isn't she? You have to arrest them. I know who did it. It was the Amaranthines. Polly and Rupe. I knew it. They just left her there, didn't they?" Hyatt was both horrified and thrilled by the concept. Part of him was thinking that it was no problem if Carmen was dead. He could still make it work. He would be the bereaved fiancé, the survivor of a heinous crime, witness to the horrors visited upon the innocent by the blood-drinking Amaranthines.


Polly entered the hospital room. "Dr. Bell says the girl's going to be all right. She's lost a lot of blood, but she'll be fine."

"Good," said Rupe. He was propped up on the bed, a cool, wet towel draped over his face and forehead. They were back at Youthmark, Dr. Bell's private hospital in Rochester. Dr. Bell had given him a couple of capsules; his headache was beginning to subside, but the nausea that had plagued him for the past few weeks was stronger than ever. Sunrise was an hour away.

"I'm not so sure it *is* good. What are we going to do with her? I told you Hyatt was up to something." Polly sat down. "Maybe we should have let her bleed to death."

"Don't say that, my sweet." Rupe pulled the towel away from his face. The bandages were gone. The flesh around his eyes looked swollen and tender.

"Why not? You realize that we are about to be savaged, don't you? Look what he's done to us!"

"Nothing. He's done nothing to us. We have a situation, that's all. Hyatt will go to the police and make a few wild accusations. The police will go to Stonecrop. They'll find nothing. We will be here. Dr. Bell said he would vouch for us."

"In exchange for a small donation, yes. I don't trust him any more than I trust Chip."

"How is he doing?"

"He's sleeping. Dr. Bell gave him a pain shot. A rather potent one, I believe."

"Good. The man was in pain."

"He's lucky he's alive. I could have shot him for a prowler."

Rupe shook his head. "No one should die at Stonecrop. You did the right thing."

"At least we won't have to worry about him for a few hours."

Polly stood up and went to the window. "Do you know what this is going to look like? The Amaranthine elders at a plastic surgery clinic? Look at my face! I'm red as a tomato, and you with your eyes all puffy and sore from your surgery. And down the hall we've got a bride who was kidnapped by one of our employees, who is a few rooms down the hall with second-degree burns on his scrotum. Even if we can prove that this was all Hyatt's doing, the press will strip us bare. It's all about to blow up, Rupe. Between the media and the police and the rest of the hyenas, they'll rip us open like a wounded lion."

Rupe grimaced. "That's disgusting." He replaced the moist towel across his face. "I wish you wouldn't watch those nature shows. They're all Death Programming."

"That's how it'll look. We're facing our Watergate, our Waco. What do you think will happen when they start talking to Chip?"

"Chip will tell the truth."

"That's what I'm afraid of. He'll tell them about our surgeries, our actual biological ages, the whole bit. He's been spying on us, Rupe. I doubt there's anything he doesn't know. It's one thing to have Hyatt out there making wild accusations, but Chip and Hyatt together—that's really bad. Even if we're off the hook for the kidnapping, the rest of it will sink us. How many of the Faithful do you think will keep writing us checks when they find out we've been lying to them?"

"Possibly most of them. They want to believe, Polly."

"And those that don't? Stonecrop is going to look to them like a giant scam. How many of the Faithful have you promised private cottages?"

"Everyone will be taken care of, dearest."

"Only if half of them die. Chip is going to sink us, Rupe. He knows everything, and he's going to talk. He's lost his faith, just like Hyatt."

"You told me he repented."

"Yeah, he repented with six ounces of boiling hot tea in his lap and a gun to his head. But what happens when his blisters heal and some reporter gets hold of him? He'll repent every which-way. The man is a dog, Rupe. As for the girl, who knows? I'm still not clear on whether she's working with Hyatt, or if she even knows what was going on at all. She could've died if we hadn't pulled that tube out of her arm."

"We saved her life," Rupe said. "When we found her she had lost a whole champagne bottle of blood, and then some. She didn't even know who she was. We should be heroes."

"That's not how the media will see it."

They sat without speaking, listening to the faint early morning buzzes and hums and respirations that filled the small hospital. Rupe could hear his pulse thumping in his right ear.

After a time Rupe said, "Are you sure about that, love? At bottom, they are all Pilgrims."

*Everyone should have enough money to get plastic surgery.*

—*Beverly Johnson, Supermodel*

CROW WAS STILL AWAKE AT dawn, standing at the window, watching the sky lighten, waiting for the sun to mount the horizon. The rain had stopped, the clouds were all but gone. At seven o'clock he realized that he was facing west. He reached up with both hands and rubbed his jaw muscles, willing them to relax. His gums hurt from clamping his teeth, and his brain felt heavy. He had mentally rehearsed his next conversation with Debrowski too many times. It no longer had a logical thread, only a kind of dirgelike inevitability. He would confront her with his feelings, support his position with a structure of facts and, if necessary, delineate for her the inevitable balance between rights and obligations in all human relationships. He was sure she'd be impressed.

Crow returned to the bed. After a time, he slept.

His first visitor, Wes Larson, was sitting quietly in one of the plastic chairs when Crow awakened.

When he saw Crow looking at him, Wes nodded. "Good morning." Wes Larson was not smiling, but he looked content.

Crow raised the head of his bed, bringing him up to the same altitude as Wes's thumblike head. "How's it going?" he said, figuring that Wes would take the question literally and talk for a while, giving him a chance to wake up.

Wes said, "You awake enough to answer a few questions?" There was a heartiness to his voice, along with a self-assuredness that Crow had never before heard from this social maladroit.

"I could use a cup of coffee," said Crow.

Wes fixed his eyes on Crow, giving him a disconcerting I-am-a-giant-thumb-and-you-are-under-me look. "I don't think they let you have coffee here," he said. "You look better than you did last night."

"I'm conscious. That's got to help. Why are you looking like that, Wes?"

"This is how I always look."

"No it's not. You usually look stern and uncomfortable. Today you just look stern."

A ghost of the old Wes appeared and disappeared. "I'm here on business," he said.

"Oh." Crow understood. The last time he'd seen him, Wes was being "old friend." Now he was being "peace officer," a role with which he was far more comfortable. "I thought you BCA guys didn't step in till the locals yelled uncle."

"We're flexible. In this case, I had a prior relationship with one of the parties involved." Wes removed a small spiral-bound notebook and a pen from the inside pocket of his gray suit.

"And that would be me?"

"That's correct. I'd like you to tell me what happened yesterday afternoon."

Crow took a few moments to adjust his blanket and drink some water. He had no reason to hide anything. On the other hand, he didn't know anything. His memory cut out after seeing that look of surprise on the clerk's face. But if he said he remembered nothing, he'd get nothing in return.

"Why don't you bring me up to speed," Crow said. "Tell me what you've got, and I'll fill it in for you. If I can."

"You were driving a limousine registered to Biggle Industries, correct?"

"That's right."

"But you are not employed by Biggle Industries."

"That's right. Look, Wes, I'm sort of under the weather here. Haven't even had my breakfast. I don't know how many questions I'm going to be able to answer. Maybe you should just tell me where you're at instead of asking me for answers you already got."

Wes glowered at him for a few seconds, then said, "Fair enough. What do you want to know?"

"Maybe you could start by telling me whether you've found the bride and groom."

"No and yes." He consulted his notebook. "Hyatt Hilton showed up with the limousine at four o'clock this morning at the police station in Prescott, Wisconsin, just the other side of the St. Croix. He drove his vehicle directly into one of their patrol cars, then proceeded to tell the officer on duty that his bride had been kidnapped by vampires."

"Vampires? What about the bride?" Crow asked.

"Carmen Roman is still missing."

"The vampires have her?"

"According to Hilton, yes. He said they were doing some sort of weird cult ritual, these—" Wes checked his notebook. "Amaranthines. He reported that they were draining out her blood. The Prescott cop figured he had a chapter fifty-one, but apparently Hilton convinced them to take a ride out to this little church up on the bluffs, where he claimed he'd last seen Miss Roman. There was nobody there. No evidence of foul play. That's it."

"That's what?"

"That's where we're at."

"Where is Hyatt now?"

"We don't know."

"You couldn't figure out some excuse to hold him?"

Wes shrugged. "The Prescott police had him. Like I said, they thought they had a psycho, holding him on a chapter fifty-one, but he walked."

"You're kidding. They just let him leave?"

"The way the Prescott cop told it, he just turned around and Hilton disappeared."

"Turned into a bat or something?"

"All I have is what the Prescott cop said. At the time, they thought he was just another nut job. They didn't even know that his missing fiancée even existed. They probably left him unattended, and he walked off. Okay, that's all we got. Now how about you tell us who it was hit you."

"I don't remember."

"You don't remember?"

"I didn't see him."

"It was a he?"

"It could have been a hermaphroditic Martian, for all I know. All I remember is going into the Clark station, and then I woke up here. That's it."

"So it could have been anybody hit you. It could have been Hilton."

"I suppose. Why don't you talk to the clerk? Didn't he see the guy?"

Wes frowned and put away his notebook. "He gave the investigating officers a statement, but when we attempted a followup interview we were unable to locate him. He gave us a fake name. We believe he was an illegal. Or maybe he was in on it."

"In on what?"

"Whatever. We're trying to get hold of the station owner. It's not clear from what the clerk said, in his initial interview, what actually happened. He just said a 'man in black' came in and clobbered you and stole all his Snickers. It could easily have been your buddy Hilton."

"You like Hyatt for kidnapping his own bride? Why would he do that?"

"We were hoping you could tell us."

"Sorry. I think you got yourselves a mystery."

"Good morning!"

Crow looked past Wes and saw Debrowski holding a Starbucks tray, two tall coffees. A small duffel bag was slung over her shoulder. She walked in and set the tray on the bedside table.

"You were sleeping so hard before, I thought you could use some real bean."

"Wes has been helping me to full consciousness," Crow said.

Debrowski nodded to Wes. "You want a coffee?"

"No thanks, I was just leaving." Wes stood abruptly. "We'll talk later," he said to Crow.

"Anytime," said Crow.

Crow and Debrowski watched him leave, then looked at each other.

"Was that fun?" Debrowski asked.

"A blast." He decided to plunge. "We have to *talk*," he said, giving the word a portentous ring.

"Oh?" Debrowski drew back, startled. "You mean you and me?"

"Yeah . . ." Crow faltered. "Uh, they told me Hyatt turned up in Prescott."

"That's right. How are you feeling?"

"Not too bad, but I still don't remember anything. Wes seems to think it was Hyatt that bopped me."

"That's not what the clerk said."

"They told me the clerk disappeared. All he told them was it was a guy dressed in black."

"Yeah. A stocky guy dressed up like a ninja. That doesn't sound like Hyatt. Is that what you wanted to talk about?"

"No. I want to talk about you and me."

"Oh!" Debrowski looked down at the bag in her hands, thrust it toward him. "You want to check out of this dive? I brought you some clothes."

"Yeah." Crow sat up. "A ninja? A Japanese guy?"

"He didn't say that. What he said was, 'a ninja with a nose like a pig.'"

"What's that mean?"

"I don't know. Is that all you wanted to 'talk' about? I was hoping for something juicy."

"Just a second." Crow held up a hand. He felt a memory coming, a black, gauzy image. Black shoes. "Just a second." Blank pants. He closed his eyes and remembered being in the Clark station, seeing the clerk's bored eyes widen. He remembered turning to see what the clerk was seeing. A pair of nostrils.

"Crow?"

Crow opened his eyes.

"You okay?"

"I remember now, the guy that hit me. You want to know something amazing?"

"Always."

"I think Hyatt Hilton might be telling the truth."

♠

Carmen woke up in the land with thick air. It was a familiar atmosphere, but an unfamiliar room. She sat up slowly, the air sliding past her face. A motel? The furnishings—a bed; a bedside table; a television mounted high on the wall; thick, ugly curtains over the window—had the anonymous quality of a Motel 6. She swung her legs over the edge of the mattress, let her feet touch the floor. Cold linoleum. She had never been in a motel room with linoleum floors. But she *had* been stoned before. She was stoned now, on something really strong. She hadn't felt like this since she'd tried Quaaludes, back when she was just thirteen.

Carmen looked down. She was no longer wearing her wedding dress. She was wearing a loose cotton gown, open at the back.

She remembered riding in a car with pig-face Chip, an older man with a bandage over his eyes, and a woman with big hair. She remembered waking up later and watching the fat doctor giving her something in her arm, smiling as he did it. Whatever the stuff was, it had knocked her out long enough for them to undress her and get her into bed. The fat doctor had probably intended for her to sleep for hours, but he hadn't taken into account the size of her liver. Carmen stood up. Her legs were a bit wobbly, but the thick air helped. She moved toward the window, eight slow-motion steps, and parted the curtains. Bright daylight flooded the room. She was on the first floor, looking out onto a small park with benches, picnic tables, and dew on the grass. She could be anywhere. She did not know how long she had slept. She was sure of only two things: That Hy's plan had gone kablooey—no surprise there—and that it would be in her best interest to get out of this place. She considered simply climbing out the window. Why not? She raised the window. No alarms, but the cool night air raised goosebumps. She would go, but first she needed to find something to wear.

Daytime drama star Wayne Savage, recovering from a chin and hair implant doubleheader, was awakened from his morning nap by a soft, clicking sound. In his dream, the sound had been a pair of geishas making music with chopsticks. He opened his eyes. A long-haired figure in a hospital gown stood at his closet looking through his clothes. The sound was that of plastic clothes hangers clacking together. Wayne worked his tongue around his mouth preparing to say something when he noticed that the back of the gown was open, revealing a nicely rounded female posterior. He decided to withhold comment and see what developed.

The girl suddenly froze, then turned her head and looked back at him. Wayne remained very still, watching through nearly closed eyes. A pretty, sleepy-looking girl. She watched him for a few seconds, apparently decided he was still asleep, and shrugged the gown from her shoulders. Her body was full and round and much appreciated by Wayne, who had had his fill of the emaciated Hollywood type. This girl would look like a cow on film, but live in person she was a goddess.

She returned her attention to the contents of his closet and came up with a pair of his chinos and a UCLA T-shirt. She dressed slowly, starting with the T-shirt, pulling it down over her head, over her breasts—a striptease in reverse. Grabbing her long hair and tugging it up out of the T-shirt. Stepping into each leg of the chinos. Tucking in the shirt, pulling the belt tight, rolling up the cuffs to keep them from dragging. She tried on his Bally slip-ons, but they were too big on her, like clown shoes.

She was going through the pockets of his jackets when Wayne broke his silence.

"You won't find it," he said.

The girl stopped and turned slowly to face him.

Wayne said, "My wallet is on the table here, but you can't have it."

"I wasn't looking for your wallet."

"Oh?" Wayne sat up, letting the sheets slide off his upper body to give her a look at his chest. "What were you looking for?"

"I was hoping for a set of car keys," she said.

"Sorry. I didn't drive."

"Oh, Well, thanks anyway." The girl backed toward the door, then was gone, with his clothes.

Wayne smiled. A fair trade. This was what he needed to cut through the boredom of his stay at Youthmark. Something pretty.


Whatever drug the doctor had given her, Carmen liked it. Instead of being nervous taking that guy's clothes, she had felt totally calm, even after she'd realized he was Wayne Savage. She'd actually talked to him, and she was wearing his clothes. This was even better than the time she'd served a bean taco to Kevin Bacon. Or anyway a guy who looked like Kevin Bacon. She was pretty sure it had been him. Whatever.

She exited the building through a side door into a parking lot containing half a dozen vehicles. Beginning with the Mercedes, she began to check for hidden keys. Hyatt had once told her that one out of every four vehicles had an extra key hidden somewhere on or in it. She got lucky on her second try—the Range Rover was unlocked and a set of keys was stashed above the sun visor. In minutes, she was on something called County Road 2. She planned to drive until she reached the next town, then stop and ask for directions, but the drug in her bloodstream began to assert itself anew, and a few miles later she found herself drifting in and out of her lane. Trying to make the vehicle easier to steer, she sped up. Fields of corn and soybeans flashed by, became a blur. The landscape warped, an ocean of cornstalks rose up before her, the vehicle bucked and heaved. A roaring, grinding, and crunching preceded a loud pop. The airbag hit her in the chest and face. All motion stopped. The air was filled with dust from the field and talc from the airbag. Dazed, Carmen took in her surroundings. Cornstalks lay across the hood and pressed against the glass on both sides. Behind her lay a swath of crushed stalks. As far as she could tell, she was unhurt and remarkably calm. These things happen, she thought. She closed her eyes, feeling safe in the arms of the corn. After a few minutes she slipped into a deep sleep.

*Marriage and hanging go by destiny; matches are made in heaven.*

—*Robert Burton*

"**Y**OU SURE YOU WANT TO do this?"

"No. What I *want* is to go home and sleep for about a hundred years."

"How about we go home and you get started."

"Later." Crow pulled into the left lane and tromped on the accelerator. The engine roared, the hood seemed to swell, and Debrowski felt her spine sink into the vinyl seat.

"I never thought I'd say this, Crow, but I kinda miss your Jag."

"I just want to check this place out."

"I understand that's what you want. What I don't get is why you're the one that has to do it. Call your friend the cop. You got his card."

"I'm the one who made it all happen. I'm the one that brought Hyatt and Carmen together. I'm the one who got the Amaranthines all stirred up. I'm the one who arranged for the limousine, and I'm the one who was driving it. The rest of them—Axel, Hyatt, Carmen, and the Amaranthines—they're all victims of circumstance."

"Crow, the universe does not tremble when you scratch your ass. Didn't they teach you that in AA?"

"I don't see it that way. If I put a bear and a tiger in the same cage, I'm the one who has to clean up the mess."

"People aren't animals."

"Oh really? You should talk to Axel sometime."

"I wonder how he's doing. Still trying to figure out what to do with the left-over food." Debrowski rested a boot on the glovebox. "You never know what's going on in these old guys' heads."

"They're all mourning their wasted youth. By the way, how did your date with Sam go?"

"Your dad's a real character, Crow."

"Uh-huh."

Crow came up behind a slow-moving Ford, rode its tail for a quarter mile, then passed it on the right.

"You keep driving like this, you'll be dead anyway."

"Look, you don't have to be here."

"Oh yes I do."

"Really." Crow's mouth went small. Debrowski had seen Crow angry be-fore, but it had always been directed at others. He twisted the wooden shift knob, grinding it into the stick. "You stay in France for three months, and all of a sudden you have to be here?"

"I'm here now."

"Yeah, because things didn't work out in France."

"If things *had* worked out I'd have been back sooner," Debrowski said, sur-prised to hear the defensive note in her voice.

"Most of the time I didn't even know how to get hold of you."

"That's my fault? That you never asked me where I was? You know, Crow, I've got one hell of a phone bill waiting for me. I called you almost every day. I got a better relationship with your goddamn answering machine than I do with you."

"That doesn't surprise me."

"Furthermore, I didn't much appreciate you leaving me alone in Paris. You could've stuck around, you know. It wouldn't have hurt you to stay another week or two, just to help me get the project rolling. Maybe if you'd been there, maybe things wouldn't have gone sour. But you never even considered that, did you? You and your goddamn cat. You think he missed you? Your cat? Would you slow down?"

Crow eased up on the gas, letting the speedometer drop from eighty-five to eighty-three. He was being childish and he knew it, and he didn't give a damn. If he had to act like a brat to have this conversation, so be it. One way or an-other, he had to let her know how he felt.

He said, "If you'd wanted me to stay you could have said so."

"You didn't give me the option. One day we're eating crepes, and the next thing I know you tell me you're leaving."

"You told me it was a good idea. You said you'd be busy."

"What was I supposed to do? Beg you to stay? Jerk."

"Jerk?"

"You don't like 'jerk'? Try asshole. Pull over. You want to go get tossed in another dumpster, I want no part of it. Maybe it's where you belong."

"Now just a minute—"

Debrowski lifted her left boot from the glove box and kicked the shift lever into neutral. The car slowed rapidly.

"Hey!" Crow put the GTO back in gear.

"You let me out of this ridiculous car, or I swear to god Crow, I'm gonna kick out your goddamn windshield."

"Okay, okay, you mind if I find an exit? We're on the freeway." Ridiculous car? Of course it was ridiculous. Didn't she think he knew that? It was *supposed* to be ridiculous.

"Right up here. Johnson Street. You let me off on Johnson Street, wherever the hell that is."

"Why should you be mad? I'm the one should be mad."

"Look at me, Crow."

Crow, who was trying to cross two lanes of traffic to get to the exit ramp, caught a glimpse of glittering blue eyes and flared white nostrils. Debrowski had both boots pressed against the dash, her arms wrapped around her knees, her hands balled into white-knuckled fists. She didn't move. The GTO rolled up the exit ramp; Crow pulled over and brought the car to a full stop.

"You're doing it again," she said.

"I'm not doing anything."

"No, you're not." Debrowski uncurled her fingers. "You're just sitting here by the side of the road having your own little premature midlife crisis." She opened the door and got out. "You could've at least argued with me." She slammed the door.

Crow sat in his car, stunned, watching her walk away. Argued with her? Was she talking about now? What did she think he'd been doing? Or was she talking about before, in Paris? He watched her leather jacket receding. "The hell with you, then," he muttered. His words lacked conviction. Debrowski was now so far away that she was recognizable only by the angry tempo of her gait. A hollow, panicky feeling came over him, the same feeling he'd had in Paris when the taxi had pulled away and he'd looked though the rear window to see Debrowski standing on the sidewalk lighting a cigarette, getting smaller.

Crow moved the gearshift into first and went after her.

♠

Drew Chance had worked on a lot of promising news stories that had gone nowhere. He'd followed politicians, chased down anonymous tips, and scrolled miles of surveillance tapes searching for stories that simply weren't there. Sometimes, when the effort became too expensive to simply write it off, he'd done the story anyway. Like the one on the St. Cloud mayor who, after months of suspicious behavior—caught on tape—turned out to be innocent of philandering, drug abuse, accepting bribes, and fixing parking tickets for relatives. Drew had titled that *Hard Camera* segment "Innocent!" Rather to his surprise, the mayor had been furious.

As for the wedding story, that one could go either way. The footage they'd got of the bleeding chauffeur was good, but the story still proved elusive. A bride and groom kidnapped? Such had been Hy the Guy's promise, but the police were not calling it a kidnapping, and Drew was getting vibes from his police contacts that it might be nothing. Maybe the couple had simply eloped and the chauffeur had fallen down and hit his head. If that was the case, the story would not be *Hard Camera* material.

But Hy the Guy had clearly indicated that there would be a real story here, so Drew remained hopeful. For now, he was waiting for the phone to ring which, eventually, it did.

"Mr. Chance? I've got Mr. Hilton on line two."

"Thanks Melissa . . . Hy? What's happening, man? How's that little fiancée of yours?"

"Did you look at it?"

"Look at what?"

"The *tape*. The tape I sent you. You didn't get it?"

"Um. Let me check." He put Hyatt on hold and buzzed Melissa. A few seconds later he was back on the line. "Yeah, I got it. It came in by courier, but I guess it got mixed in with the mail."

"Jesus Christ! You call yourself a news organization? Jesus Christ."

"Take it easy, Hy. I'll look at it. So, what happened? You get kidnapped or what?"

"Just look at the goddamn tape."

"You seen how they do," Chuckles said. "Just talk. Secret is, you say a few things simple, over and over, and you don't stop long enough to let nobody think too much. Like preachers do."

"My mother did that," Flo said. She was sitting with Chuckles in the Security Annex at the Amaranthine Church of the One. Chuckles had given her the tour. She'd seen the place before, but last time she'd been running pretty hard and hadn't noticed much.

"Mamas do that, too," Chuckles said, flashing his gold canine. "Sometimes they right."

"You really expect to live forever?"

"Why not?" Chuckles leaned back in his chair and stretched. His brick-colored wrists came out of the sleeves of his white silk jacket and kept right on going, the longest arms Flo thought she'd ever seen. The sight of them sent a shiver up her ribcage; Flo forced herself to look away from him, fixing her eyes on the bank of video screens. Chuckles said, "I know one thing for sure. If I'm gonna die, I don't want to know nothing about it till after."

That made sense to Flo. She liked his perspective on the whole immortality thing. In fact, she liked a lot of things about this Chuckles. He understood her. He knew how to make her comfortable. Even now, sitting in this little room with all the TVs, he made sure there were a few feet between them, made sure he didn't get between her and the door. He respected her space.

When he had taken her for that limo ride to Iowa last night, he'd never touched her with his hands, or even threatened to. All he'd done was drive and talk, reaching out to her with his big, soft voice. And when they'd finally stopped at that truck stop he'd given her every opportunity to bolt. She'd stayed on. Chuckles interested her. He wasn't pushy like Solid Sam, or sneaky like Bigg, or standoffish like Joe Crow. Chuckles was just there. On the ride back to Minneapolis she'd sat up front with him, watching the dashed centerline flash by, listening to the big man talk. She hardly remembered being dropped off at her condo, long after midnight, Chuckles opening the door for her but keeping his hands to himself, not even looking as if he expected her to say goodnight.

Eight hours later he'd been back at her condo, in a yellow Corvette this time, asking her if she wanted to see where he worked. The Corvette was even smaller inside than her Miata, but with the elbow-high console between them, Flo had felt completely comfortable. Chuckles's sense of personal space was impeccable. Flo believed that when the time came he would lay his hands upon her, and she would melt like hot wax over a candle.

Chuckles said, "You notice how all them folks at the aging clinic were about the same age?"

"All old."

"Not so old. Most of 'em about forty, fifty, right in there, most of 'em women. You know how come that is?"

"They see wrinkles."

"Huh-uh. What it is, they got husbands that just figured out they gonna die. You know?"

Flo shook her head.

"Husband got the middle-age blues, what he gonna do? He gonna be think-ing the best part of his life is over, and he gonna regret he wasn't payin' attention all them years when his dick was standin' out like a steel pipe and all his head was cover with hair. He gonna be figurin' he got maybe twenty years left before he have to start wearin' diapers again, and twenty years ago the other way when he was, say, twenty-five, that seem just like yesterday to him. So what he does, he start lookin' at sweet young things like you. So then the wife, she start lookin' round for something, too. Maybe she figure she like to live forever. Maybe she bring her man to the meetings, maybe she don't. Maybe she like to spend his money, give it to Rupe and Polly before the husband give it to some little gal name of Bambi."

Flo was trying hard to understand what he was telling her. She said, "So the idea of the church is to help women get through their husband's middle-age crisis?"

"You got it, only it gets more complicated, on account of you got to throw in menopause and empty nest, too. Point is, you got to have your base of Faithful to make the seventh step, which is what Rupe and Polly done. You want to live forever, you got to have people working for you, making it happen. That what Rupe and Polly got going for them, they on top. You know what I'm saying? The way it is, I maybe live a long time, but I be working for them."

Flo thought about her job at solid Sam's. "Everybody got to work," she said. Damn, she was talking that way again.

"I rather be working for me."

Flo looked away from the TVs and back at Chuckles. "You going to start your own church?"

Chuckles grinned. "I knew was something about you I like."

Flo looked back at the TVs. One of the screens caught her eye—a man entering the building. "Somebody's here," she said.

"People here all the time," Chuckles said. "They can talk to Benjy."

"I don't know," Flo said. "I think this one might be here to see you."

Benjy Hiss, an unsettled person by nature, was not enjoying his stint at the Amaranthine Church's headquarters. For the better part of a year he had been working on Stonecrop, where his focus had been on building, dealing with contractors and suppliers, and working with Rupe on transforming the vision into stone and mortar. It was hard work, but it was real. Each passing day had provided new signs of progress, and Benjy had never lost sight of what he was doing there.

Running ACO World Headquarters, that was anything but focused. The phone calls alone were enough to drive him batty. He'd gotten a number of calls from various police agencies, all demanding to speak with Rupe and Polly. Benjy had tried to explain to the first caller, a man named Larson, that the elders would not be available for another four weeks. Larson had not been satisfied with that, so Benjy simply routed his call, and all subsequent calls, to Rupe's voice mail. So far, none of them had shown up in person, but it was still a hassle. And to make things worse, the two guys he'd been counting on to help him run things were turning out to be totally unreliable. He hadn't seen Chip since yesterday, and Chuckles had just waltzed in three hours late with a little chiquita by his side, giving her the tour, not even bothering to apologize for being late for work, treating him like a servant. Benjy had never much cared for Chuckles and his attitude.

On top of everything else, Sissy Walmurt had called in sick, leaving Benjy stuck behind the receptionist's desk all day. He was brooding on these developments when a man wearing red, white, and blue warm-ups and a large bandage on his head entered the foyer and approached him.

Benjy said, "One God."

The man stared at him blankly.

"Can I help you?" Benjy asked. He rather hoped that he could not. The man had a dangerous look to him—big, brutal, and angry. Spots of blood had soaked through the white bandage, which covered most of his forehead. His left eye was swollen shut, his right was shot with red veins. One nostril appeared to be stuffed with cotton. A second bandage ran along the line of his jaw. The man rested his thick, stubby fingers on the edge of the desk.

"I'm looking for Charles Thickening," he said, producing a smile made ghastly by a freshly broken tooth. "Chuckles."

"And you are . . . ?"

"Arling Biggle. A friend of his. A good friend." Biggle sniffed through his good nostril, producing a liquid gurgle in his sinuses. "He's a member of my health club."

Benjy noticed that Arling Biggle's rather large hands had clenched into fists. He smiled. "Would you like me to page him?"

"How about if you just tell me where he is. I'd like to surprise him."

Benjy's smile broadened. "I understand. Just go on up to the second floor." He pointed to the stairway at the far end of the foyer. "Turn right at the top of the steps, go all the way to the end of the hall, and turn right again. You'll come to a door marked 'Maintenance.' That's the Security Annex. I think Chuckles is in there."

Biggle nodded and headed off toward the Security Annex. Benjy looked up at the security camera mounted on the wall and wished that such things worked in both directions. It would be interesting to observe Chuckles's reaction to the appearance of his good friend Arling Biggle. He was thinking about going up there himself to watch when the front door chimed again, announcing the arrival of yet another bandaged man, this one accompanied by a leather-jacketed woman.

*If pregnancy were a book they would cut the last two chapters.*

—Nora Ephron

"It's a good thing I don't play games," Debrowski said. "You'd be too confused to breathe."

Crow laughed. "What do you call jumping out of the car and walking away? That's not playing games?"

"That's reality, Crow. It's not a game unless you give do-overs. You weren't going to get a do-over."

"Yeah? I'm not so sure I like the sound of that. In any case, I really am sorry. I was an idiot. I really did think you wanted me to leave and go back to the states."

"Crow—you're doing it again. Don't try to make it right. Just be sorry."

"Hey, cut me some slack here. I'm trying." Crow turned into the parking lot of an old school building.

"Me, too. Is this the place?"

"This is it. You want to live forever, this is where you buy your ticket."

"Tell me again what we're doing here?"

"Just stirring the muck."

The slim, dark-skinned man at the reception desk greeted them with a cautious smile. "One God?" he asked.

"Two," said Crow. The guy didn't get it. No sense of humor. He said, "I'm looking for a fellow who works here. I don't know his name."

The man peaked his black eyebrows, waiting for more.

Crow used his middle finger to push up the tip of his nose, giving the man a look into his nostrils. He held the pose until the man's confused look suddenly gave way to comprehension.

"Oh! You are looking for Charles Bouchet!" He laughed. "We call him Chip. He's our Security Chief."

"Is he here?"

"No he's not. I haven't seen him yet today."

"Do you expect him?"

"Yes. No. I mean, I expected him this morning, but apparently there was some error in our scheduling. I really couldn't say when he'll be in. Is there something I could help you with?"

"Is Rupert Chandra in?"

"Dr. Chandra is on sabbatical."

"Do you know how I can reach him?"

The man shook his head. "I'm sorry. He won't be available until September sixth."

"Where is he?"

"I can't help you with that. I'm sorry."

"Let me ask you something, ah, what's your name?"

"Benjy."

"Benjy. Thank you. Suppose that an insanely violent man walked in here and threatened you, and only Rupert Chandra could convince him to spare your life. How would you go about contacting him?"

Benjy licked his lips. "The situation seems unlikely to arise."

"Really?" Crow look at Debrowski. "What do you think?"

"It could happen," she said. "I've seen it happen."

"In such a case, I would probably offer to make a phone call," Benjy said quickly. "But it might not do any good."

"And why is that?"

"I have Ms. DeSimone's cell phone number. They might choose to ignore it. In fact, they've as much as told me they would not be taking any calls."

"Who is 'they?'"

"Dr. Chandra and Ms. DeSimone."

Crow picked up the telephone handset and pointed at the keypad. "Punch it in," he said.

Benjy slowly punched in a number. Crow listened to five rings before a sleepy woman's voice at the other end said, "Hello?"

"Hello. Who am I speaking to, please?"

"Depends," said the voice. "Who are you?"

"This is Joe Crow."

Crow listened to the response. He turned to Debrowski and said, "It's Carmen."

"Oh man!" Chuckles groaned. He was staring at the monitors, following Arling Biggle's progress through the building. "He's comin' right on up here. What was my man Benjy thinking? I'm gonna have to have me a talk with him."

"Maybe Bigg just wants his limo back," Flowrean said.

"My guess, the man wants a piece of me first." He stood and opened a tall white cabinet by the door. Inside were two shotguns, a rifle, and assorted other weaponry. Chuckles selected a twelve-ounce leather-and-lead slapper sap. He closed the cabinet, reconsidered, went back in, and slipped a stun gun into his jacket pocket.

"I mention step number eight?" he asked.

Flowrean shook her head. "You said there was only seven."

"I add my own. It's the same as the Boy Scouts." He smacked the slapper against his palm. "Be prepared."

"How about if I go talk to him?" Flowrean said.

Chuckles pointed at monitor number three, which showed Bigg advancing down the hallway. "If you gonna do it, you best do it now."

Flo did not know exactly what had happened between Bigg and Chuckles, but judging from the condition of Bigg's face, it had been unpleasant. They stood facing each other, ten feet apart, in the hallway outside the security annex. Bigg's mouth was open, but nothing was coming out.

Flo smiled and tossed Bigg a set of keys. Bigg caught them, recognized the key fob, and grunted as if he'd been elbowed in the gut.

Flo said, "It's parked downtown, on Tenth between Hennepin and LaSalle."

Bigg said, "You okay?"

"Of course I'm okay."

"I wondered what happened to you," he said. "I tried to call you last night from the hospital."

"I wasn't home," she said reasonably.

Bigg looked pointedly at the door marked "Maintenance." "Is 'Chuckles' in there?"

"He said to say he's real sorry about what happened."

"I doubt it." He looked again at the limo keys and pocketed them. "What about you? You want to explain to me how come I got hit over the head? I thought we had a date."

Flo felt a twinge of guilt. "I'm real sorry about that, too. I got into the car, I thought it was you driving. Where were you?"

"I was in the alley, stuck in between a couple of dumpsters, knocked out cold by your friend in there."

"Oh." She had thought it might be something like that. "I didn't know that."

"Why did he do that, Flowrean?"

"I think maybe he was mad about the gym. You know. When you talked to him. He didn't like that."

"I did that for you. You said he was bothering you."

Another twinge of guilt came and went. "I didn't know him so good then. Chuckles is really a nice guy, Bigg. You don't have to be mad at him anymore. You could go get your limo now. Everything is even-steven," she said brightly.

"It doesn't feel even-steven to me. He hit me with a wrench. He coulda killed me."

"Chuckles would never kill anybody. He just wanted to meet me." She smiled happily, hoping to infect Bigg with her cheer.

Bigg regarded her balefully for several seconds, one red eye blinking. He thrust a forefinger at her. "You want to know what I think, Flowrean? I think you set me up."

"Me?" What was he talking about? She hadn't even wanted to go out with him in the first place, and she certainly hadn't wanted to be kidnapped by Chuckles—though she didn't mind it so much after the fact.

"You're crazier than a fucking fruitcake, you and your dead fish. Where do you people come from? What the hell did I do to deserve this shit?"

Flo's smile collapsed. She was trying to be nice, and he was being mean to her. "You look at me," she accused. "In the mirror."

"I look at you all right. So what? That makes it okay for your boyfriend to crack my skull open? You better find a new place to work out, honey, 'cause you're not welcome at Bigg's anymore. You or your nigger boyfriend."

Bigg made a move toward the door. Flo stepped back. Let him go in, get himself hurt. See if she cared. She backed off a few more steps. Bigg had one hand on the knob and was pulling the door open when she saw a revolver appear in his other hand. Flo's heart stopped; she reversed direction, forcing a great gout of energized air out through her throat. The resulting shriek, had it been a half step higher, might have shattered every window in the building.


"Where is she?"

"Where are you, Carmen?" Crow's brow furrowed. "She says she's in the middle of a cornfield. She—what's that?" He blinked, then said to Debrowski, "She says she met Wayne Savage."

"Who is Wayne Savage?"

"I have no idea."

"He's on TV," said Benjy.

Crow opened his mouth to ask Carmen what she was doing in the middle of a cornfield talking on Polly DeSimone's cell phone when she said, "If you see Hy, tell him I'm not gonna do it."

"Do what? Get married?"

"You tell him and his pig-nose friend I don't wanna do it."

An enraged banshee or some similar creature chose that moment to let out a heart-stopping shriek. The sound echoed through the halls, raising the hairs on the back of Crow's neck.

"Lord God in heaven, what the hell was that?" asked Benjy.

Crow looked at Debrowski. Her eyes were as wide as he'd ever seen them. He said to Benjy, "You don't know what that was?"

Benjy shook his head.

"Then tell me this: Is there a young woman named Flowrean on the premises?"

As Benjy nodded, they heard the sound of three gunshots.

Over the past twenty-four hours, Chuckles's thinking had become remarkably clear. The ongoing conquest of Flowrean Peeche—one inch at a time—had boosted his self-confidence far above its usual plateau. Every increment of his ongoing seduction had come off perfectly. He had waited patiently for the opportunity, he had grasped it, and he had never once lost sight of his goal. This was power, such as he had never before experienced. He now saw himself as a force of nature, a conductor of life. He saw himself as a player.

Was this the seventh step? Be God? If so, there was irony here, for his new vantage point revealed the church as a simple conceptual tool, a way of thinking that could be subsumed into a larger world view, embracing not only the Amaranthine Precepts, but also Flowrean Peeche, his Good Luck Charlie tattoo, and chocolate-frosted longjohns.

The visit from Bigg was a minor ripple in the overall plan, an easily handled glitch, nothing more.

Chuckles' strategy was simple. As soon as Bigg came through the door—assuming that Flowrean couldn't get rid of him—he planned to zap him with the stun gun, then give him a tap on the back of his head with the slapper. The combo should be as effective as the pipe wrench, maybe better. He positioned himself beside the door, the stun gun in his left hand, ready to jab it into Bigg's gut and squeeze off a bolt. He wasn't even nervous. It might be interesting. He'd never had the chance to use the stun gun before.

He could hear Flo's voice and Bigg's muttered replies. The handle turned, and the door was pulled open. He saw Bigg's bandaged face and began his thrust when Flowrean's scream hit him in the back of the neck.

Chuckles's body remembered that sound. His thigh went weak with remembered pain, his knees liquefied, and the stun gun dropped from his fingers as his hands moved to protect his groin.

The paralyzing effect of the scream lasted only for an instant. Bigg jumped back into the hall slamming the door shut between them.

♠

Bigg was also affected by Flo's outburst—the scream caused him to freeze momentarily, almost long enough for Flo to reach him, but not quite. He saw her coming in time to swing. His fist caught her high on the chest, knocking the wind out of her. She dropped to her knees, gasping for air.

Bigg pointed his revolver at the door and fired three shots through the door. The reports were sharp and loud and echoed for a full second in the empty hallways. He turned back to Flo, who had regained her feet, and pointed the gun at her face.

"I don't want to hurt you," he said. He backed away a few steps.

Flo coughed, holding her hands crossed over her chest. All her attention was on the door with the three bullet holes.

"He had a gun or something," Bigg said.

Flo called out, "Chuckles?"

No reply.

Bigg turned and fled.

Without a doubt, one of the oddest hallucinatory experiences in Carmen Roman's adult life—and there had been many—was waking up to the sound of a ringing telephone and finding herself in a strange vehicle, alone, in the middle of a cornfield. And then answering the phone and having it be Axel's friend Joe Crow, asking her a bunch of questions. And then something happening in the background, and Joe Crow tells her to hold on. Hold on for what?

While she sat waiting for him to come back on the line she noticed that her borrowed chinos and the driver's seat of the Range Rover were soaked dark red. Carmen's first thought was that she had bled from her arm, like in the chapel, but her arm looked fine.

So where was all the blood coming from?

Benjy jumped up at the sound of the shots, started running toward them, changed his mind, ran back to the desk, then looked helplessly at Crow.

"What should we do?" he asked.

Crow handed Debrowski the phone. "You talk to Carmen. I'll go see what happened."

"Crow, if you get yourself shot, I swear I'm gonna just let you die."

"I'll be careful." Crow trotted toward the stairs.

Debrowski watched until he disappeared, then put the phone to her ear. "Carmen? This is Laura Debrowski. You there?"

♠

As Crow reached the top of the steps he heard footsteps slapping the worn linoleum floors and saw a man with a gun running down the hall. It looked like Arling Biggle, and it was.

Crow shouted, "Hey! Bigg!"

Bigg stopped and raised the gun; Crow ducked back into the stairwell and shouted, "It's me, Bigg! Crow!"

"Crow? Are you in on this, too?"

"In on what?" Crow peeked around the corner. Bigg was walking quickly toward him, looking back over his shoulder.

He reached the stairwell and stopped, looked at Crow. "You look worse than me," he said, pointing the gun. "I'm holding you responsible."

The revolver looked small in Bigg's hand, but it was big enough to scare Crow. "Responsible for what? Was that you shooting?"

"I just shot the door. Think I slowed him down. He had a gun, something in his hand."

"Who? You're not making sense, Bigg."

"Him and that bitch Flowrean."

"Flowrean?"

"And that big black son-of-a-bitch. Look what he did to me! You see this face?" He started down the stairs, shouting, "I want my limo back, Crow."

Crow let him reach the bottom of the stairs, then followed. He wanted to make sure Bigg and his gun left the building. Debrowski and Benjy were still standing by the front desk. Bigg ran past them and out the front doors. Crow ran back up the stairs and down the hall. He heard a voice and followed it to a small room where Flowrean Peeche, sitting on the floor holding a phone, cradled the head of a large man with a gold canine tooth—the warm-up act from the anti-aging demonstration. Crow's eye was drawn to a bright red blossom on the lapel of the man's white sport coat, but it wasn't a rose at all. It was blood.

Flowrean dropped the phone. "You be okay, baby. Ambulance coming."

The man coughed and blinked. Crow knelt and pulled the pocket square from the man's breast pocket, slipped it inside the sodden shirt and pressed it gently to the wound. "Hold that there," he said to Flowrean. "Is that the only place he got hit?"

"I think so."

"You called 911?"

"I called," said Flowrean. She sounded very young.

Crow stood up. "He's gonna be okay. He's gonna make it," he said, not believing it.

"I know that," said Flowrean. "He immortal."

♠

Debrowski was still on the phone when Crow returned to the foyer.

"You still talking to Carmen?"

Debrowski shook her head and held up a hand, bidding Crow to wait. "Yes, that's the cell phone number. She said she's losing blood, I don't know why. She's in a cornfield, so I assume it's out of town. In a Range Rover. Look, why don't you call her? She was getting pretty woozy there, but she might still be able to answer the phone. You can locate her from the cell phone, can't you?" She listened for a moment, then smacked herself on the hip with her fist. "Listen, I'm just telling you what I know. The girl is missing, she was kidnapped yesterday afternoon. I'm telling you how to find her . . . yeah . . . yeah. Just a sec." She moved the phone away from her mouth. "Crow what's that cop's name? Your friend?"

"Wes Larson."

Debrowski spoke into the phone, "Wes Larson, with the BCA. How the hell should I know? Okay." She read the number off the telephone, then hung up. "I think Carmen's bleeding to death," she said to Crow.

A siren sounded in the distance, getting louder. Crow said, "She's not the only one."

*The best argument I know for an immortal life is the existence of a man who deserves one.*

*—William James*

"Rupe! wake up! we have to get out of here."

Rupert Chandra erupted from a deep sleep, sat up quickly, his heart suddenly accelerated, his pulse drumming in his ears. "What? What's wrong?" He threw off his covers; the room came into focus. "Polly? You scared me."

"Good. Listen, put your shoes on. We have to go."

"Why? What happened?"

"The girl is gone."

Rupe took a moment to wipe his eyes, trying to think. Recent events assorted themselves in his mind. "The girl? Gone? What do you mean?"

"I mean she's gone. She stole my Range Rover. We have to get out of here, Rupe. If she goes to the police, and they find us here . . . I can't even think about it. Dr. Bell has a car we can borrow." She pulled on his arm, causing a spasm of pain to travel from his wrist to his chest.

"Give me a moment, my sweet." He drew a deep breath and stood up shakily. He still felt woozy from yesterday's anesthesia. The floor appeared to be about ten feet below him. "I'm feeling a little tall," he said.

"Rupe? Are you all right? You look pale."

A lead weight had materialized inside his ribcage. "I'm feeling tall and heavy," he said. His knees buckled and he fell forward, felt Polly catch him and lower him to the floor. He heard her shouting for Dr. Bell, and he heard the murmur of the Faithful and, closer at hand, the high-pitched keening of his cells.

Chip Bouchet, between oblivion and consciousness, saw himself as a throbbing moon of pain spinning through space. The sound of running feet and excited voices tugged him toward wakefulness. He opened his eyes and the floating, weightless feeling receded. The moon shrank and located itself in the vicinity of his scrotum. He lay there without moving for several minutes. The distant sound of voices was interrupted by an approaching siren, the siren was replaced by new voices. A few minutes later the siren reasserted itself, then a quiet descended upon the hospital. For the next half hour, Chip waited for someone to come to him, to bring him another pain pill. Apparently he had been forgotten. Maybe that was good. Other than to think about how much pain he was in, Chip's mind had not performed a great deal of strategic mentation since his conversation with Polly back at Stonecrop.

Maybe he should do some reconnoitering. Get the lay of the land. It might even be possible to exfiltrate the arena. Very carefully, he rolled onto his side and swung his feet over the edge of the mattress, let them descend until he felt the cold floor on his feet. He stood up. Keeping his legs well apart, he waddled to the door of his room and looked down the hallway. Other than the fact that he was wearing some sort of blue cotton nightshirt, and that walking was incredibly painful, there appeared to be nothing to prevent him from exfiltrating.

Chip found a pair of paint-spattered coveralls and a painter's cap in one of the storage closets. Ten minutes later, disguised as a house painter, he was walking with great care down the road with no goal other than to put as much distance between himself and Polyhymnia DeSimone as possible.

♠

"Tell me about her."

"Who? Flowrean?" Crow pulled out of the ACO parking lot.

"Yeah."

"I don't know much about her. She works out at Bigg's, she's strong as a horse, and she wears a necklace strung with rotting goldfish. They smell pretty bad. Nobody likes to get too close to her."

"I didn't see any dead fish."

"She wears them when she works out."

"What was she doing there? Is she an Amaranthine?"

"I don't think so. I saw her there when I went to that anti-aging sideshow. She got in some sort of altercation. As a matter of fact, that was what got me in trouble. I sort of intervened."

"For a woman you hardly even know?"

"You know me. Damsel in distress, I'm there."

"So how good do you know her?"

"Like I said, we both work out at Bigg's. I've had maybe one conversation with her, ever. Look, I just spent half an hour answering questions for the cops. What's your problem?"

Debrowski lit a cigarette, flicked the stick match out the window. "Maybe I'm feeling a little insecure."

Crow looked at the woman sitting beside him. How could anyone wearing thirty pounds of leather and steel feel insecure? Or maybe it was the other way around.

"You've got nothing to feel insecure about."

"Good."

"We're doing okay. You know who should be feeling insecure? Arling Biggle. Right about now a couple of cops are sitting in front of his place waiting for him."

"Tell me about this conversation with Flowrean."

Crow took a deep breath, held it as long as he could, then told her about his lunch with Flowrean. Debrowski listened, stone-faced. Midway through the story, Crow turned onto an I-94 entrance ramp, downshifted to second, and tromped on the gas. The GTO took four noisy seconds to reach cruising speed. Crow shifted directly to fourth gear.

"Feel better now?" Debrowski asked.

"A little."

"Where are we going?"

"Over to Axel's."

"I thought we were going home."

"Somebody has to tell him what's happening with Carmen. I thought we should go over there."

"Fine. So finish your story. Flowrean orders a salad and tells you she's been following you everywhere. She followed you to the anti-aging thing, she knows where you live, the whole weird stalker deal. She's in love with you. Then what?"

"I told her I was unavailable."

"And?"

"She was fine with that," Crow said, unable to keep the disappointment out of his voice.

Debrowski laughed. Crow frowned. His face felt hot.

"You know what I love about you, Crow?"

"Don't tell me. You love me for my car?"

Debrowski smirked. "I'll be damned," she said. "You got it first guess."


A few years back, *Hard Camera* had aired an exclusive home video of bigfoot raiding a salt lick in Ely, Minnesota. The husband of the camera operator—Drew remembered his name as Slooch Nygaard, something like that—had taken a shot at it with his 30.06, but bigfoot had run off into the brush, apparently uninjured. The entire event had been videotaped at dusk, in a snowstorm, through a plate glass window, from a distance of approximately sixty yards, using a camcorder Mrs. Nygaard had recently purchased from the Wal-Mart down in Cloquet. The exceptionally poor quality of that video had been such that Drew Chance had been ridiculed by local media and viewers alike and had been flooded over the following weeks with "yeti-in-a-snowstorm" home videos.

The tape that had arrived by courier that morning was equally unconvincing. It looked as if the camera operator—Drew assumed it was that idiot Hy—had run the camera without the autofocus engaged and the shutter speed turned all the way up and the microphone turned off. The images were dark, fuzzy, and poorly composed. Drew thought he could make out a woman in a big white dress lying on a picnic table, squirming and shouting silently at the camera operator.

The camera moved in for a close-up of her arm. It looked like a red tube taped to the inside of her elbow, but he couldn't be sure. The closer he got, the further out of focus the picture became. Drew hit the fast forward and watched another five minutes of visual gibberish, then turned it off. Hy the Guy. He should've known it would go nowhere.


Officer Brett Grossman rounded the corner at thirty miles per, the back wheels of the LTD breaking loose as they left the pavement and hit the dirt, slewing around just so, bringing the squad car into perfect alignment with the camel-back road. He punched the accelerator, sending up a storm of dust and rocks, and fishtailed up the dirt road, his steely blue eyes flicking from side to side, scouring the unbroken rows of corn.

This was why he had become a cop. A young woman was in danger, and Brett Grossman was on duty, pushing his equipment to the max. There were eleven other cops out combing the countryside. The cellular phone company had located her cell phone to within a five-mile radius of County Road 2 and East Circle Drive—nearly eighty square miles of land, a good third of it cornfield. Their best bet was the chopper, but the Rochester P.D. only had one. Grossman figured he had a good chance to be the hero. He had an instinct for these things. He could cover more ground than anybody. He knew the land; he'd grown up there. He knew just what to look for, the distinctive signature of an out-of-control vehicle leaving the road and plunging into a cornfield. Some of the guys he worked with would drive right by it, but not Brett Grossman.

He blew past the old Aamold place doing sixty, then turned back south toward County Road 2 and brought the Ford up to eighty, heading away from town. He passed a barefooted man walking along the shoulder wearing white coveralls and a painter's cap. What was a barefooted house painter doing out here on County 2? Brett briefly considered checking the guy out, but first things first. He decided to stay on County 2 until he reached the perimeter of the search area, then circle back toward town on a network of farm roads that would take him through thousands of acres of corn. It was a good plan. Brett imagined himself receiving a commendation. The image was so vivid that he nearly missed the broken rows of corn to his right.


The limo was right where Flowrean said it would be. Bigg parked his Blazer at a meter across the street, grabbed the parking ticket off the limo's windshield, and got in. The smell just about made him lose it—all those flowers had been sitting in there all day long, baking. He rolled down all the windows and cranked up the air conditioning. He would drive it back to the gym, then get somebody to give him a lift back downtown to pick up his Blazer.

He was trying not to think about what had happened at the Amaranthine Church. It was probably nothing. A few holes in a door. How much trouble could that cause? He was sure he hadn't hit the guy on the other side. Even if he had, the bullets would be going pretty slow after hitting that door. He had other things to worry about, like what had happened to his other limo, smashed up in some place called Prescott. That was the next thing he had to be concerned about. By the time he reached the gym, the incident at the church had all but left his mind. He parked the limo and walked into Bigg Bodies, not even noticing the two suits get out of the gray Ford and follow him inside.

♠

There was a white light ahead, warm and inviting. Behind him lay cold and noise and chaos. He felt hands, soft and dry, urging him gently forward. There was no pain. Not even a hint of discomfort in any part of his being. He realized now that for his entire life he had been in pain. There had never before been a moment when something did not hurt, if only a little.

Was ecstasy the absence of pain?

He felt himself moving forward, drawn by the light. As he moved toward it, it seemed to recede. The noises behind him became strident, insistent. He tried to speed up, to immerse himself in the light, to escape the jangle and confusion. Suddenly his chest exploded in an agonizing flash of light that left behind a cloud of smoky fog shot with blue sparks. The voices became louder, hurting his ears. He searched again for the light, trying to see through the roiling fog—there! A glimmer, but so far away now. He heard a man's voice shout "Clear!" and once again a bomb went off in his chest.

Rupe's eyes popped open. He gasped, "No!"

A man wearing a blue cotton cap and holding two metal paddles grinned and said, "We got him."

Rupe began to weep.

*Kidnapped by Vampires, Groom Claims*

—Pioneer Press *headline*

"—**W**ITH MORE ON OUR STORY about the Minneapolis couple who were allegedly kidnapped on the way to their wedding. Tom? What do you have for us?"

"Thank you, Robin. I'm standing here in front of American Legion Post 684 in South Minneapolis where a wedding ceremony was scheduled to take place yesterday afternoon, until the bride and groom were apparently kidnapped in their limousine on the way here! According to police—"

Sophie grabbed the remote and hit the off button.

"What are you doing?" Axel said, lunging for the remote.

"It's the same thing, over and over. I can't stand it anymore!" Her eyes were red and wild. "Why can't they find her?"

"Give me that!"

Sophie threw the remote at Axel and went out on the deck. Axel turned the TV back on. The news anchor was saying, "—No word on the woman at this time, but we did catch up with the fiancé for an interview you'll see only on Channel Nine." Hyatt Hilton's face filled the screen.

Axel shouted, "Sophie! Hyatt's on the TV!"

Sophie ran back inside. Hyatt Hilton was saying "—the next thing I knew, we were tied up in the back of the limousine being carried off."

The image cut back to the news.

"And we'll be airing the rest of that interview at five. And now here's a story that's going to make a lot of Twin Cities commuters happy—"

Axel turned off the TV.

"Was that it?" Sophie asked.

"Yeah. I guess it was just a teaser. They're going to show the interview at five. Do you know what I wish? I wish I'd had a chance to see her in her wedding dress. I'll bet she was beautiful."

Sophie didn't say anything.

"What did you say it was called? That dress?"

"The Madonna." Sophie sat down on the sofa beside Axel and hugged herself. She looked small. "How can Hyatt be on TV? I thought the police were looking for him."

Axel nodded. "The cops that were here were asking a lot questions about Hyatt. Like they thought he was the one responsible. Maybe they think if they find him they'll find Carmen."

Sophie said, "What if they don't?"

Axel looked at the woman beside him, hardly recognizing her. He had seen Sophie scared and uncertain and angry, but never like this. Her face seemed to have collapsed, her red eyes had grown large and waiflike. She looked both older and younger, a frightened child in a body drained of youth.

She said, "What if they do?"

When Crow and Debrowski pulled up in front of Sophie's, Axel was out on the deck cleaning his Weber. He looked up as they got out of the car, nodded, then continued to scrape at the grill with a metal spatula.

Crow said to Debrowski, "Don't mention that Carmen is bleeding, okay?" He raised his voice and directed it at Axel. "Heard anything?"

Axel said, "Hyatt is going to be on TV. In an hour. They say that it was some sort of cult."

"Have the police called you?"

Axel shook his head. "Sophie's pretty upset." He looked tired.

"I talked to Carmen," Crow said.

Axel stared at him, his mouth moving soundlessly.

Crow climbed the three steps onto the deck. "I talked to her on the phone, less than an hour ago. She didn't know where she was, but the police are looking for her. They know to call you here, don't they?"

Axel nodded slowly and sat down on the bench. "How—why did she call you?"

"Joe called her," Debrowski explained. "He got the phone number of the people who supposedly kidnapped her, and he called it and she answered."

"She's okay then?"

"The police are trying to find her."

Axel stood up. "I have to tell Sophie," he said. He went inside.

Crow followed. "Mind if I use your phone? I'll give Wes a call, make sure they know to call us here."


Shortly before five, the phone rang. Sophie picked up. "Hello?" She listened, handed the phone to Crow.

"Crow here." They were sitting at her kitchen table nursing cups of Axel's powerful coffee. Sophie and Axel's eyes were locked on Crow. Debrowski was out on the deck smoking.

"This is Wes. You called?"

"Yeah, I called about five times. Did you find her yet?"

"I return my calls, Crow. Yeah, we found her. She's in Rochester General."

"She going to be okay?"

"They aren't sure. She lost a lot of blood. Listen, Crow, you heard from your buddy Hilton? I'd really like to talk to him."

"Sorry, I haven't seen him. Rochester General? You got a number?"


Ten minutes later, Axel and Sophie were in Axel's pickup truck, headed south. Crow and Debrowski got back in the GTO.

Debrowski said, "Can we go home now, Crow? You're supposed to be putting in sack time, let your brain heal."

Crow nodded. He knew he was tired. His brain was numb, his face felt like a slab of meat, and his neck hurt. "Okay," he said. "But first I gotta check something out." He started the engine.

"I don't think I like this."

"One more stop, then we go home. I have an idea where Hyatt might be." He guided the GTO through the narrow streets of Landfall, drawing looks of envy from middle-aged men and kids too young to know better.

"Why didn't you tell Axel what Carmen said?"

"Might not be true. All she said was that pig-nose was a friend of Hy's."

"And she said, 'Tell Hy I'm not gonna do it.' That's enough for me."

"I want to talk to Hy first."

"Why?"

"Right now, he's all I got."

"Thanks a lot."

"You know what I mean."

"Yeah, yeah, you've got no career, no calling, no mission in life. You feel guilty inhabiting your own lousy body sucking up all that free air, so you try to fix other people's problems. You know what they call a person like that where I come from? A busybody."

Crow focused his thoughts on shifting from second to third gear. He said, "Where did you come from, anyway?"

"I'm from Cincinnati and, believe me, there are a lot of busybodies in Cincinnati. My grandmother was their leader. She was just like you. Her own life just didn't cut it. You know what you're doing, Crow? You're acting like a cop. Just looking for trouble, looking for a chance to be a hero."

The challenge of driving while listening to Debrowski was too much for Crow's bruised synapses. He pulled over, set the brake, and massaged his temples with his fingertips.

"The thing is," Debrowski continued, "nobody cares where Hyatt Hilton is except you and that other cop, that friend of yours. I doubt if even Carmen cares. Nobody knows whether he did anything, or didn't do something he should've done, or what. But it'll all come out, Crow. You've done the one thing you could've done that mattered—you saved that girl's life. Assuming she survives."

"Debrowski, I really need you to do something for me. Would you please stop talking?"

"Stop talking?"

"Yes."

"I'll make a deal with you. We go home, I put you to bed, I make you a nice cup of cocoa, then I shut up. You get some rest, tomorrow you can do what you want. Go be a hero."

"What kind of deal is that?"

"It's the best offer you've had lately. If I were you, I'd go for it."

♠

All four of his office TV monitors were running, but the one that had Drew's attention was WCCO, which was showing an aerial shot of a cornfield with a green sports-utility vehicle parked right smack in the middle of it. The camera backed off to show the crushed cornstalks where the vehicle had entered the field, and the paramedics carrying a blood-soaked figure toward the ambulance parked on the shoulder of the highway. The search-and-rescue footage had come on just after the interview with Hyatt Hilton on KMSP.

Drew's jaw pulsed as he listened to the announcer crowing about their ex-clusive footage. His phone began to ring; Drew leaned forward and hit the speakerphone button.

"Yeah."

"It's Mr. Hilton on line three."

"Yeah? Put the son-of-a-bitch on."

"Drew?" Hyatt's voice squawked from the speakerphone.

"Ah! Our intrepid reporter, Mister Hyatt Hilton." Drew Chance leaned back, his eyes on the TVs. KMSP was now showing the same cornfield tape.

"Are you on a speakerphone? I can hardly hear you."

"It must be the connection," said Drew. There was no way he was going to pick up for Hy the Guy. "What can I do for you, Hy?"

"Did you look at the tape?"

"Yes indeedy, I did," said Drew. "Very interesting technique. You never ran a camera before, did you, Hy?"

"What? Speak up, would you?"

Drew leaned toward the phone. "I said, *'The tape sucked!'* You hear me that time?"

"What do you mean?"

Drew's face had gone scarlet. "You couldn't run that piece of shit on public access, you dumb fuck." He put his mouth right up to the microphone. "And while I got you—for the last time, I hope—what the fuck were you doing talking to Channel Nine?"

"Hey, that wasn't my idea. They came to me!"

"You're dumber than I thought, and you know what, Hy? I always thought you were pretty fucking stupid."

After a moment Hyatt said, "Does this mean I'm free to sell my story to other news organizations?"

"Furthermore, the one chance we got to be there when something actually happens, I don't hear shit from the intrepid Mr. Butt-fuck Hilton. What kind of exclusive you think I'm gonna have, them running tape of your rescued bride on six fucking stations?"

Hyatt said, "Did you say rescued?"

"Turn on your TV, dumbass." Drew hit the disconnect button. He touched two fingers to his jugular and counted heartbeats, waiting for his pulse to drop back to its normal 120 beats per minute. So much for Mr. Hyatt Hilton. He should've known from the get-go that little Alan Orlich the clairvoyant finger-painter was his best bet.

*Many a good news story has been ruined by oververification.*

—*James Gordon Bennett*

THERE WAS A WORD THAT would stop the ringing. What was it? Joe Crow swam through crevasses, opened drawers, turned over cards. His hand, more awake than he, grasped the offending object and brought it to his ear. The word popped off his tongue: "Hello?"

"Crow, this is Zink. You asleep?"

"I don't know."

"Turn on your radio."

"Zink?"

"Yeah. Turn on KSTP. Now." Zink hung up.

Crow looked at his clock-radio. A few minutes after nine. The last thing he remembered, Debrowski had been massaging his forehead. That was twelve hours ago. She must've gone downstairs to her half of the duplex. He sat up. That felt pretty good. He turned on the radio, adjusted the tuner. A woman's strident voice came over the tiny speaker:

"Now let me see if I understand what you're saying to me, Mr. Hilton—*Hy-att* Hilton—tell me Hyatt, I want to know, is that your real name?"

"Yes it is. I—"

"It's all right if I call you Hyatt, isn't it? What do your friends call you? Do they call you Hy? I'm going to call you Hy. Hy, if I'm understanding you, the leaders of this organization—and I call it an organization, not a church—these people actually believe—and I'm just going by what you tell me—these people actually think that they're *immortal?*"

"That's right, Barbara. I—"

"Now stop me if I'm off-base here, but I'm sure my listeners are wondering this, as I am—isn't that just a little bit naive? I mean, what makes them think— what makes them think that of all the people who have ever lived that they— and I'm talking here about the leaders of this so-called Amaranthine whatever-it-is—why should they think that they are immortal?"

"You know, I—"

"But you were actually a member of this organization for quite some time, isn't that true? In fact, you were one of the founders. Are you immortal, Hy?"

"No, actually I'm—"

"But you left the, ah, organization. Now tell me, Hy, these immortals, this, ah, Rupert Chandra and Polyhymnia DeSimone—am I saying their names right? Well, who cares. These two con artists—is that too strong? I'm going to get myself in trouble again, but I call it the way I see it—these con artists claim to have discovered the secret to eternal youth—we're not talking Retin-A here, ladies and gentlemen—but from what you're telling me, they actually were hav- ing plastic surgery. Now is that a fact? Or are you just guessing? Tell me, Hy?"

"It's true. But the really bizarre part of the story is what they did with Car- men."

"Yes, Carmen is your bride—or rather your fiancée—who you say was kid- napped."

"We were both kidnapped and—"

"But she was found yesterday, I understand, in a bean field—is that right? Rob? A bean field? A *corn*field. Rob, my producer, tells me it was a cornfield. And isn't there some question about the alleged kidnapping? I understand she was found in her car, and she's all right? I heard she was fine. Have you talked to her?"

"Not yet. I just—"

"Because if I was lying in the hospital I'd want to hear from my fiancé. But I'm getting off the subject. Back to this plastic surgery—we'll talk about the kidnapping—the alleged kidnapping—in just a minute, but let me understand something—what exactly, what work did these two con artists have done? I've seen pictures of this couple, and I have to tell you that they're a handsome pair. But the photo you showed me, Hy, that was taken before their surgery, is that correct? What exactly did they have done?

"I'm not one hundred percent sure—"

"Then how can you sit here and tell me that you know for a fact that the surgery took place? You see, this is what I'm talking about. People accusing public figures of doing things when they don't actually have the facts—not that I'm defending these so-called immortals, understand, but—case in point—you, Mr. Hilton, cannot actually say that you have seen, with your own eyes, this plastic surgery? Am I correct or am I right?"

"Uh, you're right, of course, but the surgery—"

"*Alleged* surgery."

"Right. But that's incidental to my story. We were *kidnapped* on the way to our *wedding*. These people are real-life vampires, Barbara."

"Did you know—I had a doctor on my show a few months ago—did you know that they are actually using leeches again? In the United States of America?"

"No, I—"

"We'll be right back, ladies and gentlemen to talk more with Hyatt Hilton, whose bride-to-be was *kidnapped* on the way to their wedding, and we'll talk some more about plastic surgery; and I'll also be telling you about my experience with plastic surgery—and I'm not talking about my tattoo, ladies and gentlemen. Now I *know* you can't see me over your radio, but I have to tell you—let me just say that I considered it the thoughtful thing to do, and anyone who knows me knows that I'm a pushy broad but I'm one of the most *thoughtful* people I know. That's right. And out of respect for the people who have to look at me every day, I try to keep up appearances, and I might not be immortal but I care about how I look. So. You know me. I love quality, I *love* my pearls and my gold jewelry, and I *love* my jeweler; and if you love quality and if you care about how you look, *you'll* love my jeweler too . . ."

Hyatt felt as though someone had given his brain a hotfoot. Yow! Thirty minutes of being grilled by Barbara Carlson had cooked his synapses good. Oh well, maybe it would get the ball rolling, get some of the other media interested. He might work his way up to Imus or Larry King. And then the biggies, the TV shows: *Geraldo Rivera, Ricki Lake, Maury Povich*. He hoped he'd sounded okay on the radio. Serious, but entertaining. That was what they wanted, what they would pay for.

He rested his hand on the phone. What next? Maybe call that morning guy on KQRS. Or should he go straight for the national exposure? No, start local. That was what Chip would call the *strategic* approach. Or maybe the strategic approach was to go straight to the top.

Maybe he should call Rochester again, see if he could get through to Carmen. See if she was still alive. The way to really work this media thing was to do it as a couple. If there were two of them, people would believe. Get Carmen's pretty face on the tube talking about the vampire church, and people would sit up and listen. The two of them on *American Journal*—that would be perfect. He wondered what had happened to her. He'd tied her up good. She hadn't untied herself, so it must've been that idiot Chip, getting it wrong. But how had she ended up in that cornfield, and where was Chip? For that matter, where were Rupe and Polly?

Too many questions. Hyatt opened the refrigerator and looked again for something edible. All he saw were the same dried up pizza remnants—some of them had no doubt been in there for months—and scraps of wire neatly tied in bundles and sorted by color. Jimmy Swann had lived on pizza, and he liked to keep his wire collection below forty degrees.

He wondered what had happened to Jimmy.

Having no cash and no place to go, Hyatt had arrived at Jimmy Swann's doorstep yesterday afternoon, hoping that Jimmy had forgotten about their last meeting. It was worth a try—assuming that Jimmy didn't have another tinfoil-wrapped shotgun. He had approached the front door cautiously. When his ringing and knocking produced no response, Hyatt had twisted the handle and found the door to be unlocked. Jimmy was gone.

Hyatt would soon be gone, too. He had called every pizza joint in a five-mile radius, and every one of them had refused to deliver. Jimmy Swann scared off all the pizza delivery guys, which was probably what had ultimately forced him to leave. Starved out. Ventured back out onto the street, where the police might find him. He wasn't sure why they were looking for him, but whatever the reason, he was sure it would only serve to cramp his style. It would be tough to do media interviews from a jail cell. Find a new base of operations. Jimmy's place was too damn weird. Besides, it still reeked of Jimmy. That son-of-a-bitch Drew—*Andy* Greenblatt—was going to miss out big time. Story of the century, and he walks away from it. He'd be damn sorry when he turned on his TV and saw Hyatt Hilton being interviewed by Katie Couric.

He wished he could get through to Carmen.

What he had to do, he had to get on the phone again. Keep working the phone. That was the secret.

He had just been put on hold by the assistant to Jenny Jones's producer when someone knocked on the front door.

Crow stepped back from the door, the foil-wrapped, antennae-studded shotgun in plain view, holding it in what he hoped was a nonthreatening manner. He'd found Hyatt's BMW tucked back in the alley, but he wasn't sure who or what else lurked within this old house.

A curtain moved. Seconds later, Hyatt Hilton opened the door.

"Am I glad to see you!" he said.

Crow said, "Really?" He peered past him into the dim interior. "Is your friend here? I want to return his magic gun." Crow held up the shotgun.

"I can take it."

Crow handed Hyatt the gun. "It's not loaded." He followed Hyatt inside. "Your friend likes to read," he said, noticing the piles of magazines.

Hyatt leaned the gun against the wall. They stood in the cluttered hallway, facing each other.

"I'd offer you coffee, but I'm fresh out."

"How about you just tell me what you and Carmen have been doing. Why stage a kidnapping? I don't get it."

"I'm just glad you're okay," Hyatt said, ignoring the question. "I heard you were in the hospital."

"I'm fine," Crow said. "But I wouldn't mind sitting down for a minute."

Hyatt led him through the hallway. The smell of beer and sweat became stronger. They entered what had once been a sitting room. Hyatt pointed at the sagging, unfolded sofabed. Every other item of furniture was covered by magazines and empty pizza boxes.

"Maybe I don't need to sit down," said Crow. "You know, the cops want to talk to you."

"They should be talking to Rupe and Polly. I'm the victim here, Joe. Nobody seems to understand that."

"I heard you on the radio this morning."

"Oh? How did I sound?" Hyatt sat down on the edge of the mattress.

"Like a guy looking for attention. I didn't believe anything you said."

Hyatt wrinkled his forehead. "Really?"

"Yeah. Yesterday I thought maybe you were telling the truth. Today I think you're full of it."

"Was it something I said?"

Crow laughed. "Yeah. You said, 'You can't believe what anybody tells you.'"

Hyatt looked thoughtful. "I might've said that."

"I talked to Carmen."

"You did?"

"She said to tell you she's not going to do it."

Hyatt frowned. "She's not? Do what?"

"That's what I want to know. What's really got me curious is why? I know you arranged for that Chip guy to hit me and drive off with the limousine—"

"That's not true!"

"And I'm pretty sure that the elders of the Amaranthine Church are not bloodsucking vampires. Bloodsuckers, maybe, but not in the literal sense. What I can't figure out is, what's your angle? Were you planning to somehow extort money out of them? Embarrass them? Or is this just your way of keeping yourself entertained?"

Hyatt said, "Joe, all I ever wanted to do was get married and settle down. You know how old I am?"

"Forty-four."

Hyatt jerked as if from a mild electric shock. "I was going to tell you forty," he said, wagging his index finger, chiding. "But obviously you've been snooping. Anyhow, when you get to be my age, Joe, you'll understand. You got one last chance, one more load to shoot, so to speak, before you wake up and look down and see you got one foot in the grave."

"I know that feeling."

"You're too young to know it. By the time you're my age I'll be a few years short of getting screwed out of my social security. All that money I put into the system, poof. How do you think that makes me feel?"

"Hy, you never put a dime into the system."

"That's not the point. Me and Carmen, we're a team. We're going to reschedule the wedding and get married. That's all I want. Also, I've been talking to a lot of media people. I'm going to get on TV and tell my story. Once they hear how it was, they'll understand. It's a great story."

"It sounds like that's all it is."

"You don't understand," sighed Hyatt. "First of all, I didn't do what you say. And second, even if I had, don't you think I'd have done a better job? I mean, what a mess! Media people don't like things messy. They like stories that are nice and neat, like the guy whose wife cut off his dick. That was a good story."

"Maybe you should try that."

Hyatt sighed. "Right now, it feels like maybe that's what I did."

Someone knocked on the front door.

"Who's that?" Hyatt asked.

"A friend of mine," said Crow. "Name of Wes. I told him to meet me here."

Laura Debrowski was sitting in the GTO trying to open the combination padlock Crow had left on his dashboard. It was one of her hobbies—usually she could crack a lock in about three minutes, but she'd been working on this one ever since Crow had entered the old gray house. At one point, ten minutes after he'd gone inside, she'd nearly abandoned the project to go in after him. But then the two cops had shown up, so she'd gone back to work on the lock.

A few minutes later, Crow got in the car wearing a faint smile.

Debrowski said, "How'd that go?"

"It went fine. He was there."

"He tell you what you wanted to know?"

"I'm not sure what I wanted to know. I think Hy just wants to be on TV."

"That's what this was about?"

"I don't think we'll ever know. But I found out something else. I found out that Hyatt Hilton and Joe Crow have something in common."

Debrowski held up the stubborn lock. "Impossible to open?"

"Yeah, that, too. But mostly I found out that we're both mortal."

♠

As soon as he heard the news that Hyatt Hilton had been arrested, Chip Bouchet decided that his best strategy would be to head for the Pacific Northwest and find a militia to join up with. He spent several hours reconnoitering and surveilling the Minneapolis apartment building where he had lived for the past several years, then went in and grabbed his bug-out bag. One hour later he was on a Greyhound bus heading west on I-94.

He began rereading *The Turner Diaries,* which described the coming collapse of the United States government. It was a very good book. He finished it just as they were passing through Bismarck, North Dakota.

Having just emerged from the future described in *Diaries,* Chip began to look at his fellow passengers in a whole new way. There was one guy he was sure was a Jew, and there were no fewer than six negroes, who were enslaved by the Jews although they did not yet know it. And then there was the man with the radio transmitter affixed to his head. Possibly a communications expert, but for which side? The longer Chip looked at him, the more convinced he became that the man was in contact with one of the militia groups he was hoping to join. The copper wires and tubes might not be a transmitter at all, but a scrambling device designed to prevent the government from monitoring him.

As the bus entered Montana, Chip decided to make contact. He moved up the aisle and accidentally on purpose dropped his copy of the *Diaries* on the man's lap.

The man looked down at the book and said, "The day of reckoning is upon us."

"Amen, brother," said Chip, taking the seat across the aisle. "Amen."

*Prosper, and Live Long.*

—*Third Maxim of the Amaranthine Church*

THE AMBIENCE AT BIGG BODIES HAD not improved in Arling Biggle's absence. Beaut, still nursing his broken foot, was opening up late every morning, closing early at night, and doing little else. The place was falling apart—dumbbells racked out of order, mirrors smudged with oil and chalk dust, and the lat machine suffering from a broken pulley. Piles of lint were growing in the corners, and the locker room floors were unspeakable. Beaut had dragged Bigg's comfortable leather chair out of his office and put it behind the front counter. He spent his days slumped in the chair reading magazines—today it was a dog-eared copy of *Fem-Physique Quarterly*—his bad foot propped on one of the weight benches. Beaut hadn't shaved lately; his eyes were bloodshot, and his skin was saggy. Every few minutes he took a sip from a plastic Spiderman cup.

Both Beaut and Bigg Bodies looked as if they had been neglected for months on end, but it had only been six days since Bigg's arrest. Crow marveled at how quickly things could fall apart. Beaut was a mere husk of his former overinflated self. Both Beaut and the gym were slowly crumbling. Rupe might have something to say here. Something about short telomeres.

Crow loaded another pair of plates onto the bar and did a set of bench presses, ten nice, slow lifts. He racked the bar and sat up, then noticed a blocky man in a blue suit come in through the front door. Not until he saw Beaut sit up and drop his magazine did he recognize Arling Biggle, the sequel.

The new Arling Biggle had removed his Fu Manchu mustache and his sideburns, and his previously clean-shaven head was now dark with new hair growth. Even more startling: a pair of wire-rimmed eyeglasses teetered on his thick nose.

Bigg exchanged a few words with Beaut, then spotted Crow. He approached, his demeanor uncharacteristically subdued.

"How's it going, Crow?"

"Not bad," Crow replied. "You made bail, huh?"

"I had my lawyer sell one of the limos. I'd have sold both of them, except the one I let you use is still impounded."

"You'll get it back."

Bigg shrugged, bent over, and picked a piece of lint off the rubber floor mat. He looked around, seemed to take in the general neglect, and dropped the lint back on the floor. "The place looks like hell."

Crow wasn't sure whether he should agree or disagree.

Bigg said, "I just got done talking to my lawyer. You know what he told me? He said I'm probably going to jail for a while. He wants me to plead something. Reckless endangerment. And all I did was shoot at a closed door. Besides, I hear the guy's immortal. How can they charge me with trying to kill somebody that can't die? They don't even care about the fact that the day before, the guy hit me over the head with a wrench. You know what I'm talking about. You got clobbered, too. What are you supposed to do, you run into the guy that hit you? You going to say, 'I forgive you, brother?' You going to turn the other cheek?"

"Truth is, I'm hoping I never run into him."

"Really? Maybe find him standing on the edge of a cliff or something so you can give him a little nudge? You don't think about stuff like that?"

Crow said, "You want to know what I really think?"

Bigg grunted.

"I think we both ran into bad weather. We're both lucky we didn't get killed. I figure, why fight the wind?" Crow stood up, pulled a plate off the bar, racked it. "You've got a business here, something to do when you get out. Reckless endangerment? What's that? It's like accidentally backing over your brother-in-law with a lawnmower. You'll be out in thirty-six months." He pulled a plate off the other end of the bar. "Hire somebody to run the place for you."

Bigg said, "How about you?"

Crow managed not to drop the plate on his foot. "No thanks." He racked the plate. "I don't want to work for anybody except me."

"That's what I'm talking about, Crow. Buy the place off me. Wouldn't you like your own business? Be your own boss?"

"No thanks."

"Think about it. A young guy like you, lots of piss and vinegar, you could make some money here. Give those assholes at Bally a run for their money. What are you? Thirty-seven? Eight?"

"Thirty-five."

"That's a good age. I could finance part of it for you. You come up with, say, thirty thousand against a purchase price of two-twenty, pay me a couple thousand a month, you'd own it free and clear in a few years. Think about it."

Crow said, "I don't have to think about it. I'm not interested."

Bigg shrugged. "Maybe I'll sell it to Beaut. Of course, you realize that your membership deal won't transfer."

"Oh?" Crow looked around. "That's fine by me. The place is going to hell. I was thinking about joining the Y anyway."

To celebrate Carmen's homecoming, Axel had invited Crow, Debrowski, and Sam over for Conitas. On their way to pick up Sam, Crow told Debrowski about Bigg trying to sell him the gym. Laughing at the idea as he told the story.

Debrowski said, "Do you want to run a gym?"

Crow wasn't sure how to answer that. He said, after a driving a few blocks, "What difference does it make? I'm not going to buy it."

"Why not?"

"No money."

Debrowski nodded. "So what the hell is a 'Conita?'" she asked.

Carmen seemed, for Carmen, unnaturally chipper after her stay in the hospital. She sat on the deck railing, chattering away about meeting Wayne Savage, telling Crow and Sophie all about the character he played on his soap opera, Johnny DeMars. She said she was going to send him a letter. Then she shifted topics, talking about a pair of shoes she'd seen at Dayton's. The effect was somewhat unnerving—instead of her usual sleepy, bored, mildly surly self, she had become suddenly interested in the world around her, even going so far as to suggest setting up the volleyball net.

"The doctor said you should take it easy for a few more days," Sophie said from the aluminum and plastic chaise lounge. "You just had a miscarriage." She took a sip of her wine. "Besides, I don't have a volleyball net."

"Oh." Carmen's lower lip popped out, and her eyes went dead, recalling her more familiar self, then she brightened. "Let's buy one!"

Moments later the phone rang. Debrowski answered, then called to Carmen. "It's for you, Carmen. Somebody named Drew Chance." Carmen ran inside.

Crow checked the coals in the Weber and adjusted the vents. Sophie watched him. She lit a cigarette.

She said, "I wonder how long it'll last."

"What's that?"

"Carmen being in a good mood."

"It's sure different," said Crow.

"You know what she needs? She needs to get married. I mean for real. To some nice guy. One of those doctors."

"I'm sure she'll find somebody."

"That's what I'm afraid of." Sophie climbed to her feet and disappeared inside. Moments later Axel came out carrying a platter loaded with strips of marinated beef and chicken.

"Where's Sam?"

"He's out back doing something to my car. Said it didn't sound quite right on the way over."

Axel began arranging the strips of meat on the hot grill. "Your old man, he's one of a kind."

"Tell me about it."

"You got some of it too, Joe. You know, I maybe never thanked you proper for saving Carmen's life. She'd be dead now if you hadn't made that phone call."

"I just dialed a number. I didn't know Carmen was going to answer."

"I still appreciate it." He gave Crow a searching look. "You know, Joe, I've got a little money socked away. I'm looking to invest a chunk of it."

"Oh? Like in what, stocks? I know a stockbroker you should avoid."

"I was thinking more along the lines of putting it into a business. You know. Something small, but with good management and lots of potential. Maybe a health club, something like that. What do you think?"


The first official gathering of the New Amaranthine Church was held in the basement of a Unitarian Church in Richfield.

Benjy Hiss had spent much of the previous week phoning the Faithful, trying to convince them that just because the former leaders of the ACO had been exposed as frauds, the core values and beliefs of the church remained alive in the hearts and souls of its immortal members. The fact that the physical assets of the church had been seized by the government in no way lessened the truth of the Amaranthine teachings. Most of the Faithful listened, but it was no sure thing that any of them would actually show up. Many were concerned about the lack of leadership.

"That is why we are meeting," he told them. "The torch has been passed. Polyhymnia DeSimone and Rupert Chandra violated the Amaranthine Principles. Others have stepped forward to take their places. As for the buildings— what are they? Bricks and mortar."

It turned out he had nothing to worry about. The Faithful had come. The small room was packed. Benjy greeted them, and when everyone was seated he told the gathering of that fateful afternoon at ACO World Headquarters when a madman with a gun had broken in and fired a .357 slug through Charles Thickening's stomach and into his spine. Most of them had heard or read about the shooting, but Benjy's firsthand account proved riveting, particularly the part where the doctor said that Chuckles would never again walk, speak, or feed himself.

"My friends," said Benjy Hiss, "in that moment I felt as though my world had ended. Just that morning I had learned that we had all been betrayed by the elders—and then to hear this pronouncement of doom on my dear friend Chuckles. I confess to you, the faith left me. I could have embraced death in that moment, and I might have were it not for Flowrean Peeche. She saw my distress, and she laid one hand upon my wrist and she said to me, 'Be there.' In that moment, I felt her power enter my cells."

Chuckles, who was standing outside the room with Flowrean, said, "Damn! He good!" Chuckles wore a white on white suit with a tie the color of blood. Something to remind them of his ordeal.

"He should be," Flo said. "We've been working on it all week." Flo, they had decided, should stay with her techno-Amazon look, only in copper. Even her nails were clad in copper foil.

Benjy continued: "And then she led me to Chuckles's side and she laid her hands upon him, and I saw, with my own eyes, I saw the color of his skin change. I saw his eyes open. I called for the doctor, and when the doctor arrived at his bedside Chuckles lifted his hand, and he opened his mouth and he spoke. He said, 'Believe.'"

Chuckles sat down in the wheelchair and said, "Let's go get 'em, sister."

Flo released the brake and wheeled him into the room and up the aisle to the front. She turned his chair to face the audience. Chuckles waited for the gasps and whispers to subside. He began to speak in his low, confident voice. He spoke for nearly an hour without stopping, though it was clear within the first few minutes that he had grasped the mantle of leadership. He had been accepted. Chuckles had planned to stand up at the end of his talk, to give them a miracle by which to remember that great day, but the Faithful were already so enthralled by their new leadership that it hardly seemed necessary.

He decided to save that move for later.

"Each of us was placed upon this earth for a reason. Some of us came to till the soil, some came to create works of art. Some came to wage war, others to make peace, still others came to make children. More often than not, our purpose in this life remains veiled. Some of us fulfill our roles early on, others go on for many years doing nothing but filling privies. But fulfill our purpose we do, each and every one of us, whether we know it or not.

"And once we have done what we were sent here to do, we die." Rupeek Chandarama pressed his palms together and smiled. "But not before." Beads of moisture formed on his pale forehead, dancing in the flickering candlelight.

"Forty-two days ago, I died. My heart stopped beating. I was dead for seven minutes and twenty-six seconds. For seven minutes and twenty-six seconds I was in the light."

Tears mounted his eyelids and spilled one at a time down his gaunt cheeks. He separated his hands and displayed pierced palms, now slick with blood. A young woman in the audience moaned; her eyes rolled up and her head flopped back. Apollonia Desiree rushed forward from the back of the small room and helped the woman lie down on the floor. The other Seekers—there were twelve of them this week—ignored the prone woman. Their attention remained riveted to the man sitting lotus-fashion on the low dais.

"I came back," said Chandarama. "Against my will. I was drawn from the light as a child is wrenched from his mother's womb. I was forced to return to this world for one reason only. I came back to fulfill my purpose, to tell you of the light. To share the joy of passage, to celebrate the inevitable transition between this world of discord and chaos and the next world, the world of freedom and light. And only when I have reached enough of you, only then will I be permitted to make my own passage. I pray to be taken soon."

A man in the audience cried out, "No, Chandarama!"

Chandarama smiled. "You must accept what is to become. As it is written in the Thanatonic Coda: To live, one must be willing to die."

*Never bet against yourself.*

*—Crow's rules*

THE TV ROOM IN THE Hennepin County Correctional Facility, like every other area of the prison, had both written and unwritten rules by which it operated. Hyatt did not know how the television channel was selected, nor how it was decided who was permitted to sit in the chairs and who had to stand—as he always ended up doing—at the back of the room, leaning uncomfortably against the wall in his blue on blue two-piece ensemble, four inches of ankle showing between the tops of his canvas shoes—also blue—and the hem of his trousers. Today they were watching *Wheel of Fortune.* Every few minutes some literate type would shout out the puzzle solution, but most of the talk had to do with Vanna White's long white legs.

Hyatt wasn't taking in much. Mostly he saw a roomful of blue poly-cotton shirts with "HCCF" stenciled across the back. He didn't care about Vanna White; the show going on inside his head absorbed most of his attention, even though it was another rerun of his star-crossed wedding day. Unbelievable, really, how many things had gone wrong, and none of them his fault. It was the same old story. You just couldn't count on anybody. Carmen, Chip, Andy Greenblatt—every one of them had failed to do their part. It was almost as if it had all been a conspiracy to destroy him. It wasn't fair. If everybody had done their part, he'd be on TV instead of watching it.

For no apparent reason, one of the guards walked over to the TV and switched the channel, producing a low muttering that lasted only a moment. Complaints would quickly result in a blank screen, so vocalization was kept to a minimum. It didn't matter to Hyatt. He figured he'd be out in a few weeks. The charges were bullshit. He hadn't done anything wrong, an important fact that would doubtless come out during his hearing, even with that pissant public defender talking. He hadn't been the one to steal the limo. Chip had done that. And as far as the assault charges, that had been consensual. Carmen had been in on it since the beginning. Besides, she would never let those charges stand. She loved him. He was surprised she hadn't already recanted.

What else did they have on him? Chuckles had reported him for shooting his vette. They called that reckless something-or-other, but it was clearly self defense. Other than that, nothing. Worst case, he'd be out in a month.

An image on the TV caught Hyatt's attention. Drew Chance, looking right at him, talking.

"A few weeks ago, this young woman—" A photo of Carmen. "—was on her way to the altar with her fiancé when, out of the blue, the young couple was kidnapped and driven nearly a hundred miles to a small church in a remote area. The fiancé was not harmed, but the young woman was subjected to a strange and bizarre bloodletting ritual.

"When she was finally found in the middle of a cornfield, near death from loss of blood, many questions remained unanswered. The police claimed the the kidnapping was bogus, a staged event. The fiancé insisted that they were the victims of a strange cult. But why was her blood drained, and by whom? Why was this young woman chosen, and how was the kidnapping—bogus or not—engineered? Was this the work of vampires? Chupacabra? The Red Cross?

"Today we have in our studios Miss Carmen Roman, the kidnapping victim

herself who, in this exclusive interview, will tell us for the first time the astonishing true nature of this crime. She will reveal that what the police called a *bogus* kidnapping was in fact a *real* kidnapping. But it was not some strange cult.
No, as is often the case in crimes of passion, it was someone very close to her."

Drew's face was replaced by a headline:

MY FIANCÉ, THE VAMPIRE

Drew reappeared, the camera backed off to reveal Carmen—looking very
schoolgirlish with her hair tied back in a ponytail and a fuzzy white sweater—
sitting beside him, smiling into the camera as if she *knew* he was watching. Hyatt let himself slide slowly down the wall, his loose shirt riding up, bunching
under his armpits. He wrapped his arms around his long white shins and rested
his chin on his knees. He couldn't see the television from that position. He took
a deep breath and held it until her words became mush in his ears.

Chester and Festus began baying for no apparent reason. Sam, who was leaning against the front fender of a rusted-out 1968 Roadrunner smoking a cigarette and surveying his kingdom, banged on the hood and shouted a string of
obscenities to no effect. Chester charged the fence on the south side of the yard
and leapt. His front paws missed the top by a good six inches; Chester fell to
the ground, picked himself up, and howled his fury, joined by Festus, his less
assertive number-two hound. A few years back, Chester had been able to claw
his way over the top of the fence. He'd made it his custom to disappear for
days at a time, servicing every uncaged bitch in a three-mile radius. But Chester had been younger then. These days, being a middle-aged hound, he was
more subdued. Not that he couldn't spread his seed from one end of St. Paul to
the other—Chester's jewels were working fine—but these days he took his own
personal comfort more seriously. He liked his old mattress and his food bowl.
Sam figured that on a good day, Chester could still make it over that fence. He
just hadn't done it lately.

A few seconds after the howling began, Sam heard the throaty sound of a
400 cubic-inch Ram Air III engine coming up the block. His damn kid, getting
the dogs all riled up. Sam smiled. He screwed his cigarette into the corner of
his mouth, hitched up his jeans, sauntered toward the gate, opened it up. The
kid pulled in slow, revved the engine a couple times, shut it down.

As soon as the dogs recognized Joe Crow they quit barking. Sam asked,
"How's she runnin'?"

The kid got out and gave the dogs' heads a scrubbing. "Pretty good," he
said. "Real good, in fact."

"How 'bout that little health club? How's that going?"

"Great. I talked to a reporter from *Mpls./St. Paul* magazine this morning. They're doing a feature on us."

"Well, don't that beat all! How 'bout Ax—he keeping his nose out of your joint?"

"Axel's fine as long as he gets some kind of check every now and then. You hear about him and Sophie?"

"Sure did. Gettin' hitched. Like once little Carmen's wedding deal didn't work out, Sophie still needed her wedding fix. I get to be best man. Get to use my suit again."

Joe laughed. He seemed a lot happier these days. Now that the kid had a business to worry about, he wasn't brooding so much.

Sam said, "Carmen's gonna be maid of honor, if they can get her out of that little car of hers." Carmen's brief media adventure—there was a week there when you couldn't hardly turn on the TV without seeing that little face—had landed her a little chunk of cash, which she'd immediately dropped on a teensy black Porsche, nothing but a glorified 150 mph Volkswagen; cost a fortune to fix when it broke down, which sooner or later it damn sure would.

Joe said, "I'll be there, but I won't be driving a limo this time."

"I'm sure Ax'll be real disappointed."

"Yeah." He looked at his watch. The kid was all the time looking at his watch these days. "Sam, I got this problem. It seems like now that I've got this gym I'm always needing to haul stuff around. Like this afternoon I've got to pick up a couple benches. I need a van or something."

"That a fact?" Sam jerked his thumb at a GMC he'd been working on, on and off, for the past few months. "How about that'n?"

"What's wrong with it?"

"What makes you think it's broke?"

"Just a feeling."

"She's got a little rust, and she might need a tranny rebuild pretty soon. She'll get your benches delivered for you."

"I was thinking of something more permanent. You know, a swap."

Sam said. "You sayin' you want to trade the Goat?"

"Right now I need a van. Only I don't want one that's going to die on me."

"Tell you what. You want to swap me your Goat for that van, I'll make you a deal." What the hell, the kid was his own flesh and blood. "I'll fix 'er for free anytime she breaks, plus I'll throw in a tranny. You change your oil every couple months, she'll run forever."

"You sound like an Amaranthine."

"I don't know what one of them sounds like."

"You want to know what amazes me, Sam? That whole crazy mess with Hyatt and the Amaranthines and so forth, and nobody got killed. Maybe some people really are immortal."

"People die, son. Just a question of when." Sam had made peace with his own mortality back before they put seat belts in cars. His philosophy was, you get ready to go, then you don't think about it no more. He said, "You want the van, or not?"

"You say it'll run forever?"

"Son, I guarantee it."